GUARDIAN OF LATOVIA

VALLA SERIES - BOOK THREE

ANNA REZES

ALSO BY ANNA REZES

Valla Series:

Unraveling Emily ~ book one
Descendant of Valla ~ book two
Guardian of Latovia ~ book three
Broken Alliance ~ book four

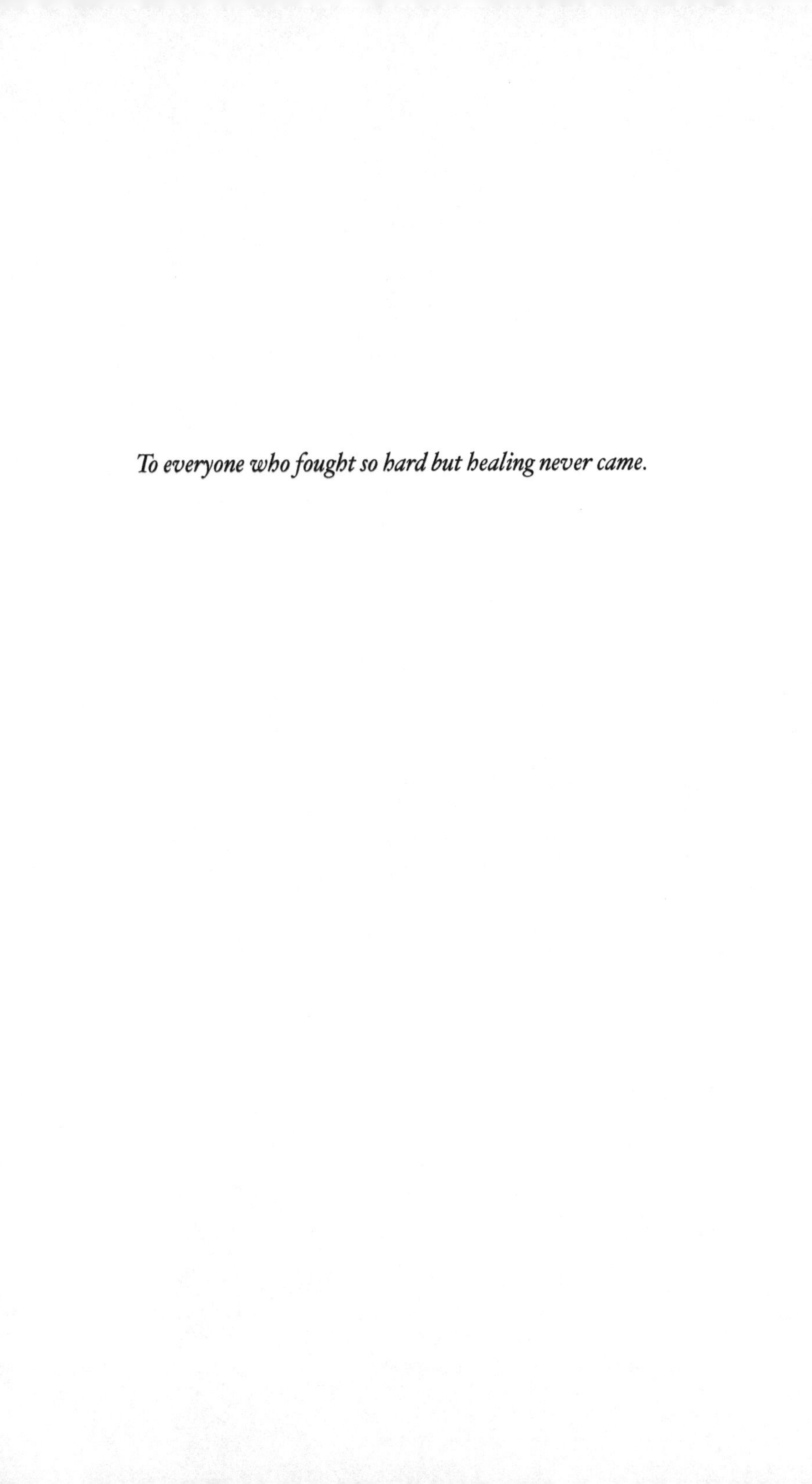

To everyone who fought so hard but healing never came.

PROLOGUE ~

EVERYONE BORN WILL EVENTUALLY DIE. It's a fact so basic, so logical, so inevitable, yet it's something most of us are never ready to face. Is it fear of leaving those we love or fear of the unknown? No one can be sure when death will strike, but every day is priceless to those who acknowledge the Grim Reaper lurking just over their shoulder.

If we knew when we were going to die, would we live our lives differently? Would it change our decisions?

The casket at the front of the room stands like a declaration of failure. He watches from the balcony, separating himself from the people pouring into the room below. It makes him angry to see how many gifted individuals show up today. He wants to berate them for being here. They don't belong here, but then again, neither does he. After all, he let this happen.

CHAPTER ONE ~

THREE MONTHS earlier ~

LATHE PACES THE HALL, crumpling the sheet of paper in his hands. With powers of healing, mental manipulation, and mind-reading, it is vital to have someone police the gifted Olvasho group. The Olvasho Council was created to do just that. It was originally set up to run like a democracy. Their primary job was to prevent the Olvasho from causing harm while keeping them safe from discovery, but during Sky's long reign, it became corrupt, running like a criminal organization.

The night Sky died, the council lost four members to abandonment and death, leaving only eight members in their council seats. Now, nearly five months later, the Olvasho are about to vote for a new leader and council members.

Lathe knows the next head of the Olvasho needs to inspire change in order to fix the corruption. Unfortunately, the list of candidates is anything but hopeful.

Lathe pulls out his phone to call Patrick.

Answering with a sigh, Patrick says, "You're losing your edge, Lathen. Your predictability is getting old."

Lathe growls, "You know why I'm calling."

"To wish me a Happy New Year?"

Lathe rolls his eyes and says, "They announced the final four candidates."

"Don't spoil it! I missed last night's episode."

Lathe grinds his teeth. "You think this is a joke? This is the future of the Olvasho."

"You have no sense of humor, Lathe." Patrick sighs. "Do I know any of them?"

"Three are sitting council members and the fourth is just for show. I've never heard the name, and no one will vote for him."

Patrick scoffs. "Of course, they rigged the election. They need to make it look like someone outside the council has a chance at winning. Is Keith on the list?"

Lathe groans, rubbing at his facial scars. "He's favored to win."

Keith had once been eager to become Sky's second in command. He would carry out all kinds of nefarious deeds, trying to capture Sky's attention. It was never Patrick's desire to be Sky's *protege*. He would've handed it to Keith in a heartbeat if Sky had let him.

After Sky's death, Keith did a one-eighty, preaching anti-Sky to the masses to gain their support. It made Patrick hate him even more.

Lathe continues, "The Olvasho respond to power above all else. Emily has power. The people love her. She has the blood of a leader, and the backing of the prophecy." He has no doubt his half-sister would win, but she still refuses to run.

Patrick sighs. "I can't make her do it, Lathe. And she is sick of hearing about the prophecy. She said she's not going to let a poem decide her fate."

Lathe's mother had premonitions of the future and years ago gave a prophecy they believe to be about Emily, though they didn't know until recently.

Bred to be orphaned, pursued but not found,
The weak build the strong to find light underground.
Rising from nothing to fight for a cause
A victim, a killer, an innocent one.
Finding freedom for souls, we believe to be lost,
By crossing lines that cannot be crossed.
Fear breeds allegiance that is easily broken,
While love builds loyalties that remain unspoken.
Rising from evil, from death, from ash
To encompass abilities no other can have.
Garnering gifts from mother and father alike,
Her blood will awaken three sisters to fight.
Saving us all, for it is fated,
Unless she befalls, incinerated.

Lathe offers, "Did you tell her I would take on Leona if she takes leadership?"

"I did, and your ultimatum didn't go over very well with her." Patrick sighs. "She's too involved with getting her life together. She's not about to throw it away to lead a group she doesn't like or trust."

Lathe huffs, "This is our window! It's our chance to change everything, and you're coddling our most powerful asset!"

Patrick remains unruffled. "I'd love for her to run, but I can't make her. You have power, Lathe. Your mother might be the most powerful Olvasho alive. If you're so keen to change things, why don't you run? Why don't you give up your life to serve the Olvasho? You can't expect your sister to give anything to the people who have persecuted her. To her, they are all like Keith."

"That isn't a fair assessment, Patrick. Most of the Olvasho are innocent. They have every right to be frightened. Their leaders have misled them, but we can put an end to it!"

"Sounds like your campaign speech is practically writing itself. The people will love your conviction."

"I can't run!" Lathe barks.

"Why? Being the head of the Olvasho will still allow you to look after mommy dearest."

A growl comes through the phone. "Don't pretend to understand my life!"

"Stop being so touchy."

"You're not taking this seriously!"

"Lathe, I don't have time for this. I have to get myself and Maggie ready for a wedding."

"I'm trying to save the future of the Olvasho, and you're going to a wedding?"

"Yes."

Lathe lets out a long sigh, trying to calm himself. He grumbles, "Who gets married on New Year's Eve?"

"Samantha. You know, your half-sister's sister."

"Fine, but while you're there, try persuading her to take leadership."

The line goes dead, and Patrick looks to Maggie and shrugs. "Some people take life too seriously. Come on girl, we have a wedding to prepare for."

Patrick jumps up and Maggie follows. The scarred Doberman Pinscher has basically become Patrick's dog since Emily has been staying with Ben. Not to mention, the dog can sense the entities living inside of Emily and they make her uneasy.

Adelaide is evil and must be destroyed, but to get rid of Adelaide, they must awaken the three creators of the Olvasho. Emily already possesses Valla, the first of her bloodline. And a few weeks ago, Patrick took on the spirit of Isa, the first of his bloodline. Except for making him more powerful, Isa is an amiable presence in his body. The only entity missing is Leona.

Patrick knows they need Lathe to take on the spirit of Leona, but he doubts Emily will ever give into Lathe's demands. Either way, he doesn't have time to think about it now. They have to get ready for a wedding.

"IT'S GOING to drop down into the twenties tonight," Ashley says, as she pushes Emily down into the chair in the fancy bathroom that adjoins to the ballroom. "Let me fix your makeup."

"Ash, my makeup is fine, and you know I don't want to look all made up."

"That's too bad because this day isn't about you. It's about Samantha and Dan, and they told me to make you look smoking hot."

"No, they didn't!"

Ignoring Emily, Ashley pulls out a giant bag of makeup and sets it on the counter. "Now, close your eyes."

Ashley's face is already done up with smoky eyes and bold lipstick. Her ultra-blond hair is spun into an outrageous updo. Put together with her willowy frame, Ashley looks like the love child of a supermodel and a rock star.

As Ashley works, Rochelle, the only bridesmaid Emily likes, hurries into the bathroom, complaining, "Alison and Eva might be the most depraved human beings I have ever met. They are out there rationing rice cakes. Rice cakes!" She throws herself into the lounge chair next to Emily. "And here we are hiding out in the bathroom while they get the bridal suite."

Ashley uses the makeup brush to point to the crystals sparkling in the chandelier above her head. "At least it's a nice bathroom."

"That's true," Rochelle admits. "Would you have time to do my makeup, too?"

EMILY WALKS to the bridal suite to help her sister into her dress. As she enters, her sister pulls her into the adjoining dressing room, pleading, "Emily, they are driving me crazy! They told me I wasn't allowed to eat anything because I didn't want to look fat on my wedding day. I am starving, and they won't shut up."

"Who? Eva and Alison?"

"Yes!"

"I'll take care of it, Sam. Stay here. I'll be right back with some food."

Emily walks past the girls in the bridal suite and goes out into the hall.

For a while, Sam thought she would have to postpone the wedding because her dad was in a coma and Emily was missing, but a few weeks earlier Patrick brought Emily back to town and that same week their dad, Mark, woke from his coma.

To explain her four-month disappearance, Emily told Samantha she suffered from amnesia. In truth, she suffered the spirits of her ancestors, Valla and Adelaide, who share possession of her body. Where Valla is benign, her mother Adelaide is cancer. For four months Adelaide had control over Emily's psyche, living through her body until Patrick found a way to suppress her temporarily. Now Emily is doing everything she can to make it up to her sister.

Emily walks down the hall to the room where Patrick is keeping Maggie. Entering the room, she pauses. Patrick's dazzling sapphire eyes settle on her, and she melts a little. His usual unruly blond hair is exquisitely groomed, and his contoured cheeks sport a natural glow despite it being winter in Ohio. A perfectly tailored black suit showcases his tall, lean body. "Wow, look at you! You look . . ." She doesn't know what's safe to say and she doesn't like her reaction to him, so she says, "You're going to break some hearts tonight."

She's wearing one of the silk floral robes Sam bought for all her bridesmaids. As she stands there stumbling over her words, Patrick feels the charge between them intensify. He's having enough trouble holding out against her increasingly tempting looks, so he's relieved she's been staying with Ben for the last two weeks. She and Ben have been friends for a long time, but ever since they started dating, nothing has gone smoothly.

"Beautiful doesn't even begin to do you justice, love."

Maggie nudges against Emily's leg, drawing her attention away from Patrick. "Maggie," she coos, bending to pet her dog. Years ago, Emily found the emaciated Doberman Pinscher curled up on her front doorstep. The dog's ears were clipped, her tail docked, and the scars down her sides were evidence of abuse. Emily adopted the pup and named her loyal companion, *Maggie*. "You are just the girl I was looking for." Glancing at Patrick, she says, "I need to borrow her. Would you do me a favor and grab some food from down the hall and bring it to the bridal suite? Lunch was catered, but Samantha didn't get anything to eat."

"Sure," he says, walking out behind her. While Emily and Maggie enter the bridal suite, Patrick continues down the hall to find the food.

"What is that dog doing in here?" Alison says, backing to a wall.

"This is Maggie. She's the ring bearer."

"What! I was expecting like a poodle or something."

"Nope, this is Maggie. I have to get her ready. I think this might go better if you're not here. You're making her nervous." Right on cue, Maggie starts growling. "See?"

Alison and Eva back to the door and slip out. Leah, the groom's sister and Emily's former bully, stays in the lounge chair, pulling her legs up as if that will protect her from Maggie.

"Relax, Maggie won't hurt you," Emily says, glad she and Leah worked things out. Maggie circles around to find a good spot on the floor while Emily calls, "Sam, it's safe to come out."

Samantha comes out of the dressing room and looks relieved to have both girls gone. "Where's Rochelle?"

"Ashley is doing her makeup. They should be done soon."

"It's almost time to change, and I'm still starving!"

"Don't worry. Patrick's bringing food."

After a small knock at the door, Rochelle enters carrying a platter piled with food. "Patrick asked me to bring this in."

"God love that man!" Samantha says grabbing a few finger sandwiches before Rochelle can set down the tray.

AN HOUR LATER, the girls in the wedding party are back together in the bridal suite.

"The guests are arriving," Leah says, peeking out the window.

Couple by couple they arrive dressed to the nines and carrying gifts. The black-tie event has women wearing evening gowns and men sporting tuxedos. Guests pile their offerings on the gift tables, check their coats, and allow the ushers to escort them to their seats.

Eva and Alison push Leah out of the way and peer through the window, searching for eligible bachelors. "I still call dibs on the dog handler," Eva says.

From the side, Leah sniggers, "Good luck with that."

"Ooh, what about him?" Alison says, pointing toward Alec. "Isn't that the girl who was doing your makeup, Rochelle? What's their story? Are they together, together?"

After Ashley finished Rochelle's makeup, she left to pick up Alec, who doesn't look happy to be here. Of course, Ashley talked him into coming in hopes that he and Morgan could work things out, but Morgan is bringing her boyfriend, Preston, tonight.

"He's spoken for," Emily cuts in. "As is the dog handler." She is fine with Patrick finding someone tonight, but it isn't going to be Eva or Alison.

A light knock has Emily turning away from the window to open the door for her dad. Mark takes in the room filled with beautiful women, but his eyes stop on the girl in white. "Samantha," he says softly, as he walks forward, "you look stunning."

"Thanks, Daddy," she says, tearing up. She wasn't sure he would be healthy enough to attend her wedding, and now here he is to walk her down the aisle. She couldn't be more pleased.

Samantha steps forward, and Mark whispers, "Don't cry, sweetheart."

"I'm just so happy you're here. You and Emily," she says, stepping into his arms.

Judy, the mother of the groom, bustles into the room, announcing, "It's time."

Before she knows it, Emily is walking down the aisle. She holds her flowers with both hands, attempting to match her pace to the lovely music Ben is playing at the front of the room.

Ben is the epitome of tall, dark, and yummy. His hair is as dark as night, and his eyes are warm chocolate to make one melt with hunger. Surrounding those delicious eyes are lashes long enough to make any girl envious. Teaching Taekwondo has enhanced his already broad shoulders and kept his muscles toned. Emily is distracted by his body until their eyes find each other. Love fills her heart, and she gives him her warmest smile.

Following Emily down the aisle is Dan's five-year-old cousin. She's wearing a miniature princess dress with pink bows adorning her cascading curls. She does her job perfectly, dropping flower petals as she goes. Her dad is one of the groomsmen, and when she sees him, she runs up to him, gaining her an "Ahh" from the guests.

Maggie walks in, and Patrick closes the double doors behind her. She has flowers draped over her shoulders and is holding a small white basket in her mouth. She saunters down the aisle coming to sit right in front of Emily.

Then the music changes and the double doors reopen. All the guests stand, turning to get a look at Samantha on her dad's arm. They glide forward, Samantha's gown and veil flowing elegantly behind her.

Both Dan and Samantha tear up during the ceremony. When

prompted, Maggie steps forward with the basket of rings, and the service continues. The couple is pronounced husband and wife and the crowd cheers as they kiss.

After an hour whirlwind of posing for photos, they announce the bridal party to the reception. A live band is playing, bringing the party to life. Food is passed around, the open bar is handing out drinks, and Samantha and Dan have their first dance before Emily can break away.

She finds Ben at a table with Morgan and Preston, Ashley and Alec, and Morgan's sister and her boyfriend. Emily sits in the empty chair next to Ben and gives him a kiss. "I can't believe I'm just now saying hello to you. This day has been one thing after the other. I am never having a big wedding."

Ben pulls her close and whispers, "I need you to come with me for a minute." Not waiting for an answer, he grabs her hand and drags her from the room. Ben seems to be searching for somewhere to go, so Emily takes charge, pulling him into the bridal suite down the hall. Once they're inside, Ben attacks, groping and kissing and doing everything aside from stripping her naked and having his way with her.

"Ben," Emily pants, pulling away. "Ben, we can't miss the whole evening."

Ben rests his forehead against hers, trying to rein in his desires. "This dress is going to kill me, Emily."

She smirks. "Sounds like a good way to go."

Ben pulls away. "I'm serious. You look so sexy in that dress. I hate that anyone else gets to see you in it."

She caresses his cheek. "But you're the only one who gets to peel me out of it later."

Something between a groan and a growl emanates from him, and he's ravishing her mouth again. She rarely gets to witness this side of him. He's always so controlled, and she loves the possessive glint in his eye that promises so much pleasure.

They eventually make it back to the reception and Ben leads

her directly to the dance floor where a love song is playing. He doesn't want to miss the opportunity to hold her. He notices Mark and makes a mental note not to grope her . . . too much.

They enjoy a few slow songs before a groomsman taps Ben on the shoulder. "Hey man, sorry, the band is asking if you'll move your guitar."

Ben nods and says to Emily, "Let me just run it out to my car. I'll be right back."

"Should I go with you?" she offers with a hint of teasing.

"If you go with me, I won't bring you back," he says, leaning in to kiss her before moving away.

"Emily," Sam says, rushing up from behind. "They said they're going to lock the bridal room. Will you help me get a few things out of there?"

"Sure," she says, following her sister. They pack up Samantha's things, and Emily helps her load it into the limo parked out front. It takes longer than expected, and Emily searches the parking lot, spotting Ben's Corvette but not Ben. He's probably inside looking for her.

Once back in the reception hall, Emily goes to sit at Ben's table. He isn't there, but Ashley and Alec are, and currently, they are having a contest to see who can hold a spoon on their nose the longest.

After watching Alec lose, Emily asks, "Have you guys seen Ben?"

Ashley puts a hand on her hip. "What? Are you embarrassed to be seen with us?"

"Of course, she is. You guys are children," Patrick says from over her shoulder.

Emily spins in her seat. "Hey, where have you been?"

"I had to run Maggie to my uncles. I didn't realize it would take so long. Traffic is a nightmare. There are DUI stops everywhere."

"Thanks for taking care of her, Patrick."

"I couldn't deprive Samantha of a family member. Come dance with me, love." He offers his hand.

"I'm waiting for Ben."

"He can come steal you away from me. Come on, just for a moment."

"Okay," she says, as he leads her to the dance floor.

CHAPTER TWO ~

ALEC IS STANDING with his back against the bar sipping his drink while watching Morgan on the dance floor. Alec heard she already met her boyfriend's parents at a fancy-schmancy Christmas party. They loved Morgan. Alec isn't surprised. Morgan is pretty hard not to love. The look on her face as she dances with Preston makes Alec grind his teeth.

Ashley nudges him, saying, "You've got a real stalker vibe going. Come on, tiger, let's go get some air."

"It's freezing outside," he says incredulously.

"It'll be good for you to cool off. I'm not taking no for an answer."

He downs the remainder of his drink and sets his glass on the bar. They grab their coats before exiting.

"Brrr, it's freaking freezing out here," Ashley complains, leaning against the side of the building. "You better cool down fast."

Alec's phone vibrates, and he pulls it out to find another message from Sadie, his ex. He broke up with her earlier this month when he found out she had faked a pregnancy as a way to trap him. She's been trying to win him back ever since, but he is relieved to be done with her and the nude photos she sends him don't tempt him the way they once did.

Ashley peeks over. "Is that Sadie, again?"

He nods and ignores the text, putting his phone away. Alec is trying to get his life together. He continues to work for the father who walked out on his mother when she was pregnant with him. Alec hates the man, but he needs the money and the experience, even if it means spending time with the devil.

"Are you still looking for your own place?" Ashley asks as she blows on her hands to warm them.

"I don't think I can afford it, but I'm trying."

"You have, like the best mom in the world. No one could blame you for staying there forever."

"I need my own place, Ashley. As much as I love my mom, it's time to prove to myself and Morgan that I can make it on my own."

Ashley exhales loudly and watches her breath in the freezing air. "This night isn't as much fun as I thought it'd be. I feel like everything has been weird since Emily came back. Like, have you noticed people acting different lately?"

"Weird shit's been going on longer than that, darlin."

Ashley sighs. "I keep throwing myself at Patrick and nothing! He's like, always with Emily, like lurking over her shoulder or something. He's even more of a stalker than you. Don't get me wrong. I like Patrick. He can follow me around like that anytime, but Emily doesn't seem interested in him. I don't know, their relationship is . . . Shit, I'm gossiping! I don't mean to be gossiping about this."

"Patrick and Emily slept in the same bed together. I mean, he . . . I don't get it. I don't know how Ben puts up with it. I've known Em for a long time, and she seems . . ."

The screech of tires steals their attention, and they watch a black car speed through the parking lot. Just beyond the first row of cars, the vehicle slows. The back door opens just long enough for something to tumble out. Then, the car speeds off.

Alec steps away from the building to get a view of the license plate as it pulls away.

"What was that?" Ashley asks.

Alec heads into the parking lot. "I'm gonna go check."

"Be careful!"

Peering around vehicles to get a better look at whatever fell out of the car, Alec sees a shadow on the ground and shouts, "Ashley, get over here!"

He rushes to the shadow, not just a shadow, a body. Ben is lying on his side, clutching his chest.

"Fuck!" Alec shouts. "Ashley, call 911!"

Rushing over to join him, she pulls out her phone.

Alec gets down on the ground and curses, pushing Ben to his back. "Ben, what the . . ." He reaches out but doesn't know where to touch his barely recognizable friend. Underneath a torn suit jacket, blood soaks through his white dress shirt. His face looks like someone smashed it in with a baseball bat. Alec swallows hard to hold back his emotion. "What happened to you, man?" Alec stumbles over his words, as he scoots closer to his friend.

Ben's lips are moving, but no sound escapes.

"It's okay, man, you don't need to talk," Alec soothes.

"Oh, my God!" Ashley gasps and hits *send* on her phone.

Alec continues reassuring Ben, "An ambulance will be here soon. Hang on, bro. Hang on."

Blood is dripping from Ben's moving lips as he keeps mouthing the same thing over and over. Alec leans closer, asking, "What's that?"

"Em," Ben breathes. He coughs, and blood sputters out of his mouth.

Ashley paces in the background, talking rapidly into her phone.

"Ashley, give them the address, tell them to hurry!" Alec urges.

She stops pacing to look for the number on the building.

Ben is choking, and Alec turns him on his side, but that only seems to make matters worse, so he rolls him back.

"Ben . . . Shit! Just . . . Shit! Hold on!"

Ben's body convulses, fighting to survive while he drowns in his own blood. Alec doesn't know how to fix this. Tears pool in his eyes and he yells, "There's gotta be a doctor in there!"

Ashley hangs up, wiping at her eyes, smearing black eyeliner across her cheeks. "Stay with him. I'll go get help."

Alec runs his hands through his hair, disheveling his chestnut waves. He leans back down to Ben, who is turning blue. Ben's body stills and his head lolls to the side.

"No, no, no, Ben, no, come on man! No, come on!" Alec puts his ear against Ben's chest but doesn't hear anything. He checks for a pulse, but his own heart is pounding so hard, he can't feel anything but his own thunderous heartbeat.

"Fuck!" he yells, as he starts chest compressions. "Ben, come on man!"

PATRICK AND EMILY sway together on the dance floor. "You're terribly clumsy, aren't you?" Patrick says in a deep silky voice. "Those were my first words to you. You've certainly proved me wrong."

In a mock baritone, Emily says, "It's rather endearing to find such a beautiful woman whose movements completely contradict the elegance a body like yours suggests." Switching to her normal voice, she says, "You were such an ass."

Patrick smiles. "I must have made an exceptional first impression since you still remember my exact words."

"Do you remember my first words to you?"

"You were yelling at me for laughing at you and calling you clumsy."

"That sounds right," she says, as they continue to sway.

"Patrick, none of this would've been possible if you had given up on me."

"I'd do anything for you, love."

"Do you think—" Her words end abruptly and her face drains of color. She looks toward the doors leading to the parking lot. "Patrick, do you feel that?"

"Wha—"

"Something's wrong," she gasps, taking off at a frantic pace, pushing and weaving her way through the crowd of dancers. Patrick follows close behind. As soon as they reach the foyer, Emily spins around. "Patrick, something has happened to Ben. He's . . . It's . . . something's happened."

"Emily, it's all right," he soothes, moving forward to console her.

She backs out of his reach, shaking her head. "No, Patrick, it's not all right!"

He catches a glimpse of a panic-stricken Ashley as she bursts through the glass doors from outside. Her black eyeliner is running, ruined by the tears streaming down her face. Her lips quiver as she looks at Emily and shouts, "We need a doctor! Now!"

Patrick steps forward. "Ashley, what—"

Emily shoves past both of them, darting out into the cold night. Before the door closes, she hears Patrick instruct, *"Ashley, go get Morgan and only Morgan!"*

Emily runs out into the deceivingly calm lamp-lit parking lot. Then she hears Alec simultaneously counting and shouting at Ben. She heads in that direction to find Ben lying on the ground while Alec performs CPR. Emily falls to her knees next to them.

"Come on, man! Fifteen, sixteen, seventeen . . ." Alec sees Emily and shouts, "Some fuckers just threw him out of a car and took off!"

Emily cradles Ben's head in her lap, his blood dripping onto her black gown. She closes her eyes and tries to focus on his injuries, but his body is rocking with each compression.

"Alec, stop!"

"The squad is on its way," he says, continuing his compressions.

She doesn't hear sirens yet, which means she might have enough time. She shoves Alec to the side. "Sorry, Alec, we don't have time for this."

"Emily, what the—" heavy footfalls cut off his complaint.

Patrick arrives, as Emily rips open Ben's shirt and places her palms against his battered chest. She cries out at the contact and closes her eyes, leaning into him.

Alec is shouting, "Emily, he needs CPR!" He makes a move to grab her, but Patrick catches his wrist. Alec spins to shove Patrick away, demanding, "Let go!"

Patrick comes right back and gets in Alec's face. "Do you want him to die?"

Alec is shaking his head.

"Then step back and let us save him."

Emily cries, "Patrick, I need your help!"

In a second, he's on the ground next to Emily as she instructs, "Get his head."

Ashley arrives with Morgan in tow.

Morgan gasps, "How did this happen?"

Ashley takes in the scene with astonishment. "Oh my God, what are they doing?"

"Morgan," Patrick instructs. "Deal with them while we fix this."

Morgan searches for an answer without giving away a secret she can't take back. "Umm . . ."

A light green haze covers Ben, growing until it encompasses his entire body.

"Well, that's going to be hard to explain," Morgan mumbles.

"Oh my God!" Ashley exclaims, staring at the unexplained glow.

"Eh' . . . you guys trust me, right?" Morgan asks them.

Ashley accuses, "You're a part of this! You know what's going on, don't you?"

"Fletch, what are they doing?" Alec can't stop shaking his head in bewilderment.

"They're helping him," Morgan explains.

Ben groans and coughs, still unconscious, but alive.

"No, no this isn't possible," Alec says, moving toward Ben while Ashley keeps repeating, "Oh my God!"

Morgan grabs Alec's hand. "Alec, I need you to trust them. If you can't do that, then trust me."

He breaks his focus on Ben as he hears sirens in the distance.

Patrick says, "Emily, we need to hurry!"

"Alec, please," Morgan begs, squeezing his hand.

Alec turns to Morgan completely speechless.

"Please," she mouths, again.

He searches her face. "This is why you changed over the summer," he says with realization.

While she swallows the lump in her throat, Ashley breaks their moment by saying, "Are you guys seeing this?"

They look toward Ben. His color is coming back, and his chest is moving up and down. They watch as the deep gash along his cheek begins closing up, healing on its own.

"Oh, thank God," Morgan sighs, placing her free hand against her chest.

Sirens wail and they see flashing lights in the distance.

Ashley leans into Morgan, saying, "They're amazing! I totally knew something was going on, but, like, I never dreamed . . ."

"I know," Morgan says.

"Why the fuck are you so calm?" Alec questions Ashley.

An ambulance pulls into the parking lot, and Morgan warns Patrick and Emily, "Guys, you need to wrap this up. The ambulance is here."

Patrick whispers, "He's going to be all right, Emily. We need to get out of the way and let the paramedics do their job."

The healing glow dissipates as Emily sits back on her heels. "We can do more than they can!"

"Yes, and we've already saved his life and patched up some injuries, but that is all we can do for now. We have to let them take him to the hospital."

"Then I'm going with him," she argues.

"Fine," Patrick says, "just let me do the talking."

Patrick turns to Alec, handing him a handkerchief. "Wipe your face and hands."

Alec gladly wipes the blood off himself, and Morgan helps him with his face.

The squad turns off its siren as it nears them. Curious wedding guests are making their way outside. Among them are Mark and his assistant, Chris, who arrive just as the paramedics reach Ben.

Morgan, Ashley, and Alec back up as Patrick begins speaking to the paramedics. Mark makes it to Morgan, asking, "What's going on?"

"They saved Ben's life."

"What happened to him?" Mark's eyes move over the group.

Ashley explains, "This black car just came screeching through and tossed him out and then took off. We didn't realize it was a person. Alec went over to check it out and yelled for me when he saw it was Ben."

Alec adds, "It was a newer Ford Mustang, no plates."

Paramedics load Ben onto a stretcher, and soon they are moving him into the back of the ambulance. Emily climbs in with him while Patrick heads to the front to sit shotgun.

Turning to Mark, Morgan says, "The three of us watched them save his life."

Mark cautions Alec and Ashley. "I'd think twice before sharing what you saw here tonight."

"Are you kidding me!" Ashley exclaims, "I'm totally psyched! I've always wanted to be part of some big secret!"

Alec is looking at Ashley like she's lost her mind. Once he

realizes everyone is waiting for him to respond, he says, "Yeah, sure. I can keep a secret, but I have some questions."

Now that the adrenaline is starting to fade, Morgan begins shivering. Alec feels her shaking and immediately removes his jacket and drapes it over her shoulders.

"Thank you," she says, looking up at him. He tugs at the sleeves of the coat, pulling Morgan into his chest. He wraps his arms around his oldest friend—the love of his life—and she returns his embrace. It feels natural to hold one another, but Preston ruins their moment when he breaks through the gathering crowd to claim Morgan. "Oh, God, Morgan!"

She pulls away from Alec and goes to reassure her boyfriend that she's okay.

Ashley moves in next to Alec and nudges him with her shoulder. "Sorry I made you come with me tonight."

Alec wears a blank expression. His adrenaline is fading, and before an almost unbearable reality sets in, he wanders off through the crowd of annoying gawkers, making his way back to the reception hall. The music is still blaring inside the ballroom, and there is a group of drunk girls on the dance floor entirely oblivious to what's going on outside.

Alec approaches the bar and orders a rum and coke. They haven't been asking for his ID all night, so he gulps it down and orders another. He wants to forget tonight ever happened. He just watched his best friend die—a nightmare come to life. Even if Ben is going to be okay, that image will continue to haunt Alec. He fingers his empty glass, noticing blood on his hand—his best friend's blood. He orders another drink and wipes his hand on a napkin.

As he finishes drink number four, a bridesmaid stumbles over and leans onto the bar, saying, "Scuse me, Mr. Bartender. Could I trooble you fur a vodka cranberry?"

"Sure, doll," he replies.

Alec watches him make her drink. "Damn, that's a strong drink," he mumbles.

The bridesmaid notices him and leans his way. "Wha'd you say?"

"Nothing."

"You sure?" she asks, moving closer.

The bartender sets her drink on the counter, giving her a wink before someone else pulls him away.

She grabs the glass and taps it against Alec's empty glass. "Cheers to an open bar! Oh no," she pouts, "yours is all gone."

"Yeah, he doesn't make mine quite as strong as he makes yours."

"Wha'd are you drinking?" she slurs.

"Rum and coke."

She grabs the bartender's attention and asks for a rum and coke as she curls her lips around her straw to sip her drink. When he sets the new glass on the counter, he says. "You don't want to drink too much, babe."

She smiles at him and slides the drink and her attention back to Alec.

"Thanks," he says, before taking a sip.

"Better?"

"Stronger, for sure."

"He was making you weak drinks, the bastard!"

Alec laughs. "You saved my whole night, but you might have gotten yourself cut off. The bartender looks pissed."

"I don't need any more to drink after this, so I was done with him anyway. You on the other hand." She strokes a hand down his chest. "Yum-my. What's your story? Are you taken?"

He hesitates, looking toward the door. Just then, Morgan walks through with his blood-spattered jacket over her arm and Preston's arm around her shoulder. He watches as Preston leans down while Morgan tilts her chin up. Their kiss isn't anything spectacular, but it's enough for Alec to say, "No, no, I'm single."

The drunk girl grabs his tie and pulls him in for a kiss. She whispers against his lips, "How about you meet me in the ladies' room down the hall in two minutes."

He grins against her lips, and that's all the answer she needs. "See you there," she says before wandering off.

He's not far behind her, but when he reaches the hall, he has to weave through the crowd of people still gathered. By the doors, he sees Morgan huddled with Preston and Ashley. As if his eyes are magnets, Morgan looks directly at him. He spins away and walks down the hall to meet his bridesmaid.

Morgan watches Alec head down the hall. He looks pissed, and she wonders where he's going. Her phone chimes and she reads the message. "Patrick says they took him to Grant Hospital."

"That's not far from here," Preston says. "Do you want to head over?"

"I still have Alec's coat. Why don't you get the car while I run this to him and let him know where we're going?"

"Okay," Preston agrees, kissing her cheek before exiting the building.

"I'll come with you," Ashley offers.

"No, give me a minute," Morgan responds. "I need to talk to him."

"Sure," Ashley says, hanging back as Morgan fights her way through the crowd. She heads down the hall and passes a few empty banquet rooms and sees a few closed office doors. When she runs out of hallway, she turns around, wondering where he went. The only place he could've gone is the restroom. She waits outside the men's room, but after a moment becomes impatient and sends him a text.

When she doesn't hear back, she enters the woman's restroom thinking she must have missed him. She freezes in the open doorway when she sees a couple pressed up against the counter kissing as they race to undress one another.

Holding in her gasp, she silently backs out of the bathroom, eyeing the two going at it. They don't seem to notice her as she slips out into the hall. She rushes back to the lobby and is halfway out the door when Ashley intercepts her.

"Morgan," she says, grabbing her arm.

Morgan spins, throwing Alec's coat at her. "Here, you give it to him!"

Ashley takes what's thrown at her and watches Morgan stalk off to Preston's car.

"What the hell?" Ashley mutters to herself. Looking back the direction Morgan came; she narrows her eyes and heads down the corridor to give Alec what's coming to him.

CHAPTER THREE ~

ALEC BREATHES out a curse as his bridesmaid—*what the fuck was her name again*—begins undressing him. He slides a hand up her leg, lifting the silky material. She tugs at the hem of his unbuttoned shirt. He lifts her to sit on the counter. Her legs wind around him, and he presses his body into her. She unhooks the button on his dress pants, undoes the zipper, and reaches down to set him free. He groans, shifting to give her better access. He catches his reflection in the mirror and abruptly pulls away, severing her hold on him.

"Hey!" she complains, "What are you doing?"

"You're not Morgan," he answers.

"Baby, I'll be anyone you want me to be."

Alec shakes his head. "Do you even know my name?"

She looks at him like he's crazy. "Does it matter?"

"It does to me," he says, as he refastens everything she's undone.

"Are you kidding me?" she huffs, pushing herself off the counter and back onto her feet.

She curses at him, but he doesn't care. He checks his reflection before walking out the door. He promised himself he was done with this. If he hurries maybe he can catch up with Morgan.

On his way to find her, he sees Ashley leaning against a wall not far from the bathroom, his coat draped over her folded arms. "That didn't take long."

"What?" he asks, stopping next to her.

"Hope she was worth it," she says in a bitter tone, as she pulls away from the wall.

"Did Morgan leave?" he asks, eyeing his coat.

"She left after she saw you in the bathroom with Eva."

Eva! That was her name.

"What were you thinking, Alec? I brought you as my guest so you could work things out with her, and you go and screw a bridesmaid in the bathroom."

"Ashley." He grabs her arm and spins her to face him. "Nothing happened in there. I didn't do anything. I stopped it."

"So, Morgan didn't see you making out with the slutty bridesmaid?"

Realizing what she must have seen, he grabs a fist full of hair and shouts, "Fuck!"

"Yeah . . . now get your ass in the car so we can go to the hospital."

He follows her out to her car. He may not be completely drunk, but he is far from sober. "God damn it, Ashley. I keep screwing this up."

"Yeah! You do!"

"Why is she with that douche?"

"Cause he's nothing like you. He's a nice guy, a safe guy, and he spoils her. Did you really think she was just gonna like, wait around for you forever, while you're out there screwing other girls?"

"I don't do that anymore!"

"Actually, you do! Saying no to one skank after making out with her for ten minutes doesn't make you a good guy, Alec."

"Ben died in my fucking arms, Ashley. He died!" He shakes his head, attempting to collect his thoughts. "Doesn't it piss you off they've been hiding this from us? I mean . . . what the hell? Nothing makes sense tonight. I had Morgan in my arms. And Ben died. And what did Emily and Patrick do? This sci-fi bullshit is too much. That bridesmaid hitting on me is the only thing that made sense tonight. It's what I know. Just like you said . . . it's what I do."

Silence lingers in the car, turning the rumble of the Mustang's engine into a formidable noise. The street lights saturate the dark night as they near the hospital.

Ashley sighs. "If it makes you feel better, tomorrow you probably won't remember tonight."

"You think I'm just going to forget?" he asks, doubtfully. "I'm not *that* drunk."

"I think they're gonna make us forget," she says. "I overheard Morgan talking with Emily's dad. I think Patrick is going to do it when we get to the hospital. He's gonna rewrite our memories for tonight."

Alec shifts uncomfortably, asking, "Can they do that?"

Ashley shrugs. "I don't know."

"Do you think they've done it to us before?"

Ashley shakes her head, saying, "I really don't know."

"Can we make a stop before going to the hospital?"

"Of course we can. I'm in no hurry to have my memories erased."

"The less I remember about tonight, the better," Alec says. "But there is something Ben will want if he wakes up. I want to do at least one thing right tonight. Turn left up here."

Alec guides them to the opulent Cetrone mansion.

Months earlier, Ben's parents had kicked him out and cut him off. He doesn't miss his parents, but he has been complaining about the separation from his fifteen-year-old sister, Molly. The two were close until she felt Ben had abandoned her. Her stubbornness and assumption of betrayal prevented her from accepting Ben back into her life, but Alec knows she loves her brother and will want to be there for him.

Ashley shamelessly pulls the car right up to the front steps, and she and Alec walk to the front double doors. Alec rings the doorbell, and a moment later the door opens.

"Hey, Natalia," Alec says, giving her his sexy dimpled grin.

The Cetrone's young housekeeper returns his flirtatious smile. "Alec," she greets with a hint of an accent.

"Oh my God," Ashley exclaims. "You're like a life-size Barbie!"

Natalia is taken aback by Ashley's outburst, and Alec gives Ashley an incredulous look. He draws Natalia's attention back to him, saying, "I know security has probably already been notified, but Ben was severely injured tonight. We're here to pick up Molly before we head to the hospital."

Alarm registers on her face, and she stutters, "Alec, I . . . I'm not supposed to—"

"They had to resuscitate him. He could die, and I know he'll want to see Molly."

Natalia stands there biting her lip, looking unsure.

Ashley pipes up, "Listen, I get that you're scared of Ben's parents. They're your employers, but you care about Ben, too."

Natalia's eyes flip back to Alec, and she says, "I'm afraid, I cannot help you. You are trespassing on private property, and you have approximately . . ." she looks at her watch, "six minutes and twenty seconds to leave before the police arrive. Goodnight."

She closes the door between them, and Alec repeatedly curses until Ashley tugs at his sleeve and drags him back to the car. After a moment, Alec questions, "Why aren't we leaving?"

Ashley smiles. "Silly boy, she was totally helping us out. She told us exactly how much time we have instead of telling us to leave immediately. I guarantee you that woman is talking to Molly right now, and Molly has . . ." Ashley looks at her phone.

'Four minutes and fifteen-seconds' to get her ass in this car so we can leave before the police get here."

Alec frowns. "You got all that from what she said?"

"Duh, I may look like an airhead, but it's all brains up here," she says, pointing to her head.

"Ashley, you've lost your fucking mind. You don't know these people."

"I'm a great judge of character."

"Really? Don't forget I've met some of your exes."

Ashley raises a shoulder, saying, "Even jerks can be fun for a time. Are you telling me you never spent time with a bitchy girl just because it's what you were in the mood for at the time?"

"That . . . that has nothing to do with this."

"Of course, it doesn't." She rolls her eyes. "You and I are alike in a lot of ways. I'm just slightly better in every way, but then again, how can you get better than this?" she boasts with a provocative shimmy. "The only reason you're not all hot and bothered right now is cause Morgan has your heart all constipated."

"You think what you have is better than this?" He waves a hand down his body in mock seduction.

"Oh, Alec, your brand of yummy is so off limits. Besides, even if we wanted to, this . . ." she motions between them, "would never work."

"Oh, and you know that because you're such a good judge of character?"

"Exactly."

"Then where is she? It's been two minutes."

"Trust me, she'll be in this car before we pull away," Ashley says, starting the engine.

"What if the police get here early?"

She puts on a panicked face and tears well in her eyes, "Oh my God, I swear officer, we tried to leave, but my car wouldn't start. It took like forever, to turn over or whatever and I . . . Oh, please don't arrest us. I would lose my scholarship, and like, I didn't even know we were trespassing—"

"I get it," Alec says. "And that's terrifying. Remind me not to get on your bad side."

Her face straightens before a cocky grin sweeps her lips up and she wipes away the tears from under her eyes. "Alec, get out so we can let her in."

"What?" he questions, as a tap comes to the window. He turns to see Molly standing outside his door, and he immediately jets out of the car and folds down the seat to let her crawl into the back.

Once he's back in the car, Ashley takes off before he has the chance to close the door. "Hey, I'm Ashley," she greets, splitting her attention between the rearview mirror and the driveway. "You must be the infamous, Molly."

Molly glares at her through the mirror, before turning her head to look out the window into the darkness.

"Okay," Ashley comments, "I see brooding is a family trait."

Molly and Ben have a lot in common. They both have their father's dark features, bronze skin, deep brown eyes, and nearly black hair. While Ben has his father's height, Molly takes after their mother's petite, ballerina build, all elegant grace. She also inherited her mother's ringlet curls. She looks older than fifteen, a side effect of turning into an adult long before she should have, but surviving in the Cetrone mansion meant acquiring certain traits. Where Ben maintained his kindhearted demeanor, Molly gives off an air of cold-hearted bitch.

Alec spins in his seat to look at Molly. "Hey," he coaxes, as they pull out onto the street.

Her eyes flash to his, her body remaining stiff. She opens her mouth to speak, but her voice breaks and she looks back out the window, clearing her throat, and tries again, "What happened to Ben?"

Alec takes a deep breath, all the humor from a moment ago, long gone. "We're not completely sure. We were all at a wedding tonight, and Ben said he was taking his guitar out to his car. The next thing we know, he's been brutally beaten. His heart stopped, but they got it going again. He was doing a little better by the time the paramedics took him."

"Who's she?" Molly tilts her head toward Ashley. "Your girlfriend?"

Ashley laughs, "Not even close. I'm a friend of Alec and Ben, you know the brother you said was dead to you."

"Easy, Ashley," Alec warns. "Her brothers in the hospital."

"Alec, why is she here?" Molly asks, "Why aren't you driving?"

"He's a bit intoxicated," Ashley answers.

Molly huffs, "Of course you are."

MOLLY IS the first through the doors of the hospital. Morgan had sent a message to Ashley telling them where to meet everyone. Molly follows the signs, not caring if she loses the others. She bursts into the waiting room like a flash of lightning, demanding, "Where is he?"

Morgan stands from her chair. "Molly, you're here! Wait, how did you know?"

Alec enters the room behind her, and Morgan's eyes soften. Alec meets her gaze and looks away. It seems like every time Alec hurts her; he does something to make her fall for him again, which only confuses her more.

"He's still in surgery," Morgan answers, sitting back in her chair. Preston reaches for her hand, and she gives it to him, along with a sad smile. He's trying to comfort her, but Morgan feels he shouldn't be here. She doesn't know how to tell him to go or even that she really wants him to leave; she just knows he doesn't belong.

Looking around the room, Alec asks, "Where is everyone?"

Morgan explains, "Patrick said he knows one of the residents. I guess they are letting him and Emily observe the surgery."

"Is that even a thing?" Alec questions, "Is that allowed?"

"See," Preston comments, "I'm not the only one who thinks it's weird. There has to be protocol against it or—"

"I guess I've heard of it before," Alec interrupts after seeing Morgan's panic. "I just didn't know Patrick had that kind of pull. I'm glad they're with him. It seems like they're his guardian angels."

"It was your quick action that saved his life," Preston says.

"Excuse me, I believe I deserve some of that credit, too," Ashley says, entering the room. She looks between Molly and Alec, miffed. "Really, guys, go on ahead," she says sarcastically, "Leave the girl in heels and a gown behind to fend for herself." She slaps Alec's shoulder with the back of her hand and goes to sit next to Morgan, complaining dramatically, "I could've been kidnapped!"

"Nah," Alec jokes, "You would've fought 'em off with your bitchiness and sarcasm."

Molly interrupts, "So, we're just supposed to sit here?"

Morgan nods. "For now, yes. That's all we can do."

"How about finding out who did this to him?"

Morgan stands to place a comforting hand on Molly's arm, but Molly jerks out of her reach.

Morgan says, "The police are investigating. I know you want to do something, but just being here is enough. I promise, he's going to be okay. He has the best team working on him."

Morgan has every confidence that Ben will be okay because she knows Emily will go to any length to make sure of it. She caught the look in her eye back at the venue. She saw anger and determination, but no fear. Patrick spoke to the police and since Mark couldn't leave his daughter's reception, his assistant, Chris, was tasked with pulling up any surrounding surveillance feed.

Molly huffs and goes to wait on the other side of the room.

A FEW HOURS LATER, a nurse comes into the waiting room. "Are you the family and friends of Benjamin?"

Molly stands. "Yes."

The nurse says, "He's out of surgery. We have him medically sedated, but you can come back to see him now. We ask for no more than two visitors at a time."

"I'm going," Molly says.

The rest of them look around at one another until Ashley speaks up, "Alec, you should go back. He's your best friend, and you need to get those images out of your head."

Alec looks to the floor, rubbing his fingers over his chin.

"Go on, Alec," Morgan encourages.

He stands to follow Molly and the nurse back to Ben's room.

Molly enters the room timidly, but as soon as she sees Ben, she rushes over to him, completely ignoring Patrick and Emily.

Alec enters slower, taking in the room and the people in it. Patrick looks as pristine as usual except for slightly messy hair and blood on his sleeve. Emily, on the other hand, looks like she walked straight out of Hell. Still in her black gown and heels, she leans on the windowsill, the city lights sparkling through the night behind her. She stares at Ben with her fingers tapping against her lips, showing off her blood-stained hands. Flecks of blood are scattered across her chest like freckles and Alec swears the large green pendant around her neck is nearly black.

Alec blows out a breath. "You okay, Burk?"

She doesn't look at him as she responds. "That's a complicated question. I don't have an answer for you."

Patrick says, "She'll be okay because Ben will be okay."

Pushing forward off the windowsill to stand over Ben, Emily snaps, "I want to hunt down and murder whoever did this to him."

Patrick moves closer, saying, "Emily, they are already looking into it. We won't let them get away with this."

Molly's eyes are wide as she stares across the bed at Emily.

Emily glances up at her and shares, "He'll be happy you're

here even though you've been a shitty sister. His world fell apart, and you ignored him." Tears leak from Molly's eyes, as Emily continues, "I was killing myself to get back to him, and you fucking ignored him!"

"That is enough!" Patrick grabs Emily's arm, pulling her toward the door, but she jerks out of his grip. Patrick steps between her and the others. "Emily, you need to take a break."

She takes a breath to yell at him, but Alec calmly says, "Burk, you were a shitty sister, too."

Emily blinks, and Patrick turns to look at him, wondering if he has a death wish.

Alec continues, "You disappeared when your sister needed you. Nobody is perfect, and life can be fucking brutal, but you saved Ben's life. You saved me from years of nightmares. You're a hero." He puts his arm around Molly's shoulder. "Don't let your words turn you into something you're not. We're all doing the best we can here."

Emily takes a sighing breath, leans over the hospital bed and kisses Ben tenderly on the cheek. Standing straight, she says, "I'll be back." Then she turns to leave.

Once inside the public restroom, she allows the feelings she's been repressing all night to break through. She places her hands on the counter, leaning over to catch her breath. Tears pool in her eyes, spilling down her cheeks when she squeezes her lids tight to shut out reality. She wants to scream, but it wouldn't do any good. She lifts her head and stares, startled by her reflection in the mirror.

Her plunging, silky, black halter dress is still intact. Her hair looks beautiful in its messy, undone waves as if it were skillfully tossed from its sleek updo. Her porcelain skin is radiant against the dark material of the dress in spite of the crimson bloodstains spattered across her bare skin.

She will not forget tonight. She will never forgive the person responsible. She grabs the side of the sink as she leans in closer to the mirror. She wants revenge. Wiping away her tears, she steps back. She debates washing her hands of the bloodstains but decides she likes it better this way. It makes more of an impression.

She doesn't alert Patrick to what she's doing because he will try and stop her. She takes the elevator down and exits through the lobby. She reaches out with her mind to find the most eligible driver. She sees a man parked two rows from the front entrance. He just got off a twelve-hour shift working in the E.R. She enters his passenger side door, and he makes a sound of surprise. "What are—"

"We met earlier. You agreed to take me to my friend's house once you got off your shift."

His confusion melts away as her words implant themselves in his head. He nods, saying, "Oh yeah, where was that again?"

She gives him the address to enter into his GPS, and they pull out of the hospital parking lot.

"It's the strangest thing, but I can't remember how we met. I guess it's been a really long day."

"Let's not talk," she suggests.

He nods, readily agreeing and they drive the next three hours in silence.

A month ago, Patrick took Emily to an Olvasho meeting in Fort Wayne where Emily discovered she has a half-brother, Lathe, on her biological father's side. After the long car ride to reflect over what happened to Ben and the magnitude of its meaning, they finally pull up in front of the well-maintained mansion. She hadn't expected Lathe to stoop to this level, but she knows very little about him. Emily exits the car, saying, "This won't take long. Stay here."

PATRICK PACES the hall outside Ben's hospital room. He can't believe Emily took off without warning. He's called her at least a dozen times, even though he knows she didn't have her phone on her. He worries she might do something reckless.

He rubs a hand over his face, as Morgan comes down the hall.

"You okay?" she asks.

"I'd be better if I knew where she went and what she was thinking right now. I can't believe she would leave Ben like this, especially after all she did to save his life. And now I have Ashley and Alec to contend with. The longer I let them know the truth, the higher the risk of brain damage."

"So, you're going to erase their memories of tonight?"

"It isn't a safe secret, Morgan. Knowing only puts them at risk."

"I know. It would just be nice not to lie to them all the time."

Patrick looks down at his phone, hoping Emily will call to let him know where she went and what he should do.

CHAPTER FOUR ~

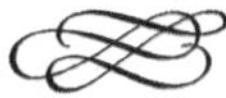

STARTLED AWAKE, Lathe opens his eyes to find a shadow looming over him. As he sits up in bed, he reaches out with his mind.

"Emily?" he questions.

"Brother."

"What's this about?" he says, reaching for the lamp next to the bed. Dim light floods the room. Lathe stifles a gasp, studying his beautifully sinister half-sister. Her sleek black gown and heels paired with bloodstained skin are more than a little alarming.

She steps forward, demanding, "Was it you or one of your men who attacked Ben?"

Wiping the sleep from his eyes, he says, "You'd make our father proud with your flair for the dramatic, but I'm much less impressed." He returns her cold stare, but insecurities rise up hideous and uninvited. He doesn't like how exposed he feels sitting here bare-chested, his scars on full display. "How about I get dressed, and we reconvene downstairs in five minutes?"

"I'll give you two." She turns and walks out of his room, closing the door behind her.

Lathe jets out of bed and grabs the hoodie and jeans he left lying over a chair from the night before. He throws on his clothes and heads down to see why his sister decided to show up in the wee hours of the morning dressed to the nines and coated in someone else's blood.

His feet are silent on the stairs as he descends and finds her waiting at the bottom.

She looks lost, but as soon as she notices him, her face hardens. "Did Sky demand control or did he manipulate everyone into voting for him? It's been bothering me since the Olvasho meeting."

"He was voted in," Lathe answers.

"How long did he hold control before everyone realized their mistake?"

"I suppose some knew right away, but by the time the others figured it out, his powers were impossible to overcome, and no one was brave enough to run against him, so he ran unopposed for over a hundred years."

"Cowards!" Emily spits. "Didn't anyone wonder why he wasn't aging?"

"No, everyone knew what he was doing, but we couldn't stop him. Some tried to fight back, but we lost too many good people. Your mom was one of them."

"But at least she fought."

"And lost," Lathe says. "If Valla blood couldn't win against him, what chance did the rest of us have?"

"So you just gave up!"

Through clenched teeth, he growls, "I never gave up."

"And what about me? Do you fear me, Lathe?"

"As long as you're in control of your mind, no."

"Why? Everyone else does. They fear me enough to hand me Sky's position of supreme ruler. You want to hand it to me, too. If it's not because you fear me, then why?"

Lathe rubs at the scars on his face. "I looked into who you were before you knew what an Olvasho was. You haven't coerced any of your friends, yet they would die protecting you. We need someone worthy of that kind of loyalty."

"So, was Ben willing to die for me? Is that what this is?"

"I take it that's his blood all over you, but it wasn't me."

"I will cause pain to anyone who tries to hurt the people I love, Lathe. Honest to God, I don't want this responsibility, but whoever did this will pay and if I have to be a leader to ensure justice, then so be it."

Lathe smiles, coming forward. "So, you accept?"

Emily glances up at him with angry eyes and mentally assaults his body. He shrieks, grabbing his head and dropping to his knees. Emily moves forward, continuing her attack. Once she is standing over him, she lets the pain disappear from his mind. The entire incident lasts only a few seconds but leaves Lathe crumpled on the floor fighting for his next breath.

He looks up at her with wild eyes. "What the hell!"

She leans in. "You might think I'm worthy of protection, but I don't need it."

"Noted," he grumbles, getting to his knees.

"I'll be your leader, and the first thing I will do is tear down this broken system and find something that works for everyone, not just the elite few."

"A welcome change," he says, standing to his full height.

She looks up at him. She may be small, but she's a force to be reckoned with. "You better pray he doesn't die because if he dies, I'll be back here for you, Lathe."

"It wasn't me!"

"Then find out who it was!" she shouts, before turning to leave.

Lathe watches Emily push her way through the solid oak doors, wondering if she even realizes she's leaving burn marks in the wood. Her powers are manifesting physically now—a chill of thrilled terror slices through him.

He picks up his phone to make a call, and it only rings twice.

"Lathe, to what do I owe the pleasure?"

"Your cruelty knows no ends, Patrick. Just when I was beginning to think you truly cared for someone other than yourself, you go and pull something like this."

"I'm afraid you're going to have to be more specific."

"I hope you know what you're doing. We might agree Emily is the best individual to appoint as Olvasho leader, but you and I both know she doesn't have the discipline needed to lead. Even now, she's one dead boyfriend away from a meltdown. I will not take the blame if he dies."

"Lathe, there must be a miscommunication. You seem to think I'm the one who put Ben in the hospital."

"He's your competition."

Patrick laughs into the phone, mocking, "My competition? If I wanted to hurt Ben, there are cleaner ways. Emily needs me, but she also needs Ben, at least for now. I suspect she will eventually need your help as well, so as much as I appreciate your accusation, your assumption is incorrect."

"She just came here to accept leadership and threaten my life should anything happen to any of you."

"Sounds reasonable."

"I have nothing to do with what happened tonight."

"Then I suggest you find out who did."

"Wow," Lathe says, "you sound just like her, or maybe she sounds like you. Either way, why would she assume I had anything to do with this?"

"She doesn't trust the Olvasho, and she feels like you threatened her. Her experience with our kind has been tenuous. Her body was taken over for months by an Olvasho claiming to have her best interests at heart. Before that, her biological father—the leader of the Olvasho—tried to manipulate, then murder her. And then there's me, the Olvasho she trusted the most who betrayed her. She's forgiven me, but you can see the pattern."

"That is not who we are. I thought you were showing her differently."

"I've changed, but my past remains, Lathe. I have manipulated and murdered. Perhaps if someone more honest had taught her, she wouldn't be so leery, but had it not been me, Emily would not have defeated Sky. I'm doing the best I can for her. She'll come around and in the meantime, find the responsible party. Ben should survive this, but only because Emily and I got to him before the paramedics."

"What if it wasn't an Olvasho, Patrick? What if someone has a vendetta against the guy?"

"You've met him. Does he seem like the type to be wrapped up in something untoward?"

"Then maybe it was random. Wrong place at the wrong time."

"They plucked him out of a room filled with three hundred people, beat the life out of him before we even realized he was missing and then dropped him off to Emily by throwing him out of a moving vehicle. They were sending a message, Lathe."

"Who would benefit from pissing off Valla blood?" Lathe asks, before sighing. "I'll look into it."

PATRICK HANGS up and approaches Ashley and Alec in the waiting room. "That was a brilliant thing you did, bringing Molly here. I know Ben will appreciate it. Now, if you would follow me, I need to talk to both of you about what you saw earlier."

Alec looks to Morgan. With regret written across her face, she turns away, knowing what Patrick has planned for them.

Ashley's eyes flare, and she grabs Alec's hand, squeezing tight. She doesn't want to forget. She knows it isn't up to her, but she damn well is going to plead her case. Together, they get up and follow Patrick out of the hospital waiting room.

Alec continues to hold Ashley's hand, feeling melancholy. Alec doesn't want to remember this night. Ben died in his arms, and he messed up with Morgan, again. But it doesn't matter if he forgets that second part, because Morgan will remember, and he will be clueless to the pain he has caused her.

Patrick leads them into an empty patient room and closes the door.

Ashley says, "So you have, like superpowers?"

Patrick smirks. "Something like that."

"Are you going to make us forget?" she asks.

A look of sympathy crosses Patrick's face while Alec grumbles, "Just get it over with."

Patrick inspects Alec and says, "Before I reach into your mind and pull out the information, I need to know this is what you want. There are risks involved when altering such a traumatic memory. I will leave as much as I can, but the strong emotions surrounding tonight's events will make it difficult to replace the memory. You will have gaps and everything about this evening will feel blurry."

"Just do it," Alec says.

Patrick nods and turns to address Ashley.

"I won't tell anyone, I swear. You've gotta believe me."

Giving a warm smile, Patrick reaches out to tilt Ashley's chin up. "You remember Lathen. Lathe is skilled in memory care, which is the Olvasho's name for altering memories. You remember his name, his face, and even pieces of your conversation with him. I'm afraid you have a very rare genetic component that will render any of my memory tampering useless as you are partially immune."

She looks at Alec who wears a worried expression. "So, why won't you let him remember, too?"

"He doesn't want to remember."

"Alec?" she questions.

Alec looks down. "I don't want to remember the death and resurrection of my best friend."

Patrick says, "He's smart to forget. This secret will only place him in danger. The Olvasho like to kill outsiders who know our secrets."

"But Morgan knows, Mark knows. And I suspect Ben knows."

Patrick gives her a look as if the answer is right in front of her. When she fails to see it, he explains, "Mark was beaten within an inch of his life and left in a coma for four months because of this secret. Ben was beaten to death tonight, likely by Olvasho. Morgan has people looking out for her and watching her closely. It is a dangerous secret, Ashley. Forgetting is the safest thing for Alec. You, unfortunately, don't have a choice."

CHAPTER FIVE ~

Ashley is let in on the Olvasho secret only to be dismissed. As soon as Ben is out of the hospital, Emily and Patrick pack their bags and move to Fort Wayne so she can take leadership of the Olvasho. Morgan spends any free time she has with Preston. Ben, making a full recovery, works all of the time. Alec has been avoiding her. Her BFF, Jeremy, spends all of his time in a new relationship. Ashley has other friends, but recently she finds them too shallow or annoying.

So, a month after she learns the truth, Ashley finds herself alone in this seedy bar. She tells herself to stop coming here, but she is a woman obsessed. She can't stop thinking about Lathe, and every time she comes to the place they met, she remembers more of their conversation. Patrick said Lathe is skilled in altering memories, and Ashley wonders if Lathe would have been so revealing had he known she would remember their entire conversation.

Tonight, at the bar, guys are hitting on her, but she doesn't pay them any attention. She takes another swig of her drink and realizes she is brooding. She needs to go home. She grabs her phone to get an Uber when her *Spidey-senses* tingle and she looks up. And there he is standing in the entrance.

LATHE HAD to get her out of his head, so he finally broke down and made the drive to Columbus. He doesn't like the idea of her spending so much time at this bar, but then again, she is only here because she is looking for him.

Her inky eyes land on him almost immediately as if she was expecting him. She watches every step he takes as if she can't quite believe he's here.

He stops in front of the table. "Ashley," he says, his voice deep and sultry.

"Lathe," she returns.

He gestures to the table. "Mind if I sit with you?"

She tips her head and leans back on her seat. "I was hoping I would see you, again."

He takes the seat to her left. "Is that why you're here in this bar tonight?"

"Yes."

"You should stop coming here."

"And why's that?"

"It's not safe."

She lifts her drink to take a sip. When she sets it down, she asks, "How's your mom?"

Her ability to surprise him hasn't changed. "She's the same."

"Still alive because of you."

Her words feel like a challenge. "Yes."

She leans back and twists a strand of her platinum hair. "So, what brings you here tonight, Lathe?"

"I wanted to talk to you."

The fingers twirling in her hair pause, then drop. "Should I feel honored or frightened you came all this way to see me?"

"I thought you weren't frightened by me."

"I'm not, but I don't want to hurt your ego."

"Why aren't you afraid of me?"

"You've given me no reason to be frightened. You even sat on my left to hide your scars from me."

She notices everything. He makes himself turn to face her, revealing his scars, hoping to—what? He doesn't know what he's trying to accomplish. He wants to impress and evade her. He leans forward, saying, "You remember . . . everything, don't you?"

"I remember you. I remember our conversation." She places her hand against his scarred cheek. "Patrick said that's unusual."

She is challenging him, again, this time with her touch. Since she is expecting him to pull away, he makes himself sit still, savoring her delicate hand on his disfigured face. He swallows and says, "Patrick is down-playing it. You are one in a billion."

"What about you? He said your powers are—"

Lathe pulls back, out of her reach. "My abilities are not something we should talk about."

She sets her hand on the table between them. "Why?"

"It's not something you should know."

"You mean it's not something a layperson like me should know. What happened to one in a billion?"

"It's dangerous for you."

"So, I've been told. But don't worry, they stuck me at the kid's table so I wouldn't hear the 'grown-ups' talking about the important stuff."

"The kid's table?" Lathe asks.

Ashley rolls her eyes. "Never mind. What did you come all this way to talk to me about?" Her manicured nails tap against the table and steal Lathe's attention long enough that he doesn't notice the man approach from behind.

"Shit, it's Brent," Ashley mumbles.

Lathe looks to Ashley just as her eyes go wide and her mouth gapes, but the warning doesn't spill from her lips in time. A bottle cracks open over the back of Lathe's head, and the world blinks out around him. He feels his body fall from the chair, but he has no way of stopping it.

His earth rotates, gravity pinning him down. Slowly his eyes open and the world comes back into focus. Ashley is screaming as a dark-haired man with a lip ring holds her back.

Ashley shoves against the man's chest, but he grabs her wrists, twisting them. Ashley curses, "You son of a bitch, you—ouch, you're fucking hurting me, Brent!"

Brent is not alone. Lathe notices a posse on the other side of him. There are only three others and none of them look particularly sharp. They think they are, but Lathe doubts any of them have ever been in a fair fight if they've fought at all. If Ashley hadn't been distracting him so much, he would have felt them coming.

Brent slams Ashley's body up against his and Lathe snaps out of his half-conscious state. With his mind, he reaches out and tries to take control over the man holding Ashley, but his head is throbbing, and he can't see straight, let alone take over someone's psyche. Ashley pulls back enough to knee the guy in the nuts.

The posse advances and Lathe peals his body off the sticky floor. He is tall and lean with broad shoulders and a deceivingly strong body. He is sinew and muscle, and they have no idea what he's capable of doing to them. He tries to manipulate them with his mind, but the roaring in his head won't allow him to use that particular skill. As soon as he stands to his full height, the posse collectively takes a step back.

"Holy shit! Look at this freak!" one of them says.

Something warm coats the back of Lathe's head. He touches his hood to find his head is bleeding. He staggers, closing his eyes to the dizziness.

He hears Ashley's voice through a tunnel. "Lathe? Oh my God, Lathe? Fuck you, Brent! He's hurt. You hit him in the head, you psycho!" Hearing Ashley's worry touches Lathe somewhere deep. No one ever worries about him.

Apparently, no one else feels touched, because while Lathe stumbles, a guy advances to throw a punch into Lathe's gut. Lathe barely feels it, but it pisses him off. He removes his hood and places a palm over the deep gash on the back of his head. The guy keeps throwing ineffective punches while Lathe mentally stitches his scalp back together.

Where is security? Someone should have broken this up by now.

Realizing his punches are ineffective, the guy shoves Lathe who takes a step back. His head is still cloudy even after his wound is healed. He must have a concussion, but there is little he can do about it now.

Lathe's eyes pop open, and he takes one good swing. His fist connects and bones crunch. The guy goes down hard, and the posse advances on Lathe. He dodges their sloppy swings and counterstrikes, knocking them around.

Brent turns away from Ashley, more interested in Lathe beating the shit out of his friends. Lathe is concise with each strike—a controlled violence. Brent picks up a stool to use as a weapon and Lathe puts an end to the fight by ripping the stool out of his grip, chucking it across the room, and knocking Brent to the floor with an uppercut.

Once everyone is down, Lathe's ice-blue eyes focus on Ashley. He tries to reign in the force emanating from him—his mental gifts aren't working, but his physical gifts seem to be overcompensating for them. His power should frighten Ashley, but she's leaning back against a table biting her lip and staring at him with lust-addled eyes.

She looks at him like he's handsome, like he's every girl's dream, like he isn't covered in horrific self-inflicted scars.

He moves forward, drawn to her like she's reeling him in and he has no say in the matter. He stops a breath away from her, wondering why he let himself get so close.

"Your head!" she says, pulling it down to run her fingers over his scalp, searching for the wound.

"I'm fine," he rasps, marveling at the feel of those delicate hands against his skin. He wants to feel those manicured nails scrape down his back. Shit! He pulls his head out of her grip. "What'd you do to piss those guys off?"

She bites her lip. "A while back Brent called me a whore and offered me a pity fuck, so I threw my drink in his face and told him he had a small penis. That was like two months ago! What an asshole! You should press charges." She reaches for him. "How's your head?"

Lathe escapes her hands by grasping her wrists. "I'm fine."

She inhales sharply. "You healed it yourself, didn't you?

But . . . Emily said that's impossible."

"Nothing is impossible," he says, letting her go.

Her ultra-dark eyes bore into him. She is so close—closer than she's ever been. She gently places a hand on his scarred cheek as if he's fragile or precious, but he is neither; nor does he like to be touched. Except her touch feels so damn good.

She lifts onto her toes and kisses the side of his head, whispering, "Thank you."

He pulls away. "I gotta go," he huffs, and without further explanation strides out of the bar.

Ashley rushes after him. "What? Wait, Lathe!"

He spins around on the sidewalk. His brain rattles and he winces, cursing.

Ashley steps forward reaching out to him. "I . . . I . . ."

He glares at her. "Stop coming here."

She lowers her arm. "Then give me a way to reach you!"

"This isn't your world, Ashley. Playing with people like me will get you killed. You need new friends. You need to move on."

She steps back. "Are you kidding me! What is wrong with you?"

Lathe knows he needs to keep her away in order to protect her, but she won't understand and she won't let him go without a fight. His voice turns to stone. "I owe you nothing."

The air around them pulsates, and Lathe grabs hold of the breeze, thrusting it toward Ashley in a gust of wind. The wind circulates around her, catching her in the eye of a small tornado.

Ashley tries to move forward through the current, but the air is like sandpaper against her skin. She jumps back, realizing Lathe has trapped her.

He watches from the outside, his cold glare sending a shiver through her. Without another word, he turns and strolls off, fading into the dark night. The wind-stream dies down the further away he goes and he drops it altogether when he climbs into his car and drives away.

CHAPTER SIX

"Not again," Alec groans.

Alec stands in darkness. Cars are collected in rows surrounding him, and a shadowy figure lies on the ground. It's a man, and he's panting, coughing, choking. Overhead a street light flickers to life, illuminating the face of the dark figure. His best friend, Ben, lies on the ground trying to mouth something, but blood seeps between his lips, and he sputters. Alec shouts at him to stay with him, but Ben stops breathing anyway.

"No, no, no, Ben! Come on. No, come on!" Alec rolls Ben's limp body over. His own thunderous pulse is beating violently, yet Ben's pulse is completely absent. Compressions. He must do compressions. He gets down on his knees and starts pumping at his best friend's chest.

A grief-stricken scream comes from behind him just before Alec is shoved aside. Going numb, he allows this unknown force to drive him away. He looks down at his bloody hands and tears leak from his eyes. It happened so fast. It happened too fast, and now Ben is gone.

Alec wakes up panting, reliving a nightmare, reliving a reality he aches to forget. Sitting up in bed, he wipes the beads of sweat from his forehead. He is drenched. He can't breathe. Cursing, he rips his shirt over his head and runs his hands against the back of his scalp.

"Fuck it," he says, grabbing his phone from the nightstand.

It rings twice before a groggy voice comes on the line. "Damn it, Alec, do you know what time it is?"

Alec lets out a sigh of relief and smooths his knotted hair. He can breathe again, but he doesn't want to admit why he's calling at three in the morning. From the other end of the phone, he hears a sigh, and the voice turns gentle, "Still having those dreams?"

Alec rubs a hand back and forth over his lips wondering how to respond. "That's just the thing, man. They're not exactly dreams, are they? That shit happened to you."

Ben sighs into the phone. "Alec, I'm still here. I'm still breathing."

"I'm sorry to call you again. I just . . . I can't get rid of this feeling. In my dream, you always die."

"But I didn't die. You saved my life, man. I owe you, but dude . . ."

"I know." Alec needs to stop calling Ben every time he has this dream, but he doesn't know how else to reassure himself that his friend didn't die that night a month ago. "Shit, I'll let you go. Sorry, man."

"I'm not going anywhere, Alec."

"Yeah, I'll talk to you later, man. Sorry." Alec disconnects and lays back in bed, wide awake. His mind goes back to the night Ben died. He was doing chest compressions when the ambulance arrived and the paramedics were able to revive Ben. They said if Alec had stopped, Ben would've died.

But something felt off. Alec could've sworn someone pushed him away. It's a feeling more than a memory. In fact, whenever he focuses on that night, he can't shake the feeling that something is missing.

Emily is propped on an elbow watching Ben reassure his best friend, yet again. She feels guilty, knowing Alec is only having these nightmares because they stole his memories and his mind can't make sense of the details left behind. His subconscious is fighting to restore pieces that can't be put back together.

As Ben hangs up, he turns to Emily, saying, "There has got to be a way to make this better."

"I'll have Patrick talk to him. Take the edge off."

"Hasn't he done enough? Why did he tamper with Alec's mind like that?"

"Alec didn't want to remember."

Ben shakes his head. "That's what you keep saying, but it's Alec. His knee-jerk reaction is to ignore anything difficult, so of course, he would say he didn't want to remember."

"Patrick left everything he could. He didn't want to do it."

"But you weren't there to help make that call."

Her head jerks back, a glint in her emerald eyes. "Don't do this."

"Do what?"

"Blame me."

"I'm not blaming you."

"Ben, you died," she whispers. "Your heart stopped. Alec isn't the only one messed up over this. I was angry. I had to get out of the hospital before I hurt someone I cared about—someone you cared about. Patrick was the only one with a level head. He and Alec made the decision together. If you don't believe me, ask Ashley."

Ben closes his mouth; afraid he'll say something he'll regret, but his silence doesn't keep Emily from feeling his anger.

She rolls out of bed and Ben calls, "Em, where are you going?"

She throws her robe around herself and pulls her long blond hair out of the collar as she heads for the door, saying, "To hunt down the fucker who did this to us."

He rises to follow her, but she's already slamming the

bedroom door between them. Letting out an exasperated sigh, he falls back on the side of the bed. His head falls into his hands. He can't chase after her. Not here. The Fort Wayne mansion is enormous and filled with Olvasho. He feels like a human living among vampires. Any of them could listen to his thoughts or mentally manipulate him. Ben has seen the way the Olvasho revere Emily, so even though they don't harm him, they treat him as if he's Emily's favorite pet, not even human. He hates coming here, but it's the only way he can see Emily. She hardly makes it home these days. Her new role of leading the Olvasho has stolen all of their time together.

She didn't want to move here, but it's where the Olvasho conduct their business. It is where the council convenes. Technically there was no vote to give her leadership, but that's only because it was a unanimous decision. No one had a chance at running against her, not when they believe she was some prophesied savior.

Emily begged Ben to move here with her, but this isn't the life he wants. It's not even the life *she* wants, but it's the life she was forced to choose in order to better hunt down the person responsible for Ben's attempted murder. So far, she has found zero proof that it was Olvasho related.

Ben wishes he could remember, but he still has no memory from the night of his attack. He remembers eating breakfast the morning of Samantha's wedding, and then he woke up in a hospital bed with Molly holding his hand while Emily was off accepting leadership of the Olvasho. Ben wants her to slow down, but she is incapable of stopping to take a break or letting too much silence fill the space between them.

Things have been off since he survived his death. Ben misses Emily. He misses the girl he could share silence with, the girl he could talk, tease, and laugh with. Ben was able to smooth Emily's sharp edges over the years, but now those edges have turned to barbed wire, and he doesn't know how to handle her anymore.

EMILY RUSHES DOWN THE HALL, her emotions overwhelming her, even as she tries to convince the spirits inside her to shut up.

Emily regained control of her body when Patrick tricked Adelaide into wearing a special necklace that contained her power, but the necklace is a temporary solution to a long-term problem. Emily feels the necklace's hold waning. There are days she can barely handle her own emotions, let alone the feelings from Valla and Adelaide. The times she spends with Ben seem to bring the most significant internal turmoil. The more she loves him, the more Adelaide fights her, consuming her mind with conflicting emotions.

Valla tries to stop Adelaide from interfering, but it only makes the emotions more complicated. It is time to free herself from Valla and Adelaide before she ends up hurting someone or going completely insane.

Once she reaches the end of the long corridor, she pounds on the solid oak door. After no response, she pulls at the handle, but it's locked. Rattling the locked door, she starts pounding again. "Come on, Patrick, wake up!"

PATRICK WAS SIXTEEN YEARS OLD, sitting in the study waiting for Sky to arrive. His mother had been dead for a year, now. Patrick had tried to end his life several times, but Sky watched him too closely. He laced his fingers together, setting them in his lap to avoid throwing something.

Sky sauntered into the room. "Patrick, what a pleasant surprise!"

With a monotone voice, Patrick said, "Why are you keeping me alive? Why not kill me and take my spirit to add to your collection?"

Sky seemed to sober and for the first time talked to Patrick like a peer. "I have had fourteen children from fourteen women. All of them have been disappointments. Lathe, I had high hopes for, but he's a lost cause now, and his mother is a catastrophe. He's better off as her keeper than he would ever be as my protege. None of my children turned out the way I desired.

"But where all of my children failed me, Patrick, you shine. You fought till the very last with your mother. I felt your strength. I want that enthusiasm by my side. I see potential in you, dear boy. I see a bright future before us, one where I share my gifts and secrets with you."

"You made me kill my mother."

"I made you stronger," Sky argued. "That was the first lesson I taught you. We kill what makes us weak and your mother was a weakness, Patrick. Without her, you have nothing tying you down. You have nothing to fear."

"You've taken away my reasons for living."

"Only so you can see what is really important. Suffering is a part of life. It makes the good seem brighter."

"What good?"

Sky crouched in front of Patrick. "If you stand beside me, I will fulfill all your desires."

Patrick hears Emily's voice. *"Come on, Patrick. Wake up!"*

Patrick's dream melts away, and he hears Maggie whining in the bed next to him. He sits up, and she barks, jumping off the bed. Emily rattles the handle, and Patrick rushes to the door before she burns the whole thing down.

When the door swings open, Emily barrels into the room. "I can't do this anymore, Patrick. I need them out of my head!"

Patrick steps back, saying, "No, please, come in, I insist. I wasn't sleeping or anything."

"You can sleep later. I need Adelaide out!"

Maggie whimpers, darting out the door before Patrick closes it and walks over to where Emily is pacing. Patrick steps in front of her and even now just after waking, his tired eyes give off a smoldering look. She tries to ignore his look while he puts his hands to his boxer-clad hips. "Emily, it's three in the morning. Why are you in my bedroom?"

"Alec called again."

Patrick sighs.

Emily continues, "And Ben and I are arguing. I don't know how to feel when it comes to him. Adelaide still won't let us have sex. And it's getting worse, even being with him has become painful. I can't live like this Patrick. I need her gone!"

Patrick sits on the edge of the bed and puts his head in his hands. He is so tired. Isa is curious about his past with Sky, so every night while Patrick sleeps, she riffles through his history while he dreams about his life.

Pulling his face out of his hands, he says, "Maybe we need to find someone else. Lathe's demands are too high."

Patrick and Emily nearly died taking on the spirits of Isa and Valla, and believe Lathe is the best candidate to take on the spirit of Leona because one must possess great strength to survive the transfer. Lathe is the logical choice since both of Lathe's parents hailed from the Leona bloodline and were exceptionally gifted.

His father, Sky, led the Olvasho with brute strength and oppression, while Evelyn, Lathe's mother, looked into the future like the average person looked out a window. Evelyn is easily the most powerful Olvasho alive, but after Sky married her, he pushed her over the edge of her sanity. One day, ten years ago, Evelyn became confused and accidentally killed several people in her living quarters. Ever since, she has been locked away, and Lathe is the only one to have contact with her. He refused to abandon his mother, so when it was time to become Sky's protege, Lathe disfigured his face and Sky left him alone to care for the violent woman.

Emily steps forward. "I need to meet her, Patrick. I need to try to fix his mother."

"Evelyn is too dangerous. She will kill you."

"Not if Lathe goes with me."

"Lathe will scrape your mutilated corpse from his mother's floor."

She grabs the sides of her head and whispers, "And even that would feel better than this. I can't do it anymore!" Her chest rises and falls with exasperated breaths while angry tears leak from her eyes.

Having one entity is giving Patrick nights of tossing and turning. He can only imagine what Emily must be going through and he hates when she's in pain. There is a growing ache in his chest, a byproduct of being madly in love with her. He represses his intrinsic need to get up and comfort her.

Since the very first time they met, Patrick has been drawn to her. He was sent by Sky to track down the Valla blood, but everything about Emily cried out to his soul, giving him another chance at life. Instead of turning her in, Patrick trained Emily to defeat the father she never knew she had. Patrick has already gone to the ends of the earth for her. He will do anything for her, which is why he's not comforting her now. Emily chose Ben and Patrick doesn't want to confuse her by confessing his love.

He clears his throat to speak. "I'll talk with Lathe's mother."

Emily scoffs, "I have a chance of making it out unharmed. There is no question she will kill you, Patrick. Look what you've done to her son."

"Emily, we go together or not at all."

She throws her arms back and growls her frustration. "Screw this! I'm gonna go talk to Lathe now."

She storms out of the room and Patrick groans from the bed before getting up and putting on some clothes. Through their mental link, Patrick tries to reason with her one more time. *"It is the middle of the night, love. Can't this wait until morning?"*

"No."

"Fine, I'm right behind you."

Lathe's room is in the South wing closest to the horse stables. Patrick and Emily are staying in the West wing because logistically it makes the most sense. The walls are all reinforced, and there are escape exits should they need them.

Patrick arrives at Lathe's room to find Emily leaning in the open doorway with her arms crossed and emerald eyes glowing with barely contained rage.

Patrick asks, "What is it?"

"He's not here," she growls.

Patrick looks into the room and suggests, "He could be down with his mother."

"At three a.m.?" She glares at him for a moment before pushing off the wall to head downstairs. While walking down the winding staircase into the foyer, Maggie barks and the front door opens. Lathe walks in with his hoodie covering his head. It looks like an egg cracked over his head and the yolk soaked down to his shoulders, except in this case the yolk looks remarkably like blood.

He bends to stroke Maggie's head, so he doesn't notice Patrick and Emily until he's climbing the stairs and Emily says, "What happened to you?"

Lathe looks up and winces at the wave of dizziness. He grabs the railing and pauses on his step.

"Where were you?" Emily demands.

Lathe pulls himself together and says, "I was out. Why are you up?"

"I was looking for you."

Lathe blinks back the dizziness and continues up the stairs. "Why?"

"Where were you? Why are you bleeding?"

"I'm not bleeding." He pushes back his hood as proof.

"Anymore," Emily observes. "What happened to you?"

Lathe passes them on the stairs and keeps going. "It's nothing. No one died, and the police aren't involved. If you don't mind, it's been a long shitty night, and I have a concussion. I'm going to bed."

Emily stomps up the stairs behind him. "You can't go to sleep if you have a concussion!"

Patrick notices the change in Emily. She is still angry, but her priorities realign, and she goes from formidable leader of the

Olvasho to concerned sister in the blink of an eye. The way Emily and Lathe interact rarely makes sense to Patrick. Some days they act as if they have known each other their whole lives, while at other times Emily complains that Lathe is enjoying her suffering. Patrick stays neutral where Lathe is concerned, which is the only reason he isn't interrogating Lathe right now. Besides, Emily will get the truth out of him. Lathen has a weakness for his sister.

Patrick follows the arguing siblings back to Lathe's room, where Emily confirms Lathe has a concussion. She tries to heal him, but when that fails, she decides to stay with him until morning to make sure he's okay.

Patrick goes back to his room and falls onto his bed, not bothering to undress or cover up. The moment his eyes close, he's already drifting back to sleep. A moment later he's sucked back into his past life with Sky, as Isa sorts through his memories.

CHAPTER SEVEN ~

"Brains are tricky things. The damage has healed, but he's not up to par yet. We're going to have to wait," Emily says, sitting at the desk in the study.

"That's it?" Patrick tries to tamp down his surprise. "You're fine with waiting?"

"Well, I can't exactly do anything about this. Lathe is still the best person to take on Leona, so we'll have to wait."

Patrick sits forward in the lounge chair, resting his elbows on his knees. "Okay, but last night you were so miserable, you woke me in the middle of the night, telling me you couldn't wait another minute. And now you say you're okay waiting another two weeks?"

Emily looks down at the legal papers in front of her and flips a page. "I had a bad night, Patrick. I'm sorry."

"Please tell me you at least found out what happened to him?"

"Of course. He went to meet a friend at a bar. He was distracted by a girl, and the girl's jealous ex-boyfriend hit him over the head. Lathe defended himself and got the heck out of there. He said he wouldn't do anything that stupid again. I'm inclined to believe him."

Patrick doesn't feel so accepting. "And who healed his head?"

"He said an Olvasho did it. It was probably the friend he was meeting."

"Does this friend have a name?"

Emily looks up from her stack of papers. "Is this an interrogation? Should I have my lawyer present?"

Patrick backs down. "No. Just curious."

She goes back to her paperwork, flipping through the pages while she says, "The brain is a tricky thing. I couldn't fix my dad without Valla's help, and I can't risk taking the necklace off right now so Valla can help fix him. Lathe's mind will heal. It'll just take a little longer. We can wait two weeks."

Patrick reminds himself to breathe. What was Lathe doing at a bar in the first place? Patrick contains his anger and in a calm voice asks, "Is Lathe still demanding we heal his mother before he attempts to take on Leona's spirit."

Emily nods, "Yes."

Patrick sighs and rubs his temple. "So how are we supposed to heal Lathe's mother when we can't heal a concussion?"

"With the three of us, we may have a chance and maybe Valla—"

"Absolutely not! You just admitted Valla is struggling to hold Adelaide back. If Adelaide regains control of your mind, we are all dead. I will not be in a position to deceive her a second time."

"We need him, Patrick." Emily picks up another page and begins reading.

Patrick fights an eye roll. "Perhaps once he takes on Leona, we can try to fix his mother, but without Leona, I don't think it's likely or even possible to heal her. Some broken things can't be fixed."

She puts the page down and looks at him, searching for the right words. "What would you give to have your mother back, Patrick?"

"Anything," he answers.

"Me too, but that isn't possible for either of us. There is a chance for Lathe. There is a chance for Evelyn. We have to at least try."

There is a knock at the door.

"Come in," Emily calls.

The solid door opens, and Jerrick steps into the study with Maggie on his heels. Maggie runs past him and darts over to Patrick.

"Traitor," Emily murmurs to Maggie even though she knows Adelaide's presence is the reason her beloved dog keeps choosing Patrick over her.

Emily looks up to Jerrick in the doorway. Olvasho are known for their blue eyes and blond hair, but Jerrick breaks the stereotype. He is beautiful like all the Olvasho, but his skin is a dark mocha, his black hair is buzzed short, and his muscles aren't that of a model, but those of a bodybuilder. Muscles strain beneath the material of his t-shirt. Piercing blue eyes shine from his symmetrical face.

Jerrick was appointed to Emily when she took on leadership. He is her administrator and bodyguard, even though the thought of her needing a bodyguard is laughable. He helps guide her with the laws and regulations of the Olvasho. Patrick helps where he can, but even he doesn't know all the rules because in his time with Sky, the laws were irrelevant.

The Olvasho believe in Emily—the prophecy—but feel she is still a child and in need of a babysitter. Jerrick is that babysitter. At twenty-four, he is six years her senior. Their relationship is strictly professional, but there is something about his eyes that always make it hard for her to look away. Emily has found herself lost in those eyes on more than one occasion. As if realizing the effect he has, Jerrick usually avoids long periods of eye contact. His voice rumbles out of him, a deep baritone. "I'm sorry to bother you, Emily. I've been informed about a possible Olvasho murder. The family reported him missing two days ago, and they recovered his body this morning. It's a suspected power killing."

Emily's eyes fall closed. Murder is a familiar thing with the

Olvasho. When an Olvasho kills another of their kind, they gain power by absorbing the souls of their victims. It is how Sky maintained power for so long. In the years he ruled, it became horrifyingly common to steal souls in hopes of becoming stronger. Emily has seen firsthand how horrific the consequences were for the devoured souls when she freed over two-hundred of them from the mind of her father. She vowed to put a stop to it when she assumed leadership of the Olvasho.

Emily blows out a breath and opens her eyes. "Where?"

"Connecticut."

She sighs. "Give me an hour."

"Yes, Vezetö." He steps out of the room and closes the door.

Emily puts her face in her hands. "I wish everyone would stop calling me that."

"It's a sign of respect. He's acknowledging you are in charge."

"I don't want to be in charge."

Patrick stands. "Come on. We've got an Olvasho to stop."

With her head still in her hands, she says, "How am I supposed to tell Ben I'm leaving again?" She drags her head up. "He hates coming here. I persuaded him to stay with me for the weekend, and then I run off in the middle of the night, and now I'm leaving town." She rubs her temples. "I miss my life."

"I know, love." He gathers the papers on the desk into his arms. "You can sign these on the plane. I'll go get the car ready while you say goodbye."

"Thank you."

She makes her way back up to her room. The bedrooms are all large, with wooden paneling to accent the Victorian style of the house. The main areas have been modernized, but there was no shortage of woodwork throughout.

Emily knocks softly as she opens the door, walking into her own room like a guilty puppy with her tail tucked between her legs. "Hey, Ben."

He's sitting on her bed scrolling through his phone. He drops it on the bed and stands as soon as he sees her.

She moves forward and he meets her in the middle of the room. He scoops her into his arms and kisses her. Pulling back, he says, "I'm sorry. I never should've said those things last night. I never should've pushed blame on you."

She looks up at him with her arms around his back and she smiles. She loves this man. He's so willing to forgive and ask for forgiveness. She feels undeserving.

"Are you still mad?" he asks.

She shakes her head, "No. I know you're frustrated. I am too. I wish there was more I could do for Alec, but I don't know how to help him, and telling him the truth will only take us back to where we started. It's not safe for him, Ben. Look what happened to you."

"We don't know that it was Olvasho related."

She looks down, not wanting to say the next part.

"What is it? Did you find something?"

"No, not about that, but I just got a call." She watches the disappointment wash over him. "There was another murder. A power killing. I have to go deal with this."

His unhappiness clouds the room and he shakes his head. "I don't like you going after murderers."

"It's not like Sky. I'll be safe and Patrick and Jerrick will be with me."

"Where are you going?"

"Connecticut. I leave in forty-five minutes."

His palm caresses her cheek and he says, "I understand. I know this is something you have to do. But come back to me, okay?"

She stretches up onto her tiptoes and her lips brush against his as she says, "Always."

IT IS SNOWING WHEN EMILY, Patrick, and Jerrick land in Connecticut. They travel snow-covered roads to get to the average looking home in the middle of a residential neighborhood. Emily steps onto the wooden porch of the victim's home and rings the doorbell.

A moment later, a woman answers the door, sadness and fear emanating from her. Emily knows right away that she's the victim's widow. Patrick moves closer—his calming essence seeping out of him in hypnotizing waves—putting the woman at ease. The wails of a crying baby ring out from somewhere inside and the woman opens the screen door, inviting the three of them in. She guides them down a hall into a sitting room, offering them drinks. She sits when they decline. A child runs into the room, barreling into her mother, complaining, "Emilie's crying, again!"

"Hush, sweetie, we have guests."

The girl turns to peer at the strangers, saying, "Who are they?"

"Go play with your dollhouse, Sarah. I'll come to get you when we're done."

Sarah doesn't listen. Instead, she says, "Are they from the council, Mama?"

"We are," Patrick says, kneeling next to the child. "Will you take me to your baby sister?"

The girl's eyes become wide with excitement as her mother sucks in a breath. Patrick's reputation precedes him, and the thought of her daughters being alone with Patrick terrifies the grieving widow.

Emily speaks up, "Patrick, stay here with me. Jerrick will look after the girls."

Jerrick stands, his giant hand taking the little girl's, and she leads him to the crying baby. After a moment the crying subsides.

Emily says, "Your baby's name is Emilie?"

"Yes, after you, the prophecy, the one we've been waiting for. It's such an honor to meet you. I only wish my husband were here." She stifles a sob and says, "I know who did it! I know who murdered my husband."

"Please explain."

The woman gives details about her late husband's gifts, abilities, and lineage. After several minutes, Jerrick comes back into the room holding a baby with the young girl trailing behind him. It is such an absurd picture, this giant man holding such a fragile being.

The woman stands and takes the baby from him, whispering, "Thank you."

"My pleasure, ma'am. You have beautiful children. Don't forget they need you now more than ever."

She shakes her head. "I won't. I won't forget."

He offers, "Should you need any help, give us a call." He hands her a card. "I'll send someone out to help you."

Emily smiles. This is why she needs Jerrick. He puts people at ease. It's funny how Jerrick and Patrick are from the same Isa descent, yet their gifts are vastly different. Patrick, like most Olvasho, is secretive, hiding his thoughts and emotions, using his gifts to soothe and manipulate, while Jerrick is an open book, very diplomatic, wishing to upset no one, and at the same time, he is battle-ready. She is grateful they chose Jerrick to be her babysitter.

CHAPTER EIGHT ~

ALL OF LATHE'S investigations have shown that Ben's attack had nothing to do with the Olvasho. Lathe never really believed it had. It just didn't fit their MO. The Olvasho were much more likely to manipulate Ben into committing suicide than resort to physical violence. In general, Olvasho avoided physical altercations.

So, when he finds out there hasn't been any progress on Ben's case in weeks, Lathe makes the three-hour trip to the Columbus Police Station despite the fact he shouldn't be driving with his concussion.

He sits across from the lead detective, listening to all the reasons they've let Ben's case grow cold: department cutbacks, lack of evidence, overwhelming workload, yadda, yadda, yadda.

Lathe leans forward, placing an envelope on the desk between him and the detective, saying, "I need you to keep looking. Look into every avenue, every aspect of Ben's life if you must, but you need to find out who did this."

"Sir, I just said, with budget cuts—"

Lathe taps the envelope. "There is enough here to keep you going for at least the next few months, but the sooner, the better. You can keep whatever is left over."

In general, the Olvasho are a wealthy group, but because of Sky's investments and shady dealings, the Olvasho had nearly a billion dollars stored up. Lathe had access to some of the accounts, and although he had to answer for the money he took, ninety-thousand dollars wouldn't be missed.

Walking out of the police station, Lathe looks down at his phone, viewing the feed from the surveillance cameras installed in his mother's living quarters. He watches his mother pace in her living room. She is talking to herself. That is usually a dangerous sign.

Lathe gets in his car to make the long trip home to Fort Wayne. By the time he arrives back at the mansion, his head hurts, but he needs to soothe his mother before she hurts herself.

He takes the back staircase down into the basement and places his face against the scanner, then types in the code to unlock the intricate system. The door clicks open, and Lathe enters his mother's underground apartment.

The lights remain steady, but his mother doesn't seem to register his presence. She is petite—almost looking frail with wild blond hair streaked with grey He stands, leaning on the doorframe, rubbing at his temples, willing away his constant headache.

After several moments, his mother spots him. "*You!*" she booms, her voice deep and otherworldly. "I have seen her death!"

Lathe's skin pricks and an icy chill sweeps down his spine. He stays motionless, feeling her out, hoping she's just having a delusion and not a prophecy. Everything will be okay as long as she doesn't start rhyming. Nothing good ever comes from her rhymes, especially when it begins with death.

She continues, her words echoing through the compact space. "Her blood runs through your veins. A relative she remains."

Shit, she's rhyming.

"She won the battle of her mind, regaining her strength of life. She rises only to fall. She will die to protect them all."

"Shit," Lathe breathes.

Her words are on repeat. "Soon she will breathe her final breath, for I have seen her death. Her blood runs through your veins, a relative she remains. She won the battle of her mind, regaining her strength of life. She rises only to fall. She will die to protect them all."

She repeats it over and over until her voice becomes hoarse and her body becomes tired.

Once she is quiet, Lathe says, "Mother?"

His mother looks up and recognition sparks. Her eyes widen, and her voice is raspy as she begins again. "Soon she will breathe her final breath, for I have seen her death . . ."

Lathe opens the door to leave, and his mother's words stop abruptly. He looks back at her, and her voice becomes clear. "I am ready to meet her, Lathen. Bring me the girl. Bring me the prophecy, and I will save her."

"Mother?"

"Do it, Lathen. It is important it happens soon."

"Why?"

"Because death waits for no one and soon she will breathe her final breathe, for I have seen her death . . ."

Lathe slips out of the room, chills prickling down his spine.

THE BALCONY of their Connecticut rental house opens to the ocean. The sunset stretches across the sky in a kaleidoscope of colors, from brilliant orange to navy blue. The water reflects the sky, doubling the magnificence. It makes Emily feel so small and unimportant. Patrick comes up from behind her, wrapping a woven blanket around her shoulders. She grabs the soft material, pulling it tighter, whispering her thanks, afraid to speak any louder for fear of upsetting the precarious balance on which they currently stand.

"It calls to me," Patrick says, slicing through the silence. "The ocean, that is. I suppose it has always appealed to me, but never like this before."

"Isa misses the water?" Emily speculates, brushing back her windblown hair to look at him.

"It's where she feels the most at peace. She is stronger here."

"How so?"

Patrick flicks his chin toward the water and moves his hand in a come-hither movement as if summoning the ocean. The wave coming toward them grows, arching out above the surface of the water before splashing against the side of the balcony. Emily steps back, thinking she's about to get soaked, but the water obeys Patrick's command, and the droplets ricochet back down into the water below.

"That's amazing," Emily breathes, moving forward to peer over the railing.

"That's the power of Isa."

She looks to Patrick in astonishment and sucks in a breath as the balance between them shifts. He is a picture of perfection. She has always been attracted to him, but standing here at the edge of the ocean where he looks most at peace—and not the self-induced calm he portrays—she has to steady herself. Curious blue eyes stare back at her, and she turns away to take in the sunset.

"Thank you, Patrick," she says to the ocean.

"For what?"

"For all of it. For never giving up on me. For moving with me to Indiana even though it reminds you of Sky. For being—" she stops herself from saying more than she should. "For putting up with me."

Patrick's voice is smooth like velvet. "We are dancing, you and I. We feel the music. It's deafening, tormenting us because it won't stop. It won't let us go. It only becomes more painful to ignore. Sometimes it's too difficult for me, love, especially when you look at me like I'm the only one in the world that will make you whole."

She looks at him, her glistening eyes pleading for him to stop.

But he continues, "I've tried to talk myself out of saying anything because I only want happiness for you, but lately, you are the antithesis of joy."

She wants to deny his claims. She wants to walk away like he means nothing to her, but she can't. She has tried to control the way she feels when she's with him, but she can't.

Patrick continues, "Your life has changed dramatically, yet you exhaust yourself by trying to make things work with Benjamin. Every time the two of you argue, you run to me." She cringes at his words, but he keeps going. "When you need advice, or support, or a shoulder to cry on, you come to me. I give you whatever you need, and I will continue to do so because I'm in love with you.

Emily takes a step away from him. "I come to you because no one else understands me the way you do. I'm not trying to hurt you, Patrick. The last thing I want is to hurt you."

"Are you still in love with Ben?"

Emily thinks for a moment before saying, "Sometimes love is a choice. It's not always an easy gushy feeling. If everyone turned their back on love every time they 'lost those loving feelings,' couples would cease to exist."

"I'm not asking about the essence of love. I am asking—"

"Stop!" Emily says desperately. "You have to stop, Patrick!" Tears threaten, and she takes a shaky breath. "I love him! I love him, and I'm terrified that means I'll lose you. I . . . I don't know what I'd do without you. And I shouldn't need you as much as I do."

Patrick's heart twists in agony as he steps forward to embrace her. "I'm not going anywhere," he says into her hair.

Her tears wet his shirt, reminding him that she is only human. She is an eighteen-year-old girl trying to navigate pressures that would cripple most adults. Because Emily needs him, he shoves back his feelings and offers the part of himself she will allow. It is a bittersweet entanglement.

Jerrick opens the door, and Patrick and Emily step away from one another as Jerrick says, "The suspect was spotted at the marina."

THE SUSPECT'S name is Jay Allensworth. Jay is in his mid-thirties. He is tall with a muscular build, blond shaggy hair and a beard. In his insulated flannel shirt and work boots, he looks like he belongs alone in a log cabin in some remote part of the woods, not at a marina.

"He looks like a lumberjack," Jerrick notes.

Patrick turns to Emily. "How do you want to go about this?"

"Just make sure he doesn't run away," she says, strolling onto the dock. As she approaches, she opens her mind to unleash the magnitude of her power.

Jay senses her presence immediately and releases the rope holding his boat in place. That's as far as he gets into his escape. Patrick stills the water around him to keep the boat captive. Emily easily delves through Jay's psychic barrier and scrolls through his mind to find not one Olvasho, but three spirits Mr. Allensworth stole.

Emily has become proficient in freeing souls, but emotionally it takes an enormous toll on her. First, she releases the souls from his mind by absorbing them into her own. She feels them with her senses, sees them in the confines of her mind, tastes their essence, hears their cries, smells their despair. Her mind swells to make room for them until she frees them into the after-life. Every time she goes through this process, her soul cries out for eternal peace, but she reels her spirit back into her human body, a body brimming with pain and deep conflicting emotions. She knows that if she were to let her soul free to unburden her own pain, Adelaide would gain her body and destroy the world and all the people she loves.

Jay sags onto the floor of his boat. Emily doesn't have to question him. She already knows the how and why and she knows where the remaining bodies are buried. She came here to free the souls of her Olvasho and put a stop to a murderer, but she is not the judge and jury. Jay will be taken to the council for a trial and sentencing.

Jerrick puts mental restraints on Jay and drags him back up the dock to the back of their specially equipped SUV. Encased in the back is a steel jail cell of sorts where they can contain their prisoner as they transport him back to Fort Wayne where he will stand trial.

Patrick waits until they are out of earshot before asking, "You okay, love?"

"Yeah, give me a minute. I'll be right there."

Patrick nods and follows after Jerrick while Emily gets her bearings. Her mind hurts. Her heart breaks every time she does this. Valla struggles to hold back Adelaide who is cursing Emily for harming herself to help the dead.

Eventually, she drags her weary body to the vehicle so they can go home.

Emily walks through the door, exhausted and ready to stretch out in her bed. That idea is thwarted as soon as she sees Lathe on the stairs. Though he appears calm and cool, the fact that he has been standing there waiting for her, tells her something is not quite right. Patrick comes up behind her. He places a hand on the small of her back to get her attention without making her jump. She jumps anyway, but not with fear. She has been diligently avoiding Patrick's touch ever since their talk by the ocean. When he touches her, she begins entertaining ideas she has no business entertaining.

"Sorry, love. Didn't mean to startle you," he says for everyone else's sake because Lord knows he feels it too. The connection between them is nearly unbearable now that Patrick spoke his feelings aloud. In the five days they were away, the spark between them grew into full-fledged fireworks. Emily closes her eyes, pretending not to feel her body vibrate from the internal explosion.

"We are dancing, you and I." His words come to mind, and Emily steps away from him, saying, "Lathe, are you the welcoming committee?"

"No, I need to talk to you."

Emily looks to the massive staircase and then down at her luggage, saying, "Elevator." She rolls her suitcase through the foyer and hits the button for the elevator. It opens, and Emily, Patrick, and Lathe get in. Jerrick is already climbing the stairs, two at a time. His room is on the third floor, and he prefers sprinting up those three flights. The doors close and the elevator begins its ascent.

Emily asks, "What is it, Lathe?"

"Mother is requesting to see you."

"No!" Patrick says the same time Emily asks, "When?"

"Soon," Lathe says, "but she's having a rough night. Perhaps in the morning."

"Absolutely not!" Patrick insists as the elevator doors open on the second floor.

Emily steps out, rolling her suitcase behind her. "Patrick, we talked about this."

Patrick sighs, "Fine. Then I'm going with you."

Lathe is already shaking his head. "My mother hasn't seen another person in ten years. I'm not going to spring two new people on her at once."

"I thought we discussed how this was a stupid idea," Patrick says. "You can't heal her without Valla and Valla is the only thing holding Adelaide back."

"She's not the only thing. I'm holding her back, too."

"More reason not to go," Patrick insists. "Lathe, we can heal your mother after you acquire Leona's spirit."

"You know my stipulation. Months have passed, and you haven't even tried to fix her, but that's not why she's asking to see you now. She had another prophecy."

Emily continues to walk to her room. She is so close to her bed and sleep is closing in on her, but she can't resist asking, "How often does she do that?"

"Emily," Lathe grips her arm, and Emily turns to look at him. "It doesn't happen often, but her predictions have never been wrong."

Emily sighs, and with hesitation asks, "What did she say?"

"She saw you die."

Emily stares at him for a moment before throwing her head back and saying to the ceiling, "Of course she did."

Patrick chimes in, "Did she say when? Her first prophecy about Emily was given sixteen years before it came to fruition. What did she say exactly?"

At this point, Lathe has his mother's words memorized. "Soon she will breathe her final breath, for I have seen her death. Her blood runs through your veins, a relative she remains. She won the battle of her mind, regaining her strength of life. She rises only to fall. She will die to protect them all."

"Soon?" Emily questions. "She said *soon*. When is *soon*?"

Patrick demands, "There has to be a way to get a more precise timeline so we can avoid such an event."

"We'll have to talk to her, but as I said, she's having a bad night. Maybe in the morning."

"She came to me at my sister's wedding rehearsal. She said something bizarre before vanishing. I just ignored it because it was gibberish, but what if that's what she was trying to tell me?"

Lathe shrugs. "Well, now we know what it means," he says before leaving.

Emily remains in the middle of the hall. She can't believe he walks away after telling her she's going to die, *soon*. Suddenly, everything feels much more critical than it did a moment ago. She knows her life is dangerous, but to be told by someone who is never wrong that she is going to die . . . It's a little too much.

She feels Patrick's presence behind her. He places his hands on her shoulders and pulls her back. She leans into him and eventually turns in his arms to rest her head on his shoulder. He combs his hand through her hair, reassuring her without giving her empty words and promises. For a moment it's blissful, and she feels like everything is going to be okay as long as she stays right here. But then she feels the music Patrick was talking about and she remembers right here is not a good place for her to stay. Right here is in Patrick's arms. Right here is dangerous.

She pulls away and grabs the handle of her suitcase. "Thank you. I needed that. I'll see you in the morning, Patrick. Goodnight."

He doesn't make any indication to move, as he says, "Sleep sweet, love."

CHAPTER NINE ~

Evelyn has several bad days in a row. At first, Emily accuses Lathe of stalling until he shows her the video surveillance of his mother. A frail-looking woman with wild hair stands in the middle of a room while papers, pillows, and utensils spin around her in a chaotic whirlwind. It's enough for Emily to cease her argument.

It is ten days later when Lathe finds Emily in the study with Jerrick. He pokes his head in and says, "Hey, you feeling up to meeting her today?"

Emily smiles. "About time!"

"Come on. We can go down now."

"What about Patrick?"

Lathe scoffs, "I never invited Patrick."

"He'll be pissed if I go without him."

"When did he become the leader of the Olvasho? I mean, should I assume since you run all of your decisions by him that he's in charge?"

"Shut up. Let's go." She pushes him out the door, saying, "Jerrick, I'll be back."

Lathe guides the way to his mother's basement corridor. They stand outside the door of his mother's room, and Lathe says, "Hide behind me if things go badly and we will back up slowly to the door."

"Lathe, I can protect myself."

He shakes his head. "Emily, she's like nothing you've ever seen before."

"No offense, Lathe, but I think I can manage."

He sighs. "You're not taking me seriously. If Mother attacks, do not fight back. Get out."

She gives him a look as if he's crazy.

Lathe reaches for the doorknob and stops with his right arm out. With his left hand, he flicks open a blade and draws the sharp edge down his arm, leaving a surgical incision in its wake. Before Emily registers what he's done, Lathe hands the knife to her and drags his left palm back up his right arm, instantly healing the self-inflicted wound.

Emily gapes at him, and he swipes the knife out of her loose grip, explaining, "I wanted to heal my mother, but I never could. I didn't think I was capable of healing. Then one day my mother had a bad day. She didn't recognize me when she hit me with a slice of wind. It broke my left arm in four places. That's when I accidentally discovered my healing abilities."

"Did Sky know about this?" she asks.

"When Patrick told Sky that my scars were self-inflicted, Sky attempted to have me killed, but it was a half-hearted attempt at best, and in the end, I think he didn't care enough to put effort into it. He never suspected I could heal myself or it would have piqued his interest."

Emily pulls herself together and mutters, "I heard it was possible, but . . ." She grabs his arm, looking for a scar or some evidence of his dramatic demonstration. Finding none, she looks up and asks, "How long have you been able to do this?"

"You're asking if I could've healed my burns. Yes, but then I would've become Sky's second in command, and I had no intention of letting that happen." There is silence for a moment, and

Lathe says again, "Hide behind me if things go south and we will back slowly to the door."

She nods, and he opens the door.

Evelyn is sitting at the dining table sipping tea and reading a newspaper. When Lathe enters, she sets down the paper and tilts her head, trying to get a look at Emily.

"Lathen, my son, did you finally bring Katie by to see me?"

Emily cringes at the mention of his dead girlfriend, but Lathe's voice is even, his face untouched by his private grief. "No, Mother, I brought Emily to meet you. She is my half-sister, remember? You requested I bring her by for a visit."

Lathen's mother looks down into her teacup and stirs the empty cup with a tiny spoon. "I don't remember much these days." She sets her spoon down and takes a sip of her non-existent drink.

"Mother, do you know who Emily is?"

Evelyn looks up, her glassy eyes unfocused, her blond hair pulled back into a frizzy ponytail. "She is your sister on your father's side. Sky's daughter. Sky tricked me once. Did he trick her too? Is that why you brought her here?"

"You asked me to bring her to you."

"I can't see her with you standing in the way," she reprimands.

Lathe slowly steps to the side, exposing Emily. Evelyn's blue eyes spark to life in a panic, and she tries to shove back from the table, but the chair is bolted to the floor. She slips out of her seat and spins away from Emily. Breathless with hysteria, she whispers, "Why have you brought her here?"

Lathe motions with his arms for Emily to stay where she is while he takes tentative steps toward his mother. Softly, he says, "Mother, I brought her here because you asked me to. You said it was important that I bring her soon."

He touches Evelyn's shoulder, and she turns to him. Her trembling hands rise to cradle his cheeks between her delicate fingers. "I did, but I was hoping it wasn't so soon. I wish we had more time. That is why my mind has been so unstable these last few weeks. You are my boy, and I don't want to cause you pain."

Lathe's head spins to warn Emily to run, but his mother's hands become firm on his face and power pours from her palms into Lathe's mind.

"What are you doing to him?" Emily demands, moving forward.

Evelyn releases her son and his unconscious body sways. Giant torrents of wind come out of nowhere to rake across the room and lift Lathe from the floor. He hovers there, his shoes inches from the ground.

Emily gasps and grips a chair to keep from being blown over. Evelyn's back is to Emily as she watches her son. "I never wanted this for him, but he needs you more than me," Evelyn says, turning with a tear-stained face. She sounds like a worried mother instead of a crazed killer.

Emily asks again, "What are you doing to him?"

Tears drip from Evelyn's cheeks, and the current around them fades. "I'm forcing him to awaken Leona."

Emily's eyes go wide, and she stutters, "But . . . but we were—"

"Waiting until you fixed me." Evelyn shakes her head. "I cannot be fixed, dear. Lathen knows this in his heart. My days are numbered, but he thinks he can still save me."

"What you're doing could kill him."

Her words turn angry. "I will *not* kill my son."

Emily holds her breath, waiting for Evelyn's wrath, but her anger seems to melt out of her and she stares back to the son she clearly adores. When she speaks again, her words are gentle. "My son . . . he needs you, Emily, from the Valla and Leona bloodline." She turns her gaze behind Emily. "He will need you too, Patrick Glenn, from the Isa bloodline."

Emily spins around to find Patrick right behind her. "What are you doing here?"

Lathe moans and the three of them turn to watch him writhe

in pain, his skin going pale. Evelyn suspends his thrashing body in the air, while Emily holds her breath, and Patrick inches forward.

Strained words come from Evelyn. "I am using all my strength to maintain control of my psyche. Once this is done, you will need to get Lathe and leave quickly. I'm afraid the longer I hold control, the more violent I am afterward. Do not let Lathe come back to see me for at least three days. He will want to, but tell him I made you promise."

"Of course," Emily breathes.

"Do you know what is happening?" Patrick asks, looking at Lathe, "Is it working?"

Evelyn grimaces, the groove between her eyes deepens. "She's rejecting him," Evelyn gasps. "Leona is rejecting my boy, my bluebird."

Patrick and Emily steal a worried glance.

"Oh, no," Evelyn says on a breath before a deranged scream rips from her throat.

The lights go out and silent darkness reigns.

Emily's skin prickles just before power surges through the pitch-black. Inside Emily's mind, Valla screams, *"Get Out!"*

Emily yells, "Patrick, grab him!"

"I'm trying," he says. "I can't see."

The air in the room tingles and the lights flash on and off in a strobe light effect. Suddenly, everything that isn't bolted down gets tossed into the air like floating debris. Patrick and Emily grab hold of Lathe at the same time, but when they attempt to move him, Lathe doesn't budge.

Patrick shouts, "The air has a grip on him!"

They both turn toward Evelyn. The woman's eyes have lost focus, and the eerie wind stirs her wild hair out around her head. Sudden power erupts out of her, stirring up a cacophony of roaring winds. The dizzying currents lash at them, causing Patrick's knees to buckle from the suffocating force.

Emily was able to keep her mind focused when she fought

Sky, but the immense power emanating from Evelyn is all-consuming, like being wrapped in a hurricane. Now Emily understands why Lathe's warning was so adamant. The power tears at her mind, ripping its way through her defenses.

Emily grits her teeth and yells, "If we don't get out, we'll all die!"

"Emily, go!" Patrick demands, regaining his feet and tugging at Lathe's body. "I'll get Lathe. You go!"

They will never get Lathe out while Evelyn is focused on her son. Her hold is too strong. Emily needs to distract her so Patrick can move him. As Emily moves towards Evelyn, she reaches inside herself. *"Valla, I could use some help."* Her arms stretch up to unclasp her necklace, but Valla's warning stops her.

"It is not safe, Emily! Adelaide is too strong. Do not remove the necklace!"

Emily's steps falter, and a blast of wind nearly knocks her over. Evelyn isn't trying to hurt her. She's just giving off so much energy that it's ricocheting off the walls. Emily uses the gifts of her Leona heritage by taking hold of the air around her, controlling it. She wears her power like a buffer, commanding the wind to dissipate before it reaches her body.

Emily grabs onto Evelyn's arm. Experiencing the sheer power, an immediate scream claws its way out of Emily. Holding Evelyn is like grabbing hold of a lightning bolt. She is unforgiving energy with a mind incapable of steering. But if they are going to get out of here alive, Emily must steer that power.

She adjusts to the feeling of being electrocuted and begins digging away at Evelyn's psyche. Evelyn must sense the threat because she starts to shove Emily away, blasting her with energy. Emily becomes a sponge, absorbing all that is thrust at her. She hopes like hell Patrick is getting Lathe out of this room. By now Evelyn's hold on him has to be waning.

Emily can't hold on for much longer. She's fighting with everything she has to keep Evelyn distracted while keeping herself alive. Emily uses all the power her Leona blood allows, while she struggles to hold back the flames of her Valla blood. She doesn't want to hurt Evelyn, but once Emily takes in as much as she can handle, her gifts begin pouring out of her in streaks of fire. She directs the flames away from Evelyn, but where they are connected, she singes Evelyn's skin.

The smell of burning flesh fills the room, and Evelyn cries out. Emily fights to pry her hand from Evelyn's wrist. When she lets go, Evelyn yanks her arm back, cradling it as she curls into a ball on the floor. The wind dies, and the powers seep back into Evelyn as she sobs like a broken child on a playground.

Emily looks around, relieved that Patrick and Lathe are gone. The walls and furniture have been scorched, and the mighty woman is sobbing as she rocks herself on the floor.

Emily knows she should get out. It's not safe in here. It's a wonder she is still standing. With careful movements, Emily sits on the floor next to Evelyn. Cautiously, she slides her arm around the damaged woman and consoles her, healing her burns at the same time.

Emily notices movement across the room and looks up long enough to see Patrick peeking in the door. Emily shakes her head no and goes back to healing the woman who has already been hurt too many times.

After the injuries are mended and the woman stops crying, Emily leaves, glancing back at Evelyn as she closes the door between them. Clear blue eyes stare back at her, a tender grin crossing her face. The door latches between them and Emily turns to see the damage to Patrick and Lathe, except they aren't there.

"Emily, come to Lathe's room, now!"

Emily rushes up the stairs. The door stands ajar, and Lathe lies unmoving on the bed. Patrick paces the floor, his arms folded on his chest as Maggie is growling by the foot of the bed.

When she walks in, Patrick demands, "Did you know?"

"Did I know what?"

Patrick waves his hand at Lathe's unconscious body. That's

when she notices the skin puckered and pink across his exposed leg where his jeans had burned away. Her flames must have hit Lathe, and now his rare Olvasho gifts are working to mend the burn. After a moment there would be nothing left, no scar, no evidence that he was ever injured.

Emily blows out a breath. "You scared me, Patrick. I thought he might be dead."

Patrick looks betrayed, and Maggie growls louder as she feels the tension rise.

"Hush, Maggie," Emily says, and Maggie leaves the room.

"Did you know he could do this?" Patrick asks.

"I only found out before we went in to see his mom. Is he okay?" Emily walks to the bed and sits beside him. She reaches out for his mind and gets a big fat nothing.

Patrick is shaking his head. "It doesn't make sense. He's not even conscious, and his body is healing itself. That means . . . That means when he burned himself, consciously, he had to decide not to heal himself. I've heard how violent his mother was, but I never experienced it. And she wasn't even trying to hurt us! I thought she had a soft spot for Lathe, but that's not it at all. When she loses control, she doesn't recognize him. Lathe hasn't once in the time I was with Sky reported injuries or reached out for help with healing his injuries. She's been hurting him this whole time, and he's been hiding it. He's been hiding his gifts."

"Can you blame him?"

"I blame him for a lot, and I wondered why Sky let him live after he sabotaged his own face. I guess now we know he's hard to kill. I always wondered if Sky was afraid of Lathe." Patrick moves to the bed, looking over Lathe. "I thought that seemed crazy, but it wasn't crazy at all." He looks at Emily. "You felt that power down there. Don't for a second believe Lathen didn't inherit some of her power. When he wakes up, he had better explain why he had the potential to kill Sky and sat on it. He said he hated Sky, yet he sat back and watched innocent people die and did nothing to stop it. He *is* going to tell me why!"

As if his anger can no longer be contained, Patrick strides out of the room and slams the door. Emily looks down at the half-brother she barely knows. She never got the feeling he was hiding something, but perhaps he had more of his father in him that she wanted to admit.

She looks over his scarred face. He was beautiful once. His features border on pretty, except his hard jaw and broad shoulders are too masculine. The skin on the left side of his face is discolored and rigid from the oil burns he inflicted on himself. The pain had to be excruciating; yet, he didn't let his body heal. He had the means to escape the pain and suffering, and he lay in the hospital bed and endured it, probably fighting to stay awake so his body wouldn't accidentally heal it should he fall asleep. If he had enough control to do that at fifteen, what is he capable of doing at twenty-two? Patrick has valid points, and Emily is going to stay right here and wait for him to wake up so they can get some answers.

EMILY AND PATRICK take turns watching over Lathe. He still has yet to wake. It's been nearly a week since they dragged him out of his mother's lair. Emily has been going down to check on her and make sure she's eating. With her Leona powers, she can counteract Evelyn's abilities when she gets violent, at least long enough to get out of the room.

Emily enters Lathe's room to relieve Patrick. The crescent moon glares through the window, casting Lathe in shadows. Everything outside is quiet and still as if the wind took the night off.

Shortly after Patrick leaves, Emily hears footsteps coming from the library next door. No one should be in there at this time of night. She reaches with her mind to feel the person next door but feels nothing. A creak in the floor alerts Emily that whoever it is, keeps moving. Emily holds her breath, listening to the nearly silent footfalls. The footsteps stop.

Silence.

She steps back, hiding her body behind a large dresser, primed to grab hold of her gifts if needed.

The wall on the other side of Lathe's bed, the one leading to the library, is silent as a panel opens and two human eyes peek out. The eyes look around the room and find Lathe lying in the middle of his king-sized bed. The panel is thrown open, and a child pops out of her hiding place to run and hop onto the bed.

Emily gawks in surprise. The girl—no more than seven years old—crawls over to Lathe to pat his cheeks and shake his body, trying to rouse him. Her voice comes out small and frantic. "Wake up, bluebird! We need you." Tears drip from her coal-black eyes down her pale cheeks. Black hair hangs in her face.

Emily steps out from her hiding place, and those coal-black eyes swing to her and open wide, as a gasp escapes her. The girl jumps from the bed and sprints across the floor into the opening in the wall.

"Wait!" Emily calls, trying again to reach out with her mind only to come away empty. She saw her with her own two eyes, but according to her gifts, the girl doesn't exist. "What the hell?"

Emily runs to the opening in the wall. She finds a passageway between walls and ducks into the small space to follow the girl. The child is too fast, and the pathway turns into a labyrinth inside the walls. Emily practically travels the length of the estates, going down two flights before she realizes the girl is long gone. There are so many hidey-holes along the way, Emily could have passed right by her without knowing.

And she doesn't have a clue how to get back to Lathe's room. *"Patrick!"* she mentally calls out, hoping he isn't sleeping yet.

"Yes," his voice comes.

"I need you to go to Lathe's room and keep an eye out until I get back."

"Where are you?"

"*In the walls,*" she admits sheepishly. "*Apparently there are more passageways than we knew.*"

"*I know them all.*"

"*Did you know about the one leading to Lathe's room?*"

There is silence for a moment followed by, "*No.*"

"*Then you don't know them all, but I bet you Lathe does.*"

"*How did you find a passage in his wall?*"

"*A little girl came out of it.*"

"*What?*"

"*Yeah . . . I think our list of questions just got longer.*"

"*I'm in Lathe's room. He's still here. I see the open panel.*"

"*I'm backtracking, but it's a maze in here.*"

"*Take your time, and when you get back, I say we jump on Lathe until he wakes up.*"

CHAPTER TEN ~

MOLLY IS FRANTIC. "Ben . . . Oh my God, Ben, I don't know what's happening! There are all these people here, and they took Dad!"

"Calm down, Molly," Ben says into the phone. "I can barely understand you. Where are you?"

"At home!" She continues to panic. "I don't understand what's going on. They just arrested Dad and Mom is running around the house packing all her jewelry, and there are all these people here. They're taking our things, Ben! I . . . I don't know what's happening."

"Where are you exactly?" Ben says, heading to his car.

"Max and I are locked in my room."

"You're gonna be okay, Weasel. I'm on my way."

"Hurry, Ben!"

By the time Ben arrives at the Cetrone mansion, home sweet home, cops are everywhere, and a news van is parked out front. "What the hell!"

He dials Molly.

"Ben!"

"Molly, I'm outside, but I can't get to the driveway from here."

"It's all over the internet! They're saying Dad stole millions. He . . . he's been embezzling. They're saying he's a criminal. And it . . ." her voice breaks and she can't seem to get the rest of her words out.

"Can you get to my old room, Molly?"

She sniffles, and there is a pause before she whispers, "Yes."

"Good. I'll meet you there. I'm coming around from the golf course."

"B . . . Ben, they say h . . . he's involved with—"

"It's okay, Molly. I'll be there soon. Just keep the doors locked until I get there."

Ben swings his car around almost hitting a media van. Shit, he doesn't want Molly to be exposed to the madness in their front yard. He winds his way around until he gets to the country club. He knows this golf course like the back of his hand. He and Molly used to sneak out onto it when they were younger. He parks by the dumpsters and jumps out, heading for the woods. He jogs down the narrow deer path out onto the seventh hole. Hole eight is right behind the Cetrone mansion.

Molly didn't listen to him. She didn't stay put. As soon as he reaches the eighth hole, Molly and her gargantuan dog, Max, sprint across the frost covered grass.

"They didn't see me," she says, rushing up to him.

The fluffy brown Newfoundland trots up with his tongue lolling out, excitement in his eyes, enjoying the adventure. Molly is trembling with fear as tears stain her cold, rosy cheeks. She looks like her whole world is falling apart, and she needs her brother to catch her on her downward dive into Hell. Ben grabs her, wrapping her in a hug. He takes the leash and guides them back up the trail to his car in silence. Ben has no idea how the three of them are going to fit into his two-seater, but they pile into the Corvette to drive the short distance to Alec's house.

Ben's apartment doesn't allow dogs, and there is no way the three of them could risk the crammed drive there anyway. Alec's house is the closest safe place.

Alec isn't home, but Cindy is. They pour out of the tiny Corvette, and Ben knocks at the front door. Cindy opens it, taking in the giant hairy dog, and saying, "Oh, my." Then she looks at Ben and Molly. "Oh, honey, sweetheart, come in, come in." She holds the door open. "What's wrong?"

Molly's tears have dried, but it is obvious she has been sobbing. Ben says, "I . . . We needed a place to go for a bit. Sorry to barge in on you."

"You're welcome here anytime. You know that. Is this the sister I've heard so much about?" Cindy gives Molly a warm smile, and Ben wonders what she's talking about. He rarely talks about Molly, but Cindy's words bring a small smile to Molly's lips.

Cindy places a comforting arm around her shoulder. "Honey, you look like you need a cupcake and some ice cream. Come with me. I'll make you both some dessert and hot chocolate while you tell me all about it."

Molly goes with Cindy and Ben follows, wondering how Alec isn't six-hundred pounds with a mom like Cindy.

THE NEWS IS on mute in the background as Molly and Ben sit on the sofa in the living room. After Cindy coaxed them into a sugar coma, bribing all the information out of them, she regretfully had to head to work for a few hours. Max lies on the floor in front of the couch, full of the ground beef Cindy made for him.

Molly has been holding back the most sensitive piece of information. She almost can't bring herself to say it out loud, but she has to tell Ben. She whispers into the silence, "I wasn't supposed to be home."

Ben turns to her, concern in his expression.

She stares at the TV as she continues, "I stayed at Ava's last night, and I was supposed to ride to school with her today, but I felt sick, so I had her sign me in at school while I came home to take a nap before going in late. Everyone thought I was at school. That's why the detectives, or cops, or whoever they were, weren't looking for me. They were calling for the dog, but when they couldn't find him, they assumed he ran out through an open door."

"You think they had this all planned out?"

"I know they did," she breathes, wiping her tears.

"How?"

"I heard them talking at the house. Natalia was there. I heard her. Except her accent was gone and she . . . she's one of them." Molly wraps her arms around her legs, hugging them to her. "She's been undercover this whole time."

"What?"

Molly's chin quivers as she forces herself to continue. "She was telling people where to find things, like hidden things, and she said, and I quote. 'The bastard is finally going down.' Ben, they think he's involved in human trafficking."

Ben knew his parents sucked at being parents, but he didn't realize how much they sucked as human beings. If what his sister says is true, their dad is a monster. Ben wants to believe better about his mother. "What about Mom?"

Molly shrugs. "They didn't arrest her, but she was freaking out about her things and screaming about her accounts being frozen." Her voice becomes small as she asks, "Ben, what's going to happen to me?"

Molly is only fifteen. She attends a prestigious prep school and is used to a life of luxury. Aside from her parents, she has no other family except for Ben. He would give her the world if he could, but for now, she'll have to settle for him. He wraps an arm around her shoulder. "You'll stay with me."

"How? You live in a studio apartment."

"We'll figure it out, Weasel. We always do."

ASHLEY WAKES with her face against the solid wood of her vanity. A textbook lies next to her head. She swears she got into bed last night. She lifts her head and wipes away the drool. This is the third time in the last two weeks she has awakened somewhere other than her bed. At least she is in her bedroom this time. A few days ago, she awoke at the kitchen table with her laptop in front of her and a half-written paper. Last week she woke up in her car after dreaming she was late for an exam. The keys, thank goodness, were still tucked neatly in her purse.

These exams are going to be the death of her if she doesn't stop this sleep-studying. Her future is riding on her acing the exams this week. She can't wait until next week is over, so her life can go back to normal, well, normalish.

She has stayed away from her gifted friends and thoughts of Lathe don't come to her nearly as often, but she still thinks about the last time they saw each other. He had wrapped her in a real-life tornado which had left her terrified and questioning her sanity.

Her stomach growls and Ashley leaves her room in search of food. In the kitchen, Bethany, one of her roommates, sees her and snaps, "Don't touch my mac and cheese."

Ashley snaps back, "I don't want your mac and cheese."

"I know you ate it last time."

"Oh, my God! Let it go! That wasn't me, Bethany!"

Bethany huffs, saying, "I can't wait to move out."

Ashley rolls her eyes. She can't wait either. "No one is making you stay."

Bethany gasps. "I still have classes, you whore."

There is no reasoning with crazy, so Ashley moves around Bethany to get yogurt out of the fridge. She grabs a spoon and leaves her bitchy roommate behind. Ashley used to look forward to spring break, but this year her plans fell through, so she will be stuck here with her bickering roomies. Ashley walks into the living room where her other roommate, Reilly, sits on the couch with her laptop propped on her legs and earbuds in her ears.

When she spots Ashley, she pops an earbud out and warns, "Stay away from Bethany. She had an extra helping of crazy this morning."

"She seems normal to me," Ashley comments.

Reilly spins her computer to Ashley, saying, "Isn't this your friend?"

Ashley leans in to see Ben in the center of the screen. He's posed for a family portrait. His mother and sister stand on one side, while his father—an older more polished version of Ben—stands next to him. There is a red circle around Ben's father.

Reilly says, "It came up on my news feed, and he's hot, so I clicked on it. I thought he looked familiar. This guy," she points to Ben's dad, "stole millions."

"No way!"

Ashley pulls her phone out and types in Ben's last name. News articles populate by the dozens, all with today's date. "Thanks, Rei," she says, before leaving the room to call Ben, but his phone keeps going straight to voicemail.

Alec notices Ben's car in his driveway as he pulls up to his house. He wonders why Ben is here. When he enters, he hears a loud woof and then a giant brown dog rounds the corner to slather Alec with kisses.

"Hey you," Alec says, rubbing the dog's head.

"Max!" a female voice calls. Alec doesn't recognize it right away, and then Molly rounds the corner. Her hair is back, and she's wearing her pajamas, looking more at home than he's ever seen her.

"Hey, kid," Alec says, squeezing Molly in a bear hug. He picks her up off her feet until she demands to be put down. He sets her down and asks, "What're you doing here?"

Before she can answer, his mother rounds the corner, wiping her hands with a dishtowel. "Hey, baby. Molly and Benjamin are staying with us tonight. Oh, and Max," she says, as he nearly takes her out by jumping on her.

"Down!" Molly shouts, and Max returns all feet to the floor. "Sorry," Molly says to Cindy.

"No worries, dear. He's a sweet dog." She turns to Alec, saying, "Ben is in your room."

Alec heads off to his room, hoping to find answers. His bedroom door is closed, and he thinks about knocking but decides to walk in. Ben is pacing as he talks to someone on the phone. He says, "I understand that, but . . . Okay. But it's been paid up front. I don't see what—" There is a pause and Ben shakes his head at whatever the person on the other line is saying. "So, you are happy to keep the embezzled money, but you draw the line at teaching an innocent girl!"

Alec sits down at the end of his bed and waits, trying to pick up the missing pieces.

"But doesn't the Bible also say to help those in need," Ben shoots back. He waits, then responds, "Yes, yes, thank you for your compassion. Your empty words fill my soul with peace. I'm sure God is truly proud of you, Sister." Ben hangs up, throwing his phone onto the bed and grinds out, "Bitch!"

Alec can tell the situation is not a laughing matter, but he can't help his smile, asking, "Did you just tell off a nun?"

Ben shakes his head. "I don't know if she's really a nun. It's a Catholic school, so I thought I'd go with it."

"So, what's going on, bro? Your sister is hanging out on my couch in her jammies; your dog basically molested my mother, and you're chewing out nuns."

Ben takes a seat on the bed and drops his face into his hands. He drags his hands over his face and then explains, "My father was arrested today for embezzlement, fraud, and they suspect he's involved in human trafficking. I just found out my mother is now MIA, and as it turns out, Natalia, our housekeeper is an undercover FBI agent."

"What the fuck?"

"Right?" Ben shakes his head. "Molly was home when they arrested our father. It was a mess, and now her school won't let her come back, because they can't be affiliated with bad apples like us Cetrones. They said it goes against their morals, but you know it's all about money."

Alec points out, "You know those bitchy girls would make Molly's life a living hell."

"You're probably right, but it's still not right that Molly is being punished for something our father did."

"So, what's gonna happen to her?"

A knock sounds at the bedroom door, and Alec goes to see who it is. He opens it and steps back to let Morgan in.

"Hey, Alec," she says tentatively, and then she sees Ben and rushes over to him. She pulls him into a hug and holds on for a long time. Eventually, Ben's shoulders relax, the tension draining as Morgan holds him, sharing his burden, letting him know he's not alone.

Alec's heart aches. This is just one of the many ways Morgan amazes him. She always seems to know exactly what people need.

When she finally pulls away, Ben asks, "Who told?"

"Who didn't? First Cindy called me, then Emily, and Ashley called me on my way over. You know, you're not answering your phone."

"I don't feel like talking to anyone," Ben justifies.

Morgan asks, "Do you know what's going to happen?"

"I don't know exactly, but first concern is taking custody of Molly so she doesn't end up in foster care."

The silence that follows feels heavy, no one knowing exactly what to say.

"You'll get through this, and we're right here with you through every step," Morgan reassures.

Alec turns to Morgan, ratting out Ben, "He yelled at a nun!"

Morgan laughs, saying, "Well, she probably deserved it!"

Ben laughs. He doesn't get to pick his family, but he gets to choose his friends, and he has damn good friends.

EMILY PACES the length of Lathe's room feeling like a caged tiger. It's her turn to watch Lathe, and it's killing her to be stuck here watching him instead of being with her boyfriend when he needs her most.

She sent Jerrick to help Ben and Molly. Jerrick knows more than she does when it comes to legal issues. He knows the laws and can sway people to his way of thinking even without his Olvasho gifts. In the five days that have passed since Mr. Everette Cetrone was arrested, Mrs. Renee Cetrone has fled the country. Jerrick helped Ben through the process of taking custody of his sister and found them a larger apartment. Today Jerrick facilitated the move into their new two-bedroom apartment. Jerrick also raided the Olvasho funds to purchase the majority of the furniture for the new place. Ben would normally refuse the help, but he wants to make the transition as painless as possible for Molly. It is difficult, however, for Ben to accept the state-of-the-art security system provided by Burk's Security.

Ben complains into the phone, "Emily, this is too much."

"Please, Ben. It's killing me not to be there. Please let them install the security system. It's not only for my peace of mind, but it's also for Molly's."

Ben huffs. "You always have to throw her name into this."

"Yeah, to help you remember why you're doing all of it."

Instead of telling her she's right, he changes the subject. "Alec called me again last night. I was going to check on him later, but I can't get away with all these people here."

"Have Ashley check on him. She and Alec are close." Emily pauses. "I'm sorry I can't make it back until this is resolved. I've turned into a crappy girlfriend since taking on the Olvasho responsibilities, but right now I can't leave until things are straightened out with Lathe, and he still hasn't woken up."

Ben sighs. "I know. I just wish you could be here."

"I do too."

They exchange their "I love yous" before hanging up, and Emily throws her phone into the padded chair, turning to a comatose Lathe to yell, "You manipulated me into leading the Olvasho, and you didn't have the decency to tell me what you've been hiding! Wake up, Lathe!"

Patrick opens the door. "Sounds like things are going well."

"What if he doesn't wake up? I mean, neither of us can reach him. Neither of us can bring him out of this thing. What if it's permanent?"

"It isn't."

"How do you know?"

He shakes his head. "Because Isa is telling me it isn't."

"That's great because Valla isn't telling me shit."

"Didn't you say she's struggling to hold Adelaide?"

An exasperated Emily throws her arms out, "Another reason we need Lathe to wake up!" She grabs her phone and plops down in the chair, shaking her head. "What was the little girl doing? She called him *bluebird*. Does that mean anything to you?"

Patrick says, "His mother called him bluebird."

"Do you think Evelyn knows what he's up to? I could try to question her."

"Don't." A broken voice comes from the bed.

Emily stands and she and Patrick advance, hovering over a barely conscious Lathe.

Patrick puts his arm out to stop Emily, mentally saying, *"You're too angry. Let me talk to him."*

She scoffs, saying aloud, "Fine, but I'm not leaving."

Lathe chokes, "How long was I out?"

Emily steps forward. "You don't get to ask questions!"

Patrick sighs and gives her a look. She steps back, unapologetic.

Lathe groans as he sits up in bed, looking at the IV in his arm and the . . . He lifts the blankets. "Why do I have a catheter?"

Patrick's voice is calm with a hint of disdain. "Would you rather lie in a puddle of urine?"

Lathe's glacier blue eyes narrow. "I don't need any of this shit. How did I get here? What happened?"

"We didn't place the catheter personally, but the nurse explained to me how it stays in place. Did you know they inflate this little balloon at the end of the tube once it's reached your bladder? If you were to try and pull out the tube without deflating the balloon first, well . . . I'd be delighted to try it for you. I'm sure you'd heal up in no time."

"I get it," Lathe says with a flat voice. "You guys are mad. I told Emily before we went in that I could heal myself. Did my mother lose control? Why do I have no memory of what happened?"

"That's a lot of questions," Emily remarks from the other side of the room.

Lathe watches her pace. He takes in the room and notices the wall panel standing slightly ajar. More forcefully, he asks, "How long was I out?"

Patrick responds, "Long enough for someone to come looking for you."

Lathe tries to get up and then remembers the catheter. "You guys don't understand what's going on here."

"By all means, enlighten us."

"Is my mother okay?"

Patrick pulls a chair next to the bed and sits. Leaning forward on his legs, he steeples his fingers. "Your mother's abilities far exceed Sky's gifts. She could have taken out this whole compound if she so desired, so why didn't you sic her on Sky?"

"She's not a dog!" Lathe seethes. "Sky manipulated her. She thought they were in love. She did everything for him. By the time she realized who he really was, it was too late. Her mind was too broken, and she didn't have enough control to kill Sky, but she had enough power to kill a lot of innocent people. That's why I didn't *sic* her on Sky!"

"So, what's your excuse?" Patrick chides, "Even if you have only a fraction of your mother's gifts, put together with your healing abilities; you had a chance against him."

"It was supposed to be Emily and me with my mother. Why did you come in?"

Patrick reclines in his chair. "We saved your life and if you're unwilling to answer our questions, we'll be forced to interrogate the dark-haired girl who came to check on you."

Lathe tenses—a muscle twitches beneath the skin. Hair rises on the back of Emily's neck as she senses the magic of Leona's bloodline in the air. It fills her with sizzling energy as a warning breeze emanates from Lathe and rustles through the room.

Patrick's chair skids across the floor, sliding several feet before it comes to a stop. Lathe throws his blankets aside and stands wearing nothing but a hospital gown. He grips the catheter tube and in a single thrust, rips it from his own body, growling, "Fuck!" He drops it on the floor, blood dripping from beneath his gown.

Emily pales, and Patrick flinches.

Lathe steps forward, looming over Patrick as he grinds out, "Pain doesn't scare me, which means your empty threats definitely don't scare me. So, go ahead and pretend you've captured someone." His eyes flick to Emily. "You can torture me, but you'll just piss me off, and I know you both well enough to know you wouldn't dare hurt a child.

"The only card you have to play is my mother, but you won't get anywhere. Neither of you want to hurt her; otherwise, you would have. I'm sure our exit wasn't a pretty one, which means you fought our way out and we're all still standing, even her, according to you." He looks at Emily. "If you didn't hurt her then, you won't hurt her now. That's not how you work. So, go ahead, try to interrogate me. Try to intimidate me. I've prepared my whole life for this."

Patrick stands from his seat and growls, "You could've put an end to Sky. You could have stopped it all. Instead, you hid in that fucking basement with your mother and let innocent people die. You blame me for killing Katie when you had the power to stop it all along." He turns on his heels and walks out.

Emily watches for Lathe's reaction, but his face doesn't reveal anything. He turns, making eye contact with her as he walks into the bathroom. Emily hears the shower turn on and she sits back in the same cushioned seat as earlier. She folds her arms over her chest, crosses her legs, and waits.

CHAPTER ELEVEN ~

"Ashley," her dad calls. His hand lands on her shoulder, and she spins, hating the concern on his face. "You're only going to make things worse if you walk away."

"I can't talk to her when she's like this. Daddy, this isn't what I want."

"I know pumpkin, but you have to trust she knows what's best for you."

"I'm twenty-one years old, Dad. I don't need her to make my decisions for me."

He knows it's the truth, but that doesn't matter. "You're a smart girl, Ashley. We don't want that to go to waste. You can quit the store. Consider this your notice. We'll take care of everything until you've finished school. Your mom will find the perfect place for you. You won't have to worry about anything in life."

She shakes her head. "But it won't be my life, will it? It'll be hers, and I can't do it anymore."

"Yes, you can. Ashley, we're so proud of you."

Disappointed in him, Ashley wipes her tears. "Nothing will ever change." She brushes past him. "We're not a happy family, and I can't keep pretending." She slams the door behind her and runs out to her yellow mustang.

She peels out of the driveway, watching as her mother steps onto the porch. The woman is intimidating even without her stiletto heels and fitted dress. She radiates dominance. Today her brown hair is pinned back in a *chignon*. Ashley looks so much like her. She has the same long legs and statuesque frame. She has the same dark eyes, long lashes, and the same chestnut hair. But Ashley spends a small fortune bleaching her chestnut waves, going back every two weeks for touchups to maintain her platinum blond. It's the only thing about her that she gets to choose. That and her clothes when she's not home.

The woman, along with the house, disappears from her rearview mirror and she cranks up her music as she drives toward freedom. The snow is melting along the sides of the road, and Ashley hopes spring will arrive soon.

Her phone rings and she almost hits ignore, thinking it's her dad trying to convince her to come back. But it's Ben.

"Hey, Ben. How are you?"

"Frustrated. We moved into the new apartment, and now Emily is insisting on a security system."

"That doesn't sound like a bad idea. How's Molly?"

"She's coping."

"How's Emily?"

"Angry."

"So, like super serious and scary?"

"Those aren't my words."

"No, they're mine but it sounds like you agree. Doesn't mean we don't love her. She's a badass, and she saved your life. Any idea who killed you, yet?"

"Stop saying it like that."

"Well?"

"No. No leads, yet."

"Too bad. Make sure you call me when you find out. I want

to give them a piece of my mind before Emily gets a hold of them."

"I'll do what I can. In the meantime, Ashley, could you do me a favor and check on Alec today?"

Ashley knows Alec hasn't been the same since New Year's. While she remembers everything, Alec had parts of his memories erased from that night and has since been unable to reconcile his memories and emotions. "Did he have another nightmare?"

"Sorta. I guess you could call it that."

"Ben, it was traumatic."

"I know!" he snaps.

"Hey, don't yell at me. I didn't do it. Alec didn't want to remember, and now it seems like he doesn't want to forget. I'm not sure how to help him, but I'll check on him."

"Thanks. Sorry to snap. It's been a frustrating day."

"Do you know if Alec is even home today?"

"Yeah, he took the day off to get things ready to move. At least that's what he said last week."

"Okay, I'll head there now."

"Thanks, Ashley," Ben says before disconnecting.

"Good to talk to you, too," she says to no one.

A few minutes later she pulls up in front of Alec's house. As she approaches the door, Alec's mom swings it open, a cake box in hand. "Hello, Ashley," Cindy calls in surprise. "Where is your coat? It's only forty degrees out here."

Ashley smiles at her motherly concern. "I have a coat in the car, but it's bulky, and I wasn't planning to be outside for long." Ashley grabs the door since Cindy has her hands full.

"Well, go on in. Alec is in his room."

"Do you need help?" Ashley asks, gesturing to the cake.

"I've got it. Thank you, dear."

"See you later, Miss Garner."

"Please, it's Cindy. Bye, sweetie."

Ashley closes the door behind her and walks down the hall. "Hey, Alec," Ashley says, peeking her head into his room.

Alec is standing by his bed, putting things in boxes. He spins around as soon as he hears her. "Ashley, what are you doing here?"

She shrugs. "Just came by to see the progress."

"What progress?"

"With the move."

Alec frowns. "I backed out of it."

"What! Why?" She steps into the room and moves toward him.

He sits on the side of his bed, saying, "It was too expensive. I need to save up for a new car, and I've decided I'm going back to school. I need to go back if I'm going to make something of myself in this field, and work will pay for part of it."

Ashley sits across from him on his dresser. "I thought you were quitting that job."

"I can't. Not yet. I need them to pay for school. It's just a few years."

"Years!" She hops off the dresser and kneels in front of him, placing her hands on his knees. "Alec, what happened to a few months?"

His shoulders slump. "Ash, it's too good to pass up."

"But . . ." Her voice drops, and she looks down.

"Ash, I need them to pay for my school. We don't all have rich parents."

Her eyes jerk back to his. Her sadness is replaced by hurt.

He goes on, "I didn't mean that as a bad thing. It's just not that easy for me."

"You think my life is easy?"

He shrugs. "I don't know. You make it look easy."

She blinks slowly, painfully.

His hand touches her chin, and with a soft voice, he asks, "What's wrong? Why are you really here?"

She looks up at him, her lips in a determined line. She isn't weak, but it's been a difficult afternoon, and she can't seem to make light of it the way she usually does. Maybe it's because of today's date, but she can't make herself smile.

"Come here," Alec says, pulling her up onto his lap.

Like liquid, she glides into his lap, leaning her head on his shoulder. She didn't even do her hair today. The natural waves are all over the place, and she thought it better to forgo eye makeup as her next destination always makes her cry. His fingers brush her hair back, comforting her. She came here to check on him, and somehow the tables turned.

Pulling herself out of her thoughts, she lifts her head to look at him. Their eyes meet briefly before she takes advantage of his kindness. Her lips fall on his and instead of pushing her away, as he knows he should, he pulls her in, his tongue mixing with hers. He cradles her face. It's so natural, like two broken pieces sliding together.

It's all lips and tongues and roaming hands. It's all lust and desperation and loneliness. It's all wrong. Ashley pushes back, pulling out of his grip. She stands with her hands on her hips looking down.

"Shit!" he says, brushing a hand over his face.

She huffs, "I can't be friends with you if you're going to continue to be so . . . nice."

He glares up at her. "What?"

"I'm a fuckup, Alec. I fuck up everything I do. I thought I was getting better, but then I go and kiss you."

Alec stands up, saying, "We all fuck up, Ash. It's part of life."

Her arms drop to her sides, and she says, "It can't be my life."

"What's going on with you today?"

She pushes her hair back, and her fingers latch onto a curl, twirling the strand as if it's a lifeline. Eventually, she answers, "It's just a bad day."

"You would never accept that answer from me."

"Fine." She drops the strand of hair, realizing it's not going to save her. "I got accepted." She pulls the letter out of her back pocket and hands it to him.

He unfolds it and reads, glancing up at her a few times. After a moment, he asks, "Is this for real?"

Her eyes are glossy, and her glare melts into a look of despair as she nods.

He holds it up. "Shouldn't you be a lot happier about this?"

"I don't want to go, but like they care what I want."

"Did you just find out?"

She nods. "My mom is making me go. I tried to stand up to her, but she's impossible. As an attorney, winning arguments is her life, and my dad won't even try to help me."

"So, why'd you come here?"

She shrugs and wraps her arms around herself. "I don't know. I just like, thought you might understand. I didn't mean to kiss you. That was just a . . . Um . . ."

"Defense mechanism," Alec provides.

"I was gonna say, slut reflex."

He laughs. "I get it."

"I . . . It didn't mean anything. It's just—"

He lifts a hand to stop her. "You don't need to explain. I get it, and I think we both know it won't happen again." He folds the letter and holds it out. When she takes it from him, he says, "Congratulations, Ashley. You should be proud of this, even if you don't do anything with it."

"My mom isn't giving me much choice. I don't know what to do."

"So, naturally you come to see me, the friend who has his life all figured out," he says with a shit-eating grin.

"More like the friend who doesn't judge me, even when I stick my tongue down your throat in a moment of weakness."

He places his hands on her shoulders. "Your mom can't make all your decisions."

"Easy for you to say. You have the sweetest mom in the world."

"I do, but my dad's a dick. Nothing I do will ever be good enough for that man, so at some point, we have to stop living our lives for their approval and do what makes us happy." He steps back, dropping his arms. "I may not be the best example of that, but I'm trying."

"My mom has controlled so much of my life, and even though I fight her every step of the way, I don't know how to take control. All the times I've tried before, I've fallen flat on my face and Mommy and Daddy swoop in to save me. I don't want that to be my life, Alec."

"Everybody falls down, but I know you, Ash, you're as strong-willed as they come. You'll pull yourself back up without their help. You'll figure it out, and your mom will come around. Apparently, you're some kind of genius."

She laughs. "And don't you forget it!" She looks at the packed boxes on the floor. "If you're not moving, then what are these?"

"Things I'm getting rid of."

She flips the lid open and gasps, picking up the duct-tape-covered plastic bat. "You're giving this away?"

"Actually, that was supposed to go in the trash. No one is gonna want that."

Ashley hugs it to her. "I do. I want it."

"Sure, take it. It's junk though."

"I know you're trying to like, get your life together, but Alec, that doesn't mean you have to stop having fun."

"You liked whiffle ball?

"Like, so much!"

"Then knock yourself out."

"You too. Come on. We can get everyone together. Everyone's been so busy with their lives, taking everything so seriously. We need a good game of whiffle ball. Jeremy will come. You should call Gavin and see if he's coming home soon."

"He probably won't be back till summer. He's got a girlfriend at school, so he never comes home anymore."

"Oh, well, forget Gavin, call Ben and Emily, and I'll call Morgan and Patrick."

"Nobody will come except maybe Morgan and she'll bring her boyfriend, and I'll get to watch them make out the whole time."

"Morgan and Preston aren't that kind of couple."

Alec glares at her, saying, "I don't care what kind of couple they are. We can't relive the past."

"Get over yourself. We had fun last time, and I think we could have fun again."

"We had fun last time, but now, so much has changed."

"Fine," she huffs. "We'll all grow apart and become miserable adults, but I'm taking this." She clutches the bat and bends over to grab the ball out of the box. "And this!"

"Fine."

"I'll see you Friday?" she asks, wanting to know if he'll be at Ben's show.

"Yeah."

She gives a curt nod. "Fine, see you then." She walks out, and Alec shakes his head, wondering how the hell Ashley got accepted into law school. He knows she is smarter than she lets on, but he didn't realize how much smarter until he saw that letter of acceptance.

MORGAN AND PRESTON walk hand in hand down the sidewalk toward the project Preston has been working to complete. Morgan has seen it before, but Preston wants to stop by again to take some pictures to put on social media.

"I can't believe they're going to award me for the design," Preston says.

Morgan is tired of hearing about his project, but she is happy for his passion and success, so she doesn't interrupt him as he tells her again about how this will affect his career.

A rough-looking man approaches wearing filthy clothes and a threadbare coat that is too large. "Hey, guys, do you have any money? I'm homeless, and I'm real hungry."

Preston steps between the man and Morgan, shielding her from him. Shaking his head, he says, "No, sorry, we don't have any cash."

Morgan steps around Preston. "There is a barbecue place right over there." Morgan points across the street. How about we go in, and I'll pay for your meal."

The homeless man stares at her for a moment, unsure what she's telling him.

She clarifies, "I don't have any cash on me, but I can pay with my card. Does barbecue sound okay?"

"Eh' yeah . . . Yes, ma'am. That sounds real good."

She ignores the disbelieving look Preston shoots her and smiles at the stranger, stepping forward to the crosswalk. Preston grabs her hand and speaks into her ear, "What are you doing?"

Her new homeless friend is a few steps ahead and in a hurry to get the food as if he's afraid Morgan will change her mind.

"I'm gonna buy him a meal." The traffic stops for the pedestrians crossing ahead of them, so Morgan hurries to catch up to the homeless man.

Preston stays next to her. "Why?"

She looks up at him with defiant eyes. "Because he's hungry."

"Homelessness doesn't just happen, Morgan. He's probably a drug addict," he says, as they reach the other side of the street.

She gives him an angry look. "If I buy him a meal, I'll know that he gets fed today."

Preston pulls on her arm. "Morgan, you can't buy meals for every homeless person you come across."

She turns on him. "Preston, I'm going to do this. If you have a problem with it, I can meet you over at the project in a few minutes."

He huffs. "I'm not going to leave you alone with him!"

"Okay, then stop talking, because you're embarrassing me."

"*I'm* embarrassing *you!*"

She pulls away from his grip and enters the barbecue joint. Her homeless friend has taken a seat at an empty table by the counter. As Morgan walks up to the register, she eyes the menu scrolled across the chalkboard above the counter. She turns and asks him, "Do you know what you want?"

"Can I get anything from the menu? Even the rack of ribs?" he asks hesitantly.

Morgan replies, "If that's what you want."

"Okay, yeah, I'll get the rack of ribs."

Morgan turns to the cashier and orders the rack of ribs to go.

The cashier asks, "What's the name?"

Morgan turns to her homeless friend, and he supplies, "George."

She pays for George's meal and looks back at him. "Have a good day, George."

"Thank you. Thank you."

Morgan meets Preston at the entrance to the restaurant where he opens the door for her and they walk in silence the rest of the way to Preston's project.

Ashley puts her new athletic supplies in the trunk of her car before climbing in behind the wheel. She wonders where to go from Alec's, even though she knows exactly where she's going to end up. She drives out through the fields and pulls into the small drive, hating this time of year. The landscape is dead from months of winter, and the cold lingers in the air, making the whole place feel drearier than usual. In a month, spring will breathe life back into the foliage. The grass will be green, and the trees will be fraught with leaves. Everything will be vibrant and alive except for the monotone gravestones and the people they represent.

Ashley comes to a stop beside a daunting tree, broad as it is tall. She always wonders if the roots are reaching into the coffins underground. She shakes the thought away and goes down the line of graves. She says a few words to her grandparents, but they aren't the reason she is here. She stops in front of the next grave. The stone has been well maintained, and there are fresh roses in front of the stone.

Ashley bends down and picks up the two dozen roses. "Really, Mom?"

Maybe it makes her mom feel better to throw money at the problem, but to Ashley, it feels like a waste of two dozen living roses. Jacob can't appreciate them, and even if he were alive, he wouldn't care about them.

Ashley kneels in front of the grave. "Hey, buddy. I miss you, like a lot. I know that's a really dumb thing to say, but I do. I'm sorry I couldn't fix you. If only I knew about the Olvasho back then, I could have found someone to heal you. It doesn't seem fair that so many people get to live when you had to die."

She sniffles and wipes at her face with her sleeve. "I'm graduating college soon, only a couple months away. I've been accepted into law school, but I don't think I'm going to go. I know you always wanted to follow in Mom's footsteps, but that's not me. I even shadowed people, trying to convince myself it's what I wanted, but I don't. I never will. It was your thing, not mine. Well, like it would've been your thing. I really wish you were here to talk some sense into Mom. She always listened to you. You were the favorite. I think you still are, actually.

"It's like, super hard not to miss you, bud. I thought each year it would become easier. Not like I want to forget you, but like I would look back with fond memories. But I gotta say, this fucking hurts. I wish death chose me instead of you, but I think you would fare worse than I am. Besides, you are too good for this world.

"I've tried to stop drinking so much. I've tried to be better, someone you could be proud of, but then I start missing you and like . . . It just sucks.

"I didn't come here to whine, but here I am blubbering all over myself." She stands, pulls out a single rose, and places it on top of the gravestone. "I'm going to take the rest of these roses and hand them out to people. It's something you would've done. See, you're making people smile even after you're gone. It's your gift. I love you, Brother."

She walks away from the grave and spends her early afternoon handing roses to strangers. As evening approaches, she's still not ready to go back to her apartment, so she shoots Morgan a text asking if she can stop by. Morgan replies with a number of excited emojis, and Ashley drives over to Morgan and Patrick's place. At this point, it's mostly Morgan's because Patrick and Emily live in Fort Wayne now. Ben makes trips back and forth in order to spend time with Emily, but she rarely comes back with him anymore.

Ashley pulls up to Morgan's apartment, just in time to see Preston leave. "Oh, goody," she says to herself. "I just missed him."

Ashley gets along with Preston, but she doesn't exactly like him. She knows his kind. She would be just like him if she gave into her mother's vision of her life, but instead, she rebels every step of the way. Her mom lined up her life like a to-do list of items and events to check off along the way, but Ashley doesn't want her whole life mapped out for her.

Preston, on the other hand, thrives on his checklist life. He has the right family. Check. He goes to the right school with the perfect job and expensive car. Check. Check. Check. Then there is his pristine girlfriend, who will turn into his impressive fiancée, and eventually, he will try to mold Morgan into the perfect Stepford wife. Except that isn't Morgan. No check.

The door swings open before Ashley can knock. "Ashley!" Morgan throws her arms around her and drags her into the apartment. "It's been too long. How are you?"

Ashley rearranges her face to hide the emotion she's been swimming in all day and smiles. "I just took my last final yesterday, so I'm officially on spring break!"

"I took my last this morning! We need to celebrate!"

"Let's go out tonight."

"Yes!"

"Wow, I didn't even have to beg."

Morgan pauses in her excitement. "Wait, I thought you were going to Cancun with your roommates."

"God no! We canceled that last month. Bethany found her boyfriend cheating with another girl again, and she broke up with him."

"Cheating?"

"It happens all the time. So, Bethany canceled the trip, and now she's trying to win Sir Dickface back. I avoid the apartment as much as I can."

"Stay here with me. Patrick is barely ever here. We could be roommates."

"What about Preston?"

Morgan waves a hand. "He's always working, but then again so am I. Sometimes I'll stay with him or visit him while he's working just to spend time together. We still get our gym dates a few times a week."

"How romantic!" Ashley says full of sarcasm.

"He's driven, and right now he's focused on his new project. It's getting statewide recognition. It's amazing, actually."

Ashley rolls her eyes, saying, "He won't shut up about it, will he?"

Morgan slumps in her seat. "No, and I'm proud of him. I am, but it's all he ever wants to talk about."

Ashley gives her a flippant smile, saying, "Everything's gonna be okay, Ashley's here now." She reaches out to Morgan and strokes her hair. "I sensed your cry for help, and I'm here to take care of you."

Morgan laughs as she pulls away. "Geesh, Ash, I can't believe I haven't talked to you in so long."

"It's life." Ashley shrugs. "Have you heard from Patrick or Emily recently?"

"Everything is pretty much the same. Since Emily took leadership, she's been up to her eyeballs dealing with Olvasho issues. Something is always keeping her from coming back here to be with Ben, but no one will tell me what's going on, not Ben, not Patrick, and certainly not Emily. Oh, and Emily is still dealing with Adelaide because Lathe still hasn't taken on Leona."

Ashley hasn't told anyone about her encounter with Lathe last month. The power she felt from him was enough to drive her away for good. He scared the shit out of her, and she has no plans to reach out to him again.

"Why are your shoes so muddy?" Morgan asks, bringing Ashley out of her thoughts.

Ashley looks down at her feet. *Shit.* Mud from the graveyard cakes the sides of her shoes. She shrugs, giving a flippant response. "What? I can like, spend time basking in nature."

Morgan laughs. "Fine, don't tell me."

CHAPTER TWELVE ~

LATHE SHOWERS and shaves the stubble from his face. He wraps a towel around his hips and moves back into his bedroom to find Emily hasn't moved from her post in the chair.

He walks toward his dresser warning, "I'm going to change."

"I sacrificed my life to fight Sky," Emily reflects. "I gave up my happiness to guide the Olvasho in a better direction."

Lathe turns to look at her.

Her emerald eyes spark with emotion. "I don't know how much of your humanity you've lost along the way, but that little girl crawled up in your bed and cried for you. You can pretend you have everything figured out and you aren't frightened by anything, but I'd bet my life you would die for that girl and for all the secrets you're hiding. But for the life of me, I can't figure out when you decided we are on opposite sides. I thought we both wanted the same thing." She stands from the chair. "I wish I could trust you enough to leave this room, but I don't. For all I know you'll slip out through that passageway and come back with an army of untraceable children to conquer the Olvasho."

Lathe scoffs, turning his back to her so he can slip his jeans on under his towel. "You don't understand what's happening. I'm not your enemy, Emily."

"You've given me no proof of that."

"It's Patrick that's got your head all turned around."

"You can't blame Patrick for this one. He has every right to want to rip you apart. You claim to have moral standards, but your actions don't follow suit. You are a hypocrite, Lathe. You have no room to hate Patrick when you, yourself fought so hard to escape his fate."

"We are not the same, Patrick and me. I hurt myself to be free of Sky, while Patrick hurt everyone around him in order to stay with Sky.

"You're lying to yourself, Lathe. You blame Patrick for everything he was forced to do when you had the power to stop it the whole time."

"It wasn't like that! You don't understand."

"You're right," she says. "I don't understand!"

Lathe stays silent.

In a pleading voice, Emily asks, "Will you really not tell me, *bluebird?*"

His head jerks around. "It's not my secret to tell." He throws on a t-shirt.

"Certainly seems like your secret," Emily says, as she strolls over to him. "The girl . . . She cares about you. She doesn't look like you, but she could still be your daughter."

Lathe snickers. "I've only ever been intimate with one girl, and Patrick murdered her. The girl you saw is Deja, and she is no relation to me or Katie, but if you harm a hair on her head, I will destroy you."

"Good to know where we stand, Brother." Mentally she taps on his psyche, checking to see if there is a way to extract the information from of him. His mind is sealed up tight, his defenses impenetrable. Lathe loosens his hold over his mind to present her with an image of wicked emerald eyes, a twisted scowl, and ferocious power wrapped up in skinny jeans and a black tunic—her own reflection.

"You worry me, Sis," Lathe says, slipping into a jacket, as he walks past her and out the door.

She follows him, and he glances back. "You're gonna follow me?"

"I said I don't trust you, Lathe. You've given me no other choice."

"You could lock me away," he suggests, continuing his unhurried pace down the hall.

"How? Where? There are too many ways for you to escape."

"What makes you think I'll let you shadow me?"

"I'm not giving you a choice."

They reach the museum-sized winding staircase, and Lathe takes a step, beginning his descent into the foyer. Emily reaches inside and pulls the strength from within, charging the air around her. With a swift movement, Emily scoops up the air and throws it at Lathe's back. She wants to see what he is capable of.

Lathe spins, sensing the current just before it barrels into him. He begins to fall backward, and Emily pushes against the barrier of his mind. It's still locked up tight even as he uses his gifts to keep from falling.

He's glaring up at her. "Testing me, are you?"

Emily smirks. He has power, all right. She shrugs. "Worth a try."

His lips twitch, and he flicks his wrist toward her. Wind fills the three-story foyer. Emily grabs onto the railing and forces the air around her to act as a buffer. The chandelier rattles above them and stray papers whirl in the air as frames clatter on the walls. Before the frames fall, the wind wraps into a concentrated force around Emily, forcing her into the eye of a whirlwind, just like he did with Ashley when he needed to escape. He turns and continues descending the steps.

Emily walks through the strong current, leaving the tornado to sway off course, knocking expensive paintings off the walls. Lathe turns back surrounding himself with magically charged air. The barrier around him gives off a translucent gleam, glowing like an opal reflecting the sun. To an outsider, there would be no color, but Emily witnesses the beauty of his power.

He is not showing off; he's merely defending himself. Emily wants to see more. Touching the air Lathe charged, she draws it to herself, absorbing it and making it her own, manipulating it to obey her. Then she snaps it at him, letting it fly like a broken rubber band. It plows into him and his barrier cracks, knocking him back, right over the railing. Emily gasps and rushes to look over the railing just in time to see Lathe land softly on his feet, like Mary fucking Poppins.

His gifts come so effortlessly. This enrages Emily. She is fighting with one hand tied behind her back. Her gifts from her Leona bloodline don't come as easily or as precise as her gifts from Valla. Her Valla blood is dominant, and she is done fighting with her weaker gifts. White-hot flames fly from her palms, striking the marble floor below like a bolt of lightning.

Lathe jumps back, looking shocked. His clear blue eyes zero in on Emily, and he sees she is done holding back. She's still niggling at his psyche, trying to see what he is hiding.

His arms shoot up, and the wind slaps Emily in the face like a whip. Her face stings. Her fingers touch her cheek and come away bloody.

Post-traumatic-stress is a bastard. The memory of her fight with Sky barrels into her, stealing her breath as the vast foyer shrinks to the size of a coffin. Sky's wind lashed at Emily the same way. She thought she would die when she fought him, and technically she did, but only for a moment. Her Valla blood saved her life, and now Adelaide wants to destroy it.

Rage rips through her, and she snaps out of her panic. Fire rains over the railing, falling like drops of lava. Lathe ducks and covers himself with the opal-colored wind bubble. Fire hits the bubble and ricochets from the current. Flames are tossed like bullets causing paintings to catch fire on the second floor. Her flames aren't penetrating his defense, and she isn't even making a dent against Lathe's mind. The bastard is strong.

Patrick's voice comes from the top of the stairs. "Emily, what are you doing?" He winces, ducking to avoid a fireball.

She reinforces her flames with stronger winds. "Just a little," she clenches her teeth, power rippling out of her, "fight between siblings!"

"You're destroying the foyer!" Patrick reprimands. "Can you at least move this outside?"

She launches herself over the railing, pushing the air below to cushion her fall. She doesn't land as softly as Lathe, but she doesn't break any bones. Her voice booms, "Outside!"

Lathe's bubble reforms into a hooded cape around his shoulders. It hugs him, protecting him even though there seems to be an unspoken truce as they exit the mansion.

Once outside, Lathe is the first to attack. Emily doesn't see it coming, but her other cheek stings and blood wells and drips. He is fast and precise, and he is still playing with her.

A roar of outrage works its way out of her, and she shouts, "Come on, Lathe, I know you're holding back!"

"So are you!" he bellows over the winds howling around them.

"I have an evil being living inside me!" Emily shouts. "What's your excuse?"

"I just woke out of a coma. You couldn't have waited to pick a fight until after I ate?"

"Sorry for the inconvenience," she says, thrusting fireballs at him.

He holds a piece of the sky like a shield and deflects assault after assault and even launches attacks against her. This goes on for another fifteen minutes until they are both winded and sore, but it is Valla who ultimately demands an end to the fight by warning, *"Adelaide is quite excited. Should you continue this fruitless brawl, she may regain control."*

Adelaide enjoys the fight. So does Emily. She isn't sure it's a good thing, but it releases so much pent-up energy and relieves stress.

"Truce!" Emily calls out, bending forward to catch her breath as she explains with one word, "Adelaide."

"Fine," Lathe accepts. The wind quiets, and his legs give out, weak from his time in bed.

Emily sits down in the grass in her ripped jeans and tattered top. They ended up on the giant lawn between the house and the stables. Emily lies back, looking at the dreary March sky as dusk settles over them. A dozen feet away, Lathe lies in a similar position, fighting to catch his breath.

"You enjoy it," Lathe says. "The fight? The power?"

"Not usually, but this . . . this was the first time I've let it free without thinking I might die."

"What makes you think I won't kill you?"

She props herself on an elbow to look at him. "Because you would've done it already."

"I've also never brought an army of untraceable children to conquer the Olvasho, but you seem to think I will."

She sits up. "Why are you hiding things from me, Lathe?"

He sits up too. "You have evil living inside of you, Emily. I'll tell you my secrets once Adelaide is gone. She's the reason I've been keeping things from you. If she overpowered you with everything you know, the results would be catastrophic."

"*You're* the one who put me in this position of power, and *you're* the reason we haven't put an end to Adelaide. If you would take on Leona's spirit, we could be done with this."

"Leona rejected me," Lathe admits.

"No shit, Sherlock," Emily says. "Why?"

"For the same reason you don't trust me. I have too many secrets. She said my interests are too conflicted."

Emily heaves out a sigh. "I can't get rid of Adelaide without Leona."

"I know. I think I have a better candidate for her anyway."

"Who?"

Lathe pushes to a stand and limps over to Emily, offering his hand to her. He pulls her to her feet and says, "Have an open mind."

"Okaaay . . ." she says with hesitation.

"My mother," he offers.

"What?" she barks her laughter.

"Hear me out. My mother—" He stops abruptly, tilting his head to the side, sensing something strange. He listens carefully for something out of place. He feels the gentle breeze and then a snap, a slice through the air as a bullet heads straight toward Emily. Lathe jumps in front of her and draws up his wind barrier. He's not fast enough with his barrier, and the bullet hits Lathe in the gut. He jerks back with the impact but still manages to get his barrier in place before the second bullet hits.

Bullets ricochet off the barrier one after another and Emily mixes her gifts with Lathe's to strengthen the barricade around them. Lathe reverses his energy back into himself to attend to his gunshot wound. The first bullet tore through his insides. If he doesn't heal it quickly, he will go septic and die of infection.

Emily says, "Is the bullet still in there?"

"Yes."

"Don't we need to get it out before you close it?"

"My body will force it out," he grounds out, visibly shaking from pain.

"Can I help?"

"Just hold the barrier," he snaps.

The shots continue, and Emily searches the direction in which they come. "Who the hell is trying to kill us?"

"You! They are trying to kill you, Emily."

THE BAR DOWNTOWN isn't very crowded this early in the evening, so after getting their drinks, Morgan and Ashley settle into a booth. Ashley scopes the area for eligible bachelors. Finding none, she leans back, taking a swig of her drink.

"So," Morgan begins, "any new men in your life?"

Ashley rolls her eyes. "Nothing noteworthy." Spotting a group of cute guys coming through the door, Ashley twirls a lock of hair, adding, "At least, not yet." Ashley scoots out of the booth, saying, "Watch our drinks, I'll be right back. I have to use the ladies' room before saying hello to my future husbands."

Morgan laughs as Ashley walks away.

A full-length mirror shows Ashley's reflection as she walks into the bathroom. Behind her, Patrick comes barreling in. She steps out of the way and spins. "Patrick, what are you doing here?"

He holds his hand out. "Hurry, you need to come with me. It's not safe in here."

"Okay." She takes his hand and immediately jerks away from his clammy palm. "Wait, why didn't you grab Morgan first?"

He rolls his eyes, irritated with her. "Come on! Someone already got her."

They step out of the bathroom, and Ashley's eyes catch Morgan on the way out. Ashley stops in her tracks. "Wait!"

Patrick tugs her through the front door, and Ashley fights his grip. "Stop!" Ashley stomps on his foot with her heel, and he releases her.

"You bitch!" he shouts, sounding nothing like Patrick.

"Who the hell are you?" she demands.

His face begins to blur into someone else. Before Ashley gets a good look, a car pulls up, and the guy jumps in and takes off.

Morgan rushes out of the bar behind Ashley. "Are you okay?"

Ashley looks from the car to Morgan. Shaking her head, she says, "No. I don't know. I thought it was Patrick. It looked like Patrick. It sounded like him. I just . . . I don't understand."

Morgan pulls out her phone, dialing Patrick while she says, "That certainly wasn't Patrick."

Patrick answers, "Morgan, everything okay?"

"No, not really. Where are you?"

"At the mansion. Why? What's going on?"

Ashley tucks her arms around herself while Morgan says, "Someone just tried to take Ashley. She says he looked and sounded like you, so she started to go with him, but then his face changed."

Ashley looks up at the night sky, feeling scared and humiliated. How could she think that stranger was Patrick? Something catches her eye on the rooftop of the next building. A man in black is staring down at her. "What the hell?" she mumbles to herself.

Morgan follows her gaze but doesn't see what Ashley sees and soon the figure disappears.

"Did you see him?" Ashley asks.

Morgan shakes her head and into the phone she says, "Patrick, let me call you back. I'm gonna have Preston come to pick us up." Morgan hangs up and calls Preston. "He's not answering."

"He'd probably tell us to call the cops, and I have a feeling they can't help us. Maybe we should get an Uber," Ashley suggests.

"After some stranger tried to nab you! I don't feel like getting in the car with someone I don't know. I'm calling my dad."

PATRICK IS PUTTING OUT FIRES, literal fires since Emily set the place ablaze in her tiff with her brother. He wants to lecture her for her total disregard for everyone else's safety. The power emanating from Lathe and Emily was palpable. It was dominating, and even before Emily started tossing flames around, every Olvasho in the compound cleared out. No one wanted to become a victim of such power. Last year the Columbus compound had been decimated from the inside out as Olvasho under Emily's unknowing influence, beat each other to death.

Patrick almost intervened in Emily and Lathe's fight, but the siblings weren't actually trying to murder one another, and someone had to remain cognizant of their surroundings. Also, he might have been tempted to kill Lathe.

Where anger burned through him, now only concern remains. Morgan sounded very worried. He lifts his phone to call her back when he feels a snap in the air. A gunshot! Fear streaks through him and Maggie barks, registering his tension. Patrick bolts down the stairs and throws the door open. Maggie takes off as more shots ring out. Patrick moves in that direction, his mind calling out to Emily. *"Love?"*

"I'm here. I'm fine," Emily says through their mental link. *"Lathe's been shot. We're heading toward the stables. Shots are coming from the south wing."*

Patrick stops. *"They're coming from inside the mansion?*

"Yes."

"Shit," he swears, running back inside to sprint to the south wing. He feels a faint Olvasho presence, but whoever it was is gone before he arrives.

"They're gone," he says.

"They tried to kill me, Patrick."

Patrick pulls out his phone and calls Morgan.

"Sorry, Patrick, we were trying to find a ride."

"Call your dad and get somewhere safe. Someone just shot at Emily."

EMILY BRUSHES her hair from her face. She is sweating and winded, exerting herself to the limit with the effort it took to get Lathe into the stables. Curious horses peek out from their stalls as she lowers a bloody Lathe on a bench. One horse is bucking its head, irritated by their presence. Emily mentally calms the mare and pushes her mind out toward the mansion, searching for the culprit. The whole place feels empty aside from Patrick, but that can't be right.

Maggie barrels into the barn, and heads straight to Emily.

"I'm okay, Maggie." Emily reassuringly pets her head.

Lathe groans.

Emily spins to him, asking, "What can I do?"

"Don't fucking let them shoot me again."

Emily gives him an irritated look. "You're the one who jumped in front of the bullet."

"To protect you," he reminds her.

"So, let me help you."

"Not yet!" he growls in pain.

Emily leans into the wall, watching Lathe writhe in pain until finally, he says, "Towels, will you get towels?"

She hops to her feet to begin searching, as Patrick strides into the barn, saying, "Whoever it was, is gone now."

"I'm not sensing anyone," Emily says, as she opens and closes cabinets.

"Everyone cleared out while you two were fighting," Patrick says, looking to Lathe. "Does he need help?"

"No, he's got this," Emily responds.

Patrick is doubtful that Lathe has got this unless *this* means shock. In that instance, Lathe has a wicked case of *this*. Currently, Lathe is huddled on a bench; his blood-soaked shirt pulled up to reveal blood oozing from the bullet wound in his abdomen. Meanwhile, his greenish tinted skin is glistening as his trembling hands draw poison from his body. Sure, he can heal himself, but it would go much faster if Lathe would accept their help.

"What does he think he's doing?" Patrick asks, as Emily continues her search.

Lathe looks at Patrick, beads of sweat dripping down his forehead. "Ah, just chillin'. What the fuck does it look like I'm doing?"

Emily places a stack of towels next to Lathe as she addresses Patrick. "It's a gut shot. He's trying to bleed out the infection before closing the wound."

"Keep up the good work," Patrick says. "You're looking good."

"Thanks, asshole."

Patrick turns his attention to Emily. He reaches out, capturing her face between his palms. At first she's nervous and then she feels the heat from his hands and remembers the slashes on her cheeks.

Once he's finished, he steps back, saying, "I checked in with Jerrick on my way over here. He said Ben is safe, but just before someone shot at you, Morgan called to tell me that someone posing as me tried to abduct Ashley. She and Morgan are with Morgan's dad now, but should we be worried about your dad or sister?"

Lathe grits his teeth and growls, "It was an inside job. How well do you know the people around you? Why isn't Jerrick here? Is he . . ." Lathe groans, "trustworthy?"

"Yes," Emily says. "I sent Jerrick to help Ben with some legal issues."

Patrick agrees, "Jerrick is solid. He wouldn't betray Emily."

Emily asks, "Could it be an Olvasho reacting to our fight?"

Patrick scoffs, "Well, you certainly cleared out the mansion, all except for the shooter. We'll need to look over the security footage. No one, except us, knows where the cameras are so they wouldn't know to hide from them. But to answer your question, I don't know if your little power show brought on these attacks."

Lathe says, "I've been watching Ashley for a while now, ever since—" He passes out mid-sentence.

Patrick jumps into motion, digging out the first-aid kit while he directs, "Elevate his legs above his head."

Emily lifts his legs while Patrick breaks open the smelling salts and waves them in front of Lathe's nose. Lathe snaps to, swinging an arm to shove Patrick away.

Still gripping his feet, Emily asks, "Will you let us heal you now?"

Lathe takes in the scene and says, "Go ahead. The infection is out."

"Good!" She lowers his feet and mops at the blood with a clean towel before Patrick heals the wound.

Emily and Maggie find the stable kitchen, where Emily grabs some juice and snacks. Lathe is sitting up when she returns. She hands him the juice first, prompting, "You were saying, about Ashley?"

"I was keeping an eye on her before I went into the coma, but I was out for what, two weeks?" Emily nods confirmation and he continues, "Who knows what happened in that time. What is today's date?"

"First, why were you keeping an eye on Ashley?" Emily demands.

"I'll explain later. What's the date?"

"March sixth."

"It's a new moon tonight," Lathe notes.

Patrick and Emily exchange a look, and Emily asks, "Are you into astrology?"

"Sorta," Lathe divulges. "It works in our favor."

Emily gives him an irritated look. "Could you be any more cryptic? And you wonder why I think you might lead an army of untraceable children to raid the mansion. Wait! It wasn't them who shot at us, was it?"

Lathe scoffs, "They are children, Emily. They have nothing to do with this. Come on," Lathe pushes up to his feet and sways.

"I don't think it's safe for you to walk, yet," Emily notes, shoving snacks at him.

Patrick sighs, "So we're back to taking his word for it?"

"He took a bullet for me," she justifies.

Lathe grabs the wall and stumbles down to the mare Emily had to soothe when they first arrived. Lathe opens the stall, and the horse steps out, lowering her head onto Lathe's shoulder. Lathe leans against the mare, stroking her before stepping back and with a swift, practiced motion swings up onto the horse's broad back. He rides over to Patrick and Emily. "We've got work to do. Come on. We'll talk."

The three of them head back to the mansion, Lathe on a horse and Emily with Maggie attached to her side like a Velcro-dog while Patrick lags behind, vigilantly searching their surroundings.

EMILY TAKES a quick shower to wash away the blood and slips into new clothes. The first call Emily makes is to her father. She fills him in, and he goes to be with Samantha, while Chris digs through the surveillance. Patrick drives out to Columbus to help protect Morgan and Ashley while Emily and Lathe gather as much intel as they can from their end.

At first, Emily is nervous when Lathe disappears, but he shows up after getting a bag of IV fluids and eating a proper meal. His color is better, and he's no longer walking like an old man. Lathe reports that the surveillance he placed outside Ashley's apartment picked up someone following Ashley for the last two weeks.

"Lathe, why have you been watching Ashley?" Emily queries.

"I'll tell you everything once we get rid of Adelaide."

"Again, there is no way your mother can handle Leona. She can barely handle herself, and I'm not going to put her through that process."

"Then I guess you're gonna have to accept that I have secrets. Are you sure it's a good idea to leave Jerrick with Ben?"

"Yes."

"I think you're being stupid."

Maggie growls at his tone. She was instructed by Patrick to watch Emily's back while he was away. Emily glances at the dog, then back to Lathe, saying, "I think you should rephrase that statement."

He says, "You sent away the two Olvasho you trust the most. You left yourself wide open for attack."

"That's exactly right, and people think you and I hate each other because of our fight this afternoon, so I'm making myself look like an easy target. I'm hoping to weed out those who want me dead."

"What if you can't handle them?"

"Then we will let your mother out to play."

"That's not funny."

"You thinking I can't handle myself isn't funny either," she sneers. "Now let's call Ashley and see what she can tell us about this stalker your camera picked up."

COLD CHILLS SWEEP through Ashley after her conversation with Emily. She runs to Morgan's bathroom to puke. Someone has been stalking her. Could they have manipulated her, and she can't remember it? But that's impossible. She remembered Lathe even though he is skilled in memory care. Could someone be better than Lathe? Have they been manipulating her for weeks?

Ashley holes herself up in Morgan's bathroom. She doesn't want to leave. While she thought she had been sleepwalking, someone could have been interrogating her in her kitchen, her car, and her bedroom. She feels violated. What if she spilled Olvasho secrets? She splashes water on her face and wonders how this could be happening.

A tap at the door has Ashley blowing out a breath and sliding the door open into Morgan's childhood bedroom. Instead of Morgan greeting her on the other side, a stranger stands there with a malicious grin.

"Boo," he says, throwing the door to the side. He wrangles her into a chokehold causing her to blackout in a matter of seconds.

MORGAN KNOCKS as she enters her own bedroom to warn Ashley she's coming in. She knew Ashley needed some alone time, but she didn't want to leave her alone for too long.

"Ashley, it's me," Morgan says, entering the empty room. The bathroom door is closed so she taps at it, calling, "Ashley?"

She calls her name a few more times before trying the door. It's unlocked so she slowly slides it open, finding it empty. The Jack and Jill bathroom is empty, but the door into the empty guest room is open.

"Ashley?" she calls, getting nervous as she feels a cool breeze that spreads chills down her arms.

"Ashley?" she says louder, walking through the bathroom and flipping on the light in the guest room.

The room is empty, but the window facing the front of the house is wide open, leaving the curtains to flap with the wind. Panic seizes Morgan, and she screams for her dad.

CHAPTER THIRTEEN

Ashley wakes in an enclosed dark space. It takes her a moment to realize she's in the trunk of a moving car and even longer to remember how she got here. The man at Morgan's had knocked her out. It all happened so fast. There was nothing she could have done to stop it.

Her wrists and ankles are tied securely behind her back. Slowly she works the gag out of her mouth and spits out the remainder of whatever drug they had slipped her, but she is already feeling dizzy from its effects. Desperate, she begins working on loosening the rope around her wrists, but it only pulls the restraints tighter, the frayed rope carving into her skin.

The car rocks, throwing Ashley against the back of the trunk as tires squeal and the car comes to a stop. There is commotion outside followed by shouting and then silence. Ashley's heart is racing, her breathing loud in the silence.

There is a scrape, and the trunk pops open. Ashley recoils, waiting to be assaulted, but nothing happens. Standing above her is a dark-skinned man, the color of midnight with dreadlocks down past his shoulders. The moonless sky spins behind the man wearing a black leather jacket and dark jeans. She squints and tries to focus on him. She doesn't know who the hell he is, but he looks pissed.

He snaps open a knife, and Ashley prepares to scream.

Seeing her alarm, he clarifies, "It's for the rope." His voice is deep and raspy. "To cut it off. I need you to turn around."

She stares at him, forgetting how to move. "Who the hell are you?" she finally manages.

"I'm your best bet of getting out of here, princess." He winks.

Ashley thinks through her options, and as much as she doesn't want to give him her back, she has no way to defend herself, so she rolls onto her belly. She feels the rope tighten and then release to free one extremity at a time.

"Done," the rough voice tells her.

She flips over and tears the gag from around her neck and rubs at her bloody wrists. "Bastards," she whispers.

She looks into the dark eyes of the stranger as he helps her out of the trunk. She stumbles, nearly falling, but he steadies her. She steps away from him thankful she hadn't lost her shoes in the struggle.

They are on an empty country road. She peeks into the front seat of the sedan she just crawled out of. Two dead bodies are slumped across the dash while blood paints the windshield.

Ashley steps back, muttering, "Are . . . are they . . ."

"No need to worry. They're dead. They won't hurt you anymore."

Ashley recoils and rushes to the side of the road to heave, but her mouth feels chalky, and nothing comes up.

Behind her, she hears the stranger say, "Should've made it more painful for them for what they did to those delicate wrists."

Ashley turns and watches him pull a first-aid kit out onto the seat of his motorcycle. Of course he was on a motorcycle. "Let me help you there, princess," he says.

She lets him bandage her trembling wrists. Once he's done,

he heads to the front of the car, pulling a camera out of his pocket. He snaps photos of both men before walking back to his motorcycle. He climbs on and looks to Ashley. "Come on, princess. I don't bite."

Ashley doesn't move. "You killed them."

"Yes." His voice doesn't carry an ounce of remorse.

"But . . ."

He leans on his handlebars. "Listen, we're running out of time here. Sooner or later a car will come along. We need to be on our way." When she still doesn't move, he gives her an exhausted look. "Come on. I'll take you back to your friends."

"How do I know I can trust you?"

"Either you trust me, or you stay here with the corpses and wait for more Olvasho to come kill you."

"You know about the Olvasho?"

He smirks. "Of course, I do."

She looks into his dark eyes and says, "But you're not one of them."

"No, I'm not. I'm like you. Immune."

"But, I'm not immune."

"You are. You're just new to this. Now come on. We've got to get going."

Against her better judgment, she dives deeper into the bazaar dream-like reality by climbing on the back of the bike. "Where are you taking me?"

"To the leader of the Olvasho."

"You mean Emily? But I need to get back to check on my friends."

He pulls a spare coat out of his saddlebag and hands it to her. "Your friends are fine. You were the target."

"But why?" she asks, slipping into the warm coat.

He shrugs and starts the motorcycle. "Hold on."

She wraps her arms around him loosely, but when they start forward, she grips him tighter.

As they ride away, the car they left behind explodes, and Ashley clings to the murderer who saved her.

TWO HOURS LATER, Emily paces in her office while she talks to Patrick on the phone. "How did they get to her without anyone realizing it?" she asks.

"Judging by what Morgan said, these guys must be Olvasho. They're skilled at cloaking themselves. Tom didn't sense them at all. She was only left alone for ten minutes, but they were long gone by the time they realized she was missing."

"It's been hours, Patrick. I'm losing my mind here. What could they possibly want with her?"

"We'll find out soon, and then we'll get her back," Patrick reassures. "What did the surveillance footage show?"

"Council members, Joseph and Marcus shot at us, and then they escaped through another hidden passage we weren't aware existed."

"Did Lathe know about it?"

"Yes, but he doesn't know how they found it. A private emergency meeting for the council members has been called. It's just a ruse to get them here, but they should be arriving any second. All eight members are coming. Lathe will detain Joseph and Marcus as soon as they arrive.

"Are you sure Joseph and Marcus will come?"

"Of course. It will look suspicious if they didn't show and they don't know about the surveillance cameras, so they have no reason to suspect we know it was them. Lathe will interrogate them, and together we will deal with them."

"Remember to keep a level head."

Emily looks at Maggie sitting next to her. "That'll be easier when I know Ashley is okay."

"I'm pulling up to my uncle's now. I'll let you know if we find anything new."

"Thank you."

"Of course, love."

"Do you have to do that?"

"Do what?"

"Call me love?"

Patrick snickers, "I thought that didn't bother you anymore?"

Lathe knocks, poking his head into Emily's office, saying, "It's time for you to make your appearance."

"Patrick, I gotta go."

Once she hangs up, Lathe says, "I'll be hanging back, out of sight. Let me know if you need my assistance."

"Wait," she calls, "did Marcus and Joseph show?"

He nods. "They won't be able to make it to the meeting. I escorted them to their assigned rooms, and I'm planning to have a few words with them while you're in the meeting."

"Keep them alive."

He nods. "What are you going to talk about in there, anyway?"

"I don't know. I'll come up with something. They'll find out about the shooting one way or another, so I'll probably tell them about that, but I'll keep it vague and brief. Thank you, Lathe."

Emily exits her office and moves down the hall to the council meeting room. She opens one of the heavy mahogany doors to reveal a large square room with intricate mahogany woodwork covering the walls. Twelve chairs line a u-shaped table in the center of the room which faces a judge's bench with enough space for three. The Olvasho council, usually twelve, lost four members when Sky died. With two members upstairs with Lathe, it leaves only six council members sitting in a line in front of Emily.

She doubts Marcus and Joseph are working alone and wonders how many of the other members are working against her. She takes her seat at the front of the room to begin the meeting.

ASHLEY CLINGS to the stranger as she goes in and out of lucidity. She forgets how she got on the back of this motorcycle, and she doesn't remember how long they've been riding. She looks up at the twinkling stars but can't find a moon in the vast night sky. She thinks she should be frightened, but she can't recall why. She untucks her face from the man's back and feels the rush of cold air against her face. She ducks back behind the stranger, clinging to him for dear life. Eventually, the bike slows and pulls into the circular driveway of a large estate.

"You can let go now, princess," the stranger says, looking over his shoulder.

Ashley whispers, "Who are you?"

He gives her a crooked grin, his raspy voice answering, "Name's Wolfe."

Ashley lets go of him and climbs off the bike. "Like, as in the big bad?"

Wolfe laughs, his teeth a brilliant white against ebony skin. "Sure," he says, climbing off his bike. "Big, bad, and homicidal."

A middle-aged male exits the front door of the estate and pauses when he sees the two of them standing there. Ashley feels the urge to run, but Wolfe puts a hand on her back to steady her.

The man at the door makes an unsuccessful effort to get into their minds, alerting them of his Olvasho abilities. The attempted intrusion makes Wolfe growl a warning, but the man doesn't run, so Wolfe advances, menace in every step. "Let us by," he demands.

"Not gonna happen," the Olvasho says, pulling out a taser.

Wolfe knocks it to the side, and when the man bends to retrieve it, Wolfe knees him in the ribs and shoves him aside. He turns to Ashley and motions to the door, saying, "My lady."

She stumbles into a massive three-story foyer with over-looking balconies at each level and grand curved staircases that wrap both sides of the oblong room. Each story opens to enormous landings with decorative hangings and large windows overlooking the front courtyard. The bright room is blemished with spots of charred wall looking as if someone had sporadically bounced a ball of fire around the three-story space.

Three men and two women stroll into the foyer from a first story archway.

Wolfe shuts the front door behind him, steps in front of Ashley, and announces, "Tell Emily the party has arrived."

No one moves until the guy from outside barrels in with his taser out. Ashley squeals, running for the stairs while Wolfe steps between her and the taser, saying, "You don't want to do that."

Ashley spins around on the stairs in time to watch the Olvasho become stiff. A suffocating warmth permeates the air, sweeping through the room like a dragon exhaling. In the next moment, Emily is striding into the main foyer like she owns the place and everyone in it. Maggie follows behind her, with her clipped ears pinned back and a snarl curling her lips.

All of the Olvasho stand at attention, except for the man with the taser, who takes another step toward Wolfe.

Emily commands, "Keith, Stop!" The power behind her word causes Keith to wince, curving into himself, and the taser falls from his hand.

Wolfe hesitates in his movements, watching Emily, but she pays him very little attention as she walks past him. Ashley's body shakes as Emily wraps her in a hug and guides her to sit on the steps, muttering, "What have they done to you?"

"I can only remember bits and pieces," Ashley whimpers.

Without looking, Emily thrusts her hand out and fire snakes across the already damaged floor to encircle Wolfe in flames. He seems astonished by her capabilities and doesn't even attempt to get away as she questions, "What did you do to her?"

Wolfe answers, "She was like this when I got to her."

"Keith," Emily commands, "Handcuff him."

"Of course," Keith says, stepping over his taser and withdrawing cuffs from his waistband.

Emily makes eye contact with Wolfe. "If you don't let him cuff you, then I will." She pulls the fire up as if to encircle his wrists, but just before contact, Emily pulls the flames back and extinguishes them altogether.

Keith secures the handcuffs and Emily commands, "Take him to the council room and keep an eye on him, all of you. I'll be right there."

The room clears except for Maggie who stays to comfort both the girls. Maggie licks Ashley's face while Emily takes a deep breath and says, "I was so worried about you."

Emily closes her eyes for a brief moment to pull herself together. She sighs, coming to a stand. "Come on, Ash. I'll take you somewhere we can talk."

Emily and Maggie escort Ashley to the study where Emily seats her in one of the oversized lounge chairs. Ashley curls into herself, huddled in her borrowed leather jacket.

Emily sits across from her, reassuring, "You're safe here. Can you tell me what you know?"

Ashley startles as if she forgot Emily was there. "Where are we?"

Emily hides her concern and answers, "The Fort Wayne estate."

Ashley looks around the room. "I think I've been drugged. Everything is blurry," Ashley says, her eyes cautiously flitting around the room.

Emily offers her hand, saying, "Let me help get the drugs out of your system."

Ashley blinks and takes her hand. Emily uses her healing gifts to leech the toxins from Ashley's body. Ashley gives little warning before she jets out of her chair and rushes to the half bath in the corner to retch violently, emptying the remaining drugs from her system.

Ashley sits back, leaning against a wall. Once Emily is confident her friend is done getting sick, she helps Ashley to her feet and takes her to the sofa where she lies down, falling asleep with Maggie cuddled at her feet.

Wistful and exhausted, Emily admits, "I wish Patrick were here." She looks to Maggie, whispering, "I miss that cocky bastard. I could use one of his pep talks right now."

She stays for a moment longer, observing her sleeping friend before getting up. "Maggie, stay with her. I'll be back soon," she whispers, leaving the room.

Mentally, Emily reaches for Lathe. *"Brother?"*

"Yeah?"

"Ashley's here. Some guy just delivered her to our front door. I'm going to question him now, while she's resting. How's it going on your end?"

"Joseph and Marcus just finished telling me everything they know. I have a list of names for you. Have you ever heard of the group called Trinity?"

"No."

"I'd say that's where we need to look next. I'll secure these guys and be down soon."

"Thank you, Lathe."

"Pleasure was all mine."

Emily wears a mask of confidence as she approaches the council room. She hears chattering and hesitates just outside, listening to the bickering Olvasho on the other side of the door. Her anger grows. She needs answers. Some of the council members in this room are working against her and she will find out soon enough who they are.

Emily enters through the heavy mahogany door. The Olvasho scattered around the room grow silent and the stranger watches Emily from his seat at the center of the council table. The Olvasho had stripped him of his leather jacket, revealing dark arms wrapped in intricate winding tattoos on both wrists.

Images burst inside Emily's head triggered by Valla's memories. Emily takes a step forward, uncertainty stealing some of her anger. "Your markings are hard to miss," she observes, forcing herself to remain calm. "You are an enemy of the Olvasho."

"Don't pretend to know what my markings mean," he growls.

"I don't need to pretend. I've seen those markings before, or rather," she taps her temple, "my ancestors have."

He tilts his head to the side, stating, "Your ancestors are liars and terrorists."

"My ancestors had a name for you," Emily continues. "Roughly translated it would mean night-devil. Your kind is nocturnal. Why is that?"

He glances to the skylight above. "You'll find out soon enough, Vezetö."

Emily follows his gaze. "You're afraid of the sun?" She looks at him. "Why? What does it do to you?"

"Flash explosion." He grins. "I'll take you all out with me."

"That's dramatic." Emily crosses her arms. "They referred to you as devils, and you say you catch fire in the sun. What are your thoughts on churches, holy water, crosses, garlic?"

"Even in the multifaceted versions, vampires are defined by feeding on blood in order to survive." He smirks, lifting an eyebrow. "We only do that for fun."

She scoffs, taunting, "Tell me, does your skin sparkle in the sun?"

He relaxes back in his seat. "You want to strip me down and see for yourself?"

She glares at him, unable to sense any emotions from him. He is a blank slate, mentally unreachable.

He asks, "Are you always so rude to your guests? I heard you have a violent temperament."

The man standing next to him knees him in the rib cage. Emily mentally reprimands him, and he steps away from the prisoner.

Calm and collected, Emily smiles. "Our mental gifts allow us to go unnoticed. We have no reason for brutality except in extreme cases."

He tosses his head, moving the dreadlocks out of his face. "Yes, I couldn't help but overhear you committed patricide." He quirks an eyebrow. "Was that what you call an extreme case or was it a temper tantrum?"

"Emily?" Ashley's voice is tentative. Emily whips around to see her peeking into the room with Maggie at her feet. Ashley's eyes roam the faces, and she stutters, "Eh, can . . . can I talk to you?" She is trying very hard to keep her thoughts hidden, but everyone can see she's frightened.

Emily mentally reaches out to Lathe before she makes a move to leave. *"Lathe, I could use your help here. Are you almost done?"*

"Just dropping the list of names off in your study. Be right there."

"I'll be back in a moment," Emily says to the council, moving toward the door.

Ashley and Maggie retreat halfway down the hall as Emily joins them.

"Ashley, what is it?"

"Emily, don't hurt him! He saved me. I think . . . I'm so confused. Someone has been tampering with my head."

"I know," Emily says softly. "It's okay. We'll keep you safe."

Ashley clutches her head in her hands. "Emily, something is wrong. None of my thoughts make sense, and there are chunks of time missing. Just please, don't hurt him," Ashley whimpers, fear radiating out of her in waves of putrid orange.

"I wasn't going to hurt him, Ashley. I've already contacted Lathe. He'll stay with you until I have this settled."

"No!" Ashley shakes her head. "I don't want to see him."

"You'll be safe with him until we can figure this out. Let me secure our guest, and then I'll find you."

"But Lathe is scary!"

Lathe appears at Ashley's side without a sound. She jumps, and the putrid orange turns into an anxious yellow.

Emily says, "Lathe, don't let Ashley out of your sight. Someone has tampered with her memories. It's only temporary. I have a few things to tend to first."

"You mean the night-devil you've got cooped up in there." Lathe points to the door down the hall. "I would be more valuable helping you with him than I am babysitting."

Emily gives him a stern look. "With Patrick gone, there is no one I trust more. You should feel honored."

"I feel used. I should be helping you weed through your corrupt council."

"We will have to verify that Marcus and Joseph are telling the truth and not—" Emily stops abruptly, sensing commotion going on in the council room down the hall and she cuts Lathe off. "Excuse me."

Entering, she finds her guest sitting in his chair with his handcuffs lying on the table next to him. Maggie barges in behind her and begins sniffing all six of her people lying unconscious on the floor.

"You didn't kill them," she observes.

"No, I expect you'll do that once you find out who betrayed you. I have impeccable hearing, so I heard your little conversation in the hall, and I made myself useful since we share a common goal."

"And what goal is that?" she questions.

"Ashley."

"What is your interest in Ashley?"

He grins in a way that tells Emily she won't get information out of him so easily. She looks at the people on the floor. "Knocking them out was unnecessary."

"You want answers. They wanted me dead, so I guess we'll agree to disagree."

Emily comes forward and sits in the chair across from him. "What's your name?"

"Wolfe."

"Wolfe?" she repeats with a curious narrowing of her eyes. "Okay, Wolfe, what happened tonight?"

He glances up to the skylight. "Do you mind if we have this conversation underground? The rising sun tends to make me a little edgy." He has put his black leather jacket back on in the time she was gone. Unconsciously, he rubs at his forearms but stops when he notices her watching.

She notes, "We still have a few hours until the sun comes up."

"I'd rather not risk it."

Emily sighs. "And I'd rather be sleeping, but we don't always get what we want, and you don't get anything until you tell me what you know."

Wolfe sighs. "I was on the roof across from the bar this evening when Ashley was nearly abducted. I followed her. Assuming she was safe at the house in the country, I went to fill up my gas tank, and by the time I circled back, I saw the same car from earlier screeching away. I turned off my headlights and followed. I waited until they dropped their guard and then I attacked."

"You killed them?"

Wolfe continues, "I found Ashley tied up in the trunk. Her wrists were bleeding, and her eyes were unfocused from whatever drug they must have given her." He pulls the camera from his pocket and hands it to Emily.

She scrolls through the photos, trying not to cringe at the dead bodies.

"They look familiar?" Wolfe asks.

Emily shakes her head. "No, but I want a copy of these."

"I don't want them back, and I set the car on fire to destroy any evidence leading to Ashley."

"Why were you watching her in the first place?"

"Because someone needed to," Wolfe says. "You put her in danger and walked away."

The heat in the room goes up twenty degrees.

Wolfe lifts his hands in surrender, reminding, "I saved her life tonight. Ashley will be upset if you hurt me. She knows as well as you do that I saved her life. Now, I would appreciate you taking me downstairs."

Emily glares at him for a moment before giving in. "Fine," she says, "this way."

Emily and Maggie show him to the basement. They are walking through the underground corridor when Wolfe pauses outside Evelyn's door. "Who do you keep in this cell?"

"This isn't a prison. We don't have cells."

"But she is locked up just the same," Wolfe says. "I hear her rambling."

"Then you know it's for her safety. Keep moving."

Wolfe resumes his walk, saying, "I would very much like to meet her."

"She would kill you the moment you entered her room."

"A memorable way to die."

Emily ignores his comment and opens the door at the end of the hall. She tugs a wire chain next to the door, and a soft golden light glows from behind an antique wall sconce. Despite the high-tech lock on the door, the room is quaint with ancient stone walls and a braided area rug that does a poor job of covering the cracked cement floor. A twin bed sits in the corner beside an old-fashioned dresser.

Emily says, "It's musty in here, but this will have to do for now."

"This is nicer than what I'm used to, but I'd still be more comfortable down in the tunnels."

"What tunnels?"

"The tunnels below this mansion."

CHAPTER FOURTEEN ~

A FEARFUL ASHLEY follows Lathe through an upstairs hallway. Emily said she would be safe with him, but she doesn't feel safe. She would be lying if she said she felt nothing for him. She feels something, but what that feeling is, she doesn't exactly know. Fear? Intimidation? Attraction? Is there a word to encompass all three?

Even though Emily had emptied the drugs from Ashley's system, her head still feels fuzzy, and she is second-guessing her decision to follow the man in front of her.

"Don't worry; I'm not thrilled about being stuck with you either," Lathe comments.

A door slams and Ashley jumps, grabbing onto Lathe. He steadies her, saying, "It's only the wind closing the terrace door."

Ashley turns to look at the door he's referring to. She steps away from him, justifying, "I'm not usually this scared."

He nods, turning away to continue down the hall.

"I'm really not," she says, glued to the spot.

Lathe turns back. "Believe me; I know," he says. "I had to create a tornado to get you to back off the last time."

"I'm not here by choice," she reminds him.

He shakes his head. "I was trying to keep you safe."

She scoffs, "A lot of good that did."

"You have no idea . . ." He stops himself. Why is he arguing with her?

"What's that supposed to mean?"

She's driving him out of his mind, the way only she can do. Instead of answering her, he turns and continues down the hall.

Ashley rushes up behind him, complaining, "You're not supposed to leave me."

He turns, holding his arms out to his sides. "I'm right here. What makes you think I'm leaving you?"

"You're running away!"

"I'm taking you someplace safe."

She stares at him from across the space, attempting to be brave, but her chin trembles. Lathe steps forward, looking her over. No signs of her tenacious side remain. His glacial eyes soften. "What did they do to you?" he asks, his knuckles gently caressing her cheek.

She flinches at the contact and her inky eyes touch his, filling him with an immense urge to shield her from harm. He jerks back, pulling away from the emotion. "This way."

He guides her to the library next to his bedroom. It is an octagonal room with six walls of floor-to-ceiling bookshelves, and the remaining two are graced with bare windows. During the day the windows reveal a beautiful view of the lake behind the mansion, but with the dark night, they reflect the room. Over-sized furniture is scattered through the space with a large curved sofa in the center.

Lathe closes the double doors, locking them inside. He turns to find Ashley standing by the sofa, her arms hugging her thin frame as she bites her lip. She is eyeing the windows, and her voice comes out timid. "Is this place safe?"

Their images are mirrored in the darkened windows and Lathe catches his disfigured face along with Ashley's perfect figure standing before him. He answers, "The windows are reinforced."

"That doesn't make me feel better."

"We aren't staying here. We're only stopping here until Emily is finished."

She glances at him. "And then what?"

"And then we get answers," Lathe says, as he sits on the sofa. He pulls out his phone to bring up the security feed from the hallway outside his mother's room. Ashley sits down, watching him from the opposite end of the sofa.

THE NIGHT BRINGS frigid wind to bite Alec's bare hands. Cars surround him, and a shadowed figure lies on the ground in front of him. Overhead a street light comes to life, illuminating the face of his best friend. Ben lays on the ground mouthing, "Em" over and over until blood seeps out of his mouth and Alec is screaming for help, screaming for Ben to stay with him. Alec shouts and shouts, but Ben stops breathing anyway. *The fucker never listens.*

Ben's pulse is absent. His heart stops. Alec is doing compressions when a grief-stricken scream comes from behind him, and Alec is shoved aside. This unknown force drives him away, and he looks down at his bloody hands as tears leak from his eyes.

Ben dies, and the scene morphs the way dreams often do.

Ben is in a hospital bed, and Emily stands next to him, his blood staining her hands. Emily can't have blood on her hands, because Emily wasn't there. Paramedics rescued Ben. Emily didn't get there until they were taking him away. As if knowing what he's thinking, Emily's emerald eyes pin Alec to the spot.

Alec hears himself say, "Emily, you saved Ben's life. You saved me from years of nightmares. You are a hero."

He wraps his arm around the girl next to him. He doesn't remember her being there before. He turns to find Molly standing next to him.

Alec wakes, panting, reliving the same twisted memories,

only this time he remembered more. Sitting up in bed, he wipes the sweat from his forehead. Molly has never made an appearance in his dream before, but she was there that night. She was standing there next to him looking terrified of Emily as Ben lay in the hospital bed.

Alec throws his blankets off and jumps out of bed. He pulls on a shirt, grabs his phone and heads for the door. He pauses in the door frame realizing it's only four in the morning. His shoulders slump.

He has to talk to Molly, but he can't visit her until later, preferably when Ben is gone, and he can question his sister without looking like a paranoid creep.

LATHE WATCHES the surveillance feed on his phone, noticing the moment Emily and Maggie walk past his mother's room, away from the room where she stashed the newcomer. Lathe starts a loop in the surveillance footage; then he stands from his place on the couch and turns to Ashley. "We need to go now."

Ashley looks startled. "What? Why? What did you see?"

"Come on, I'll explain on the way."

Emily told Ashley to trust Lathe, so she stands to watch Lathe open a short narrow door hidden within one of the bookcases. Ashley enters when Lathe waves her through and once she's inside, she rises to her full height. Lathe is right behind her. He shuts the bookcase, closing them off from the light, making the narrow passageway perfectly dark. Ashley grabs Lathe's arm, afraid he'll disappear.

One by one, tiny blue lights illuminate the ceiling. It's barely enough to see, but Lathe takes Ashley's hand and guides her forward through the narrow space. They come to a fork and Lathe turns left, then right. Ashley holds tight to him as her eyes adjust to the faint blue glow.

Lathe has to turn to the side in a few places where his shoulders are too broad to pass, but Ashley fits just fine. They climb down a very narrow winding staircase where Ashley slips, but Lathe catches her before she falls. Ashley wonders why they have to take this route to get to Emily, but she is beyond questioning things tonight.

Finally, Lathe opens a place in the wall, and they exit the creepy dark passageway. Ashley shudders and takes in her new surroundings. They are in a corridor with no windows. The walls are mostly bare except for a few paintings here and there. Lathe starts in a direction, no longer holding onto Ashley.

Ashley follows, asking, "Where are we?"

"We're in the basement."

"Is this where Emily is staying?" Ashley eyes the high-tech lock mechanism mounted next to a door as they pass.

"No," Lathe says, approaching the door at the end of the hall. He presses a code into the lock panel, and after a click, Lathe opens the door and enters.

Wolfe is lying on a small bed. He sits up when he sees Lathe enter. "Cutting it kinda close, my friend."

Lathe defends, "You have over an hour to get back before the sun rises."

Ashley walks in behind Lathe and pales when she sees Wolfe sitting on an old rickety bed. She chokes, "What's going on?"

Wolfe stands with a grin. "Hey, princess."

Ashley pivots to Lathe, demanding, "Why is he here? Where's Emily?"

Lathe keeps his face neutral, reminding her, "He saved your life. Now, come on, we need to move."

Ashley sucks in a breath, realizing, Lathe really means *we need to move before Emily finds us.* She darts out the door at a sprint and makes it about fifty feet before strong arms lock around her, pinning her arms to her sides. She screams and struggles against the iron hold.

"Ashley," Lathe says, his mouth pressed against her ear, his breath sending shivers down her spine.

She takes a shaky breath, and her body relaxes against him. She is weak, but his presence is intoxicating. She whimpers, knowing she should run, but his voice continues to soothe her. "Ashley, I won't let anything happen to you. Emily has an evil spirit living inside of her. It is better that she not know all of our secrets."

Ashley stomps on his foot, and his grip loosens, but he doesn't let go even as she struggles and screams for help.

Wolfe takes his jacket off and steps in front of her. He shows Ashley the skin on his arm, practically shoving it in her face before she stops screaming and gasps. Realizing what he's showing her, she gives up fighting and her eyes fill with tears. She tries to swallow the emotions, but her body begins to tremble. Lathe loosens his grip, and she reaches out with a shaky hand to touch Wolfe's arm.

The once dark brown skin of his arm has turned ashy, his tattoos almost entirely covered by his affliction. His skin is hard as stone and utterly absent of heat. Ashley looks into Wolfe's black eyes and swallows. "How? How are you still alive? This . . . this is terminal."

"It's only terminal because people don't know there is a cure, or they refuse to endure the only thing that can restore them."

Her nostrils flare with defiance. "There is no cure!"

"Shh," Lathe coos, his arms no longer restraining her. "All of us have watched people die from this. It never gets easier, but the people in our lives chose to take the risk."

Wolfe cuts in, "I'm guessing your twin brother didn't know there was a choice."

She loses her breath, shaking her head. "No, no, they said there was nothing they could do. They said Ashing's disease was incurable, that it strikes at puberty and would be fatal before Jacob reached adulthood."

"And yet, here we both are," Wolfe says.

"I never had it," Ashley says. "Believe me I wish I could've taken his place."

Wolfe shakes his head. "I don't."

Lathe says, "You are a miracle, Ashley. A miracle we've been hoping and searching for."

"Have you met your biological father?" Wolfe asks.

"Frank is the only dad I've ever known, and I've never had a desire to go looking for a guy who didn't want Jacob or me. Why would I? Mom said he was just a one-night stand and when she finally tracked him down to tell him she was pregnant he laughed, said it wouldn't last, and disappeared. She figured he was married."

"Do you know the date you were conceived?" Wolfe asks.

Ashley gives him a look. "What the hell kind of question is that?"

Lathe says, "Is it at all possible you and Jacob had different dads?"

Ashley looks at Lathe like he's lost his mind. "No. First of all, we were twins, and secondly, Ashing's is a genetic disease. We did testing when Jacob got sick, so I know we were full genetic siblings."

Lathe and Wolfe exchange a look and Wolfe says, "But he got sick and you didn't."

"Don't look so smug," Ashley berates.

Lathe doesn't look thrilled, but he realizes Wolfe is grinning. Lathe elbows him, effectively wiping the smile from his face.

Ashley blows out a breath and says, "What is the cure?"

"Latovia," Lathe says.

Wolfe adds, "We should go before this," he lifts his arms, "gets worse."

Lathe leans in, divulging, "We'll give you all the answers, Ashley. All you have to do is come with us."

Ashley wants answers. She has wanted answers for years, and no one could give her any, until now. "Okay," she relents.

"This way," Lathe says, turning to lead the way.

Ashley wipes her face. She's not an emotional person, but thinking about her brother is her kryptonite. She turns to follow, but Wolfe pauses outside the door with the intricate lock. Ashley wonders if it's a retinal scanner while Wolfe addresses Lathe, "Your mother is in here, isn't she?"

Lathe keeps walking, pretending not to hear, hoping he'll get the hint.

"Let me speak to her," Wolfe insists.

Lathe turns on him with a *do not fuck with me* glare.

Ashley misses the look, staring curiously at the door. "I hear her," she says quietly, "like, in my head, clear as day. How can that be?" Her eyes fall on Lathe, and his glare softens.

Wolfe confirms, "I hear her, too. She affects us because she's connected to Latovia. That's why her magic affects us when no one else's does."

"That is *your* theory," Lathe states. "She has never confirmed this theory, and until she does, I will not allow you to warp her mind." He looks up, feeling Emily coming like one would sense a thunderstorm just before the rain hits. "We have to go now."

They escaped through the same passage in the wall. Lathe has had the labyrinth memorized since he was a little boy and his mom introduced him to Latovia. They travel downward in the maze one staircase after the other.

"Are we traveling to the center of the earth?" Ashley grumbles. "Good lord, like, where are you taking me?"

"Almost there, princess," Wolfe says.

"There had better be an elevator on the way back up or somebody is carrying me!" The stairs come to an end in an underground tunnel large enough to fit the mansion above them and then some. The blocks around them are arched into a three-story half circle. "What the hell is this?"

"This is buried history that the world forgot," Wolfe says.

Lathe adds, "Because the Olvasho wanted them to forget."

Ashley looks annoyed. "And neither of you answered my question, like even a little bit."

Wolfe takes a step, waving her forward. "Let me show you."

They walk a hundred yards and stop outside of an ornate wooden door with carvings of vines etched into the surface.

As Ashley takes in the door, Lathe asks, "How much of the Olvasho history do you know?"

"Like none. I know about Sky, kinda. They didn't really tell me anything."

Lathe says, "A long time ago, a shaman woman named Pelagia shared her gifts with Adelaide, who went on to twist her magic. Almost a century later Pelagia's descendant, Reyshen, caught up to Adelaide to undo as much of the damage as she could, but once she got rid of Adelaide, Reyshen stayed to help raise Valla, Isa, and Leona, the founding Olvasho family. Reyshen shared pieces of her magic with them, and the sisters passed their gifts on to their children. That is the dumbed-down version of the Olvasho origin story.

"On the flip side, Pelagia, the shaman woman who helped Adelaide, came from a long line of Latovian magic. Her descendants didn't like that Pelagia shared her Latovian gifts with an outsider. They liked it even less when Adelaide twisted and changed the magic because it made her a threat to Latovian people. Reyshen was supposed to put an end to the twisted magic. She got rid of Adelaide, but stayed to protect the Olvasho girls, reinforcing their magic. In doing this, she betrayed her Latovian roots, and it began a feud that lasted centuries, until the Olvasho cursed the Latovian people and locked them away inside of Latovia, a city deep underground only accessible through portals."

Wolfe adds, "Children can come and go from Latovia as they please, but as puberty hits, so does their magic and it's that magic that will be their death. After puberty, if you leave Latovia our skin turns into fragile stone, which corrodes away until we are nothing but ash. It is a curse that was labeled a disease by those who don't understand magic. The truth is, there is no such thing as Ashing's disease."

Ashley squeezes her eyes shut, remembering the helpless

feelings as her brother suffered and died. "You think our dad was Latovian? That's why Jacob . . . got sick."

"Yes," Wolfe says. "It's the curse the Olvasho put on the Latovian people. Your father must have escaped Latovia during the new moon. It's the only time that is safe for us to leave Latovia."

Ashley takes a deep breath, trying to calm herself. "Why did you bring me here?"

Wolfe points to the door. "This is a door to Latovia."

"I want to see." Ashley can't believe what she's saying. How can she regard any of this as truth?

Wolfe steps toward the door and Lathe takes a step back.

"You aren't coming?" Ashley questions Lathe.

He shakes his head.

"Why not?"

Wolfe answers, "Because when an Olvasho goes through that door, they die. The Olvasho cursed the Latovian people to live underground. It was to keep them under control and to stop them from killing each other, so the passageway works both ways. Olvasho die if they go in and Latovian people die if they come out."

"Except for the loophole of the new moon," she says.

Wolfe looks to Lathe. "She's learning."

"What will it do to me?" she asks, "If I am just a normal human, I mean. What will it do?"

"Nothing. It will have no effect."

"And what if I am what you think I am, half Latovian?"

"Latovian powers are derived from the sun, but we are cursed, so even the slightest reflection of the sun is deadly to us. That is why we can only come out when the moon is hidden. Latovia has been losing its magic since the day we were cursed. In a few years, we believe Latovia will die and all of its people along with it.

"You, Ashley, have been walking in the sun your whole life, storing its powers. You have nothing to fear from Latovia, but we think you might be able to help us by restoring some magic to Latovia."

"What if I can't come back? What if it triggers Ashing's disease?"

"Ashing's disease is made up, but I understand what you're saying. The curse is already in place. If you haven't been affected by it yet, then going to Latovia shouldn't change that."

"So, I'm like, your guinea pig?"

"More like our savior," Wolfe replies.

"Are you going to like sacrifice me or something?"

"No!" Wolfe says, sounding horrified.

Ashley turns to Lathe. "Can I come right back?"

Lathe nods a yes, while Wolfe says, "Of course."

Ashley asks Lathe, "Is it safe?"

He nods, and she turns back to Wolfe, so she misses the look Lathe gives her. He lied. There is always a risk, and he would rather she not go, but he believes this is what Latovia needs. At the same time, he is afraid it will tear her away from him.

"Okay, I'll go," she says.

Wolfe puts on his leather jacket. "I'm glad you're still wearing the jacket I gave you. You'll need it." Wolfe opens the portal door, offering, "Right through here."

Lathe almost reaches out to stop her, to protect her, but he can't. Thousands are dying, and she might be able to put an end to the suffering.

"We walk through together," she says, taking Wolfe's hand. She glances back at Lathe just before she steps through to Latovia.

CHAPTER FIFTEEN ~

Ashley and Wolfe stand in the middle of a narrow stone cave with flecks of iridescent light emanating from a kaleidoscope of raw gemstones in the wall. Ashley looks both ways, picking up on the slight slope in the floor, but the dull light fades to black in both directions, giving her no clue what lies ahead.

Wolfe releases Ashley's hand and touches it to the low stone ceiling above his head. His fingers brush over one of the glowing gems, and the gem fades. Once the gem turns black, Wolfe lowers his hand, saying, "This way." Wolfe leads them up the slight incline of the cave.

"What did you do to that stone?" Ashley asks, looking back to see if the stone would resume glowing.

"I took its magic."

"Why?"

He lifts one of his sleeves enough for her to see his arm. "To heal my skin."

"Oh," she says.

Trudging across the slightly uneven floor, her footsteps make small sounds that echo through the cave, while Wolfe moves silently with practiced grace. "So, it's magic that makes the rocks glow like that?"

"Yes, and I took the magic to heal myself."

The incline becomes more perceptible with each footstep, but Ashley doesn't complain. They move in silence, and soon the cave tunnel evens out, expanding into an opening that branches off in three directions. Wolf ignores the three openings and goes to stand along a railing that overlooks a cliff.

As Ashley steps forward, she realizes it opens into a stadium-sized cavern with dozens of tunnels and alcoves off the open cavern. There are staggering rock formations, where the Latovian people sculpted the stones into shapes, statues, and even spiral staircases that reach up into overhanging alcoves. Ashley marvels at its size. Glittering stones and gems fill the walls of the cavern, giving off a beautiful but subdued light. A waterfall trickles down the far side of the cave and Ashley sees a few people milling around below them.

"How many people live down here?"

"Thousands, but most of them are sleeping right now. It's very early."

"Is it always this dark down here?"

"It didn't use to be, but we are draining Latovia's magic reserve, so the light is becoming dull. The dragons died years ago, and the waterfall is—"

"Whoa, whoa, whoa, you can't just bring up dragons like it's an everyday thing and move on."

"The jacket you're wearing is made of dragon skin, mine too."

Ashley gapes, touching the material of her coat.

Wolfe continues, "Haven't you wondered how something so thin could stay so warm?"

"I've had enough to focus on tonight."

"The dragons were amazing." He points to a place high up on the cavern wall. "They used to sleep up there."

Ashley gawks, then more subdued, she asks, "How did all this come to be? Has it always been down here, under a mansion in Indiana?"

Wolfe smirks, explaining, "We're not in Indiana, princess.

We're not even in the United States. Latovia has been around longer than the American people. I believe the original caves were located in what is now Bulgaria. However, Latovia has long since become its own space, void of an actual location and having no natural way in or out."

"What?" Ashley asks.

Wolfe continues, "Latovian magic comes from the sun, but practicing magic was dangerous, so the original Latovian clan would come down to these tunnels and caverns to practice their skills. As the group grew, the Latovian people noticed the walls began to absorb the residual magic. It spread throughout all the caverns, so overrun with magic that the walls sparkled, and life sprouted from within, birthing the first dragons.

"The Latovian people decided to seal up the cavernous city to keep it safe from outsiders and to keep their dragons from overtaking the world. Dragons could feel the magic. They were friendly with the Latovian people, but they did not recognize anything outside of the caves and therefore saw everything as an enemy. They burned towns to ash before the Latovian people sealed them inside the cave. Once it was all sealed up, the location of the caves became irrelevant because the only way in or out is through a magic portal. That is when it officially became Latovia.

As the Latovian people spread out, they began creating portals, so even from oceans away, they could still come home to Latovia at the end of the day. Latovia grew, rulers emerged, and a monarch prospered. With laws in place, its people thrived. Latovian people were peaceful in the beginning. They didn't use their magic outside of Latovia for fear of being found out. It was a beautiful place to live, where people bonded with dragons and laughing could be heard over the sounds of music filling the utopian city underground.

Ashley can see it, almost as if the magic left a residual shadow over the caves. "So, how did it become this?"

"War."

"Of course."

"As war broke out across the world, some Latovian people decided they couldn't turn a blind eye when they had the power to stop it. So they got involved, but not everyone believed it was the right move. It split alliances, the crown was overturned, and hundreds of people fled Latovia.

"That is around the time when Pelagia, the rightful princess to Latovia found Adelaide. Pelagia was a healer and felt a great responsibility to help the people who had suffered across the world. She shared her magic with Adelaide, hoping to make a young woman's life better.

"Adelaide used her gift selfishly and eventually Pelagia's descendant was sent to kill Adelaide, but the Latovian stayed to help raise Adelaide's daughter and step-daughters. The Latovian shared her gifts with them and that is how the Olvasho began.

The next two-hundred years, Latovia suffered as everyone fought over what we now refer to as the blood crown. Then a great king was born. He changed Latovia, reverting it back to what it once was, but the Latovian people were scattered across the world, fighting battles of their own without realizing Latovia was once again whole.

"There was a feud between some Latovian families and the Olvasho. It started a war over power and in the Olvasho's desperation to save themselves, they cursed the Latovian people as a whole. When it took effect, it killed every Latovian who was outside of Latovia.

"Thousands died. It was catastrophic."

Wolfe turns to look at Ashley. "Everyone involved in the feud died long ago and yet here we are today, dying inside this tomb because the Olvasho cursed our ancestors."

Ashley asks, "How did Lathe get involved in this?"

"His mother," Wolfe says. "Evelyn's family has been trying to set us free for years. We thought we might have a chance when Evelyn came of age. The power she possessed was incredible, but

Sky warped her mind and stole her away from us. I don't know how she managed to keep Latovia a secret from him. Once Lathe was born, he really had no one aside from his mother, and her mind was in shambles. The Latovian people stepped in to help care for him. Our children looked after him when he was just an infant, and as he grew, Latovia's burdens fell to him."

"Didn't Evelyn have parents or siblings or someone?"

"Sky killed her mother and there was no one else."

"Lathe had no one?" she asks, sounding breathless.

Wolfe studies her. "We are Lathen's family. He would sacrifice anything to save us, and we would do the same. The Olvasho don't realize all that boy has already given up."

"He's not a boy."

"You're right, he is a man, but I have known him since before he was born. Part of me will always think of him as a boy."

Ashley looks back out at the vast cave, saying, "And he's never even seen what he's fighting for."

"He knows whom he's fighting for. He knows our people; our children still visit him. They kept an eye on you too. That's how we knew you were being followed."

"Isn't it dangerous to send children out unsupervised like that?"

"Would you deprive your children of sunlight?"

Ashley doesn't answer. She gets his point, but how would it feel sending your children out, knowing you may never see them again and worse, to know you couldn't go looking for them. Helpless, this whole situation feels helpless. "If the children can go out in the sun, can't they bring its power back to Latovia?"

"They can't absorb its strength until they're older, and by then, it will kill them."

Ashley turns to face him, offering, "So what can I do to help?"

EMILY PACES her office as the morning sun rises outside the window. She is furious. Hours have passed, and she has no idea where Lathe disappeared to, but she knows he took Ashley and Wolfe with him. Mentally she reaches for him for the hundredth time and comes away empty as if he merely dissolved out of the building. Why had she trusted him with Ashley?

Before Lathe disappeared, he left the names of the corrupt Olvasho on her desk, but he also tampered with the surveillance footage, so Emily checked with the two men Lathe had interrogated and they confirmed the five names on the list. She left them locked in their holding cells on the third floor and went to check on the council members Wolfe had knocked out. Two of the five names were council members, and once the council members awoke, Emily detained the two who were suspected to be corrupt. She ordered everyone who wasn't detained, to leave. Then she called for backup.

Patrick and Jerrick are on their way, but Emily is losing her patience. "Where the hell are they?" she questions as she leaves her office and Maggie loyally follows. She stalks towards Lathe's bedroom but stops short when she hears her name.

"Emily?" Patrick calls through their mental link.

"Are you back?"

"Just pulling up."

Emily rushes to the foyer and arrives just after Patrick and Jerrick walk in. She wants to run into Patrick's arms and tell him never to leave her again, but that's just the sleep deprivation talking, so she pulls that thought from her head and says, "Come on, I have an idea."

Patrick, Jerrick, and Maggie follow her up to Lathe's room. She goes straight to the wall panel that opens and forces it ajar. She stands in the opening and looks back. "Wolfe mentioned something about tunnels under this mansion. I've tried every way I could think to get to them without any luck. Maybe it's nothing, but I think we should start here and work our way down. If there are actual tunnels, then maybe this is how we get to them." She stares at them, offering, "Unless you have a better idea?"

Patrick steps forward, saying, "Let's go."

WOLFE STANDS next to Ashley as they overlook the cavern, saying, "I'm not entirely sure you can help, other than to get your friend to help lift the curse. It's possible that you don't absorb the sun's magic, just like the children don't absorb it."

"So, you're saying there may be nothing I can do?" Ashley offers, feeling hopeless.

"You can report back what you see. Let them know we're worth saving."

"You said the dragons were friendly?"

"Yes," he says, smiling. "They were amazing creatures. The last one died twelve years ago. I wonder if they will return since you're here."

Ashley scoffs, "But you just said, I may not be—"

Wolfe's smile is filled with hope as he interrupts her. "I lied. You are without question the one we've been searching for."

"How can you say that with so much confidence?"

"Ashley, your skin is glowing."

Ashley looks down at her hands, and sure enough, they had taken on an iridescent purple sheen. She gasps.

Wolfe explains, "It's your magic. It is awakening."

Ashley looks up with eyes wide. "What do I do now?"

"You let me take you back."

"Back where?"

"Home."

"What? I want to see more!"

Wolfe shakes his head and guides her back the way they came. "You can't stay any longer, or it may become painful to leave. We are going to take baby steps because as much as I want an easy fix, this is going to take some time and endurance. I want to keep you safe, Ashley."

"You said it wouldn't have any effect on me."

"It shouldn't have a lasting effect, but I'd rather be cautious."

"When can I come back?"

"Soon, I hope. Perhaps tomorrow. I'll send a child to escort you down."

"I can't come on my own?"

"You can't open the portal on your own, at least not yet." They arrive at the portal door. "When you come through next time, they will lead you down," he points the direction they didn't take. "It leads to the cavern floor. I'll meet you there."

Ashley steps toward the door. She looks over her shoulder, asking, "You're not going with me?"

"It's been over two hours, princess. The sun has already risen. You have a lot to adjust to, and you need sleep. I'll be in touch."

She reaches up onto her toes and grazes her hand over the dull gem Wolfe had drained. With her touch it sparks to life, glowing a bright purple and the gems nearby shine brighter. Ashley smiles a brilliant smile, and Wolfe stands in awe.

She lowers her arm and feels tingling energy through her whole body. She says, "I'll see you tomorrow." She turns the doorknob and exits Latovia.

Stepping through the portal takes some effort, like Ashley's whole body is being squeezed through a vacuum and then all at once the pressure disappears, and Ashley stumbles forward, gasping as she falls. Lathe is there, catching her before she tumbles headfirst into the stone floor. She straightens in his arms and looks up into his crystal blue eyes. "Lathe, it was beautiful. How did you know about me when I didn't even know?"

Lathe wears a serene smile. "I'm glad you saw for yourself," he says.

Ashley catches movement from the corner of her eye and

spins. Emily stands with her arms folded, anger in her rigid stance. Heat seems to simmer around her, and Maggie sits at her feet, with her ears pinned back.

Patrick and Jerrick stand on opposite sides of Emily, looking tired.

In a dry voice, Emily says, "We spent an hour in the walls of this mansion trying to find this tunnel. I was starting to think it was complete bullshit, but here I am, covered in cobwebs and dust standing outside of a door that Lathe was trying to explain wasn't a door but actually a portal to an underground world that we can't enter or we'll die. Then he said you were in there with Wolfe, who is a friend of his and that you were safe. Is this true?"

Ashley nods.

Emily doesn't react except to ask a follow-up question. "Did you know about Latovia?"

"Not until tonight," Ashley says.

"And you came down here of your own free will?"

Ashley nods. "I needed answers," she says, trying not to cower.

"Did you find what you were looking for?" Emily asks. The heat wafts out from her as her hair starts to float around her shoulders.

Ashley glances at Lathe, feeling safer with him to back her up.

Patrick steps forward, saying, "It was reckless going through that portal. You have no idea what could've happened to you. You were trusting a stranger, one who murdered people tonight."

Lathe begins to speak, but Ashley holds up a hand to stop him. "No, I got this," she says, rolling her shoulders back before she begins. "Wolfe killed those men because they were going to interrogate, torture, and kill me. I don't give a shit if I've never met him before tonight. I was trusting the man who saved my life and why do you think I was in danger in the first place?"

"Ash—" Patrick starts.

Ashley cuts him off. "And what do you know of Latovia?"

"Nothing," he admits, "which deeply concerns me."

Her stance wilts, her exhaustion toppling her intensity. "Patrick, they are dying down there."

"You don't appear to be doing so well, yourself," Patrick points out.

She reaches over to Lathe, holding onto him for balance as she responds, "I don't feel well. In the last twelve hours, I've been knocked out, abducted, drugged, tied and gagged, rescued by a stranger, spent an hour on the back of a motorcycle while high out of my mind. I discovered there was a cure for the disease that killed my twin brother and I was shown a different world, a world my father must have been a part of, a world that is dying because of what the Olvasho did to them." She takes a deep breath, her body shaking with anger.

Lathe pulls her back to his chest, steadying her as he says softly, "You're okay, Ashley. You're safe. You're okay."

Her body relaxes against him, and she barely holds back her tears.

Jerrick's smooth baritone cools the tension in the room. "It's morning. None of us have slept, and emotions are running high. It's been a very stressful twenty-four hours for everyone. We need to clear the air and talk about what's happened, but for now, let's take a break and get some rest." He steps forward. "Lathe, you seem to know this place the best. Where is the safest place for us to stay?"

"There are fully stocked living quarters above the stables. There are four bedrooms, the windows are reinforced, and there is only one way in and out. No one ever stays there, and no one will expect to look for us there. I can take us straight up from here so no one sees us enter."

A calmer Emily, says, "I already cleared out the mansion, aside from our holding cells."

Patrick adds, "We don't know all the ways into the mansion. We could be sitting ducks there."

"The living quarters above the stables is the safest place for what we need right now," Lathe reiterates.

"Please, lead the way," Jerrick encourages.

Lathe offers to Ashley, "Should I carry you up the stairs?"

"No," she snaps, breaking away from him to begin walking. She looks back over her shoulder and says, "Come on, try to keep up."

God knows he's trying. He rushes forward to lead the way to the stables. They climb up without exchanging words, each of them lost in their thoughts. The passageway opens up right outside of Lathe's horse's stall.

They head up the stairs into the living quarters to find an open floor plan, kitchen, living room, dining space with two bathrooms and four bedrooms.

Jerrick announces. "I'll take the couch. Each of you grab a room and get some sleep. We will reconvene in the study at four this afternoon."

There is a general sound of agreement before they all go their separate ways.

Lathe settles into one of the guest rooms, lying down on the queen-sized bed. As soon as his head hits the pillow, he starts to drift off to sleep, but his eyes snap open the moment Ashley enters his room. He watches her close the door and turn to him. He tries to read her facial expression to get a read on the situation, but she's not giving anything away.

She doesn't say a word. She doesn't ask permission. She simply rounds the bed and crawls under the blankets. She scoots towards him, and he's glad he kept his shirt on so she couldn't see his scars. She lays her head against his chest and pulls his arm around her. His body remains taut, and he reminds himself to breathe.

Then he hears her sniffle against him, and he melts. She undoes him every damn time. He runs his hand over her back, wondering why she came to him for comfort when there are others better suited for it. He continues to soothe her, and after a while, her body relaxes with sleep. He holds her. He pretends it's because she'll wake up if he lets go, but really, he loves the way she feels in his arms.

170

CHAPTER SIXTEEN ~

ALEC PULLS UP in front of Ben's new apartment. He sees the security cameras mounted outside and his paranoia reaches an all-time high. Alec slips his sunglasses on, pulls his jacket hood up, and angles his head down as he approaches the door. He pounds three times. Hearing movement and faint murmuring from inside, Alec shouts, "Oh, for fuck's sake, Ben! Open the damn door!"

The door swings open, and Alec barrels in without looking up. He shuts the door behind him and locks the deadbolt. Then he spins to face Ben and Molly who are looking at him like he's lost his mind.

Ben says, "What's with the Unabomber get up?

Alec rips off his glasses, saying, "You think this is a joke?"

Ben turns serious. "Dude, what's wrong?"

"You know your apartment is under surveillance?"

"Yes," Ben says, "Emily's dad's company installed the cameras. With everything that is happening with our dad, they were worried someone would bother us."

Alec looks at Molly. "Ben, she was at the hospital with me."

"Who, Molly?"

"Yeah, I need to talk to her."

Ben steps between Alec and Molly, saying, "I'm not going to go through this again with you, man. You've gotta drop it."

"You don't understand, Ben. She was there! In my dream—my memory. She was there that night. She was at the hospital!"

"Okay, Alec. Let's go talk, you and me," Ben coaxes. "Come on."

Molly is backing away, and Alec stares her down over Ben's shoulder. "You remember, don't you? You were at the hospital. I had my arm around your shoulder."

Molly looks to Ben, unsure whether she should answer. She questions, "How drunk were you?"

Alec continues, "You saw Emily. She had blood on her hands. It was on her chest. She was covered in Ben's blood."

Molly volunteers, "Yeah and she told me I was a shitty sister."

"Molly," Ben whispers.

Molly says, "You stuck up for me. I was afraid for you because she was scary intense. Patrick yelled at her, too. You don't remember any of that?"

Ben drops his head into his hands, wondering what to do now.

Alec turns to Ben and says, "How could Emily have your blood on her hands when she didn't see you until the hospital?"

Ben shakes his head. "I don't know, Alec, but it's not a conspiracy."

"Where is Emily?" Alec asks.

Ben sighs. "She's in Indiana."

"Why is she there, again?"

"She's there for a job. She's helping her dad with a new security branch."

"Are you sure, Ben? What if she's—"

"Alec, get out of my house! All you're doing is upsetting Molly and pissing me off! You've known Emily and me since elementary! There is no conspiracy. What has gotten into you?" Ben shoves his friend towards the door.

Alec squeezes his eyes shut for a moment. When he opens

them, he says, "Shit, man. I'm sorry. I didn't mean to piss you off. I'm . . . sorry." He contemplates for a moment and says, "Shit, what am I doing here? I've gotta go home and get ready for work."

With that, Alec leaves and Ben sighs heavily. He hates that he has to lie to his friend, but it's to protect him. What other choice does he have?

WHEN LATHE AWAKENS, his bed feels empty without Ashley next to him. He hears talking in the common area and decides it's good she left before he woke up because he wasn't sure what to say to her. Now he can pretend she was never here. He rolls over, burying his face in the pillow, but he smells her scent and groans. "Dammit!"

He jumps out of bed, wondering what's happening to him. The clock says it's already two in the afternoon, so Lathe throws on the rest of his clothes and exits his room. Emily's door is still closed, Jerrick is missing, and Ashley and Patrick are talking in the kitchen.

Entering the kitchen, Lathe steps over a sleeping Maggie. He finds Ashley with her hand on Patrick's arm as she giggles at something he's just said. Irrational jealousy pummels Lathe, and he interrupts, "Where's Jerrick?"

Still smiling, Patrick answers, "He went to check on our guests in the holding cells."

Lathe nods, studiously avoiding eye contact with Ashley, but he feels her eyes on him. He mumbles some shit about going to check on his mother and leaves as quickly as possible.

AT FOUR O'CLOCK in the afternoon, the five of them sit at a round table in Emily's study. Everyone is showered, dressed, and recharged. Jerrick starts by giving an update on prisoners. "The four men in the holding cells have given us all the information we need. They are cooperating with Lathe and me because they don't want to face you again." He nods at Emily. "Someone from this Trinity group blackmailed them into attacking you. It sounds like they didn't want to attack you, but there was a lot of pressure placed on them to cooperate."

Emily asks, "Did you show them the pictures Wolfe provided of the bodies?"

"I did, and only two admitted to recognizing them."

"So, the two attacks are connected?"

Jerrick nods. "Yes, Marcus admitted he was told to kill Ashley, and when he eventually refused, Trinity members came. The Trinity group, from what I gathered, is led by three; hence the name. They've been active for about two years, and they kill or blackmail people in order to get what they want. We know they have people inside the Olvasho council. We weeded out all of the known associates, but Trinity has a group of followers, mostly made up of weak-minded individuals looking for power."

Lathe adds, "They had the opportunity to hurt others, but Emily and Ashley were the only targets. The two men Wolfe killed were identified as Trinity leaders, so we're only looking for one more."

Ashley offers, "They could promote two of their followers."

"I doubt anyone will want that title now," Lathe counters. "The only advantage they had was the element of surprise, and now we're onto them. The whole thing was sloppy, but they were in a hurry to have you both killed before the new moon."

"This is about Latovia," Ashley says with realization. "They must have known I was part Latovian, so they started watching and questioning me."

"I suspect the remaining leader knows about Latovia," Lathe replies, "but the men I interrogated didn't know anything more than they were told."

Ashley tries to keep her voice steady as she asks, "Why didn't he kill me? Marcus? You said—"

"He admitted he had every intention of killing you," Lathe says, "but you reminded him of his daughter, and he couldn't do it. That's why the men from Trinity came."

"But I knew nothing about Latovia until last night," Emily says. "So why did they blackmail Joseph and Marcus into coming after me?"

"You are the sympathetic leader of the Olvasho," Patrick says. "You don't crave power. You value life above all else. They see it as a threat to the Olvasho's power placement in the world."

Lathe adds, "They want Latovia to die."

Ashley and Lathe bring everyone up to speed on Latovia, filling them in on its origins and explaining how the conflict started between the Olvasho and Latovian people.

Emily leans back with her arms folded, and when they are finished speaking, Emily looks to Lathe, asking, "Why couldn't you tell me this before? Why did you sneak Ashley and Wolfe out from under me?"

"I didn't want to tell you anything until we exorcised Adelaide from your mind. If she were to take over right now . . ." He shakes his head, at a loss for words.

"He's right," Patrick says. "We've gotta get rid of Adelaide."

"I'm not the one holding us back!" She looks to Lathe. "She rejected him, so now what?"

Lathe says, "She rejected me because she wasn't sure of my allegiance. She didn't like all the secrets I held. She didn't like that I stood by and let Olvasho die, but I couldn't save them without risking the lives of thousands of Latovian people."

Patrick says, "So you admit, you let Katie die?"

"Katie made her own decisions, but if I—"

"Now isn't the time to bring up past grievances," Emily says. "Moving forward, we are a team. We've all lost people. None of us is without grief, but if we don't put the past behind us and start depending on one another, then we may as well hand ourselves over to these people, or to the next group to oppose us.

"No more secrets, no more holding on to past wrongs, no more thinking we can do it all on our own. We are a team." She looks at Lathe, asking, "Do you think Leona will accept you now that your secrets are in the open?"

"I can try, but it would be better to wait until tomorrow. I still haven't recovered fully from the coma and I'm drained from the past twenty-four hours."

"We'll try tomorrow then," she says. "Do we know what the Trinity's next step is?"

Jerrick says, "The remaining Trinity leader is a woman. She is the wife of one of the men, so I imagine she'll be looking for revenge. She will keep sending people after you and Ashley. We have to find her. Without her, the rest of their followers aren't likely to be a threat."

Emily asks, "What exactly scares them so much about Latovia?"

"Latovian magic is stronger than our own," Lathe says. "Basically, Olvasho are a dulled-down version of Latovians."

Patrick turns to Ashley. "Can you do magic?"

"Well, I was able to make a few rocks glow inside Latovia, but I'm not sure of its significance. I don't feel any different, but like, this is all new to me."

"So what would happen if the Latovian people were able to break the curse?" Patrick asks.

"If the Latovian people were able to leave Latovia, the Olvasho would no longer be at the top of the food chain, so to speak," Lathe says.

Ashley winces, realizing this could be very messy. "I can't imagine the Olvasho would be thrilled to lose the power they hold by sharing it with a stronger group."

"A stronger group who hates us," Lathe adds.

Ashley defends, "Wolfe doesn't hate us."

"Wolfe doesn't hate you or me, but our people are the reason his people have suffered," Lathe counters. "Wolfe and I have talked for years about strategies in case we find a way to break the curse. Bringing the Latovian and Olvasho people together would be our first priority. We need to make everyone understand we are not enemies and that feuding is what started all of this in the first place."

"Or we can do nothing," Emily says. All eyes turn to her. "It is not in our nature to be peaceful. We fight amongst ourselves. In my short time leading the Olvasho, I have stopped one serial killer after the other. Even the people the Olvasho elected to make good decisions have tried to kill me. The Latovian people are the same from what you've described; only they're stronger. They have the potential to breed dragons that are loyal only to them. So, essentially what you're asking us to do is unleash these people on the world and hope everything works out. These people who have incredibly strong magic and a major grudge against us!"

The silence is heavy as everyone searches for the right words.

Ashley is the first to speak. "I can't do nothing. How can you let thousands die, just because you're afraid of what might happen?"

Emily says, "Thousands of them equals nothing when considering the billions of people in this world we would be putting at risk."

Ashley makes a noise of protest and Lathe puts a hand on her arm, saying, "Ashley, she's playing devil's advocate. We have to consider all the options."

Emily continues, "We could restore the magic to Latovia and keep the curse in place."

Patrick says, "But if you've restored the magic, they could find a way out and then they'd come after us first."

"Then we could try to break the curse but make it so their magic only works in Latovia."

Lathe says, "You would be clipping their wings, and birds need to fly. You would only be giving them back half of their freedom, and if they had magic, they would find a loophole, break open their wings and clip yours so you would know what it's like."

"What if . . ." Ashley begins but seems hesitant to continue.

Jerrick encourages, "Nothing you say here will be held against you. We all want what is best, so if you have a suggestion, please, go ahead and share."

"What if we don't break the curse as a whole, but if we do it individually; if it's even an option? Like, we would only allow certain Latovians out into the world at a time."

"A slow trickle instead of an instant explosion," Patrick says. "That might work."

Lathe says, "Wolfe and I have considered all the possibilities, and that seems to be the option we keep circling back to. If we made the Latovian people take a crash course on the way the world works above ground before letting them out, they would see us working with them to break the curse. They would see we are not the enemy and at the same time, we could feel them out to see who could be a potential threat."

"There are a lot of hypotheticals," Emily says, "but at least we have a direction. Ashley, I want you to learn as much as you can while you're there tomorrow." Ashley nods and Emily continues, "Now, what do we do about this Trinity group?"

"First we need to find out exactly who we're up against," Jerrick says. "I have some of my contacts working on it, and I also spoke with your dad. He's keeping an eye on everything in Columbus as well as running some faces through a special software he's developed. Your dad is a genius." He looks down at his phone when it begins buzzing. "This is one of my contacts, now. Let me take this and get back to you," he says, walking out of the room.

Emily eyes the rest of the people at the table. "Ashley, welcome to the madness. Do you regret wishing you were a part of some big secret?"

Ashley says, "I just wish I knew how to fix all the problems."

Patrick scoffs, "There will always be more problems."

Emily sighs, saying, "I don't know about you guys, but I'm starving."

JERRICK COMES in with news while they are eating. "My brothers are coming to transfer our prisoners to the offsite holding cells. They'll stay under guard while we continue our investigation. I'll personally screen the guards."

Emily gives him a curious look. "You have brothers?"

"I have three."

"Oh!" Emily says, surprised. His family has always been a topic he wasn't willing to share, and Emily had assumed he no longer had any surviving family. "Do you want some help?"

"Not necessary, Vezetö. But I do have a few leads on the remaining Trinity leader. How would you like me to proceed?"

Emily puts down her fork, asking, "Jerrick, have you eaten today?"

"Yes."

"Do you ever take a break?"

"I prefer to stay busy."

Emily pushes her chair back and stands. "Let's go talk."

After they leave the room, Ashley asks, "Vezetö?"

Patrick explains, "It's a term of respect. He is acknowledging she is in charge."

"So why don't you guys call her that?"

Patrick snorts and Lathe smiles.

Ashley asks, "What am I missing?"

"She's not fond of it," Patrick scoffs. "She's threatened bodily harm."

Ashley wonders, "So why does Jerrick use it?"

"Because Emily doesn't correct him anymore. She knows it makes him uncomfortable *not* to use it." Patrick pushes back from the table, asking, "Lathe, did you secure the mansion?"

"I did it earlier."

"You're sure we're safe to stay here tonight?"

"Yes. I closed off all the outside entrances. The only way in and out is through the front door."

"I'll do another walkthrough," Patrick says, leaving the room.

Ashley looks at Lathe. "Does that mean they just left us to do the dishes?"

Lathe smirks and starts clearing the table.

Ashley grabs what's left and heads for the kitchen. When she enters, Lathe is already busy at work, washing dishes. She sets the dirty dishes next to the sink, remarking, "How domestic of you." She walks around him, grabbing a dishtowel. She pulls herself up to sit on the counter on the other side of him. "I'll dry."

Lathe hands her a clean plate, and she begins drying, noting, "This might hurt your badass reputation."

"What? Doing the dishes?"

She smirks. "Yeah. Next, you're going to tell me you do other house chores, too."

"Would you rather me be a slob?"

"No. It's a very sexy combination. A badass who will clean up after himself."

Lathe doesn't know how to respond. He knows Ashley is flirtatious and he shouldn't take anything she's saying to heart. But damn it, he isn't used to this kind of attention, especially not from someone looking like her, and how is he supposed to interpret her actions from last night. What was her end game and why did it matter to him? He knows nothing can happen between them, anyway.

"I think that one's clean," Ashley comments.

Lathe looks up at her, and she glances down to the sink where he's still scrubbing the same plate. In his rush to be done with the plate, he turns it, splashing himself with water, causing Ashley to giggle.

He shoves the plate at her and goes to the next one, concentrating on the task in front of him. They make it through the plates and half the glasses when Ashley says, "It feels weirdly intimate to be doing the dishes together."

Lathe turns off the water. "The rest of these can wait."

Ashley snaps the dishtowel at him, challenging, "You that afraid of intimacy, Lathe?"

He steps back, folding his arms and frowning at her—his go-to move when he doesn't want to be messed with—but, of course, Ashley blows right through his defense by mimicking him. She dramatically crosses her arms and gives him her best pouty face.

Fuck, if she isn't adorable.

Lathe turns away, saying, "Come on, I'll show you to your room." He doesn't look back to see if she's following as he walks out of the kitchen.

She catches up to him on the stairs. "You might need to work on your hospitality skills. I'd hate to leave a bad review."

Lathe glances at her. "You left this on the table downstairs," he says, holding out her phone. "You should have it in case you need to call anyone."

Ashley takes her phone flipping it in her hand. Patrick had returned it to her earlier in the day, but so far, she hadn't felt the need to contact anyone. "I should probably text one of my roommates, so they don't worry about me."

Sensing her sudden melancholy, he says, "I know there has been a lot to take in. How are you holding up?"

"I'm okay. I . . . Thank you for last night. I didn't want to be alone."

"Anytime." As the word comes out of his mouth, he kicks himself. What is he thinking, encouraging her to crawl into his bed anytime?

"How are you doing?" she asks. "Now that all your secrets are out?"

Lathe eyes her and says, "This is your room." He motions to

the heavy door on her left, and she opens it to take a look, but she doesn't go in.

After a moment she shuts the door, saying, "It's nice." She turns back to him. "Where is your room?"

Lathe points in a direction, saying, "Down that way."

"Will you show me?"

"Why?"

"In case I need you in the middle of the night," she replies.

He doesn't know how to take her answer, but he doesn't want to appear slow, so he says, "This way." He continues down the hall, stopping in front of his closed door.

She steps forward, right into his personal space. "It's not just me, right? You feel it, too."

"Feel what?"

"A connection between us," she says, moving around him to open his bedroom door. She walks in, and Lathe cautiously enters behind her.

"Your room is bigger than mine," she comments, as she wanders around his room.

"I live here. You're just visiting."

"Is that what I'm doing?" she questions. "And how long am I going to be visiting?"

"I don't know."

"It kinda feels like my life is here now," she says, picking up a snow globe and shaking it. She watches the snow fall over the little church and then places it back on the built-in bookshelf.

"What about law school?"

She flicks her eyes over to him, "How did you . . ." She stops herself, because, of course, he would know. Hadn't he already proven he knew more about her than she did? She finds a picture of a beautiful blond woman on his shelf and picks it up. "Is this your mother?"

"Yes."

"She's beautiful." She sets the photo down. "I never wanted

to go to law school. That's my mother's dream for me, not my own."

She picks up the next picture and Lathe cringes, hoping to distract her with a question. "What is your dream?"

"To be happy," she answers, then asks, "Who's this?"

Fuck. He hesitates, before saying, "Katie."

Her eyes find his from across the room. "The girl who died?"

He nods, and she sets down the picture. She walks over to him, saying, "It's a screwed-up world we live in."

He nods again, not trusting himself to speak. She places her palms against his chest and looks up at him, saying, "You're one of the good ones, Lathe. I don't know what happened to Katie, but I know you're a good man. I'm sorry you lost her."

He tries to take a deep breath, but she seems to have stolen all the air from the room. She slides her palms up his chest and wraps them around his neck, saying, "I'm not crazy, right? There is something here."

He shakes his head, denying it.

She moves her hands to hold his face between her palms. The skin on his right cheek is smooth and perfect, while the surface of the left is ridged and taut, just like him, beautiful and scarred, inside and out. His glacial eyes spear her, but she won't let him intimidate her. She rises on her tiptoes to place a gentle kiss on his lips.

His eyes close, and he pushes her away. "Ashley, it can't be like this."

"Why not?"

He looks at her. "I have a duty to my people, as do you."

"And that stops us, why?"

"Their needs will always come first, Ashley."

"Is this how it's always been?" she asks. "Their needs come first, so everything you feel is unimportant?"

"It's not like that."

"Then kiss me."

He shakes his head. "No, I can't afford a distraction right now."

Ashley gawks at him. "Is that all I am? A distraction! In that case, I think you would definitely want me right now, especially because you're about to risk your life by trying to take on the spirit of Leona. Patrick told me you almost died the last time. He said you woke from your coma yesterday!" She breaks away from him.

"Why are you lecturing me?"

"Because there is more to life, Lathe. Give yourself a fucking break! Let someone else take on Leona! Let someone else risk it!"

"No, I can handle it. I can do this."

"I love Emily, and I want Adelaide gone too, but you don't have to be the one to do it. Almost dying once is enough. You know that, right?"

He pulls away from her and walks across the room, only to spin back to her. "I gave them my word, and I will follow through."

"Fine," she huffs, moving toward him. She comes to stand right in front of him. "Then while you're still you, please put me out of my misery and kiss me! You know you want—"

He swoops in, unexpected, and his lips crush hers. He's been craving those lips and that tongue that verbally lashes him. She opens her mouth, and he gets to experience just how capable that tongue is of pleasure. A collective moan escapes them, and Ashley clings to his broad shoulders as he draws her closer.

She notices the second he remembers he's not supposed to let her get to him. She feels the change as his body goes rigid and he breaks their kiss. She wraps her arms around his neck to keep him from going anywhere, but he moves to push her away.

Before he can, she grinds her hips against him, rubbing over the proof that she isn't the only one affected by their kiss. She guides one of his hands to her waist, where he tightens his grip on her. Her lips brush his in teasingly light kisses. Her eyes are open and challenging him with a glint in their inky depth. He holds her against him, shivering at the contact.

"Don't take on Leona," she begs in a soft voice. "I've seen what it's done to Emily and Patrick. Please. Don't do it, Lathe."

His fingers stroke her face and he watches her lips, longing to kiss them again, but he doesn't. He can't. His duty comes before his feelings. It always has. Pulling away, he says, "I won't be manipulated. You don't get to make my decisions."

She backs up, putting her hands on her hips. "Obviously! God! Screw you, Lathe! You want me, or you don't, but I deserve someone who can admit that he wants me, and you . . . you can't even figure out that you're worth more than your sacrifice and duties! God, Lathe, you're fucking amazing, and it pisses me off that you can't see it! Like, figure it out!" She walks away, slamming the door behind her.

Lathe sits down on the side of his bed, burying his face in his hands.

"I like her," a small voice says, and Lathe jumps to his feet. The little girl freezes, frightened by his quick movement.

"Deja, I wasn't expecting you until tomorrow."

Pale skin and dark eyes peer out beneath strands of jet-black hair. Lathe pushes the hair out of her face and she smiles. She's a petite little thing, barely coming to Lathe's waist. She's his favorite, not that he would admit it out loud.

The little girl says, "Wolfe thought it'd be better if she visits at night until he knows how the others will react to her." She looks to the door. "Was that her?"

"Yeah."

She smiles. "She's right, you know."

Lathe gives her a sideways look, asking, "How long have you been listening?"

She looks down, her cheeks turning pink. "Do you think someone will want to kiss me like that someday?"

Shit. "It better be a long time before someone kisses you like that."

"Do you think I'll be as pretty as she is?"

"Prettier."

She shakes her head. "Do you want her to be your girlfriend? She said you're fucking amazing."

Lathe tries not to laugh at her little voice saying those words. "Deja, you shouldn't eavesdrop like that."

She looks confused. "What are you talking about? That's what you taught me to do."

"Yeah, but don't eavesdrop on me."

"I'm sorry. I didn't mean to. Please, don't be mad."

"I'm not mad." He ruffles her hair. "Come on, let's go get her."

They knock at Ashley's door, and she shouts. "Unless you're here to apologize, I don't want to talk to you!"

Lathe opens the door.

From across the room, Ashley spins to face him, saying, "I'm not fucking—" she stops when she sees Deja standing next to him. "Um, oh, sorry, I was . . ." She eyes Lathe, giving him a death glare.

He smirks, and Deja says, "It's okay. I've heard worse."

Lathe says, "Ashley, this is Deja. Deja, Ashley."

"Hi, Deja."

"You don't have to act different around me because I'm small. I'm older than I look."

"How old are you?"

"Eight and a half," Deja says, puffing out her chest. "Are you ready to go?"

"Sure, I thought I had to wait till morning, but this is even better. Keeps my mind off things." She flicks her eyes to Lathe once more.

"Deja, I trust you know the way from here," Lathe says.

"Yep," she answers proudly.

"Then I'll leave you to it." He turns to leave and pauses, looking back to instruct, "Take her through the main corridors instead of the labyrinth in the walls."

Deja's look of excitement grows. "I'm allowed?"

"This time you can, but only because the mansion has been cleared out."

"Awesome, let's go!" Deja grabs Ashley's hand and tugs her out of the room. They make it several paces down the hall before Deja drops Ashley's hand and spins to run back to Lathe, whispering, "I think you should ask her to be your girlfriend."

Ashley pretends not to hear, waiting for the girl to jog back to her so they can continue through the mansion.

Deja leads her to the basement. The opening for the stairway to the tunnels is hidden in the wall across from Evelyn's room. Ashley can feel Evelyn's magic and she hears her mumbling gibberish to herself. It makes her pause in front of the door, saying, "Hey Deja, do you know how to get into that room?"

"I'm not allowed in there."

"But how does Lathe get in?"

"Lathe uses the retinal scanner and types in the code."

"Do you know the code?"

Deja wears a sly grin. "Of course, I do. And I know how to bypass the retinal scanner. You want to break in?"

"Um . . ."

"It's okay, I won't tell. I'm good at secrets, but Evelyn is dangerous. Lathe'll be mad at me if you get hurt."

"I'm not going to go in. I just . . . never mind." Ashley shakes her head and spins toward the opening Deja created in the wall.

"It's probably good I didn't tell you; cause Lathe uses the same passcode for everything."

Ashley turns to look back at the door one more time, asking, "How do you bypass a retinal scanner?"

Deja gives a sly grin. "You pull the cord out of the back. It will give an error code so you just type in the password to correct the error and then you punch it in again to get the door to open."

"How do you know this?"

"Lathe tells me everything," Deja says, sliding the wall back in place behind them before they descend to the portal entrance.

Deja walks to where the portal should be, while Ashley looks around, confused. "What happened? We must've made a wrong turn or something. This isn't the right door."

Deja smiles and steps up to the black steel door. She places her palm against the surface, and carved vines blossom, starting in the center and spreading across the door in intricate detail.

"This is why Wolfe sent me to get you. He was afraid you wouldn't be able to get back in without me."

"The door didn't change like that before."

"It recognizes Wolfe, so it probably changed the moment you guys entered the tunnel. I'm still young. It doesn't know me as well." Letting her hand drop, she takes a step back. The door doesn't change. She backs up several more steps, and Ashley follows suit. At about ten yards out, the door melts back into a solid black door.

"Whoa!" Ashley exclaims.

Deja rushes back to the door, standing right in front of it and sighs when it doesn't change back. "Damn, it still doesn't recognize me."

Ashley moves forward. "I don't think you should say damn."

"Why?"

"I don't know, because kids aren't supposed to swear."

"That's stupid. Why are some words okay when others aren't?"

Ashley shrugs. "It's like, a thing. I don't know."

Deja steps back and motions to the door, saying, "You should try it. See if it recognizes you."

"Really?"

Deja nods and Ashley steps forward, tentatively standing before the door. Nothing happens, so Ashley places the palm of her hand against the steel and closes her eyes, afraid to look. Her palm tingles and the cold steel warms against her touch. Ashley opens her eyes, feeling the force of Latovia radiate through her body as the portal door appears in front of her.

Deja says, "It knows you're one of us."

Ashley smiles as she opens the door. "This is so cool."

BEN RECEIVES a call while he's at work. He recognizes the detective's number, so he picks up. "This is Ben."

"Hello, Ben, this is Agent Frest calling. We have some new evidence in your case."

"You mean my father's case," Ben corrects.

"No, I mean your case. The brutal attack you endured on New Year's Eve. We have found irrefutable proof of your attackers and their motive. We want to meet with you as soon as possible, so we can move forward."

"I'm just finishing up at work. I can be there in twenty minutes."

As soon as he's off the phone, he tries to call Emily, but as usual, she doesn't answer. He sends her a text. **I have some exciting news. Call me.**

SEVERAL HOURS LATER, Emily walks into her bedroom, dialing Ben.

He answers before the second ring. "Emily?"

"Yeah, I just saw your text. What's going on?"

"They know who attacked me," he says. "They caught the guys responsible. I guess there was video footage of my attack. They abducted me to collect ransom from my father, but when he refused to pay, they beat me up and sent him the live video. My father didn't give a shit, so they just kept beating me, thinking he would cave."

"Oh my God, Ben!"

"I know. Crazy."

"I knew your dad was an ass, but I never would've imagined even him stooping that low."

"He allowed them to beat the life out of me. He allowed it without blinking an eye and didn't even consider reporting them to the authorities. The cops have the video now, and the guys confessed. They admitted that once they realized I wasn't worth anything, they dumped me back where they found me. The police don't know how I survived the attack. I told them I have a guardian angel."

"Ben, that's so terrible. I'm so sorry."

"I'm not," he says. "I'm relieved. They have the guys that almost killed me. That means you can stop searching the Olvasho for my killer."

CHAPTER SEVENTEEN ~

ASHLEY CLIMBS the steps back up from the Latovia. She exits the hidden passageway into the mansion and pauses. Evelyn's door is right in front of her and Ashley can hear her more clearly tonight. Instead of gibberish, Evelyn is speaking in full sentences. Lathe told her she had moments of clarity. Maybe this was one of those moments.

"Please, Latovian child, come and sit with me," Evelyn calls out.

Ashley shouldn't have been able to hear her through the soundproofing, but it is as if she's standing right next to her.

"A short visit," Evelyn cries. *"I am so lonely."*

Deja said Lathe uses the same code for everything and Ashley watched the code Lathe typed in his phone to pull up the camera feed. She detaches the wires from the retinal scanner and types in the code, hoping she won't set off an alarm. Instead, it gives her the go ahead to enter the code and then the clink of a mechanical mechanism inside the door disengages, and Ashley opens the door.

The lights are on, and Evelyn is standing in the middle of the room looking at her. Ashley doesn't recognize her from Lathe's photo upstairs. This woman seems frail, like a breeze could knock her over. Her blond hair is streaked with grey and the frizzy mess sticks out from her head like a bolt of lightning struck her. She wears a blue cotton nightgown with a cardigan tied over her shoulders and snow boots on her feet. As if that isn't bizarre enough, she stands in the middle of the room with a cup of tea in one hand, a pillow in the other, and her eyes—the only sign of intelligence—are focused on Ashley.

"Hi," Ashley says softly. "I could hear you speaking to me."

Evelyn drops the pillow and teacup which Ashley discovers is plastic as it bounces on the floor without shattering. Evelyn looks down as if realizing she just dropped something, but her focus quickly returns to Ashley. Her voice comes out, sounding almost hypnotic in its beauty. "Take me with you, down to the tunnels."

"I can't. You won't be able to enter, and Lathe will kill me."

Evelyn smiles and Ashley sees a glimpse of the woman from the photo. "I will be able to enter because you did! I have seen it. Take me there, princess."

"I'm not a princess," Ashley says. "And Lathe will literally kill me if I let you out of here."

"Please princess, make me whole again."

Ashley shakes her head. "Let me talk to Lathe. I'll tell him what you told me and then maybe we can all go."

Without warning, absolute darkness consumes the room and Ashley freezes. Evelyn's beautiful voice is gone, replaced by a fierce growl. "You will take me where I want to go!"

Ashley backs up as the wind stirs the air. "I'm sorry," Ashley says, unsure how to get out with total darkness surrounding her. Cold air tickles her neck, and then a burning heat strikes her midsection. Pain radiates through her body, and she covers her midsection with her hands. *How did she get wet?* There is liquid dripping through her fingers. Ashley's hair blows into her face, and she closes her eyes. The last thing she hears is the lock mechanism disengaging. She falls to the floor, opening her eyes as light pours in from the hallway. She lifts a hand and tries to speak, but the crimson dripping from her hand locks her words inside her throat. She sees the panic on Lathe's face just before everything fades away.

LATHE JUMPED out of the shower as soon as he heard the alert on his phone. It goes off every time his mother's door opens, but it can't be opening. Aside from him, no one knows the code. He pulls up the feed just in time to see his mother's door close. Shit. He throws on some pants and runs out of his bedroom. He sprints down the hallway, jumps the railing into the foyer, using his gifts to soften his landing. Then he takes off again, almost running over Patrick.

Patrick watches a half-dressed Lathe sprint toward him. "Whoa!" Patrick says, jumping out of his way. Lathe doesn't respond. He keeps running like his world is on fire.

Patrick reaches out to Emily. *"Hey, something's up. You might want to get down here."*

She asks, *"Where are you?"*

"Going to the basement," Patrick says, as he follows Lathe.

Lathe makes it into the basement corridor and feels the pressure of his mother's anger. He types in the code as quickly as he can, but he flubs up and has to start over. The lock finally clinks, and Lathe throws open the door just in time to see Ashley fall to the floor. She doesn't even try to catch herself. Her midsection has been cut wide open, nearly splitting her in two. Ashley lifts a bloody hand to Lathe, and then her eyes roll back as her hand flops to the floor.

Inside the room, the lights are off, and eerie stillness fills the space. "Mother!" Lathe roars, leaving the door open so he can see. His mother steps out of the darkness—her eyes razor-focused. Lathe stumbles back. "Why?"

He expected her to be out of her mind, but she is lucid. Lathe drops to the floor next to Ashley and feels for a pulse. Unable to find one, he reaches for his gifts, but before he can bring life back to the woman before him, his mother's brutal force knocks him back. He slides across the floor, the back of his head slamming into the brick wall.

Patrick steps off the bottom step just in time to see Lathe disappear into the room. A massive thump from inside the room causes Patrick to freeze. His skin crawls as he moves closer to Evelyn's room, creeping along the wall. *"Hurry Emily!"*

"Coming!"

Wind bursts from the room, knocking Patrick back ten feet. He lands on his back, looking up in time to see a deranged Evelyn step out into the hallway. She makes eye contact with Patrick, warning him to stay down. Behind her—as if being carted out by an invisible gurney—is the mutilated corpse of his friend. Patrick's blood runs cold. Ashley's stomach is nearly severed in two, and her limp arms dangle at her sides, dripping blood from her fingertips.

Evelyn opens the wall across from her room, an opening he wasn't even aware existed, and then she disappears inside with Ashley's body. The wall closes, and Patrick stares in shock at what he's just witnessed.

"Ben, I'm sorry. I gotta go. Patrick is freaking out about something. I'll call you right back," Emily says into the phone. She says her goodbyes as she leaves her room. She slides her phone into her pocket and runs down the stairs. She pauses in the foyer, feeling a rippling of something ugly from within.

"I don't like that," Valla says.

"I don't either." She starts jogging and reaches for Patrick, but something is wrong. She can't feel their connection. She sprints, jumping down the basement steps. "Patrick!" she calls over and over. When she reaches the bottom step, she finds the floor littered with debris from the wall. Lying in the middle of it is Patrick, propped up on an elbow.

"Oh my God, Patrick! Are you okay?" She rushes over to him, still feeling that sick queasiness in her gut.

Patrick's eyes lift to Emily, and she notices the emotions radiating out of him are so potent, so concentrated, it looks as if he is sitting inside a black cloud.

"What is it?" Emily asks. She looks toward Evelyn's room and notices the door standing wide open. Emily creeps forward, coaxing, "Evelyn?"

"No, Emily," Patrick says, snapping out of his trance. He comes to a stand. "Evelyn is gone. We need to see if Lathe is okay."

"She's gone?"

Patrick ignores her question and sweeps past her, rushing into the room. Light shines brightly on the horrific scene before him. Patrick steps over the pool of blood to check on Lathe who is lying on the floor with blood seeping from the back of his head. Patrick covers the wound and begins healing the gash, barely registering Emily's frantic shriek.

"Whose blood is this, Patrick?"

"I'm not sure," he says to buy himself more time because he doesn't want to tell her that her friend is dead. Patrick pulls out his phone to call Jerrick. When he answers, Patrick says, "Evelyn's quarters, immediately!"

JERRICK HURRIES down to the basement. He gets a sick feeling as he approaches Evelyn's door. The emotions are so thick, they billow out like clouds of dark smoke. He enters to find Patrick hunched over, healing an unconscious Lathe while Emily is sitting on her knees, sobbing next to a pool of blood. He almost kneels next to Emily, but right now Lathe's injury is the priority. Lathe is wearing nothing but a pair of sweats, revealing scars emblazoned across the exposed skin of his chest. The old burns disfigure the left side of his body, from his scalp down to his torso. Jerrick never realized how severe his injuries were, but he pushes that thought aside as he uses his healing abilities on Lathe.

Within moments, Lathe's eyes open and he sits up. Patrick abandons him to comfort Emily. He wraps her in his arms and consoles her with soothing words.

Lathe rubs at the back of his head, asking, "What happened?"

Jerrick responds, "I was hoping you could tell me."

Memories come flooding back to Lathe, and he shouts, "No!" He jumps to his feet, demanding, "Where did they go?"

"Across the hallway," Patrick answers. "There was an opening in the wall."

Lathe rushes out of the room to open the secret wall entrance, and the others follow after him.

"Where does this one take us?" Patrick asks.

"The tunnel to Latovia," Lathe answers, racing down the steps.

Patrick asks, "Why would Evelyn come here?"

Lathe suspects he knows, but he doesn't want to believe it himself. He certainly isn't going to share the disturbing news with the group, not until he knows for sure.

They reach the tunnel below the mansion and walk up to a solid steel door. It is all black except for the bloody handprint in the center. Lathe pounds on the door, screaming while Emily's tears fall harder and Patrick and Jerrick exchange worried glances.

Eventually, Lathe calms down enough to explain, "If an Olvasho coats their body with Latovian blood, they can enter Latovia without any harm coming to them."

Wolfe is sitting at a table with friends when the cave gems flicker. Everyone looks up and around, searching for the cause of such a fluctuation, and when nothing is found, they look to Wolfe. He stands from the table. "I'll look into it," he says, before walking away.

Latovia feels different, but he can't put his finger on it. Thinking it might have to do with Ashley's visit earlier today, Wolfe heads toward the portal door. Before he enters the tunnel leading to the portal, magic pulsates from down the tunnel, stopping him cold in his tracks. This energy feels familiar, but different.

"I feel it too," Deja says, coming up behind Wolfe. "I don't even have my magic yet, and I can feel it."

"It feels like distorted Latovian magic, but that can't be," Wolfe says.

As they look into the faintly glowing tunnel, its gems begin to darken. The only way for that to happen is if someone is using up the magic of each gem as they pass by.

"Deja, I need you to get out of here. Go tell the Latovian Guard I need their assistance."

"Be courageous, brother," she says, giving him the Latovian send off, before running to alert the others.

Wolfe can barely make out the outline of a person walking toward him through the tunnel, but the underground passage continues to darken as the light from the magic gems continue to drain.

"Stop where you are!" Wolfe demands.

The person doesn't stop. They are only fifty yards out, and the Guard is nowhere near ready for an attack. How long has it been since another infiltrated Latovia? Decades? More?

Wolfe repeats his command, "Stop where you are, or I will crush you with the entirety of the Latovian Guard."

He hears indistinct mumbling as the person comes closer. There is a rhythm to the muttering, almost like a chant.

Wolfe pulls out his knives. One for each hand, ready to throw them right into the trespasser's throat. They continue forward, and Wolfe takes aim. The chanting grows louder and he finally deciphers the words. "Apples, peaches, pumpkin pie, if you're not ready, holler I. Apples, peaches, pumpkin pie, if you're not ready, holler I."

She repeats the words over and over, and he realizes it most definitely is a she. He knows those words from his days as a child when he played hide and seek in the mansion. Evelyn would always sing those words before she came to look for him.

"Evelyn?" he calls out, lowering his knife, but she keeps chanting and moving forward, sucking away what little remaining magic Latovia has. "Evelyn, please stop!"

At ten feet out, he notices things are worse than he thought. She is wearing a nightgown with snow boots and wild hair. She has become a shell of her former self, and right now her eyes stare straight ahead, unseeing as she continues her chant. He steps out of her way, and she walks right past him without even acknowledging his existence, but then he sees the mangled body floating behind her.

His eyes go wide with shock, and he cries, "No!" He rushes to Ashley. Picking her up, he cradles her body to him. "What did they do to you? Why?"

"THERE IS enough blood upstairs that I could cover myself and go through," Lathe says. "I can find her."

"And what?" Patrick asks. "You don't know where you're going, and if you go in there drenched in Latovian blood, they'll kill you."

"We don't even know what she's doing," Emily adds. "Maybe there is a fountain of healing in there or something."

"There isn't," Lathe contradicts, "but if I found her . . . if I got to Ashley in time—"

"Lathe," Patrick interrupts. He shakes his head, misery filling his words. "I'm sorry. I saw your mom carry her out."

Lathe feels himself being ripped in two. He wants to tell

Patrick to shut up, but he needs to hear the truth. He needs to face the facts.

"She was already gone," Patrick continues with tears welling in his eyes. "Even if she were lying in front of us now, we could not bring her back."

"Why would she do this?" Emily sobs, turning to Lathe. She shoves against his chest, crying, "Why would your mother do this?"

Lathe's anguish feels visceral as he shouts, "I don't know!" He buries his face in his hands, attempting to clear his thoughts as he says, "She's never been purposefully violent before, but this was intentional." He lifts his head. "I don't understand."

Jerrick suggests, "Maybe she doesn't want the Latovian people to be saved."

Lathe says, "That doesn't make sense. I've gotta go in after her."

"No!" they say in unison.

Jerrick continues, "You go in there covered in blood and every bit of diplomacy you've created with them over your lifetime will be gone."

Lathe steps back. "I can't just stand here."

Emily sits down on the cold brick floor. Patrick follows suit, sitting next to her, pulling her into his side where her silent tears fall against him. Jerrick slips off his jacket and hands it to Lathe before sitting down. It's only forty degrees down here and Lathe, who is still barefoot and bare-chested, slips into the coat and paces.

Wolfe cradles Ashley's body in his arms. Her skin feels cold. Too cold.

Suddenly, Evelyn's face is right in front of him, and she screams, "Holler I, holler I, holler I!"

Wolfe stares back at her gibberish and asks, "Did you do this?"

"Apples, Peaches, Pumpkin Pie! If you're not ready, holler I!" She looks frantic to make her point, but her words are meaningless.

Wolfe shakes his head, and Evelyn starts walking off only to turn back and stare at him, still chanting that damn rhyme. Deja steps out from a hiding spot and says, "She wants you to follow her!"

"What are you doing here?"

"I already told them to come, but they take forever, and you needed backup. Is she going to be okay?" Deja asks, eyeing Ashley.

He doesn't tell her that Ashley's body is getting cold and that rigor mortis would be setting in soon. He tries to switch her focus back to the more urgent matter. "How do you know what she wants?"

"I don't," Deja shrugs, "but it's worth a try."

Wolfe follows Evelyn, and her chanting gets faster as she begins to jog. Wolfe starts to jog too, watching the gems around her dim as she passes. They reach the giant cavern, the center of Latovia and Evelyn stops chanting. The Latovian people give them a wide berth, but everyone seems curious, so they don't go far. A crowd gathers on the ground floor, and the levels above them fill with curious eyes.

Wolfe knows better than to fight Evelyn. First, because he sees her as a big sister, but even if she didn't mean something to him, he knows he is no competition for her, so he stands by and prays for a miracle.

Evelyn gets to her hands and knees in the middle of the cavern with thousands of eyes watching her. She places her palms against the floor, and the cavern goes eerily and utterly dark. There is an outcry from the people as darkness consumes everything, but it is short-lived as Evelyn begins to glow, shining so bright, people look away to protect their eyes.

Wolfe makes himself look, scared of what she's doing to herself and his people. She's powerful enough to kill them all, but the Evelyn he knows is not violent. She stands up, her body radiating so much light, she could have her own solar system. Then as if she can't contain it any longer, the power bursts from her in an array of iridescent color. The people closest are knocked down by the initial flow of energy, but the magic continues pouring out of her like Niagara Falls. The gems throughout the cavern shine to life, brighter than they were before.

Wolfe still clings to Ashley's corpse, holding her as if protecting her from harm, but it's already too late to save her. Evelyn looks at him and in an otherworldly voice, says, "Bring me the girl."

Wolfe carries her forward, but Evelyn picks her up with her mind, transporting her with the wind. Ashley's body floats forward, her cheeks colorless, blood crusting on her skin. Then Ashley begins glowing from the inside out. Her body is lowered to the floor, the glow softens, and her skin remains iridescent.

Deja kneels next to her, running her hands along shimmering skin. "She's alive!"

Wolfe stares at Evelyn as her internal glow dims. She smiles at him and comes forward to embrace her old friend. As they hug, she says, "It's been a long time, my friend."

"What did you just do?"

She pulls back with subtle grace. "I restored Latovia's magic."

"But you . . . are you, you again?"

"Yes, Latovia has restored my mind, and I gave it back its power, but stronger. It is only temporary, but I will continue to restore Latovia until we find a way to set you free." Evelyn looks down at herself, saying, "Oh my, what am I wearing?"

Wolfe is very aware of all the curious eyes on him. He suspects they all want answers and he and Evelyn aren't speaking loud enough for the crowd to hear. Wolfe tilts his head so his voice will echo and reports, "Latovia's magic has been restored.

There will be an announcement with further explanation in two hours. Go about your business."

A few people leave, but the majority must feel like this is their business as they loiter close by, watching, listening. Wolfe says, "You know how to get the crowd's attention, but maybe, let's talk somewhere a bit more private."

They move to Wolfe's private quarters. Two guards and Deja stand guard outside the door. Wolfe provides a change of clothes for both Evelyn and Ashley. As Evelyn attempts to tame her hair, she says, "So, you've gone and done it. You always said you would put an end to that monster. Lathe tells me the Latovian people voted you in despite the circumstances. You are the king now."

"I don't like labels," Wolfe says with a shrug. "What about you, our Latovian savior? Words can't begin to express how grateful we are."

"You are a great king, Wolfe. I am so proud of you." Evelyn looks over at Ashley still asleep on the bed the Latovian Guard provided her.

"What happened to Ashley?" Wolfe asks.

"I killed her. I don't think I meant to. I was trying to get her to bring me to you, and she kept saying *no* and then I lost myself for a moment, and the next moment she was bleeding out on the floor. I stole her mind, her soul; I guess you could say and stored it in my body until I could bring her back to life. I just had to get us both here, and that rhyme reminded me of you. It kept me focused. If I forgot where I was going or what I was doing, then Ashley would die for good and Latovia would lose all hope. I knew I couldn't fail. I appreciate that young girl out there, Deja. She's smart as a whip."

"Your son loves her too. He'll never admit it, but Deja is his favorite kid. I don't know what will happen when she's too old to visit him. I worry about both of them."

"Hopefully we can find a solution before that day comes."

"Evelyn, why didn't you die as soon as you entered Latovia. The curse should've killed you with your Olvasho blood."

"My father was Latovian and my mother, an Olvasho. She lived in the estate with her family, and one moonless night she met my father in the stables. They fell in love and saw each other every new moon. They wrote letters to one another and children would deliver them between worlds. I was their love child, but my father died from sun poisoning before my birth. I always knew where I came from, but I was too afraid to test out if half-Olvasho was too much. I didn't want the curse to kill me, so I stayed away from Latovia and shame kept me from telling anyone the truth.

"I wanted to do this years ago, but my mind was never clear enough to explain it to Lathe. The toughest part was getting out of my room and finding someone of Latovian decent to get me into Latovia without forgetting what I was doing."

"It's great to have you back," Wolfe says.

"I would love to stay longer, but I left things a mess at the mansion. I have to go back before Lathe kills himself looking for me."

"Or her," Wolfe says, nodding to Ashley. "That one is special to Lathe." Wolfe pauses before adding, "I think he's special to her, too."

Evelyn studies a sleeping Ashley. "Does she know who she is?"

"She knows her father was Latovian."

"Does Lathe know?"

"I suppose he does." Wolfe hesitates, then divulges, "He's guarded around her."

"She and Lathe . . ." she stops herself, unsure how to finish that statement.

"I know," Wolfe agrees. "It will be complicated, for sure."

"I had better get her back to him then."

"I'll walk with you."

Wolfe pushes the bed containing Ashley like he is pushing a stroller. Deja, along with half a dozen men from the Guard escort them to the portal door and stand back. Deja reaches for the handle and offers to take Ashley through.

Evelyn stops her. "We would love for you to visit, Deja, but right now is not a good time. Will you come by in the morning?"

Deja slinks back, rejected. "Fine, I'll wait until tomorrow."

So she doesn't go at midnight, Wolfe clarifies, "Morning, Deja. Let's make it after eight."

"Fine," she whines.

"Clever girl," Evelyn says.

"She thinks so," Wolfe says before switching subjects. "Do you know when I should expect to see you again?"

"Soon, but I'll have to see what's going on out there before I know when I can come back."

"Understood." Wolfe leans in for a quick hug. "Take care, Evelyn. We owe you everything."

"You owe me nothing," she says, opening the portal door. Using her gifts, she lifts Ashley from the bed and carries her back to her son.

CHAPTER EIGHTEEN ~

LATHE JUMPS TO HIS FEET, calling out to the others when the black door begins to transform. The steel door morphs into an intricately carved wooden door. Lathe's pulse races and he hears the others come to stand behind him. Lathe gathers his gifts, wrapping the air around him like a shield. He feels the heat at his back and knows Emily is preparing to fight.

"Remember," Lathe warns, "children come and go out of this portal. Don't attack before we know who it is."

The door opens, and Lathe takes a step back, giving himself more time to react should something hostile come through. They can't see into the portal and whoever is inside can't see out.

Lathe listens to himself breathe, the tension pulling every muscle tight. A makeshift white flag is shoved through the opening, but Lathe and the others don't soften their stance. They stand alert as someone steps through the portal.

Evelyn looks different. She changed into a decent looking outfit, tamed her hair, and got rid of the snow boots. But the most significant change is the way Evelyn holds herself, not as a prisoner of her own mind, but as a self-possessed woman. Her soft blue eyes stare at Lathe and the white flag she's holding bursts into flames. Evelyn drops the flag and Lathe wraps his mother in air, shielding her from Emily's assaults.

"Lathe, what are you doing?" Emily shouts.

His protective instinct over his mother is a reaction, a reflex, but it's also a choice. As much as he hates her right now, she's still his mother, and he needs an explanation.

"Emily, back down," Jerrick warns. "He's got her."

Lathe realizes Jerrick thinks he's captured his mother. That's kind of what it looks like he's done, but that wasn't exactly his intention, although it should have been.

"This isn't necessary," Evelyn says. "I'm not going anywhere, and I would like to explain my actions."

Lathe can't take it. She's better. Her mind is whole. The thing he's wished for his whole life has come to pass, but only after she committed an unforgivable act. "Why, Mother?"

"Let me show you," she turns back to the portal.

"Don't move!" Lathe warns.

Evelyn stops. "Lathen . . ." she tries to explain but goes quiet at his look of disgust. Using her gifts, she guides Ashley through the portal opening.

Emily lets out a sob as Lathe lets out a breath he hadn't realized he was holding. Patrick curses and Jerrick stays stoic, looking calm amid the madness.

Evelyn lays it all out for them, confessing, "My father was Latovian; that's how I was able to survive in Latovia." She goes on to explain her reason for escaping, and Ashley's death. She explains how she possessed Ashley's soul while her body died and then returned it once she restored her body. She tells it all as Ashley floats next to her, her chest rising and falling with each breath, proving she is very much alive.

Once Evelyn is finished speaking, Lathe falls to his knees, overcome with emotions. Evelyn steps forward to comfort her son, but Emily steps forward, saying, "Why is she unconscious?"

"It will be more comfortable for her to wake up somewhere familiar, especially after such a traumatic event."

Patrick places a hand on Emily's arm, and they move to Ashley's side, while Evelyn drops to her knees next to her son. They embrace, Evelyn whispering, "My son," as tears rain down her cheeks.

No one notices Jerrick slip away. He climbs back up the many stairs and cleans away the evidence of Evelyn's destruction. He removes the pool of blood and picks up the array of shattered picture frames in the hall. He doesn't want anyone to be reminded of what came before.

He's finishing up when Patrick and Emily come through the opening in the wall. Lathe comes out next carrying Ashley in his arms, and Evelyn shadows him, closing the wall behind her.

Evelyn stops in front of the space that has been her home for the last ten years. Jerrick already closed the door, and Evelyn moves past it, without looking back.

With everyone following, Lathe carries Ashley to her room and lays her on the bed. Emily crawls into the bed next to her, while Patrick perches at the foot of the bed, and Jerrick watches from the doorway. Evelyn leans over Ashley to place a hand on her forehead. "Awake," she whispers into Ashley's ear.

Everyone braces, preparing for the worst. Emily laces her fingers through Ashley's just in case she needs help calming down. Her last memory would be her death, so Emily half-expects her to wake up swinging.

Ashley's dark eyes flick open, instantly focusing on Evelyn. She reaches up with her free hand to cup Evelyn's cheek. A blissful smile graces her face, as she whispers, "My fairy godmother."

Evelyn gives her a peaceful grin. "Welcome back, princess."

Ashley looks up to Lathe. "So, this is your mother?"

Lathe nods.

Ashley says, "I see why you're so protective of her." She lets go of Evelyn's cheek and turns to Emily. "I'm sorry I scared you again."

Emily doesn't know how to react to something so absurd.

Ashley should be freaking out, but instead, she is totally calm. Emily looks to Patrick to see if he understands, but he appears just as confused and turns to Evelyn for an explanation.

"When I took in Ashley's essence, our souls converged in order to survive. So, even though we don't know one another, our souls have met on a deeper level."

"So, you guys are . . . friends?" Patrick suggests.

Ashley smiles, saying, "More like BFF's."

Evelyn steps back, saying, "I'll let you guys catch up, just like my son and I have some catching up to do."

Before walking away Lathe squeezes Ashley's shoulder, saying, "I'm glad you're back."

Ashley is sorry to see him go but turns her focus back to Emily and Patrick.

Lathe passes Jerrick in the doorway. He takes a few steps down the hall and turns back to Jerrick, saying, "Hey."

Jerrick steps out into the hall, "Yeah."

Lathe says, "Down in the tunnel, I wasn't trapping her. I was protecting her."

Jerrick nods. "I know."

"So why did you say that to Emily?"

"Because even when the people we love do terrible things, we still want to protect them from harm. I wouldn't have let her get away, but I wasn't going to let Emily tear her apart in front of you."

"Glad it didn't come to that," Lathe says.

"Me too."

Lathe and Evelyn are talking together in the lounge when Emily comes down from Ashley's room. She peeks in, and Evelyn says, "Please, come join us."

Emily enters, sitting on the couch next to Lathe. Evelyn is seated across from them, sipping from a teacup. She looks at

Emily, saying, "It's hard for you, isn't it? It's hard for you to believe that the woman I am today, is the same woman you saw yesterday."

"That's not what's difficult for me," Emily says. "I have a harder time understanding how Sky could trick a woman with your incredible mind and powers. How did you not see him coming? And when he arrived, why didn't you overpower him? I know you could've stopped him."

Evelyn wears a sad smile. "Emily, have you ever been in love?"

Emily stares at her for a moment before giving a small nod.

"Does love feel practical to you? Or does it make you irrational? Does it change the way you act? For better or worse, does it help you justify things that otherwise you would never dream of doing? I saw Sky coming. I told myself not to fall for his manipulation, but then I fell in love with him, anyway. I knew he wasn't a good man, but when I met him, I didn't see the monster everyone else warned me about—that my visions warned me about. He was sweet and unbelievably kind to me. He doted on me.

"Growing up and even as an adult, people acted differently around me. They were either nervous I'd see a vision they didn't want to know, or they were expecting me to answer questions about their future. Sky was the first person to treat me like my gifts didn't matter. He wasn't nervous around me. He didn't ask me to look into the future for this or that. He was the first person who didn't expect anything from me.

"So even though the future revealed warning after warning, Sky made me feel normal. He made me believe I was more than my gifts and I fell in love with him. I couldn't imagine a life without him, and I could not believe Sky was capable of the things I foresaw. I knew in my heart Sky could change and he would change, for me. He would do anything for me, but I remained cautious.

"The first thing he ever asked of me was to be his wife and that was a year into dating. I was the only woman Sky ever married. I thought that spoke volumes about his love for me and my caution continued to slip. He tricked me slowly—the long con.

"The first time I looked into the future for him, wasn't because he asked me to, but because I was worried about his safety. I knew people would be coming for him because of the awful things he had done in his past, but I believed he was done with that life. I thought he had changed, but he had just become more devious, never doing his own dirty work.

"He had my mother killed and then stood there and held me when I got the news that she was dead. My caution evaporated, and I put all my faith in him. I put the future of the Olvasho in his hands. I never told him about Latovia because I was sworn to secrecy, but he had the rest of me.

"By the time he got around to asking me for things, I gave freely. I became pregnant with Lathen, and for the first time since I met Sky, I cherished something more than him. I didn't want to risk harming our son by overusing my gifts, so I stopped using my magic in that first trimester. It's the first fight Sky and I ever had. He showed an inkling of his true self because I cut him off from the future.

"He began spending more time away from me, and in my desperate attempt to fix things, I looked into the future and saw everything I feared and everything I didn't know I needed to fear. Sky was a monster, and I had played right into his game. I was distraught. When Sky stopped living with me, I was heart-broken, and my anger created torrents of wind that ripped this mansion apart. Half of the structure had to be rebuilt." She closes her eyes and Lathe leans forward to hold his mother's hand.

Evelyn looks up at him with a strained smile and continues, "My pregnancy made me emotional, and I couldn't reconcile Sky's betrayal. I became almost catatonic. I kept searching the future for a better outcome, and eventually, it drove me mad. Sky didn't break me, he broke my heart, and I destroyed everything else by pushing my powers too far. I gave birth to a perfect child and did my best to stay well for him, despite my first psychotic break. Lathen was the only thing to keep me a little sane.

"Then one day when Lathe was two, Sky came to visit me. I knew the truth. I knew Sky was evil. I knew it in my head, but when he came to see me, my heart overtook my senses. It was perverse, and I knew it wasn't right, but I still loved him. I can't explain it. I thought he might give me a second chance and we could be a family. He stayed with Lathe and me for a while, and on the days he was sweet, he was my whole world, and on the days he showed his true self, I told myself I'd never let him trick me again.

"I hated myself." Her look of grief turns to pain and guilty eyes peer up at Emily. "I told him—" She closes her eyes like her words are too painful.

Emily consoles, "It's okay, you don't have to tell me."

Evelyn's eyes flick open, and she says, "He told me he wanted to protect the Olvasho from Valla blood and I told him where to find your mother." She takes a shaky breath. "As soon as I told him, I saw the future change. I saw what he was going to do to her."

Tears fall from Emily's eyes, but she continues to listen in silence.

"He stood there before me, and I knew what he was going to do, so I finally fought back. I knew he wouldn't stop. He wouldn't change. He was always going to be a monster. The future came to me in vivid detail. I saw everything, every horrible component, all the pain my son would go through, all the atrocities Sky would commit. I saw you, Emily, and I knew the Olvasho needed you. The Latovian people needed you, but I couldn't justify letting him live, so I stepped forward. I was intent on killing him, but then I had another vision of the future, a future where I killed Sky. That future was far worse. My son died before his third birthday, and you, Emily, were never born. The world was chaos and Latovian dragons burned the world.

"I couldn't understand how letting an evil man live could positively impact the future, but my visions never lied to me. I lied to myself, but my visions always told the truth, so I let Sky go free, letting the future play-out, knowing if I prevented the many catastrophes, the alternative future would be far worse. That is what finally broke my mind, and it only got worse from there."

Emily wipes her cheeks and moves off the couch to kneel in front of Evelyn. "I never thought about how hard it must be to know what's going to happen." She leans forward to wrap Evelyn in a hug.

As Lathe lies in bed, he feels like his whole day has been surreal. Part of him wants to go down to his mother's room to make sure she's still in her right mind. A more significant part of him wants to stop at Ashley's room to make sure she is still breathing. He closes his eyes, remembering her body laying against his when she climbed in bed with him early that morning. Maybe he should crawl into her bed and see how she reacts. She'd probably scream. He shakes his head dismissing the ideas. A floorboard squeaks, and he opens his eyes to find Ashley standing next to his bed with her arms folded on her chest.

He sits up, turning on his bedside lamp. "What are you doing here?"

"You didn't come back and see me."

"I didn't know you were expecting me," he says, getting out of bed.

She rolls her eyes and moves forward to stand right in front of him.

He reaches out slowly, his fingers running through her hair. Their eyes meet, expressing all the things they don't know how to say. His thumb caresses her jaw as his hand moves down her neck. Breathless, he says, "You'll leave."

Ashley shakes her head. "And where would I go?"

Staring into those sinfully dark eyes, he begs, "Please."

"Please, what?" she asks. "Please, stay? Leave? Please, sit on your face? Never talk to you again? Please, what, Lathe?"

He closes his eyes and drops his hand, clearly distressed. She lifts his hand and places it over her heart, demanding, "Look at me."

She is wearing a V-neck nightshirt which leaves his hand pressed against the silky skin of her cleavage. He opens his eyes, and his hand moves up to cradle the back of her neck. His body moves in close, their foreheads touching.

"I tell myself to stop thinking about you all of the time," he admits.

"Does it work?"

"No."

She grins. "Will you kiss me now?"

He hesitates.

"What are you afraid of, Lathe?"

"I'm afraid of losing you once you realize you could have so much more."

She places her hand on his chest, saying, "I like you. I'm crazy about you, actually. I love how protective you are of the people who matter to you. I love that you are so crazy about me that you were ready to jump through a portal door that would likely kill you just for a chance to save me." She grins, saying, "Yeah, they totally told me. I love that you jumped in front of a bullet for my best friend. I also hate that you jumped in front of a bullet because you could've died. I hate that you were born into a shitty situation and that you never had the happiness you deserve, and I love how much you love your mom despite everything that's happened. She's alive and whole because of you."

"And because of you," he adds.

"See, we make a good team." She smiles.

"Ashley, I don't know how to do this, and I don't know how to come back from it after I fuck it up."

"Then I won't let you fuck it up, and we'll figure out everything else as it comes."

"What if I lose you to Latovia?"

"You won't."

"But what if I do? What if—"

"Lathe," she interrupts, "kiss me."

His lips fall on hers. It's a gentle kiss. A sweet kiss and Ashley feels herself falling for him. She's never been kissed like this before. This kiss is a breath of fresh air, it breathes life into her soul, flowing through her, refreshing her spirit. She feels like it's the first kiss, the only kiss that has ever mattered. As the kiss comes to an end, Ashley opens her eyes and studies him.

Concern fills his face as he wipes a tear from her cheek. "Are you okay?"

She should feel embarrassed, but she can't help her grin. "I didn't know it could feel like that."

"Did I do something wrong?"

She's shaking her head. "No, the opposite. I think I've been doing it wrong this whole time."

She lifts up on her toes to kiss him again, and he picks her up into his arms and carries her to his bed. Excitement blooms, but instead of stripping her naked and having his way, he tucks her in, lying next to her. He wraps his arms around her and whispers in her ear, "Go to sleep."

CHAPTER NINETEEN ~

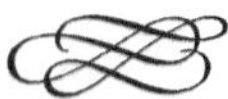

During breakfast the next morning, Ashley feels a wave of dizziness and asks, "Did your ears just pop?" Everyone at the table is suddenly very quiet as if listening for something. Ashley looks out the window just as the morning sun hides behind a cloud.

Lathe says, "The atmospheric pressure just shifted." His eyes go round, and he jets out of his seat. "She wouldn't!"

Emily gasps, "It's—"

"Leona," Patrick finishes.

Feeling the pull from Leona, they stare out the French doors overlooking the side patio as howling winds rattle the doors.

Lathe pulls up the surveillance on his phone and searches through the feed. Jerrick picks up his iPad and starts tapping away at the screen. Ashley takes another bite of her eggs because she's barely eaten anything the last two days and she isn't about to miss another meal. She stabs another fork-full of her hash browns as debris smashes against the outside wall of the kitchen. A lawn chair is thrown into the window, but it ricochets off the glass.

Ashley pauses mid-chew and Lathe says, "It's bulletproof glass."

He goes back to his phone, only looking up when Jerrick calls, "Southeast corner. By the gardens." Lathe flips screens and sees a figure standing in the center of a storm cloud. It's too obscure to make her out, but Lathe is sure he's watching his mother struggle with Leona.

"She's half Latovian. Why would she think Leona would accept her?" Emily asks.

"Leona's going to kill her," Lathe murmurs, too shocked to react.

Ashley stands. "Then go help her. Right, you guys can help?"

Patrick says, "I'll go."

"Not without me," Emily adds.

Patrick glares at her. "You can't, Emily. Adelaide is still—"

"None of you will go!" Lathe shouts. "Leona will decide whether she's worthy or not and if you help her, you will only make her look weak."

"That's not how it was with . . ." Emily stops herself because that's exactly how it was with Isa and Patrick. Valla wouldn't let Emily help him. "We can't just stand by and watch."

"He's right," Patrick says.

"So, what does this mean?" Ashley asks.

Lathe takes Ashley's hand. "It means she'll either die or possess the spirit of Leona."

The silence inside the kitchen is eaten up by the slicing winds and debris crashing outside the mansion. Down the hall, glass breaks and the howling winds sweep through the main corridor.

Then, as quickly as it came, the chaos dies. The wind quiets, the clouds clear and the sun shines down on the wreckage left outdoors. Patrick opens one of the French doors and pushes lawn furniture out of the way, making a path. Emily follows with Jerrick close behind.

Lathe continues holding Ashley's hand as she whispers, "It's better to know."

"Is it?" he questions. "What if . . ."

"Come on, Lathe. I'm right here." She kisses the hand she's holding. "We'll go together."

Emily is walking across the lawn when Valla warns. *"Adelaide senses things have changed. She knows we'll be coming for her soon and she won't give up without a fight."*

That means Evelyn succeeded in capturing the finicky spirit of Leona, creating a full-blown tornado to do it.

Emily mentally reaches out to Lathe, *"She did it, Lathe. She's gonna be okay."*

Lathe's grip loosens around Ashley's hand as he sighs with relief. He drags a hand over his face, imagining what he could've lost.

"Is she okay?" Ashley questions.

"Yeah, she is."

Ashley smiles and tugs at his hand, pulling him forward. When they arrive in the gardens, the others are around the outskirts trying to find a way through the wreckage. The winds had bulldozed the stone walls that separated the paths through the garden.

Patrick, Jerrick, and Emily begin moving the debris. Lathe notices large rocks in the center of the garden being guided back in place by his mother's magic. She's cleaning up the mess she and Leona made.

It takes nearly the entire day to get the gardens back in order and to pick up the debris around the mansion. The unsalvageable items are gathered in a large pile that Emily sets on fire. They stand around the fire as the sun begins to sink, and Ashley is really glad she ate breakfast.

Once they finally make it back inside, Emily picks up her phone from the kitchen table seeing the six missed calls from Ben. "Shit," she says, pressing the button to call him back.

It goes to voicemail, and she remembers he's performing at the coffee shop this evening. She has two missed texts from him, too.

Hey. Followed two hours later with, **You ok?**

She texts back, **Sry, didn't have my phone. I'm ok.**

THE COFFEE SHOP is swamped like it always is when Ben plays. Alec sits down across from Molly at the reserved table.

"Hey, Alec," she greets.

He forgoes the introduction and leans forward, saying, "Tell me what you know about the night your brother almost died."

EMILY WALKS into the mansion's lounge to join everyone for pizza. Before she can take her seat, splintering pain rips through her body causing her legs to give out. Patrick and Ashley are the closest, and they rush to her, but it's Evelyn who keeps Emily from falling by propping her up with the surrounding air.

Valla screams inside Emily's mind, a shriek of pure agony and Emily copies the noise as Adelaide claws through her conscious mind. Just before Emily blacks out, she warns, "Adelaide."

Things happen quickly. Patrick lifts Emily into his arms and rushes her out of the room. Lathe kisses Ashley's forehead, then shoves her at Jerrick, saying, "He'll take care of you." He grabs his mother's arm, and the two of them take off. Jerrick closes the lounge door, and Maggie growls at the tension.

Ashley stands in the middle of the room, glancing over at Jerrick who doesn't seem to be paying her any attention.

"What the hell just happened?" she demands.

Jerrick doesn't look up as he answers in his deep baritone, "Adelaide is trying to regain control over Emily's mind. We've spent months preparing for this possibility."

"Prepared how?"

"They'll take care of it."

"Shouldn't you be with them," she suggests, "helping them?"

Jerrick looks at her, hitting her with the full force of his stare.

"Holy shit!" she says, stepping back. How had she not noticed him before? The brilliant blue of his eyes stands out against his decadent milk chocolate skin, and his large frame is packed full of defined muscle, noticeable even through his fitted shirt. His physique spoke of more than just good genes, it spoke of hours in the gym and a lifetime of protein drinks and specially constructed diets. He had cultivated his look, and yet, he hid it. Ashley isn't sure how he hid it from her, but it's like before this moment he was some undefined man, and now— "You're like, every girl's wet dream."

Jerrick looks away, but Ashley keeps going. "I'm not hitting on you. I just don't understand how I've spent the last few days with you, and I am just now like, actually seeing you."

"You've been wrapped up in Lathe," he answers, and Ashley feels the rumble of his baritone.

"No, that's not it. It's like you hide yourself behind a fog until you want to be noticed. It's kinda like you have a superpower. I mean, I know you have actual powers—"

"Gifts," he corrects.

"What's the difference?"

"Power is something you accumulate; gifts are something you are born with or that are given to you."

She rolls her eyes, not seeing the big deal. Remembering why they are here, she sits down on an ottoman, "Are they going to be okay?"

"All we can do is prepare, try our best, and hope that it is enough."

"And if it's not?"

"If they can't extract Adelaide from Emily's mind, then they will kill the host."

"They're going to kill Emily?"

"Only as a last resort."

"So why are you here with me, instead of with them?"

"Because should they fail, I am the last line of defense."

"What can you do that the others can't?"

He peeks up at her, saying, "Let's hope you don't have to find out."

Ashley shivers. "Sexy and dangerous."

He lifts a brow, and she clarifies, "Again, I'm not hitting on you, just pointing out the facts."

ALEC GETS INTO HIS CAR. When Molly climbs in next to him, he asks, "How did you get the address?"

Molly says, "Emily shares her location with Ben. So I broke into his phone today and got the address."

Alec pulls out of the parking lot as Molly snaps her seatbelt in place and says, "Are you sure you want to do this? He's going to be so mad. He'll probably ground me, but he might kill you."

"I'll deal with Ben," Alec says. "I just can't deal with my friends lying to me anymore. It's driving me crazy, Mol."

Molly looks at her GPS. "Looks like it's two and a half hours from here."

WHEN EMILY WAKES, she has no idea where they have taken her. She has never seen this room before. It's the size of a gymnasium, but the walls, the floor, the ceiling are all shiny cement. The lights above are covered with wire and bulletproof glass. Emily can't even figure out how they got in here. There are no doors—no handles sticking out of the walls. The only exposed item is the sprinkler system hanging from the ceiling twenty feet above.

Emily doesn't like this. She feels trapped . . . Or are those Adelaide's thoughts? She can't tell. All the entities inside her have merged into one super spirit who craves freedom above all else and will do anything to get it.

She turns to Patrick, her eyes glittering with manipulative tears as she begs, "Patrick, this isn't right." She wraps her arms around him, saying, "I can't feel her. I don't feel her spirit anymore. Do you think she fled?"

Patrick pulls her into him, comforting her. He rubs her back and dips his mouth to her ear. "Do you remember when you begged me to kill you if Adelaide ever took over again?"

Emily's body becomes tense. She pulls back to look at him, wrapping her hands behind his neck, her fingers splaying in his hair.

Patrick looks over her shoulder to Evelyn and Lathe, instructing, "Now!"

Energy flows into her from behind. She screams, trying to get away, but Patrick holds her in place for her torture. "Why?" she shrieks, in an otherworldly voice.

"Because I made a promise. It's mercy, Emily! It's mercy, not murder!"

THE LOUNGE HAS two long couches that face one another with a table between them and comfy chairs scattered around. Right now, Ashley sits on one couch while Jerrick is on the other. A weird silence fills the air between them and Maggie whines.

"So," Jerrick says, "what is Latovia like?"

Ashley looks over at him, asking, "Do you really want to know, or are you just trying to fill the silence?"

"Both, I suppose."

"You know, it's dark and cave-like, but it's cool. There are no lights, only glowing rocks and gems that are reservoirs for magic. The brighter they shine, the more magic they hold."

Jerrick moves forward on his seat. "What do they look like?"

"They aren't diamonds and rubies. I asked. They're different sizes, shapes, colors. Each gem changes color depending on the magic that last touches it. Right now, everything is sparkling gold because Evelyn basically rebooted the magic down there. My magic is purple, so if I touch the gems, they turn purple."

Jerrick leans forward with his elbows on his knees, looking fascinated. "Do you always possess this magic, even when you're here?"

"I guess I carry magic with me all the time, but it doesn't show up except when I'm in Latovia. When I'm not in Latovia, my magic is busy keeping me alive because of the curse, but when I'm there, it manifests in different ways. I can control it."

"What would happen if you brought a gem back with you? Would it lose its magic?"

Ashley shrugs. "I don't know. It's an inanimate object so probably not, but I would never do that. Latovia is suffering as is. Taking a gem would be stealing their power."

"Ashley, you know the necklace Emily always wears?"

Ashley blanches, sitting forward. "You think the gem came from Latovia?"

"It changes color." Jerrick ticks off on his fingers. "We know it holds magic because it's held Adelaide for months. And the Olvasho have never been able to find another gem like it."

"But, does it even glow?"

"I've seen it glow when Emily uses a lot of power. But this gem hasn't been properly charged with Latovian magic for hundreds of years. We've kept it charged with Olvasho blood magic, but it is far weaker. If we had a larger gem with greater power, maybe it could contain Adelaide on its own until we find a way to destroy her."

"All you'd have to do is return the gem to Latovia and Adelaide will die because of the curse, right?" she asks.

Jerrick stands. "Come on."

BEN SEARCHES for Molly in the crowd, and when he doesn't see her for a while, he takes a break. Pulling out his phone, he notices a few new texts. He has one from Emily. **Sry, didn't have my phone. I'm ok.** And he has a text from Molly. **I wasn't feeling well, so Alec drove me home.**

He texts his sister back, **How're you feeling? Should I come home?**

Almost immediately he hears back, **I'm okay. Just needed to lie down. Finish your set.**

EMILY'S BODY gets so warm in Patrick's grip, he eventually, has to let her go. She falls to the floor and quickly flips to her feet, flames shooting from her palms toward Evelyn and Lathe. Evelyn shoves the fire out of the way with magically charged air.

Emily retreats a few steps, her flames encircling her, growing larger and hotter. The sprinkler system begins showering them with water to wash out the blaze, but it is like using a garden hose on a wildfire. Emily laughs. "You thought this would work?"

Lathe moves forward, the air covering him like armor. "No, but it is a good distraction."

Emily turns just in time to get hit with a cannonball of water. The power of it knocks her off her feet, and Patrick directs the water to douse the flames.

Emily lies unmoving on the floor, while across the room, Evelyn suddenly collapses.

MOLLY IS HAVING second thoughts as Alec repeats himself again, sounding more and more like a crazy person.

"They're involved in something bigger than us, Mol," Alec says. "I'm telling you. I think they can bring people back from the dead."

Molly looks out the window, so he doesn't see her expression. She knows Ben will be finishing up soon, so she shares her location with him. Then she texts him.

So sorry. I never should've lied to you. BTW your best friend is looney tunes, but I'm just as crazy for telling him where Emily is.

ASHLEY STANDS FROM THE COUCH, saying, "Jerrick, we don't even know if this will work!"

"Did you know that Evelyn can see glimpses of the future? She has given prophecies over the years, and despite her being completely senile, her predictions have always been spot-on. Do you know what her last vision was?" He doesn't wait for a response this time. "It was Emily dying." Jerrick goes on, "The last time the three Olvasho sisters tried to kill Adelaide, they all died. I think this might be our only chance, Ashley. You might be our only chance."

She stands with her lips parted and eyes wide. Swallowing, she says, "No pressure, right?"

Just then, Emily's phone begins ringing from the floor. Ashley jumps, startled while Jerrick bends to pick it up. "She must have dropped it."

The phone stops ringing only to start back up. Ashley asks, "Who is it?"

"Ben."

"Let me talk to him," she says, reaching for the phone.

Jerrick holds it out of her reach, and she glares at him. "Let me talk to him, and then we'll go."

Jerrick hands the phone to her, and she answers, "Hey, it's Ashley."

Ben doesn't even start with a greeting. "Alec is on his way there with my sister. They should be there in about a half an hour."

Ashley has a lot of follow up questions, but instead says, "Okay, we'll handle it."

"I have to drop my dog off, and I'll be on my way."

"Oh, you're coming too?" Ashley says, eyeing Jerrick. "Perfect. The more, the merrier."

"Where's Emily?" he asks.

"Well, we're kinda in the middle of something here so, she's tied up." Her voice goes an octave higher than usual, but he doesn't seem to notice as it continues to climb. "Not sure she'll be around tonight. But, hey, I gotta go. See you soon, Ben."

After she hangs up, Jerrick plucks the phone from her hand. "What was that?"

"Generally speaking, I don't do well in high-stress situations. And oh, by the way, our friend Alec and Ben's sister, Molly, will be here in half an hour.

Jerrick can see she's cracking, and she's just a hair from completely falling apart. He puts an arm around her and guides her out of the room saying, "Come on, I'll walk you through this."

MORGAN IS STILL STAYING with her parents. Even though Ashley was nabbed from here, she still feels safer here than at the apartment alone. She's sitting in the living room watching a movie with her parents when Ben calls.

She hops up and leaves the room as she answers. "Hey,"

"Could you watch Max for a couple of days?"

"Your dog! Of course. Is everything okay?"

Ben sighs into the phone, "Alec took my sister with him to Indiana."

"What?"

"He's been acting weird this week. It's because they messed with his head, but now he's gotten my sister involved. It's gone too far."

"I'm going with you."

"Morgan . . ."

"I'm going with you! You can drop Max off when you come to pick me up at my parent's house." She hangs up before he has a chance to argue.

CHAPTER TWENTY ~

Lathe crouches by his mother, with his body turned to keep an eye on Emily.

Patrick stands ready, in case she wakes up.

Evelyn's eyes open. "I had a vision. Fighting isn't going to work. We were never meant to beat Adelaide. We are merely vessels for the Olvasho sisters. We are the distraction because only Latovian magic can defeat Adelaide." Her eyes are grave as she looks to her son. "Ashley is going to steal from Latovia. If she does, she'll be cursed."

His heart sinks. "Can we stop her?"

"Not if we want to save Emily."

"But . . ." When does one life become more important than another? "What about the other prophecy? The one where Emily dies?"

Evelyn's eyes widen, and she shakes her head. "I don't know what you're talking about."

"You said Emily would die to protect them all."

Evelyn is still shaking her head when Patrick yells, "Watch out!"

They both throw up a barricade, but the fire burns into Lathe's side. He puts out the flames, and his body begins to heal as Emily moves forward, carried by the wind around her. She shoots more flames at him, sensing he's an easy target as his mind is distracted with thoughts of Ashley.

ASHLEY AND JERRICK go down to the tunnel. As they begin walking toward the door, Ashley watches it transform for her. It recognizes her now. She stops just outside the door and turns to Jerrick.

"A couple of things. I'll do my best to get a stone, but I'm not sure if it's even possible. I don't know if I'll even be able to find Wolfe. And I can't just steal a stone without explaining myself. Also, you might want to go up and wait for Alec and Molly. He's probably gonna be all worked up."

"I'll handle it," he says, stepping forward. "You can do this, Ashley, and I'm coming right back down as soon as I get Alec and Molly situated."

Ashley gives him a nervous smile and opens the portal. As soon as she walks through, Jerrick jogs back up the stairs, hoping to make it to the foyer before their new guests arrive.

The tunnel is shimmering gold, and Ashley touches one of the stones, changing its color. Wolfe told her he could feel when the magic shifts, so she is hoping he can feel her presence. She walks down the glowing tunnel toward the cavern up ahead.

She stops at the opening of the cavern. She doesn't want to get lost, and she isn't sure how safe it is to be here by herself. She waits, but after a few minutes, she realizes Wolfe is not coming.

She taps another gem, sharing her magic, turning the gem purple. She figures this will be her version of leaving bread crumbs, so she doesn't get lost. She heads down toward the main cavern and sees no one. Is it always this empty? The last two times she was down here with Wolfe, she at least saw people in the distance.

The cavern is beautiful glowing with golden light, but something feels off. Ashley slinks back into the protection of a dark cove. She is cold. Her long sleeve t-shirt isn't cutting it. She hadn't thought to bring her jacket and Latovia seems to stay between fifty and sixty degrees. She hugs herself and tries to feel the magic around her like Wolfe had taught. She senses something in the next tunnel over and taps a gem as she goes inside the narrow cave. About one hundred yards in, she thinks about turning back as the tunnel becomes so tight, she has to turn to the side to get through, but she keeps going, drawn by something.

The tunnel opens enough for her to walk normally again and then it takes a sharp left where it unfolds into a room. It's not a large room by any means, but there are several nooks cut out of the stone walls. Bunks, Ashley realizes when she moves forward. There are pillows, blankets, and cardboard mattresses, but no people. Ashley picks up a teddy bear wondering who would let a child sleep like this.

She hears a shoe scrape the ground and then fast footfalls that fade. If she wasn't scared before, she is now. Ashley squats to look through an opening in the wall. She sees a glimmer of light on the other side, but to move forward, she will have to crawl twenty feet through the darkness. She squeezes her eyes shut, focusing on that pull of magic she felt.

She feels it still, urging her forward. She gets to her knees and begins crawling. She hesitates before exiting the tunnel because other than a single golden gem right above the exit, the cave ahead is dark.

"I should've just grabbed a rock at the entrance and been done with it," she whispers to herself.

She uncurls from her crouch on the other side and hears people breathing. The hairs on the back of her neck rise and she reaches toward the wall, hoping to find a gem to ignite.

She finds one, and she fills it with her purple glowing magic. It's a small light, but it's enough to see in front of her. She finds another gem; this one is jagged and big. She fills it with her energy and the cave brims with light. She looks around to discover dozens of little faces staring back at her. Children. They are watching her with wide, terrified eyes. Some are standing, but most are hiding in their bunks, with only faces poking out. They live here. Where are the adults?

"Hi," she says, breaking the silence. "I didn't mean to intrude. I'm looking for Wolfe. Does anybody know him?"

No answer.

A little girl tugs on Ashley's shirt, timidly asking, "How did you do that?" She points to the glowing gem.

Ashley smiles. "You like the light?"

The little girl nods and Ashley notices several heads bobbing up and down.

"Do you want more light?"

Another head nod.

Ashley asks, "Where?"

The girl moves forward across the room to a dark corner and points up. Ashley reaches her hand up, searching until it finds purchase on a smooth gem. It comes to life and Ashley sees that it's not a corner, but an opening to another tunnel.

"Where does this lead?" she says.

A brave little boy says, "Out."

"Out to the main cavern?" she asks.

"Yeah."

Since he's talking, she asks, "Where are all the adults?"

"Hiding, probly."

"Why?"

"There was an uprisin' after that crazy lady turned everything gold and someone attacked the king."

"Do you know Wolfe? Do you know where I could find him?"

The little boy snorts, "Lady, everybody knows Wolfe."

"He's the king," another little voice says.

"What?" Ashley gasps, before pulling herself together. "Okay, do you know where I can find him?"

"Yeah, but you shouldn't go unless you wanna be killed."

"But she has magic!" A little girl says wistfully.

Ashley says, "You said the king was attacked. Is he okay?"

"Yeah, he killed that other guy."

"What about a girl named Deja? Do you know where I can find her?"

"Deja's an orphan, like us. At least she used to be. Now, she spends most of her time running errands for the king."

"None of you have parents?" Ashley looks around the room again, watching as kids shake their heads. These kids live alone in a dark hole, and Wolfe is king. What has her life become? Then she remembers Emily. "I'll be back, but right now I have something very important to do. Could you point me in Wolfe's direction?"

Ashley hears little footsteps run off.

"Sure, it's right out there." A kid points down the tunnel she just discovered. "Then turn right."

"It's left, dummy," a girl corrects.

"Um, okay. Thank you," Ashley says, moving toward the exit.

"Hey lady, thanks for the light. I hope you don't die."

With that Ashley walks through the exit. It snakes around a bit before dumping her in the main cavern. She's almost directly across from where she started. She turns to her left and starts walking toward a large opening, but someone grabs her wrist and pulls her to the side.

"Deja," Ashley squeals.

"You got a death wish?" Deja scolds. "Come with me."

Deja leads her into a fissure in the cavern wall. It becomes so narrow, Ashley barely squeezes through before it opens into another tiny tunnel. After a few turns, Deja pushes aside a wooden panel, and they enter a bedroom.

This room is not like the one with bunk beds in the wall. This is a real bedroom with a king-sized bed. Oh, and look at that, a king lying in the king-sized bed. Deja goes straight to the bed, sitting next to Wolfe.

"Wolfe?" Ashley calls.

Wolfe opens his bloodshot eyes, his head dripping with sweat.

Ashley didn't know someone with such dark skin could look so pale and grey. "They told me you won."

Wolfe says, "You should see the other guy."

"What happened?"

"Nothing new," he says, blowing it off. "I assume you came here for a reason."

"I did. I need to take a large gemstone back to the mansion with me."

Deja's eyes go wide, and she looks to Wolfe for his reaction. Taking a gem outside of Latovia was treason.

Ashley continues, "If I don't, they'll kill Emily. I'll bring it back before the night is over, I hope."

"Who's going to kill Emily?"

"Patrick, Lathe, Evelyn. And if they fail, Jerrick."

"Take what you need. I'll have one of my Latovian Guard go with you. Deja, you go, too."

"But, Wolfe," Deja complains.

"Go with Ashley, Deja."

Deja cries, "You're only saying that 'cause you think you're gonna die."

Ashley walks closer, getting that same wrong feeling she had before. She reaches out to touch Wolfe's hand. He's burning up. "There is poison in your body," she says, unsure how she can detect it by touch.

"I know," he says in his gravelly voice.

"Can I fix you?"

He shrugs.

"I'm gonna try." She places a hand on him and concentrates, but nothing happens. "How long do you think you have?"

He shakes his head, "I don't know."

"Why didn't you tell me you were the king?"

"It didn't seem to matter."

"I'll bring Evelyn back to fix this."

MOLLY AND ALEC pull up to a tremendous estate. "What is this place?" Alec wonders.

Molly rolls her eyes. "It's Xavier's school for gifted youngsters, duh."

Alec gawks at the mansion, looking far too serious.

"I'm kidding, Alec."

"No shit, darlin'. Mutants aren't real. I'm not a fucking moron."

"Are you sure? You did just drive us two and a half hours on a hunch."

He shakes his head. "You don't believe me."

"I'm just not sure this is the best way to go about this."

"We're here now. Might as well give it a go." He gets out of the car and walks up to the door. Molly catches up to him on the front steps. Before Alec can knock, the door swings open and a giant black man is there to greet them.

"Hello, you must be Molly and Alec," the man says. "I'm Jerrick. Please come in. Let me show you around. I'm afraid Emily and Ashley had previous engagements and weren't able to change their plans on such short notice, but they'll be here soon."

"Ashley's here?"

"Of course."

"How did you know we were coming?"

Jerrick says, "Ben told us you were on your way."

Alec looks at Molly, and she shrugs. They enter the three-story foyer with staircases winding to the stories above. Sporadic burn marks stain the pristine walls and Alec asks, "Was there a fire in this room?"

Jerrick sighs. "Someone thought it'd be funny to set off sparklers and toss them from the third floor. We're counting our blessings it didn't cause more damage."

"What is this place, exactly?"

"This is the Vallor mansion. It belongs to Ms. Evelyn Vallor and her son, Lathen. Friends and family often stay here."

Alec feels at ease with this man who by all rights should feel intimidating.

ASHLEY OPENS THE PORTAL. She walks through pulling a cart with a huge shiny gemstone the size of a watermelon. The gem doesn't lose its luster even after leaving Latovia. Deja walks through and closes the portal door, noting, "It's still shining."

Jerrick is waiting for them. He steps forward once the portal door closes.

"Oh, thank God!" Ashley says. "I can barely lift this damn thing. Will you carry it up for us?"

Jerrick stops about ten feet away from Ashley, eyeing the giant purple gem. He steps back. "I can't."

"What do you mean, you can't? You're like the buffest guy I've ever seen."

He continues taking steps back, his eyes never leaving the gem. "There is so much power! It's beautiful, but the second I touch it, I won't be able to let it go. The magic will consume and destroy me. I'm sorry, Ashley." He takes off up the stairs.

Ashley looks to Deja. "It's too heavy. I was counting on him. Now what?"

"You could do it, just take some of your power back from the stone and it will give you the strength to carry the burden."

"I can't. It needs to stay charged." Ashley reaches down to caress the glowing gem. As her fingers touch the stone, the magic uncurls, offering all its power to her. The magic pours into her, feeling like a natural extension. She quickly pulls her fingers back. "Oh no! I can't even touch it without absorbing its power. What the hell are we going to do?"

"I'll carry it," Deja offers.

"Deja, this stone weighs more than you do."

Deja looks down, saying in a small voice, "We have to get it to them so Evelyn can save Wolfe."

Ashley can't let everyone down. She knows there has to be a way. "Deja, give me your jacket."

Deja doesn't argue. She slips out of her jacket and hands it to Ashley who wraps the gem inside the coat and tests it again. Her fingers graze the outside of the jacket, and although she senses the magic, it doesn't freely flow into her. "Here goes nothing."

She lifts the boulder. They told her it weighed ninety pounds. She carries the stone up six stairs before her arms begin to shake. It doesn't help that the stairs are uneven and her foot slips on a crumbling step. She sets the giant rock down, complaining, "I'm going to make him install a freaking elevator!"

Deja bends over and zips the jacket around the rock, then she adjusts the sleeves and says, "You grab one side, I'll grab the other."

This gets them up another twenty steps before the sleeves rip. "We need a rope or something," Deja says.

"You stay with it. I'm going to run up and find something that will help." She runs up the remaining fifty or so steps. As soon as she exits the stairs, Jerrick is leading Alec down the basement hall to her.

Ashley steps out of the passageway in the wall, saying, "I need rope or—Alec, what are you doing down here?"

"Alec will help you," Jerrick offers, pushing him forward.

"But—"

"We're running out of time, Ashley." Jerrick's deep voice has an edge to it. "Let him help you."

"Come on, Alec." Ashley grabs his hand and drags him behind her. "I'll explain on the way."

"What is this?" Alec asks as they descend the never-ending spiral staircase. The stone steps are crumbling, the stone walls are dark, and the lighting is less than desirable.

"You're right, Alec," Ashley says, rushing down the stairs. "We've been lying to you."

Alec stops. "Why?"

Ashley turns to face him. "I'll explain everything, but I need you to keep moving."

Alec follows while she confesses, "I was with you when you found Ben that night. He died in your arms while I ran inside to get help. Emily and Patrick came out and like, magically healed his wounds, bringing him back to life."

Alec's steps falter, but Ashley continues, "Patrick offered to take your memory of the event, and you basically begged him to do it. You didn't want to know any of it and knowing would only put you in danger, so he altered your memories and ever since, you've been like, going out of your way to try to remember everything."

Before Alec has a chance to ask questions, they come upon a young girl with dark hair leaning against the stairwell.

"I brought reinforcements," Ashley says to the girl. "Deja this is Alec. Alec this is Deja."

"Do you think you can carry it?" Deja asks, gesturing to the ripped leather jacket wrapped around something big, while a purple glow emanates from the ripped seams.

"What is that?" Alec asks.

"A giant magic gem."

Alec looks around for a camera wondering if he's being recorded for some prank show. While he looks around, Deja says, "I don't think he can lift it."

"Alec, without this, Emily will die. When Jerrick said we're running out of time, he meant Emily is running out of time."

Alec is shaking his head like he doesn't believe it.

Irritated, Ashley says, "You want to know why you've been going crazy for the last three months? It's because when we tell you the truth, you freak out, but when we keep it from you, you can't deal. Alec, I need you to like, man up and deal! We're counting on you!"

"Please," Deja begs, "my brother will die if we don't do this soon."

Alec bends down and picks up the massive boulder. Without hesitation, he begins climbing the stairs.

Jerrick is in the basement corridor when they exit the spiral staircase. As soon as he feels the magic gem, he begins backing up. "Come on. I'll show you the way."

Alec asks, "Why isn't he carrying it?"

Ashley explains, "He can't. Its magic affects him."

"Is it gonna affect me?"

"Do you feel anything?"

"Yeah, I feel like I'm carrying a hundred-pound basketball!"

"You'll be fine. Just follow him."

They follow Jerrick to a room Ashley has passed many times, but never paid attention to. Jerrick opens the door and steps back ten feet, saying, "Ashley, you should take it from here." He holds out a scrap of paper. "Go into the closet. I already moved everything to the side. All you need to do is enter this code on the keypad, and the door will open. Carry the stone through, set it down, and leave as fast as you can."

Deja takes the slip of paper from Jerrick, and he moves further away. Ashley holds out her arms for the stone and Alec gives it to her. Deja runs into the room to open the closet. She types the code into a keypad as Ashley approaches. The back of the closet slides open and a giant cement room opens before Ashley.

Water splashes her feet, and wind blows the hair from her shoulders. She witnesses the brute force of Olvasho power as Patrick manipulates water, arching it above his head, before sending it flying at Emily who is hovering in the air like super-woman with flames dancing on her palms. Evelyn is floating in the center of a tornado that seems to tip off balance, and she comes crashing to the floor only to roll up to her feet and continue forward.

Lathe is across the vast space, removed from the chaos. He stares at the opened door. It wasn't the movement that caught his eye; it's Ashley. He sensed her presence like a beautiful pulsing light shining inside his mind. He turns away from the fight. They aren't getting anywhere, anyway.

Patrick and Isa had time to coexist, learning each other's strengths and weaknesses. Evelyn is just beginning to adjust to the new entity inside of her. So, while Lathe and Patrick hold Emily back, his mother and Leona struggle to work collaboratively.

While Evelyn rolls up onto her feet, Lathe leaps up, and the air carries him across the vast space to Ashley. The others hadn't noticed her yet, and he needs to keep it that way.

As he drops in front of her, he feels the magic. Wild, powerful, overwhelming magic. He pales, and his eyes widen as he looks at the object in her hands. "You didn't!"

The object in her arms is calling to him, luring him. It's a sweet temptation, radiating magic and the essence of Ashley. He steps closer, desperate to possess such beautiful, wild magic.

Ashley shakes her head. "Back up, Lathe."

He stares at the object wrapped in dragon skin, feeling high off its power. "It's covered in your magic. I feel it."

She takes a step back, "Lathe, no," she begs, "it will kill you."

He shakes his head, trying to banish the temptation. "God, Ashley, what are you doing?" He takes a step back.

She says, "You guys have to resist. Adelaide won't be able to, and the magic will devour her. She'll be trapped. Just don't let anyone else touch it." Ashley looks over Lathe's shoulder, watching Emily turn in midair, sensing the magic. Evelyn and Patrick also seem to forget what they are doing. All of them stare at the source of wild magic that is now permeating the room.

"Watch out, Lathe!" she shouts, and as he steps to the side, Ashley sets the gem on the floor, the water splashing around it. She unzips the jacket and jumps back into the closet. Deja types in the code and just before the door closes, Ashley watches Lathe step in front of the gem glowing with her Latovian magic, guarding it against the others.

Ashley leaves the closet, feeling uncontrollable anxiety. She tangles her hands in the hair at her scalp, walking to the other side of the room. "What if I just screwed them all? What if . . ." She slides down the wall, burying her face in her hands.

She feels someone sit beside her, wrapping their arm around her shoulder. Ashley opens her eyes, and her face rests on Alec's chest. Deja slides down on the other side of her, leaning against her shoulder.

Deja encourages, "Lathe will know what to do. He always knows what to do."

Jerrick walks into the room to find them huddled together on the floor. "Now, we wait."

Ashley nods, terrified of what could happen next.

CHAPTER TWENTY-ONE

BEN RINGS the doorbell and knocks, but there is no answer. He tries to open the door, but it's locked. "Did they forget I was coming?"

"Emily isn't answering," Morgan offers. "Maybe, call Molly."

Ben dials his sister, and she answers, sounding sleepy. "Hello."

"Molly, we're here, but we're locked out."

"I don't know where they went. Jerrick needed Alec's help moving something. They said they'd be right back, but," she looks at the time, "that was like, two hours ago. I must've fallen asleep on the couch."

"Will you let us in?"

"Of course, as soon as I find the front door."

A few minutes later, Molly opens the door for Ben and Morgan. While Morgan takes in the foyer, Ben focuses on the scorch marks on the wall. "Shit!"

"Yeah, I guess someone threw a bunch of sparklers from the third floor."

Morgan eyes Ben, and he shakes his head, wondering what else she's been leaving out of their phone conversations. Ben starts up the stairs and the girls follow. He's become familiar with the layout of this mansion and he notices how quiet it is compared to usual. They must have cleared the place out. After they find Emily's room empty, they go to Patrick's bedroom, but it's empty too. As they continue to search, Ben realizes who else is missing.

"Hey, Mol, have you seen the dog?"

"No."

Ben whistles and hears a bark from down the hall. They find Maggie closed inside a lounge. As soon as Ben opens the door, Maggie takes off. They follow the dog, hoping she'll lead them to Emily, but she stops at the back door.

Molly laughs. "I guess she has to pee."

Ben opens the door and Maggie runs out into the night. He looks around to make sure he doesn't miss them if they're outside, but seeing nothing, he turns and asks, "Where the hell is everyone? Every time I come here this place is packed."

Trapping Adelaide in the gem is easy. It's keeping everyone else away from the temptation that is difficult. Adelaide desires power above everything, so she can't help but latch onto the extraordinary gem overflowing with potent energy. It is a vessel for all things magic and Adelaide has to have it, so she untethers her soul from Emily and Valla, breaking their connection in order to bond her soul with the magic reservoir glowing before her. In her greed, Adelaide doesn't take into consideration that she might not be able to wield the magic flowing from the gem. The wild magic consumes her, dissolving her magic and eating her soul. The gem—now tainted by Adelaide's magic—glows emerald.

Lathe takes a breath of relief, but it's short-lived as everyone around him crumbles, crying out as they are pulled apart from the inside. They hadn't anticipated losing all their entities. They all wanted to be rid of Adelaide, but without Adelaide anchoring Isa, Valla, and Leona to this purgatory here on earth, the entities are ripped from their hosts, unable to stick around for heartfelt goodbyes. They pass onto the afterlife, leaving their hosts behind to pick up the pieces.

While Evelyn screams in pain, Patrick seems to let go more naturally, though he's still gritting his teeth. Emily's body goes limp, and she falls, cracking her skull on the cement before Lathe can react. The water splashes around her, and blood streams from the fissure in her head.

Lathe rushes over, falling to his knees next to her. Her clothes are ripped and burned from the fight. Her chest rises and falls in quick succession. Her lips look blue, and her skin feels cold. Lathe thinks about his mother's premonition. Even if she doesn't remember it, he can't help but feel like this could be it. He's determined not to let it end like this. What's the point of being warned about the future if you can do nothing to improve it?

He unleashes his healing abilities, pouring them into her, but they aren't absorbing, as if there is a barrier keeping them from getting through to her. Suddenly her back arches off the floor and Lathe sits back, wondering what the hell is happening. Then he notices Patrick kneeling on the floor with his palms hovering on the water, supercharging it with his energy. Emily collapses and Patrick crawls toward her but falls short. Emily's eyes open and her head rocks toward Patrick. She reaches out a weak arm, and her hand finds his. Patrick's fingers tighten around hers and Lathe gets up to tend to his mother who is also lying in the pool of water.

He needs Patrick to do something with all this water. After checking to make sure his mother is okay, Lathe uses the air to dry his clothes. Once he's done, Patrick is sitting up, gathering the water and directing it to the other side of the room where a drain sits in the wall. As the water drains from the room, Lathe attempts to dry the rest of them.

"Whose idea was this?" Patrick asks, looking at the boulder-sized gem.

Lathe shrugs, saying, "Ashley brought it in. I'm not sure how she got it. It's the same kind of gem on Emily's necklace, just much, much larger."

"Where did she find it?"

Lathe shakes his head. "Latovia, I think."

"How did she know this would work?" Patrick asks.

Lathe says, "I don't think she knew for sure."

"I wasn't expecting to lose Isa. It hurts," says Patrick. "I feel empty without her."

"Why didn't they give you guys more time to recover before they abandoned you?"

"They couldn't. The only thing anchoring their spirits to this world was Adelaide. With her gone, they had nothing tethering them here."

"Not even you guys?"

"They were never prisoners," Patrick says. "They were free to go. But it feels like something is missing, now, like suddenly I've lost a vital organ. That sounds crazy, but I was used to Isa being there. I depended on her." Patrick looks over to Evelyn lying unconscious on the floor. "Your mother barely had time to adjust to her entity before Leona was ripped from her. And Emily . . . " his eyes find her. "She lost two entities at once," he says. "One she relied upon heavily for her survival and one who wanted to take over her mind completely. I can't imagine how she's feeling."

"Empty," Emily says, too weak to sit up.

"I have to return this gem to Ashley. I'll take Mother and go out to explain what happened to the others. Why don't you guys take the other exit. It will lead you to the stables where you can recover without curious eyes on you."

"Are you sure you don't mind?"

"I'm sure. Just take care of one another."

Patrick knows he's really saying, "Take care of her." He nods and lifts Emily into his arms before walking to the other exit.

After the door closes behind him, Lathe turns toward the emerald gem.

ASHLEY STANDS AS SOON as the door at the back of the closet opens. She watches Lathe come through, carrying his unconscious mother. He brings her into the room and lays her on the bed.

Alec comes to a stand next to Ashley as the terrifyingly scarred man rests an unconscious woman on the bed. He wonders what the fuck is going on and why no one else looks upset. He protectively places a hand on Ashley's shoulder.

The hand on Ashley's shoulder is the first thing Lathe notices when he looks up from his mother. He knows the thought is irrational, but he doesn't like another man touching her, and what is Alec doing here in the first place?

Lathe focuses. "Adelaide is contained, and we all made it," he says, still worrying about that hand on her shoulder. He doesn't have to fret for long because soon Ashley is running to him. Lathe catches her when she leaps into his arms. She wraps her legs around his hips, her arms encircling his neck as her lips fall on his. He is as excited as he is unprepared for her sudden show of affection. She kisses him like no one is watching and soon he forgets that anything other than Ashley exists.

Alec is thoroughly confused, and Jerrick clears his throat. "We'd like to know what happened."

"What's wrong with her," Deja says, standing next to Evelyn.

Lathe breaks their kiss, answering, "She'll be fine in a few hours."

"But we don't have a few hours!" Deja cries. "It's already been a few hours! Wolfe is going to die!"

Ashley slides down Lathe, her feet hitting the floor. She's not ready to let go of him yet, but she knows how vital Deja and

Wolfe are to Lathe. They have become important to her as well. She says, "Wolfe has been poisoned."

"He was challenged," Deja adds.

"He won the challenge," Ashley explains, "but poison from his opponent's weapon made it into his bloodstream. I tried to fix him, but," she shakes her head, "I don't know what I'm doing. We were hoping your mother could help him when she was finished."

Lathe is speechless. Deja is trying her best to be brave, but she's terrified and rightfully so. If Wolfe dies, Deja's world will collapse. "Let me try to wake her," he says, kneeling by the bed.

"You said you all made it, but where are Patrick and Emily?" Jerrick demands as he looks into the cement gymnasium, finding it empty aside from the glowing emerald gem.

Lathe lays his hands on his mother, explaining, "They went out the other exit. They need time to recover in private."

"Why?" Jerrick asks.

"When the gem consumed Adelaide, the entities were ripped from Emily, Patrick, and my mother. Emily and Patrick spent months living with these spirits, and Patrick explained it was like missing a vital organ. They need time to recover."

Jerrick's phone chimes and he looks down. "The back door was just opened." He pulls up the surveillance. "It appears the rest of our guests are getting anxious."

Lathe looks up from his mother to glare at Alec. "Our guests?"

Alec shrugs and looks to the woman lying in bed. She looks like a magical fairy, and he wonders how someone so pretty and petite could give birth to such a scarred monster.

Jerrick explains, "Molly and Alec came a few hours ago. Ben and Morgan just arrived."

"Their timing couldn't be much worse," he comments, attempting to wake his mother.

"I'll see to them," Jerrick says, before leaving.

Ashley says, "Alec needed to know the truth, Lathe, so I told him as much as I could while he carried the magic gemstone up the underground staircase."

Lathe's sharp eyes flick to Alec, their hostility barely contained. He turns his head back to his mother, saying, "Let me wake her, and then we will return the gem to Latovia."

While Lathe concentrates on his mother, Ashley says, "Alec, come help me with this rock."

They wrap the coat back around it, and Alec lifts it from the ground, carrying it into the room. Ashley kneels next to Lathe, her hand softly grazing his thigh. "We're going to start down to the tunnels. Catch up to us when you can."

Lathe stops what he's doing and turns to her. "Ashley, don't go back through the portal. My mother believes you're cursed because you took a gem from Latovia."

Ashley rests her forehead against his, saying, "Wolfe gave me permission to take it, and I didn't take its power. I'm returning it with more magic than when I left." She kisses him. "But I won't do anything until you come down." She stands, turning to Alec. "Let's go."

Deja stays with Lathe while Ashley and Alec head for the tunnel. As they walk down the stairs, Alec comments, "This rock feels different now than it did earlier. That probably sounds crazy, but it's making me feel weird."

"I feel it, too."

Alec hesitates, saying, "I think it's trying to communicate with me."

"Do not listen to it. The spirit inside that rock is the reason Emily almost died last year."

Alec's eyes widen, and he desperately wants to set the rock down. Instead, he works on distracting himself. "So you and Lathe, huh?"

"Yeah, me and Lathe." She smiles to herself.

Alec laughs under his breath. "Interesting choice. I mean, your taste in men never has—"

"Don't you dare finish that sentence, Alec Garner!" She turns on him, her eyes fierce. "He is nothing like the other guys I've dated. Lathe is a good man, better than you and me. He might come off a little intimidating, but you don't know anything about him!"

"Damn, Ash," he returns. "Truce!"

Ashley spins back around and continues down the million crumbling stairs. "Watch your step," she warns.

Alec looks around the rock to see the step below entirely crumbled. He maneuvers over the missing part and continues down.

"I didn't mean to yell at you," she admits. "Lathe just means a lot to me."

"I see that."

After a while, he asks, "When did you guys meet?"

"Originally, back in November."

"What? Were you keeping him a secret?"

"Kind of. I just felt this super strong connection to him, you know, but it seemed irrational. I started looking for him everywhere I went, hoping to run into him. I didn't see him again for three months, and by then, I knew he was Emily's half-brother."

"Emily has a half-brother?"

"Oh yeah! There's a lot I need to fill you in on."

PATRICK CARRIES Emily up to bed. Her jeans and sweater are torn and burned, so Patrick strips them off, leaving her in her underwear and tank top. He tucks her in bed and moves to the door, intent on finding his own room, but her voice stops him.

"Patrick," she says, her voice trembling. "Please don't leave me."

He makes his way back to her, sitting on the side of the bed. His fingers brush through her hair, calming her until she stops shaking. His eyes close, exhausted from the day.

He wakes with a start some moments later. He sits up

straighter, stretching. He looks down to see Emily must have covered his lower half with the blanket. He so badly wants to stay here with her, which is precisely why he needs to leave. He starts to move, and she opens her sleepy eyes, asking, "Where are you going?"

"You're okay, Emily. You're safe. I'll be right next door."

"Please, Patrick," she begs. "Everything is so quiet inside. I feel hollow." Tears leak from her eyes and Patrick says to hell with it. He lies next to her and holds her. Her silent tears leak onto his shirt while he strokes her hair and kisses her forehead. Eventually, they fall asleep wrapped together.

WHILE JERRICK SETTLES MORGAN, Molly, and Ben into guest rooms for the night, Deja and Lathe escort a newly awakened Evelyn down to the tunnel. As promised, Ashley and Alec are just outside the door to Latovia and Ashley is still explaining things to Alec when they arrive.

Ashley and Alec look up as Lathe speaks. "You seem to be taking things much better this time around."

Alec responds, "Months of feeling confused will do that, I guess."

Evelyn steps forward toward Latovia, singularly focused. "Come. Let's find Wolfe."

Ashley stands, grabbing the handle of the cart that holds the giant glowing emerald.

"Wait," Lathe says, stepping forward, "What about Ashley and the curse?"

"My visions aren't always clear, but her skin is not changing. Right?"

Ashley shakes her head. "I feel fine."

"She will be okay," Evelyn says. "Alec, you should come with us so Ashley can restore your missing memories." With that, she heads through the portal with Deja following behind.

Ashley turns to Alec, a question in her expression.

"Can you do that?"

Ashley shrugs.

"She can," Lathe says, moving to Ashley, jealous that Alec will get to experience her magic when he cannot. His hand grazes her arm. "Where's your jacket?"

Ashley grins slowly. "You worried about me?" When he doesn't answer, she says, "It's in my room, but I'll be back in a little bit then you can warm me up." She presses her body against him, whispering, "I can't wait."

Lathe closes his eyes, tempted to throw her over his shoulder and take her upstairs. Instead, he says, "Be careful. Latovia is dangerous without Wolfe."

Ashley kisses him and says, "That was made pretty clear earlier. Now, let go so I can catch up to your mom."

Lathe hadn't even realized his arms had curled around her. He lets her go, and she waves Alec through ahead of her. She smiles at Lathe, saying, "Here goes nothing." She walks through wheeling the gem behind her. As soon as the gem makes it through, the portal door slams shut, instantly transforming into solid black steel. Lathe's heart pounds. He's never witnessed such a harsh transition.

The portal door slams shut behind Ashley and the emerald rock explodes, shattering into a million pieces. The power of it throws Ashley ten feet through the air, and she crashes into Alec. They are both covered in a fine dusting of shimmering emerald powder. Ashley picks herself up, recovering quickly with her Latovian gifts. Alec sits up, appearing mostly unharmed. Ashley stands and brushes herself off as Evelyn and Deja come running back toward them.

"We're okay!" Ashley calls out.

Evelyn and Deja slow, taking in the Emerald glitter covering everything. The powder touching Ashley's skin changes into a purple shimmer and she tries to clear it from her face.

Evelyn says, "Adelaide?"

Ashley nods. "I don't feel her essence anymore."

"That's a relief," she says, before turning to find Wolfe.

Ashley offers her hand to help Alec to his feet, but as soon as their hands meet, Ashley's magic sparks between them like a bolt of lightning. It rips through his flesh and bones, tearing into his brain in waves of electricity, and flows to every nerve ending. A burst of images play like a motion picture inside his skull—snapshots of his lost memories piecing themselves together in an array of movement. He's lost in pure sensation.

The pain of experiencing so many emotions at once is overwhelming, but he cannot escape. He feels it all. *The cold air against his skin. The smell of blood and a dying Ben. The panic in his soul as he watches his best friend's heart stop. Morgan's voice urges him to trust her. The feel of magic and the haze covering Ben's body. Morgan's hand in his. The sirens. Morgan wipes the blood from his face. The crowd gathers as paramedics load Ben onto the stretcher. Morgan is huddled in his jacket. The ambulance pulls away. He holds Morgan in his arms. Preston steals her away. Alcohol. Alcohol. Too much alcohol. Preston and Morgan kiss. A bridesmaid wraps herself around him. Regret. Ashley yells at him. He and Ashley arrive at the Cetrone's. Molly. Hospital waiting room. Morgan avoids his eyes. He holds Ashley's hand while Patrick explains he can take it all away.*

Alec opens his eyes. Ashley's hand is in his, and she's kneeling in front of him now. Tears carve paths through the shimmering magic powder covering her face. It's then he realizes she just experienced everything he did: every touch, every feeling, every emotion.

Very sincerely, she says, "You have to tell her."

Alec pulls his hand from hers, feeling apprehensive.

"You have to tell Morgan how you feel, Alec." She wipes her cheeks. "I shouldn't tell you this, but things aren't going well with her and Preston. It's just a matter of time until they break up."

"She doesn't want me! Why the fuck would she?" He stands as anger rushes through him. His fingers interlace on top of his head while he paces. "She wanted to talk to me that night and instead witnessed me in the bathroom with that bridesmaid. Nothing I do will change that. I've been busting my ass these last few months, thinking I might have a chance if I get my shit together. But I don't have a chance in hell." He turns to her, shouting, "She couldn't even look at me at the hospital!"

Ashley stands, still trembling from all the raw emotions she experienced.

Alec continues, "I don't understand. Why the fuck would Patrick take those memories away?"

Ashley tries to shake herself free of the harsh emotional aftertaste. "I don't know, maybe it's not an exact science, or maybe he didn't want you drowning in guilt over something you couldn't change. Either way, this is not where we should be having this discussion."

Alec looks around, remembering where they are and Lathe's warning of danger. "Sorry, Ashley."

"I totally didn't know that would happen just by touching you. Some kind of warning would've been nice."

"Yeah," he agrees. "Now what?"

"I think we should check on Wolfe."

"No need," Deja says, stepping out from a shadow.

Alec jumps, and Ashley complains, "You've gotta stop doing that!"

"Sorry, I didn't want to interrupt, and I knew you'd stop talking if you saw me."

Alec turns to Ashley, "Who is this kid?"

Deja scoffs, "I'm not a kid. I'm eight and a half!"

"If you use a half year to describe your age, then you're a kid."

Ashley interrupts, "Deja, how's Wolfe?"

"He's better. Evelyn was able to remove the poison from his body, so now he's able to recuperate. I came back to check on you guys and you were locked in some weird trance for about ten minutes. Then you snapped out of it and started crying and yelling. I wanted to let you have your moment."

"Where's Evelyn?"

"She said she's going to stay here tonight to keep an eye on Wolfe."

"I'm glad he's okay," Ashley says.

CHAPTER TWENTY-TWO ~

LATHE STOPS pacing when the door to Latovia transforms. He holds his breath as he watches Ashley come through covered in purple and green glitter. Lathe realizes it's magic dust. He can feel its pull from across the room. Alec comes in behind her, and he's covered almost as much as Ashley.

"Adelaide?" Lathe asks.

"We're wearing her," Ashley says, making a face. "That sounded grosser than I realized."

Lathe smiles. *God, she loves that crooked smile.*

"Is there somewhere I can shower?" Alec asks.

Lathe says, "I'll show you."

They head up the winding, crumbling staircase to the basement and then travel up two more flights to a row of guest rooms. Ashley recognizes this area, but it's not the same wing as her bedroom.

Alec complains, "This is way too many steps."

Lathe states, "You get used to it." He opens a door. "This is your room. There is a bathroom and help yourself to anything in the closet. "Ben is next door and Molly and Morgan are across the hall."

"Thanks," Alec says.

Lathe grabs Ashley's hand to tug her along with him. He doesn't say anything as he leads her to his bedroom. Once there, he drops her hand to close and lock the door. He turns to face her; his expression filled with need.

So far in their short relationship, Lathe has been the one to slow things down, treating her like the delicate flower she's never pretended to be. Each kiss from him has felt different, from frenzied to tender, but each one makes her feel more alive than she's ever felt before. They set her on fire, as if a live wire lives between them, sparking each time their lips meet.

Now, as he stalks toward her, she feels a thrill of excitement, wondering what this kiss will do to her. She backs up a step, suddenly intimidated by his intensity. She's nervous about letting herself feel anything more than she already feels for him. He catches up to her, capturing her face and guiding her lips to his.

Before now, he has let Ashley lead, but tonight he's in charge, his kisses are possessive. He backs her up to the wall, kissing her the whole way. His hips capture hers, and his hands move down her body, leaving a trail of heat everywhere they touch. She holds onto him, feeling lightheaded as his tongue meets her neck.

"God, Ashley, I can taste it," he groans against her skin.

She doesn't know what he's tasting, but she doesn't care as long as he keeps doing what he's doing. "Mhmm," she agrees, just to keep him going.

She parts her legs, and he presses in, rubbing against her as his tongue travels down her neck. His hands find the bottom of her shirt, and he pulls it up over her head and then his mouth is on hers again, stealing her little gasp as his thumb teases her nipple through the lace of her bra. Her tongue mixes with his, and she realizes what he was saying as she tastes her own magic on his tongue. Before now, she didn't know it was possible to taste magic. It's intoxicating.

His hips move in a rhythmic pattern, one thigh pressed against her core as his fingertips trail over her exposed skin. He slides one bra strap down her shoulder and then the other in a slow sensual movement that spreads goosebumps across her skin. Unfastening the clasp behind her back, the lacy material falls away. Cool air against her breasts is quickly replaced by strong but gentle hands.

"Lathe," she cries, needing more. Her hands pull at his body, greedy, hungry. She finds the button of his jeans, but he's already beaten her there. His pants are undone, only held in place by the friction between them. She reaches inside his boxers, finding him there. The pleasure has her moaning again, her hand wrapping around him as she begins to stroke his length. He lets out a breath and pulls away, breaking her grip on him. She starts to complain until he strips her of her jeans before removing his own. He slides her panties down, and his fingers explore, quick to find the spot that makes her body quake while pleasure noises escape.

"Fuck, Ashley." His head falls against her shoulder.

"Yes, please," she says, rolling her head to the side.

He lifts her up, her legs wrapping around his hips. Gripping his shoulders, she presses into him as he carries her to his bed. He nips at her neck and she squeals. He captures her lips with his, as she rocks against him. Lowering her down on the bed, she reaches for him, instantly missing his body against hers. Watching her sprawled out naked on his bed almost does him in, but he can't let it end that way. He continues to work her with his fingers as his mouth takes turns with her nipples. He feels her body tense, just before her release and he thanks God he's doing something right.

Ashley reaches for him, her hand tugging at his shirt. "Off," she says, running her fingers up his chest. He shakes his head, and she repeats, "Off."

"Ashley, I'm not pretty," he says as explanation.

Ashley's inky eyes grow a new depth as she glares at him, her hand running up his chest. "I know what you look like, Lathe. You are rugged and masculine and fucking beautiful, so take off your damn shirt!"

He swallows, taking her words in before slipping his shirt over his head. Ashley bites her bottom lip, running her hands over his chest and down over the muscles of his abdomen. She dips her hands lower, tugging his boxers down and he springs free. Ashley reaches for him, gliding her hand up and down. Her eyes meet his. "I *need* you."

He nods, before reaching for the nightstand. He pulls a condom out of the drawer and hopes it's not expired. Ashley takes it, rips it open and slides it on him, guiding him to where she wants him. He pushes forward slowly inch by inch, filling her until he's buried deep. She almost comes undone just by experiencing all of him, and her nails glide down his back. He begins moving, and she loses any semblance of control. She pulls his shoulders forward, demanding his mouth as she shifts against him, trying to match his pace thrust for thrust.

For once in her life she can't keep up, lost in the bliss of his movements, the bliss of him. His touch goes beyond pleasure. As his hands glide over her skin, committing her body to memory, she realizes what she has always been missing. Past experiences have taught her sex is just about getting off, but Lathe is proving it is so much more. Joy and pleasure build until her body melts a second time and she holds on to him for dear life.

He doesn't last much longer, his body becoming still above hers. He guides one of her hands up to his chest and presses it right over his heart, saying, "Do you feel that."

Ashley stares up at his tender expression while her palm becomes a witness to the galloping heart inside his chest. She nods.

"It only beats like that for you. Every time I'm with you, every time I think about you—so, all the time. You own all of my heartbeats, Ashley. Every single one is yours." He nuzzles into her neck, placing a tender kiss against her silky skin.

She attempts to hold herself together, but his words and actions strip her bare, and she does something she's never done before. She falls, falling so hard that she shatters to pieces in his arms. Her breath becomes uneven and hot tears stream from her eyes. Lathe looks up when he hears her sniffle. He pulls out, discarding the condom and lies down next to her. He tugs the comforter over them and wipes her tears, too scared to ask why she's crying. He doesn't want to be the reason, but if he is, then snuggling next to her is the last place he should be, so he asks, "What's wrong?"

She wipes at her cheeks, saying, "You."

He can't move. He can't breathe. It is him. She is regretting all of it.

She continues, "You say all these sweet things to me like I'm this special flower when I'm so ugly inside. I don't deserve to have any part of you. I pretended to hold it together after Jacob died, so my mom didn't feel like she lost both of her children, but I'm hollow on the inside. I've tried to fill it with shopping, guys, liquor, parties, school, basically anything that could distract me from the pain. I've made so many terrible decisions, like, really awful.

"I'm mean and mouthy, and I pretend that nothing affects me when really, I'm too broken to feel any more pain. Even my best friends don't know who I truly am. You talk to me like I'm better than you, like you don't deserve me, but Lathe, it's me who doesn't deserve you."

He holds her tighter, whispering, "That's not true."

"But it is," she whimpers against him. "The girl you love doesn't exist."

Lathe pulls her face to his and kisses her. Her lips work with his, desperate and wanting. She tilts her head for better access as her hand reaches for him, but Lathe pulls away, and her dark eyes look up at him, stung by his rejection.

Lathe's thumb caresses her face to soften the blow. He asks, "Did you just kiss me to fill an empty void inside you?"

Her eyes widen, looking betrayed. "No."

"Did you risk your life getting that magic gem in an effort to fix yourself?"

"Of course not."

He dips his head, softly nudging her neck. In her ear, he whispers, "I know who you are, Ashley. I had the privilege to follow you around before I knew you. I was trying to get a read on all of Emily's friends, and you know what I found out about you before I even spoke to you?"

She turns her head to him, waiting for him to finish, but realizes he's going to make her ask aloud. "What?" she whispers.

He smiles and answers, "You had a magnificent ass. I mean I really struggled, and every time you lifted your arms, I would see this belly button ring." His fingers move across her abdomen, and she tries not to smile.

"I'm not lying when I say I've never felt more like a creep than when I was in that bar watching you. I've watched a lot of people in my life, and I've never wanted a single one of them the way I wanted you, not even close."

Her sinfully dark eyes tempt him, but he continues, "Before I even spoke to you, I saw you were smart. You could read people, like the asshole playing darts with you. God, I wanted to punch him for groping you with his eyes every time you looked away, but you knew what he was doing. You were just resigned to it, and you weren't going to let him ruin your time.

"I hated your friends that night. The girls were jealous of you, the guys all wanted you, but you were an island to yourself, none of them knew you, and they didn't deserve to know you, but you still watched out for them. You started watering down your roommate's drinks to keep her from getting sloppy drunk. You kept the other girl from misplacing her phone four times, and you almost succeeded in keeping your roommate from noticing her boyfriend eye-humping you."

"Almost doesn't count," she argues.

Lathe goes on. "You didn't belong there, but you're a chameleon, pretending like nothing touches you, pretending to be a ditz when really you're the smartest one in the room. I was glad Emily had someone like you on her side, but I wondered who was on *yours*."

A tear slips from her eye, and he brushes it away. "Then you came over and ruined me forever. You called me out on my stalking you, proving even my assessment of you fell short. You were fearless. Then you reacted to my face with the innocence of a child."

"It took me by surprise," she admits. "You didn't have to insult my hair."

His fingers run through her hair. "I only brought up your hair because you were torturing me with it. You kept twirling it and playing with it, and I wanted to—" He shakes his head.

"What?" Ashley coaxes playfully, "Please go on."

"God, Ashley, you have no idea." He runs a hand over his face. "No idea."

Ashley glides her hand up his chest. "I think I might have some idea."

He looks at her and says, "You blow me away, Ashley. You are a ray of sunshine in a world of darkness."

Her eyes drop to his lips and he is tempted to give in, but he has to continue. He has to make her understand. His hand trails up her side, and he says, "After you freaked out by the sight of me, you told me I had a nice face, that it had character. I just thought you were lying, but later after you broke down all of my defenses, spilled your guts without me compelling you, and somehow persuaded me to tell you my story, you reached for me across the table. You were curious, but more than that, you were turned on. I was blown away.

"I'd had my chance at love and messed up so miserably that I figured there wouldn't be a second chance for me." He stops and his expression changes, as he looks back at a painful memory.

Her lips touch his scarred cheek. "Lathe, you are beautiful. Don't let anyone lie to you and tell you that you aren't."

Lathe sighs and tells the story he's never told before. "I grew up fast. I had to. Katie's situation was different, but she had to grow up quickly, too, so we grew up together. We were best friends, and as we got older, our relationship evolved. Our sleepovers changed, and eventually, she just stopped going back to her own bed. We started having sex way too young, but neither of us had parents around to stop us. Our lives were messy, and we relied on each other to survive.

"Then one day I came home with a disfigured face, and scarred body and Katie found her own bed, but we remained friends. We still relied on one another, and occasionally she would crawl back into my bed when the lights were off and she was desperate." Pain is wrapped around every word like he had cut open his soul and was bleeding aloud for her.

He continues, "Everyone thought of her as my girlfriend. They would marvel that she didn't leave my side after the *accident*. She hated that people thought we were together, so she decided to prove we were no longer an item by crawling into everyone else's bed. I still loved her, so I took care of her when she came to me crying or if she needed help or money. She was all I knew, and I was resigned to the fact that no one else would ever want me. I'm not sure when she stopped caring about me. Maybe she still cared in her own way, but I didn't know how to stop loving her.

"She was hanging with the wrong people and one night she fell into Patrick's bed, a dangerous place to be because everyone knew Patrick belonged to Sky. I actually felt bad for him, because I knew my father abused him in ways no one deserved."

Lathe becomes silent for a long moment, and Ashley wonders if he's done talking. She looks up to find him glaring at the ceiling. She waits silently, letting him work through the storm in his head. Her hand continues gliding over the skin of his chest from smooth, perfect skin to the ridges and valleys of his scars. Her hand goes back and forth, marveling that she found a man with so much depth and strength. His scars are a part of who he is, and she loves all of him.

Without warning, Lathe continues, "I knew Katie was in

over her head, but I couldn't go dragging her out of someone else's bed. I tried to talk her out of it, and she accused me of being jealous of Patrick, jealous of the thing I was determined never to become. It was then I realized she didn't know me anymore. Eventually, Sky found her with Patrick. He found out she was connected to me, so he made Patrick kill her."

Ashley gasps, her hand forgetting its movement against his chest. "Oh my God, Lathe. I'm so sorry."

Lathe continues, because he needs to be done with it. "They sent me the recording of her that night. Sky recorded everything Patrick did, so I got to witness all of it. I knew how it would end, and I still watched from the time she entered Patrick's bedroom to Patrick scrubbing her blood off his floor. He made it quick. It could've been a lot worse."

"Oh my God," she whispers into his shoulder.

"They expected retribution. Before Katie died, she screamed, 'Lathe will kill you for this.' Instead, I punished myself by watching that damn video over and over again. I hated my father. I hated Katie for putting herself in that situation, and I hated myself for not finding a way to prevent it. Part of me still hates Patrick, because it's easier to hate him that to hate myself, but the truth is, I never fully blamed him. I only pretended to because it's what everyone expected. I could've gone after my father, but there was a good chance he would've killed me.

"I couldn't risk it, because I was the only one besides my mother who knew about the Latovian portal under the mansion. So, I became a recluse. No one could be punished by association if I had no associates. I honed my skills, I took care of my mother, and I stayed in this mansion to protect Latovia. Everyone formed opinions about me and told stories about my upbringing. Suddenly, I became this icon, a deformed beast that refused to live by Sky's rules. It's like I woke up one morning and all the Olvasho both feared and respected me. They looked to me for guidance after Sky died like I had all the answers."

Ashley's hand resumes its calming movement over his chest

and Lathe gets to his point. "I'm telling you this so you know we both have ugly parts, Ashley. Everyone does. If I'm not allowed to put you on a pedestal, then you can't put me on one either. I thought my whole life would be desolate, but then I found a ray of sunshine in that nasty bar with those terrible people and you changed my life."

She rolls on top of him, straddling his hips and says, "No one has ever made me feel so . . . cherished. You see me, Lathe, like, really see me, and you're not scared away. She sits back, her hands fanning across his chest. "I see you, too, and you better believe I cherish the shit out of you. I'm not good at love. I don't know that I quite understand it, but the way I feel for you . . . I've never felt so much. God, I'm bad at this." A self-deprecating laugh bubbles out of her and Lathe smiles.

He pulls her down for a kiss, saying, "Show me." He bucks his hips, and she bites her bottom lip, pulling back only to rock against him.

CHAPTER TWENTY-THREE ~

Patrick wakes and for a moment thinks he's dreaming. Emily lies with her back pressed against him. His arm is draped over her midsection, his hand resting against the smooth skin of her abdomen. His thumb moves, caressing the silky skin. He can't help but notice her cleavage is more present than ever since her tank top lowered as they slept. She stirs against him, gently pushing her hips back. He is very aware of her, too aware of her. He's already lost the battle with the part of him that is pressing firmly against her ass. He tries to move his hips away, but she arches into him.

He closes his eyes trying to regroup, fighting every instinct he has to devour her. If she were his, he wouldn't let her come up for air. He would keep her in this bed and drown right along with her in blissful ecstasy. His hips move forward, rubbing against her. He grips at her waist and holds himself in place, fighting his urges and desires. Every touch is amplified, so when she responds with a soft moan as her curves rub against him, he gives in, lowering his lips to her bare shoulder. He kisses her while they curl closer together.

Her head falls back against his shoulder, and they keep a soft friction going as they rock gently into one another. His hand lowers on her abdomen, and she moans again, encouraging his descent. His tongue grazes her shoulder, and she tilts her head to give him better access to her neck. His fingers dip below the material at her hips, all pretense gone.

"Mmm, no, wait . . . Ben."

Ice runs through his veins. He pulls his hand away, pulls his whole body away as quickly as he can. He rolls off the bed and leaves the room, shutting the door behind him. His heart is beating so loud—too loud. He enters the room next door, but it's not enough. He goes into the bathroom and locks the door behind him. He strips out of his clothes, his erection not at all bothered by the ice water in his veins. It's still hung up on that supple ass, silky skin, and the soft moans that came out of those bow-shaped lips he's been dying to kiss for so long.

He turns on the shower and jumps in. And this time he doesn't stop thinking about her. He pretends she turned around and kissed him back. He pictures her wrapping her arms around his neck and her fingers in his hair as he removes every article of her clothing. He imagines the sweet taste of her on his lips. He doesn't have to imagine for long, because soon it's all too much.

He thought his release would bring relief, but his body is still wound tight as a rope. He can't keep this up. The lines are far passed blurred, and somewhere along the way, he started to allow himself to believe there was a chance with her.

He is confusing her too, which isn't fair. He promised her this wouldn't be a problem, but everything they do together is intimate. Their thoughts are intertwined, their full-body contact that used to bring comfort now brings pain, frustration, and guilt.

SHE KNEW what she was doing. She woke up with Patrick's

hands on her. She felt the evidence of his attraction pinned against her, and she wanted it. She wanted him. She wanted his hands on her body, his tongue on her neck. She craved it more than air and then she came to her senses and remembered Ben.

She rolls onto her back, alone in bed and feeling like a total bitch. She isn't making this easier on anyone. The problem is, she doesn't know how to separate from either of them. They both have a piece of her and the longer she lets this go on, the more of herself she will lose when she is forced to make a decision.

It is time to make a decision. It should be simple, but she now knows there is no such thing as simple.

AN HOUR LATER, there is a knock at Emily's door. Patrick's voice comes through, saying, "I'm going back to the main house." He hesitates, before continuing, "Just so you know, we had visitors last night. Morgan, Alec, Molly, and Ben stayed over at the main house." She can almost picture Patrick with his forehead against the door as he finishes, "I'll see you over there, okay."

She should feel excited to see Ben, but guilt eats at her. While she slept cuddled up to Patrick, her boyfriend was sleeping in her bedroom, or was he? What did he think when everyone came home but her and Patrick?

She showers and gets ready for the day, but when it's time to go back to the main house she can't. She sits on the couch and stares at the wall, feeling hollow. She is used to chaos inside her mind. She is used to Valla and Adelaide questioning her choices and putting in their two cents even when she didn't ask. She is used to their thoughts and emotions running through her twenty-four seven. She never had a single moment alone. The constant commotion in her head had slowly been driving her mad, but now that the chaos is gone, the deafening roar of silence feels overwhelmingly empty. Worse, she can no longer blame Adelaide for her mixed emotions. She can't blame her attraction to Patrick on anyone but herself. Her feelings are all her own, and she realizes with immense clarity that she doesn't like herself very much.

Before she has time to spin further into darkness, a knock comes to the apartment door. The door squeaks open, announcing someone is coming in, whether she is ready or not.

"Emily?" Morgan calls, as she walks further into the room, finding her friend on the couch.

Relief flows through Emily like a warm breeze on a cold winter day. Emily stands from the couch to embrace Morgan. Their hug lasts longer than most, and when they break apart, Morgan takes a seat. Emily follows her lead, sitting down across from her.

Morgan leans forward. "Patrick said you might need me."

Emily lets out a quick breath. Even after she was terribly unfair to him, he still sent the right person to help her.

"Morgan, I don't know what to do." She breaks down her dilemma, baring her soul to her friend, laying all the incriminating pieces at Morgan's feet, before asking, "What would you do?"

Morgan frowns. "Honestly, I don't know. I love you, and I love Ben, and I love Patrick. I hate to see you all hurting. I don't know that I'm the best person to ask."

"You're the only person I can ask," Emily insists. "You always do the right thing."

Morgan laughs. "Emily, I was praying for Alec to cheat on his pregnant girlfriend. I don't think you want relationship advice from me."

"Yes, I do. You might have been hoping, but you never would've let it happen. Even Alec knew if he cheated on his girlfriend, that in the long run, he'd lose his chances with you. I know it, and Alec knows it. You always do the right thing, even when it's the harder thing."

"The right thing would've been backing away from Alec."

"You tried, didn't you? Your friends kept bringing you back together."

Morgan shakes her head. "This isn't about Alec and me. It's about you and what you want."

"I love them both, Morgan, but in doing so, I'm torturing us all. How can I love them so much and still cause them pain?"

"Because you're not perfect. The world isn't perfect. When it comes to love, we're all victims. We become vulnerable, handing our hearts to imperfect people and trusting them not to destroy us. But imperfect people fall down sometimes. They make mistakes, they change and grow, and sometimes they hurt the ones they love. It's the human condition."

Emily leans back. "I'm afraid no matter who I choose, my guilt will keep me from moving on."

Morgan leans forward. "Then maybe don't choose either of them."

"What?"

"You shouldn't feel guilty about who you love, and it sounds like either way you lean, you're going to be unhappy about your decision, so maybe the best thing for everyone is for you to choose yourself, at least for now. Eventually, you'll find who you can't live without."

Emily closes her eyes, a sad smile pulling at her lips. "Thank you for letting me borrow your moral compass."

"Em, you have just as much of a moral compass as I do."

"No, I don't. I don't even know if I can follow through." She wipes a tear as it falls.

Seeing her vulnerability, Morgan finally caves, confessing, "I broke up with Preston."

That snaps Emily out of her thoughts. "What? When?"

"Yesterday."

"Why?"

"We're different people. He cares so much about success, and there is nothing wrong with wanting to be successful. It is part of what attracted me to him in the first place, but I care more about people than money. I see a room full of people, and I see potential friends. He'll see that same group and think of all the connections he can make. I thought he understood me, but I realized he didn't and honestly, I'm not sure I even understood him."

Emily holds in all her additional comments and says, "I'm sorry, Morgan."

"It's okay. I'm okay."

"Have you talked to Alec since you've been here?"

Morgan rolls her eyes. "Really? You couldn't hold it in a little longer?"

Emily grimaces. "Sorry, it's just so obvious."

"Emily, he really hurt me, over and over again. I'm not ready to trust him with my car keys, let alone my heart, and right now I'd rather he not know that Preston is out of the picture."

Emily nods. "I get it. My lips are sealed."

"How are you feeling now that Valla and Adelaide are gone?"

"Hollow."

"That's how Patrick described it, too." She's quiet a moment before asking, "Are you okay?"

"I will be," Emily says, coming to a stand. "We should get back to the main house."

Morgan follows Emily out. As they walk through the stables, they come across Lathe mucking out stalls. He looks up as they pass, asking, "You okay?"

"Yeah," Emily responds, "You?"

"Never better," he says, with an out of place smile.

Morgan leans into Emily after they are out of earshot, saying, "He makes me kinda nervous."

Emily scoffs, "He has that effect on people. It's part of his charm."

"Try explaining that to Ashley."

"Ashley told me he'd be too pretty without his scars. She doesn't see what the rest of us see. She's always had a way of seeing through bullshit. Lathe might be scary, but he's also incredibly smart and loyal. Once you've made it past his barriers, he's a softy."

"Somehow, I doubt that," Morgan mutters. "He left quite an impression on Molly. I think he came out here to escape her wide-eyed, nervous stare."

"I forgot about Molly. Wait. How much does she know?"

"Nothing. We've been cautious around her. Ashley filled Alec in about everything, and she restored his memories somehow, but Molly is none the wiser."

"Do you know how long you guys are staying?"

"Ben and I have to work tomorrow, so we're planning on heading back tonight. Next time we'll plan ahead."

Emily opens the back door, and they walk into the main house together, finding everyone gathered in the lounge. Ben stands as soon as he sees Emily. She goes to him, allowing his arms to encircle her. He leans down to kiss her, and she makes sure to keep it simple. They sit together, sharing an oversized chair.

"How are you feeling?" he asks, as conversation picks up in the room.

"A little better."

"Can I do anything?"

She shakes her head, pretending to tune into the group conversation. Patrick is watching her intently. His gaze becomes so intense that she flicks her eyes to him, telling him to knock it off. He stands abruptly and leaves the room. Emily pretends to look as surprised as everyone else.

Ben whispers in her ear, "Can we go somewhere to talk?"

"Okay," she says, and leads Ben to her office.

They sit together on the sofa and Ben says, "Adelaide is gone, and Evelyn was talking this morning about how she can help lead the Olvasho." He tucks her hair behind her ear. "Emily, you can come home."

Home?

"Ben, I . . . It's more than those things. My life is here now. I can't just walk away."

"Why? You did it to me."

His words cut through her, and she wants to argue his claim, but his bitterness is justified.

"I didn't mean that to sound so harsh. I just miss you, Emily. Please, come home."

She tries to find a way to make him understand. "Ben, I . . . I can't." She thinks about all the people she's helped—all the lives she's saved. She thinks about the horrible injustices she's witnessed in her few months here, and she knows she can't leave. "What I do here is too important for me to go."

"I thought you only came here to get rid of Adelaide and to find my killers, and now Adelaide is gone, and we know my father is the reason I almost died."

"That's what it was about at first, but now I've done so much good. I've helped so many people. I can't undo everything my biological father did, but I'm making a difference here, Ben."

Ben closes his eyes, knowing what comes next. He looks at her and says, "We are good together, Em. You make me happy, and I used to make you happy, but right now we are living separate lives, and I can't keep doing this."

She stares at him, afraid to speak as her world closes in on her. "What are you saying?"

There is no verbal response, but his eyes say it all. He's given up. He's done fighting for them, and she can't blame him.

Tears pool in her eyes and she whispers, "But, I love you."

"But you're in love with him."

Silence.

After a moment tears fall from her eyes, as she very quietly says, "I don't want to be."

"I don't want you to, either." He shakes his head and steals a line from Ashley. "But the heart wants what the heart wants."

"This isn't right, Ben." She wipes her tears.

"Life's a bitch."

"How are you so calm about this?" she says with bitterness. She doesn't understand how his world isn't falling apart when her heart is crumbling in front of him.

"You aren't the same girl I fell in love with, and I'm not the same guy, either. We both changed and grew into something else, Em. We love each other, but for this relationship to work, we have to put in the effort. I've tried, but I don't fit into your world, and I know you've made efforts to include me, but I'm no longer a priority. How many times has Patrick sat next to you in the place I should've been? How many times have you gone to him with your problems or for support instead of coming to me?"

Emily doesn't answer, because he doesn't need a verbal response.

He continues, "He's what you needed at first, and I understood. We all knew our places, but now . . . now you are careful around him, dodging glances and looking guilty when he's next to you." He stands and his fingers rake through his hair as he spins to face her. "God, Emily, you and Patrick stayed somewhere together last night! Tell me, did you sleep in the same bed? Was he my placeholder? Or worse . . . am I his?"

She stands on shaky legs, lifting a hand to touch him. "Ben—"

He steps out of her reach. "Your guilt and confusion are tearing you apart, and I don't want you to resent me."

"I would never resent you."

"You would, and I would resent you, too. I don't ever want to hate you, which is why this has to happen now."

"You're giving up on us."

"I'm putting an end to it before it turns ugly and you begin to hate yourself for what you do to me and then you begin to hate me for making you hate yourself."

"You think you know me, Benjamin Isaac," she says, trying with great effort to hold herself together.

He shakes his head. "I don't want to turn into a caveman and demand you never talk to him. I'm not going to ask you to cut anyone out of your life."

She steps forward, her palms landing on his chest. "You are, though. You're asking that I cut you out of my life." Her tears overflow.

His hand gently wipes her tears away. "Only because I can't keep doing this. I can't keep waiting for you to come around. Emily, you just admitted you're in love with him. Don't drag this out."

"Does this mean we won't see each other anymore? Are we no longer friends?"

"I think it means we take some time, do our own thing, but we have the same friends, and I know too much for me to ever be completely out of your life. I still love you. I just need to love you less and from further away. I need to find myself and take care of Molly."

"And you'll find someone else?"

"Maybe, and maybe we'll find our way back to one another."

Her palms form fists in the front of his shirt, and she moves into him. Her arms wrap around him, holding her friend, holding the man that used to feel like home, holding onto her past. His arms encircle her, pulling her in. She stands on her tiptoes and breathes in his scent as she nuzzles his neck. She tilts up to face him, and his lips meet hers in a desperate kiss. Their pace is frantic, but it doesn't last long, because Ben rips himself away and Emily's eyes open wide. Ben heads to the door without another word. As soon as the door closes behind him, Emily touches her lips, and her emotions spill out of her in ugly wet sobs.

Once she calms down enough to escape, she exits her office and moves a back way through the house, hoping she doesn't run into anyone before she reaches the side door, but Maggie finds her, followed by Patrick.

"Em, you okay?"

She glares at him, like all the problems of the world are his fault. "Leave me alone, Patrick!"

He steps out of her way, and she brushes past him and out of the house. "What the hell?" he says, watching her go, and wondering what's wrong.

CHAPTER TWENTY-FOUR ~

MORGAN IS BACK in the apartment above the stables. She knocks on Emily's bedroom door. "Hey, it's me. We're getting ready to leave."

The lock clicks and the door opens. Morgan takes a step into the dark bedroom where Emily is hiding out. She's lying on the bed cuddling with Maggie.

Morgan asks, "So, what happened?"

Emily recaps her conversation with Ben and Morgan frowns. Even though she knew it was coming, it is still hard to watch her friends hurt. "Do you want me to stay an extra day? I can call off work tomorrow."

"Don't be ridiculous. I'll be fine, Morgan." She hesitates and then whispers, "I'm just really gonna miss him. He's been my friend for so long, I just . . . Nobody told me it would be this hard. I didn't just lose my boyfriend. I lost my best friend. I did it to myself."

"It won't always feel this bad," Morgan says, sliding her hand through Emily's hair.

Emily nods, but she doesn't know if she'll ever be able to forgive herself for ruining what she and Ben had.

PATRICK ENTERS the foyer expecting to see Ben and Emily in the throes of their goodbye, but Emily isn't around, and he doesn't sense her nearby. Ben comes down the stairs with his sister beside him. He spots Patrick when he rounds the bottom step. "Molly, go get in the car. I'll be right there."

Molly goes on out, and it's just Ben and Patrick. Ben's emotions are circling him, flipping through different shades as he steps up to Patrick, holding his hand out. Patrick takes it, and while they shake, Ben says, "Take care of her." He breaks their contact, swallows his feelings, and he is out the door.

Patrick stands in the foyer, unable to move. Did Ben mean it? Nervous energy fills him with anticipation. He can finally act on his feelings. His excitement is short-lived as he starts wondering how it happened and if this is why Emily was so upset with him earlier.

Ashley enters the room and laughs. "Why are you standing there looking like a scorpion just crawled up your ass?"

He looks at her sideways. "What?"

"Why do you look so lost?"

Patrick stares at her for a moment, his heart beating wildly, and his feelings jumbled. "I think . . . I think they broke up."

"Oh my God," she says, rolling her eyes. "You guys make Lathe and I seem normal."

Patrick doesn't laugh. He feels like his next step is crucial. "Ashley, what do I do?"

"Are you kidding?"

He shakes his head.

"Nothing, Patrick. You do nothing! I know you're like, anxious or whatever, but Patrick, she was in love with him. Even if she's not anymore, it's gonna take her a minute to get over him. If you go in there guns blazing, she's going to shoot you down . . . hard!"

"So, what do I do?"

She shakes her head. "I told you, nothing. Just go about business as usual, except maybe give her like, a lot more space. She's her own person again. She doesn't need you suppressing Adelaide or whatever you did before. Give her time to adjust."

"Okay," he nods.

To drive it home, she says, "Do not rush her, Patrick!"

"You were quite clear, thank you." Patrick heads off, unsure how he is going to give her space when they live and work in the same place.

ALEC STEERS his car onto the highway, glancing over at Morgan in his passenger seat. "Sorry, my car is a piece of shit."

Morgan hushes him, "Shh, your car will hear you."

Alec grins, his dimples making their appearance. "Nah," he argues, "she's hard of hearing."

"Probably from listening to this music." She winces, asking, "What is this?"

"It's Dropkick Queens."

Morgan gives him a questioning look.

He clarifies, "One of the guys at work has a band. I told him I'd listen to them."

"Can you understand the words?"

"Sure," he says with confidence. "Right here I'm pretty sure they're saying purple elevator baby carriage."

Morgan laughs, "Oh, please keep translating for me."

Alec continues, "Tie my boots down, tie my boots, feed me peas, I'm wasted with a bomb, purple elevator baby carriage." He glances at her, saying, "It's pretty straightforward once you get the hang of it. Come on sing the next line with me."

She bites her bottom lip, trying not to laugh. "I just don't think I have your level of talent when it comes to music."

"Here it comes." He waves his hand at her, singing, "Tie my boots, feed me peas, I'm wasted with a bomb, purple—"

Morgan joins him, "Purple elevator baby carriage."

Now Alec is laughing, and Morgan reigns in the urge to hand over her heart. She's barely able to keep it from leaping right out of her chest and landing in his lap.

He looks over at her, noticing the sudden worry in her expression. He turns down the terrible music and asks, "What is it?"

"I've missed you, Alec. I hated lying to you about all this Olvasho stuff and I . . . I just missed you."

"Look, Morgan, I'm sorry for . . . everything. I was a total dick for treating you the way I did, and I'm sorry about that bitch, Sadie, and I'm just—"

"Alec, stop. It's okay. You're my oldest friend. We were bound to fight sometime. I just hope we're okay now." She hesitates before continuing, "We're okay, right?"

He nods. "Of course. For as long as you'll have me, Fletch. I'll always be the thorn in your side."

CHAPTER TWENTY-FIVE ~

PATRICK AND BEN. Ben and Patrick. Emily has a dream where Ben is already seeing someone. When she finds out, she goes straight to Patrick to get back at Ben, but when she storms into Patrick's room, she finds him in bed with Ben.

She stands there in the doorway, speechless for a moment until Ben speaks up. "This is what you wanted, right? You want us both. Come on, Em, join us."

She wakes with a start. "What the hell!"

Three days have passed since Ben left the mansion. She's been staying in her room most of the time because she doesn't want to see Patrick right now and Ashley and Lathe are way too affectionate.

With Jerrick's help, Evelyn has taken some of the Olvasho responsibilities off Emily's shoulders, which is a huge relief. Especially because between the deafening silence in her mind and the grief and confusion over her love life, she is having difficulty functioning as a human being, let alone a leader.

LATHE KISSES ASHLEY'S SHOULDER, breathing her in. He counts

his blessings every day he wakes up to her in his bed. He doesn't ever want her to leave, but she has already been here over a week and her life is back in Columbus. Her classes resume in a few days, and he doesn't know what that will mean for them. He wraps his arm more securely around her like it will keep her from leaving.

Ashley rolls toward him. "Lathe, why are you up so early?"

"Seven doesn't seem that early to me."

"It's early for me," she complains, her face pressed against his chest.

"Ashley, what are you going to do?"

"What do you mean?"

"You know what I mean. You've been avoiding it, but sunshine, it's killing me."

She sighs. "I'll be done with school at the end of April. I don't want to leave you or Latovia, but I've worked hard for this, and it's only a month. Then I'll have my bachelors, and I can come back here and be with you."

"I'm going with you."

She pulls back. "What? Lathe, you can't."

"Why not?"

"Well, for starters, you just got your mother back. You can't leave her. Also, you'll distract me, and my roommates are bitches. They'll give me so much hell if I bring you home with me."

"Why? Because of the way I look?"

She looks shocked. "Where the hell did that come from?"

"Are you embarrassed by me?" he asks.

"And why would I be embarrassed by you?"

"Because of my scars."

She sits up, thrown by his comment, "Lathe, you've gotta be kidding me! I think you're fucking hot! Why the hell would you think I'd be embarrassed by the way you look?"

"You've never been out in public with me when everyone stares and gawks, and then they pretend they don't notice."

She shakes her head. "Is this going to be like, a thing?" She gets out of bed and walks to the closet.

He asks, "What are you doing?"

She flips through the closet and pulls out some of the clothes she has commandeered since staying here. She starts getting dressed and Lathe gets out of bed, asking again, "What are you doing?"

She looks at him, her anger gone. "We're going grocery shopping."

He's confused. "Why?"

"Because I want to see the way people react to you in public and if you get any reactions I don't like then I'll set them straight."

Lathe laughs, his uneven smile pulling at her heartstrings. He walks over to her and begins stripping off the clothes she just put on. His lips fuse to hers, and he walks her back to the bed. She sits on the edge, and he pulls back, saying, "I'm sorry. I didn't mean to take my insecurity out on you."

Ashley gives him a sexy smile and falls back on the bed. "I guess you'll just have to find some way of making it up to me," she says playfully.

Lathe lowers himself, kissing his way down her body. He gets caught up by that damn belly button ring and then he goes lower. He kisses her hip, lifting her leg to rest on his shoulder, his hand grazes her ankle, and he pauses. He pulls back to look at her leg.

"Lathe?" Ashley complains.

Lathe forgets how to breathe. He stares at her ankle.

Ashley props herself up when he doesn't respond. "Lathe?" Then she sees it—her left ankle. She pulls out of his grip, realizing she couldn't feel his touch there. She hadn't even realized he was holding it until she looked. She knows now that Ashing's disease isn't a real illness—it's a symptom of the curse—but seeing her own body betray her like this feels wrong. For a moment she doesn't recognize the world she is living in as her mind goes numb with fear.

Lathe draws Ashley's face between his palms. He pulls her eyes up to his and says, "It's okay. You're gonna be okay."

She wants to tell him that his words are empty because they both know what this means. There is only one cure.

"It's daytime. The sun is out. This is so mild. It's nothing." He attempts to reassure Ashley, but they are both afraid of what this may be.

"Lathe," she says, interrupting his rambling. "Can you fix it?"

His eyes widen, and he lowers himself to sit on the floor, both of his hands wrapping around her left ankle. He closes his eyes and concentrates on healing her leg. His healing gifts never worked on his mother's illness, and they have never worked on the Latovian people, but Ashley isn't all Latovian, and she's lived above ground all her life.

He's still trying to convince himself that there might be a chance to save her when Ashley touches his shoulder. "Lathe, baby, you did it!"

He opens his eyes and lifts his hands from her ankle. It looks good as new. He gets onto his knees, wrapping both of his arms around her, and buries his face in her neck. She does the same to him, saying, "I love you so damn much."

He squeezes her tighter. "You are my world, Ashley. If you're going to Columbus, then I'm coming with you. Your roommates can fuck themselves."

"Or, maybe we can stay with Morgan at Patrick's apartment."

"I don't care where we stay, but I'm not leaving you."

Ashley pulls out of his grip, saying, "There you go, stalking me again."

"Sunshine, you wouldn't know what to do without me," he says with a sexy grin.

"Oh, like you would do any better without me!"

He shoves her back on the bed, separating her legs as he dips his head to place a kiss against her inner thigh. His lips tease their way up, and he says, "I barely know what to do *with* you." His breath sends a tingling through her. "But I can't fathom life without you." His tongue finds her core, and she grips the sheets.

"It's great to see you happy, Lathen," his mother says, coming around the kitchen island. "But I worry about you. Have you told her, yet?"

"No, but it won't change her mind."

"The longer you wait, the more it will feel like a betrayal."

Lathe looks to his feet, admitting, "Something happened earlier."

She lifts a brow. "Oh?"

"Ashley's ankle, it started to . . ." He can't bring himself to say it.

"Petrify?" she supplies.

"Yeah."

Evelyn reminds him. "She is Latovian."

"But she's lived here her whole life."

"But, she is Latovian."

He huffs. "Are you saying we're doomed?"

"I'm saying, you need to find a way to break the curse, so you don't lose the love of your life to a different world."

"I healed her," he admits.

She tilts her head. "And it worked?" When he nods, she says, "Interesting, that's never worked on the others."

"But," he justifies, "Ashley isn't all Latovian, and she carries more magic than most Latovians."

Evelyn corrects, "She carries more than all of them at the moment."

"Except for you," he corrects. "Technically, you are as much of a Latovian as she is."

"But my Olvasho blood neutralizes the curse."

He leans back against the wall. "What's going to happen?"

Her eyebrows crease as she lifts her hand to his cheek. "My

boy, you know there is not a set future. While some things are more concrete than others, the future changes and shifts. In one future, I see you in Columbus, and in another, I see you here."

"Where is she?"

"Her Latovian blood makes her difficult to see, but with you watching out for her, I know she'll be safe." Evelyn lowers her hand.

He sighs, not hearing the answer he was looking for. "Thanks, Mom. Have you seen Emily today?"

"She's outside with Maggie."

"Is that safe? We still haven't found the third Trinity leader and their followers—"

"Their followers have abandoned them and approached us begging for forgiveness and offering us everything they know. The last Trinity leader's name is Margaret Talle. She's forty-two, five foot six, slim, last seen with dyed burgundy hair. And she's in Europe now."

"When did all this happen?"

"While you were spending time with Ashley." She grins. "Don't worry, Lathen, we have it under control. There was no reason to bother you."

He wonders if he's been that oblivious, but he knows the answer. He's been spending a lot of time with Ashley and he's working on the stairway to Latovia, making it safer and working to install an elevator. He wants to surprise Ashley with it when they come back from Columbus. He's also been spending time catching up with his mother, but he thought she would have told him about something like this.

He asks, "Do you know where in Europe?"

"Outside of Budapest. We have eyes on her. Our contacts are happy to capture and escort her back to us."

"So, it's over?"

"There will always be new threats," she says, "but this one is about wrapped up."

Lathe is so used to working by himself, the idea of having people he can trust still feels foreign.

"Lathen," his mother says, drawing his attention back to her. "Tell Ashley the truth."

ASHLEY WALKS into Lathe's bedroom and slams the door, yelling, "Don't you dare fall in love with someone else while we're together!"

"What?"

She stalks across the room and collides with him, reaching up to hold his neck while they kiss. When she pulls back, she says much softer, "You're not allowed to fall in love with anyone else."

"I don't know what you're talking about, but you have nothing to worry about because no one compares to you."

"That's what Emily thought too, but then she fell in love with two people."

"Oh, that's what this is about." He runs a hand through her hair, saying, "There will never be anyone else for me."

"That's right. No one else would put up with your shit, anyway."

He smiles at her feisty attitude and counters, "If there is any danger of one of us falling for someone else it would be you, sunshine. And no one could love you more than I do. No one would tolerate your sass the way I do."

She smiles. "You love my sass."

"Yes, I do." He pulls her in to kiss her again.

She begins unbuttoning his pants, and he stops her, stepping back, "Wait, Ashley, I need to tell you something."

Her arms fall to her sides, and she steps back, concerned by his sudden change in demeanor.

"There's something I've been keeping from you because I didn't want to overwhelm you or make you feel pressured, but now I feel like I'm lying to you."

"What is it?"

He says, "I believe we know who your biological father was."

Ashley's shoulders relax, and she blows out a breath. "Oh, that. God, Lathe, you scared me."

"I know you don't care about the man, but he—"

She interrupts, "Let me guess. He was the king of Latovia?"

Lathe's head jerks back. "How did you know?"

"Well, for starters, Wolfe calls me princess more often than he calls me Ashley. Also, before your mom went all psycho on me, she told me I was the princess of Latovia, so that was a pretty big clue. The Latovian orphans I told you about filled in the rest of the blanks for me. My dad was a busy guy."

"How long have you known?"

"For like five days."

"Why didn't you tell me?" he asks.

"Because I figured you knew and were keeping it from me, so I was waiting to see how long it took you to break down and tell me."

He rubs his hands over his head. "You know I've been stressing over this!"

She steps forward, "Babe, you were treating me like a delicate flower after I told you not to." She grabs his hands, lacing their fingers together. "I'd like to hear it from you, though, because I did get most of my information from elementary-aged kids."

Lathe laughs. "I want to hear what they said first."

"Okay," Ashley pulls him over to sit on the side of the bed. "So, King Mazilon was not a nice guy. He took kingship by challenging the last king, which is pretty common, I guess. King Mazilon knew Latovia was dying, so in an effort to save it he would come out during the new moon, plant as many seeds as he could and return to Latovia. He did this for years before anyone knew what he was doing. Then, the children started piling up. He was hoping that if they grew up in the outside world, they would fare better through puberty, and then he could bring them to Latovia to restore its magic. But when the children reached puberty, he watched them die in droves. The Latovian people caught on to what he was doing, and while some of them agreed with him, most of Latovia found it barbaric."

Lathe cuts in, "The kids told you all of this?"

"Yes. How'd they do so far?"

"Scary accurate."

"Well, they aren't normal kids. I mean, you know. So, anyway," Ashley says. "The people of Latovia began searching for the king's children to try and save them before they reached puberty. But when the king found out, he started sentencing expulsions, which is a nice way of saying, shoving people out into the sun and letting them die horrible deaths. The crown was challenged over and over—battle to the death style—which is also like, totally Neanderthal of them, but no one could beat King Mazilon. That is until an orphan had enough of watching the king sentence his friends to death. So, a thirteen-year-old Wolfe said to hell with challenging the king. Instead, he snuck in and murdered the fucker in his sleep."

They sit in silence for a moment before Lathe says, "What Wolfe did was treason, but instead of expulsion, they took a vote. *A vote!* That has never been done before. They voted for him to be their king. He was sixteen by the way, not thirteen, but other than that, the kids had it right."

Ashley looks down at their hands, asking, "Was I the only one to make it through puberty on the outside?"

"The only one we know of. We rescued thirty-two kids before they reached puberty. A few of them, the older ones mostly, decided to take their chances above ground. None of them survived. We believed there were only twenty-one remaining children of Mazilon. Then, we found you, twenty-two. There may be others, but it's difficult to track them down. Had you not been friends with Emily and Patrick, I doubt we would have ever discovered you. But once I witnessed your immunity to Olvasho powers, I did some digging and found your brother's hospital records."

"Stalker much?" she chimes, and then more seriously she says, "Twenty-one half-siblings. What are the holidays going to look like?" she jokes.

"I have eight half-siblings."

"You do?"

Lathe nods, "That doesn't include the ones who have died. Emily and I are much younger than Sky's other children. He became picky the older he got. But Sky was procreating for nearly two-hundred years. My oldest living half-brother is eighty-five. The youngest, besides Emily and myself, is fifty-two. I know they exist, but I never felt the need to bond with them. Sky dismissed them when he saw their gifts weren't spectacular."

Ashley is quiet before bringing up, "Something else has been bothering me. I tried to ask Wolfe, but he blew it off."

"What is it?"

Ashley lets out a sigh. "All the orphan's down there. At first, I thought they were Mazilon's children, but they're too young. I asked Wolfe why there are so many orphans, and he just shrugged and said, 'Only the strong survive Latovia.'"

Lathe runs a hand down her back, saying, "Things work differently in Latovia. It's more savage, or in your words, Neanderthal. Things are improving, but the progress is slow, and the Latovian people are stubborn. Honor is big, and suicide by the sun is common. Some people would rather die than never see the sun again."

Ashley cries, "But they leave their children behind to fend for themselves. Lathe, they sleep on rocks and cardboard. They own nothing but the clothes on their back. It's horrible."

Lathe nods, kissing her temple. "I know, and now you can do something to help improve their lives. Did you hear how I met Deja?

She shakes her head. "No."

"Deja's dad challenged Wolfe and lost. Deja's mother was so disgraced, she walked out into the sun. She took Deja with her, but Deja was only three. I found her crying in the stables."

"Oh my god!" Ashley gasps.

He continues, "I kept Deja with me until Wolfe came up during the new moon. He took Deja back with him, promising me he would keep an eye on her."

"That little girl is amazing."

CHAPTER TWENTY-SIX

Two days later -

A heatwave rolls across Indiana. At sixty-five degrees with the sun shining down, Emily decides to open up the patio doors and sit outside. The sun beams down with a warming glow, teasing of summer. Soon Evelyn joins her, followed by Deja and Patrick. While Evelyn sits with her, Deja and Patrick take the next table to play a card game.

Pretty soon, Evelyn and Emily are laughing at Deja and Patrick's game of war. Deja is dominating Patrick with the card game even though he's the one that is supposed to be teaching her.

Evelyn wears a serene smile as she lifts her face to the sun. "Emily, if you knew when you were going to die, would you live your life differently? Would it change your decisions?"

Emily's smile melts with a look of concern creasing her brows. "What have you seen?"

"Relax. As far as I know, you are perfectly safe." She sighs. "When Lathe told you about the most recent prophecy, did it change the way you lived your life?"

"When he told me I was going to die soon?"

Evelyn nods.

"It scared the shit out of me, but then I pulled myself together and kept doing what I do."

Evelyn smiles. "You love what you do?"

"Yeah, I do. It's difficult a lot of the time, but I see the difference I'm making, and I remember why I'm here. I need to stop wallowing and get back to work."

"You must miss Ben, though. I know he is important to you, too."

"I do, but Ben and I want different things. We live in different worlds now. It doesn't mean I stopped caring about him. It still hurts."

"Of course it does. Anytime you allow someone to hold your heart; they take a piece of you with them when they go." Evelyn reaches over to hold her hand. "You're a strong woman, Emily."

LATHE STEPS up to the window in the library, and Ashley wraps her arms around him. Lathe looks at those gathered on the patio below. Patrick and Deja are playing a card game while Emily and his mother are huddled together having a conversation. Lathe runs his hand down Ashley's arm, feeling her perfectly smooth skin. She hasn't had another incident in the past two days. Maybe his mother's visions are slipping. Ashley hasn't turned to stone, and his mother can't even remember the prophecy she had about Emily. She'd repeated it so many times that night, that he still remembers every word.

"Soon she will breathe her final breath, for I have seen her death. Her blood runs through your veins, a relative she remains. She won the battle of her mind, regaining her strength of life. She rises only to fall. She will die to protect them all."

His blood runs cold.

Ashley looks up at him when his hand stops. "What's wrong?"

"It wasn't about Emily," he mumbles, then louder, he says, "The prophecy wasn't about Emily."

"What are you talking about, Lathe?"

He disconnects with her, his eyes distant. "The prophecy was about my mother. She saw her own death."

"But if she sees it she can prevent it, right?"

Lathe spins around, heading for the door. "I don't know."

EVELYN SQUEEZES Emily's hand while her eyes fill with tears, "I've done the best I could. My son is happy. You are a strong, compassionate leader with an incredible team surrounding you. Latovia has a fighting chance with Ashley working as a liaison between the Olvasho and the Latovian people. Don't let your emotions slow you down, Emily. Keep this momentum going, and great things will happen. Don't let your people down."

Sensing the unease, Patrick begins listening to their conversation.

Evelyn's hand releases Emily, and she leans back in her chair. "Don't let Lathe blame himself. There is no way he could have foreseen this, and I wouldn't have let him prevent it."

Emily leans forward, saying, "Evelyn, what are you talking about? You're scaring me."

By the time Emily feels the air move, three bullets slice the air. She screams and ducks, pulling Evelyn with her. She feels a blanket of Evelyn's magic before it evaporates, and the thick cedar table blocks the two of them from the shooter. For a split second, Emily and Patrick make eye contact. He and Deja are tucked behind the other table, appearing unharmed.

Emily takes inventory of herself, shaking so badly she can't see straight. When she looks down, she discovers she's bleeding everywhere, so much so that she can't tell where it's coming from. Her body is numb with shock as she turns to check on Evelyn who doesn't look right, but Emily's mind is slow to comprehend. She doesn't register her screams as she shakes Evelyn's body, demanding she wake up.

The doors to the patio fly open as Lathe arrives. Lawn furniture soars as he hurls a wind barrier around the patio, blocking further bullets. Patrick jumps up, rushing to intercept the powerful storm that wears Lathe's skin. Patrick stands in front of him, pushing back. "Turn around, Lathe. Go back inside."

Lathe shoves him out of the way, but Patrick returns, withstanding the storm to get in his face. "Lathe! Go back inside! You don't need to see her!"

Lathe stops moving and looks at Patrick with pure hatred. "Get. The. Fuck. Out of my way, Patrick!"

Patrick glances at Ashley who is hovering behind Lathe; her eyes are wide and her shaking hands covering her mouth as she witnesses the nightmare Patrick is trying to prevent Lathe from seeing. Ashley steps forward, grabbing Lathe's arm. "Lathe, baby, don't—"

He jerks his arm out of her grip, shoves Patrick to the side, and takes three steps forward before collapsing to his knees with a thunderous roar of undiluted agony. It is a soul-shattering sound. It rips Ashley in two. It curls Deja into a sobbing mess on the ground.

Patrick recognizes the anguish all too well. To avoid reliving his own pain, Patrick seeks the numbness he imposed in his time with Sky. Everything real fades as Patrick looks around, detached from his surroundings as if watching a movie. Ashley tries again to pull Lathe, but he shoves her away. She cries silent tears as she watches the other half of her heart shatter in front of her.

Deja takes off, running into the house like she, too, can escape it, but it is Emily that makes Patrick snap out of his trance. She is kneeling next to Evelyn, using one hand to staunch the bleeding from her chest wound, while her other hand is scooping brain matter back into Evelyn's cracked skull.

Patrick moves forward, putting his arms around Emily's midsection and picking her up. She tries to fight him at first, but her hysterical complaints turn into wailing sobs. He sets her down inside the house, swiping the tablecloth from the kitchen table. He goes out and lays the tablecloth on the ground next to Evelyn's body. He lifts her onto it, wrapping it around her to cover her body from view.

Jerrick appears in the door, taking in the scene. Without a word, he moves to help Patrick transfer Evelyn into the house. Emily stands in the same spot where Patrick left her in the kitchen covered in blood.

In her shock, she searches herself for a bullet wound. Patrick lifts her chin, so she focuses on him. "Emily, this is her blood, not yours."

Her eyes become wide, and she whimpers before stripping her clothes off in a panic. Patrick doesn't stop her. He wouldn't want to be covered in Evelyn's blood and brain matter either. She's standing in her bra and underwear when Ashley runs into the kitchen, crying, "I couldn't stop him!"

They all move back onto the patio to witness Lathe using his wind to reel in a body like a fish on a line from across the lawn. He slams the woman into the side of the house, and her body crumples on the pavers below.

Margaret, the third leader of Trinity, pleads with him to spare her, but he doesn't listen. He lifts her body on the wind, anger consuming him as he looks into the eyes of his mother's killer. He pulls the thoughts from her head and the air from her lungs. But watching her suffer brings him no pleasure, so with a lethal slice of air, he snaps her neck. Her body collapses and Lathe storms past the watching crowd into the house.

Ashley says, "Jerrick, will you look for Deja? She ran inside a little bit ago."

Jerrick points in the direction of the basement stairs. "She ran past me, saying she's going back to Latovia."

Ashley nods. "I'll check on her later," she says, before taking off after Lathe.

Emily is still in a state of shock, so Patrick says, "Come on, Emily." He leaves her clothes behind on the floor while he escorts her up to her bathroom to shower.

He turns on the faucet, and Emily says, "She was warning me."

He glances at her while he adjusts the heat of the water. "I know."

"She knew this was going to happen."

"It appears that way." He steps out of the way, saying, "Shower's ready."

"She didn't want us to stop her." She looks up at Patrick, saying, "I have to tell Lathe." She turns to go for the door.

Patrick catches her wrist. "Emily, you're wearing his mother all over you and you're almost naked."

She pauses, looking down at herself. Patrick pulls her back toward the shower where she steps under the spray, letting the water clean her face.

Before Patrick closes the glass door, he says, "Be sure to wash your hair."

Emily steps from under the spray, touching her hair. Her fingers brush over something sticky, and she gasps, "Patrick! I can't do this."

"Yes, you can."

Hyperventilating, she says, "No, I can't do this."

He places his hands on her shoulders, "Yes, you can. Breathe, Emily. Slowly." He demonstrates by taking several deep breaths.

She follows his lead, but her eyes are begging for help, so he steps into the shower fully dressed and closes the glass door behind them. He guides her back under the water spray and Emily tips her head back, letting the water rinse her face and wet her hair. Patrick gently rubs in the shampoo, his presence calming her. The way his hands feel against her scalp is almost enough to make her forget how they ended up here in the first place.

"Oh, God!" Emily gasps, remembering in vivid detail. Her body shakes and she leans into Patrick, crying into his chest, "She's gone, Patrick."

He embraces her, his hand stroking the back of her head and down her back over and over until she calms down. Eventually, Patrick pulls back to lather soap in a washcloth. He washes her neck, down her shoulders to each arm and she gets caught up in the intimacy of what he's doing. She steps closer to him, placing her hands against his chest.

He stops washing her, wondering what she's doing. She glides her hands across his drenched shirt and down his abdomen to begin unbuttoning his shirt.

"Emily," he says in warning.

She glances up with wanting eyes, and Patrick's body responds, even as his mind hesitates. She removes his shirt, and her fingers find the skin of his chest, gliding over every contour.

His hands gently encircle her wrists. "Emily," he warns. "What are you doing?"

"I've felt your hands all over my body; I've felt you in my mind; I've felt you in my thoughts; I've felt you in here," Emily says, pointing to her chest, "but I've never actually touched you, not like this." Her hands break from his grip to wrap around his back, and she pulls her body flush with his, tucking her face into his chest and breathing him in.

His arms encircle her, and his face falls forward, his breath falling against her neck. "Emily?"

"Yes, love," she says, looking up at him, water mixing with her tears.

He brushes the hair from her face. "Your emotions are running a bit high right now."

She closes her eyes, squeezing more tears out before returning his gaze. "I could be washing your brains off of me,

Patrick. It could've been any one of us. Our lives are too dangerous to put off the things we want," she says, gripping him as if she's afraid he'll leave her. "God, Patrick, it's torture seeing you just out of reach doing everything exactly right. I don't understand the way you love me when all I've ever done is hurt you." She releases his back, wrapping her arms around his neck. "Let me make it up to you."

He feels like a wild animal caught in a trap. His hands have become fused to her body, unwilling to let her go. To free himself, he will have to gnaw off his own limbs. "I don't have enough willpower to say no to you, Emily."

"Good." She tilts her mouth up to meet him, and he doesn't hold back. He devours her. Their lips and bodies coalesce as they tear down every last emotional barrier between them. His tongue invades her mouth, and she willingly surrenders to him, offering herself. They kiss, packing months of repressed feelings into this moment of passion.

The steam from the water floats around them as he lifts her. Her legs wrap around his hips as he pins her to the shower wall. Her fingers dig into his back as his teeth graze her bottom lip. Her hips move of their own accord, rocking against him, setting them both on fire.

Pounding at the bathroom door makes them pause, just before the bathroom door opens, and Ashley demands, "We need you guys downstairs! Right now!"

The door slams shut, and Patrick pulls away from Emily, searching her face for any sign of regret. He's met with terrified eyes as she remembers how they ended up here. He can tell she wants to cry, but she holds it in as he lowers her to her feet. She uses her arms to cover her see-through bra when he steps away. He turns off the water and wraps a towel around her. He grabs his own towel, his pants dripping across the floor. "I'm going to go change. I'll meet you outside your room."

Before he leaves, she steps toward him, saying, "I don't regret kissing you. I meant what I said."

He turns back to her. Taking her face in his hands, he kisses her fiercely, before stepping back and moving out the door.

They quickly change their clothes and reconvene in the hall to run downstairs together, stopping midway on the steps. Lathe stands stationary in the foyer, lashing out with mighty winds to tear everything apart, including Jerrick, who is bleeding from multiple lacerations, but he appears none the worse for wear. He isn't backing down, using his unique abilities to cripple Lathe by draining his energy.

Ashley screams, "What is he doing?"

Patrick witnesses for the second time in his life, the strength of Jerrick's abilities, the precision, the skill, the terrible consequences. Jerrick has refined his gifts since the last time Patrick observed them.

Two years ago, Jerrick attempted to stop Sky with his unique ability. Sky was so impressed by his attempt that he made him an offer. When Jerrick refused, Sky held Jerrick's wife and two-year-old son hostage, forcing Jerrick to comply. It worked for a year before he refused to use his abilities to torture an innocent girl. Sky had Jerrick's family murdered and threw Jerrick in prison. He was in isolation until the day Patrick freed him, two days after Emily took out Sky.

Patrick understands why Jerrick signed on to help Emily when she took leadership of the Olvasho. Jerrick would do anything for her. After all, she destroyed the man who killed his family.

Now, Jerrick lived for a purpose and stayed busy in an effort to keep from focusing on the wife and child he lost. Patrick knows Jerrick isn't heartless but watching him use his abilities on Lathe like this, makes him cringe.

Emily looks at Patrick. "You know what he's doing?"

Patrick nods, saying, "He's manipulating the water inside Lathe's body. He would only use it as a last resort. I'm going to tell him to let go. You grab hold of Lathe."

Emily nods, and Patrick runs down the stairs while Emily

launches herself over the balcony, using the air to soften her fall. She is getting better at this. She steps close to Lathe, watching Jerrick and Patrick until Jerrick's body relaxes. When Lathe's power builds, Emily steps in to wrap her power around the two of them until fire swirls around them in a glowing haze.

"You think that will stop me?" Lathe threatens, but his wind lessens.

"Why was Jerrick restraining you?"

"He wouldn't let me kill Trinity's followers. They lied to us! They gave us bad intel."

Emily frowns. "Lathe, your mother was the one to give us bad intel. She knew she was going to die and didn't want to stop it."

His wind builds as he roars, "You think this was suicide?"

"I don't think we know the whole story, Lathe, but her last words to me were to tell you not to blame yourself."

"You let this happen!" he accuses.

"I don't see the future!" she shouts back.

Her words seem to make it through his anger, and the wind around them dies down as Emily drops her flames.

Patrick is next to Ashley as she holds a notebook out to Lathe. Tears stain her face, and her hands tremble, as she says, "I found this in her room."

He looks at the notebook and then at her. He takes the book from her and flips it open.

Bluebird,

I have outrun my death many times. The truth of it is, I should've died three years ago from a brain aneurysm, but my mission was not complete, and I could not leave you alone. I foresaw my death over a dozen times and each time I changed my fate, but death will only wait so long. If I continued to prevent my death, others would begin to die in my stead. I no longer have the same reasons for staying alive. Latovia is on the way to recovery. The Olvasho have found a good leader in Emily, and she does not carry the burden alone, because she is surrounded by a team of advisors, one of which is my bluebird. You are no longer alone. You have friends, family, and a woman who loves you.

You must free Latovia. If you fail, Ashley will no longer be allowed in your world.

I'm sorry you have to witness such a gruesome death, but I needed to be sure you wouldn't try to save me or bring me back.

I will always love you, my sweet bluebird. I appreciate all of your sacrifices. You've always made me so proud. My heart is with you, my bluebird, my Lathen, my son.

Your Mother, Always

Lathe stares at the note. His mother's almost suicide note. How could she not say goodbye to him? How could she leave him? She must have known he would never have let her go. He shoves the notebook at Ashley before he walks away from the mess he's made.

As he opens the front door, he hears Ashley. "Lathe," she cries, walking after him.

He storms out of the house, slamming the door behind him.

CHAPTER TWENTY-SEVEN ~

ASHLEY IS CRAWLING into bed in the guestroom when Lathe throws open the door. Surprised by his abrupt appearance, she says, "Lathe?" She means to say more, but his intensity as he stalks towards her makes her anxious. She's gotten to know the sensitive man behind the intimidating body and scarred face, but looking at him now, she remembers he is one scary bastard. She almost forgot. She crawls backward across the bed until she is standing on the opposite side, putting the bed between them.

Confusion clouds his eyes, and he demands, "What are you doing?"

"I was going to bed."

"I mean, what are you doing over there?"

"Lathe!" She points to the full-length mirror on the other side of the room. "Look at yourself!"

He uses the air in the room to tilt the mirror toward him. He is met by a monster, complete with bloodshot eyes, ripped clothes, and dried blood across his face, arms, and knuckles. His scowl mixed with the dark circles beneath his eyes makes him look dangerous. Then, there is the storm behind his eyes. Seeing the intensity of his grief and anger is too much for him, so he slices his arm through the air, shattering his reflection as the glass explodes.

Ashley lets out a little yelp and quickly covers her mouth. He looks at her, his strong, beautiful, lionhearted princess cowering from him. Her fear spears him through his already ravaged heart. He turned into a monster today, and she was there to witness the worst of it. He murdered a woman in front of her. She watched him turn on his friends. She watched Jerrick torture him, and when she tried to comfort him, he pushed her away over and over until she finally left him alone.

She was in here, giving him the space he requested, and he burst in like a Neanderthal, scaring her half to death. He sits on the side of the bed, lowering his face into his hands. He lost his mother. He can't lose Ashley, too, but that is precisely what he is doing. He expected her to understand where he was in his head when he had barely spoken a word to her. He hadn't realized he still had the ability to scare her.

He feels the bed move next to him and then her arm wraps around him, her fingers gliding across his scalp. He tilts his head to her, saying, "I'd never do anything to hurt you."

"I know you'd never hurt me on purpose."

He winces at her words, but he can't blame her for being cautious. "Are you afraid of me now?"

"Lathe." She tilts his chin up to face her and her thumb strokes his cheek. "You lost your mother today. Anyone who knows you knows how much she meant to you. Your anger is totally justified, but it is also terrifying."

"Don't leave me," he pleads.

"I'm not going anywhere. I don't care if I fail all of my classes; I'm not going anywhere."

He buries his face into her neck and engulfs her with his arms.

In a small voice, she asks, "Are you going to get in trouble for killing that woman?"

"I just came from talking to Jerrick. Legally, I won't have trouble. The body has been destroyed and the evidence is gone, but I'll have to live with it. I promise you, Ashley, I won't ever hurt you."

CHAPTER TWENTY-EIGHT ~

EVERYONE BORN WILL EVENTUALLY DIE. It's a fact so basic, so logical, so inevitable, and yet it's something most of us are never ready to face. Is it fear of leaving those we love or fear of the unknown? No one can be sure when death will strike, but every day is priceless to those who acknowledge the Grim Reaper lurking just over their shoulder. If we knew when we were going to die, would we live our lives differently? Would it change our decisions?

The casket at the front of the room stands like a declaration of failure. Lathe watches from the balcony, separating himself from the people pouring into the room below. It makes him angry how many people are here. They wanted nothing to do with his mother while she was alive, but now that Evelyn is dead, gifted individuals pour into the room by the dozens. He wants to berate them for being here, but guilt keeps him silent. How could he let this happen?

He looks down to find Emily at the foot of the stairs wearing a sad smile. She politely excuses herself from the hordes of strangers to escape up the steps. Standing next to him on the balcony, they look down over the crowd. The Olvasho are watching their every move, waiting for their emotions to slip up. Emily's face remains stoic, but her voice is low and filled with bitterness. "Their condolences are empty."

Lathe's expression doesn't change as he replies, "Everyone is curious. They didn't think my mother could die. They had to see for themselves. If we weren't here to stop them, they'd be prying open the damn casket for good measure. But they aren't all here for that. Some came just to get a look at you. They know you're single now."

She turns to him. "How?"

He nods toward Patrick as he enters the room below. "The better question is, are you single?"

He knows something happened between Emily and Patrick, but they were acting as if things hadn't changed.

"The timing isn't right," Emily admits. "The Olvasho are my first priority."

"Are they?"

She stares at Patrick, as she answers Lathe. "They have to be. Otherwise, who else will lead them? You?" She pauses. "The only people who want leadership have an agenda. I'm the only thing standing in the way of another Sky."

Lathe glances at her. "Remember, I'm with you."

"And you want it even less than I do. It's okay. I know I'm making a difference."

They watch Patrick reach out to someone in the doorway. Emily feels the change in Lathe as soon as Ashley enters the room below. He tracks her movements, his emotions escaping his confinement, being broadcast for all those observing, as he says, "She's incredible."

Ashley's eyes rise to the balcony meeting Lathe's before a meaningful smile curls her lips. Patrick places a hand on Ashley's back to move her forward, and her eye contact is momentarily severed as she reaches out for the girl that is now standing with Patrick. Deja and Ashley link arms and move through the crowded room.

Lathe's protective instincts grow so overwhelming, he pushes back, ready to leap over the railing. Emily's hand lands on his arm in warning. "You'll make them look weak if you jump over that rail. Those ladies know how to handle themselves, Lathe."

He flicks his eyes to her. "Why are they here? The Olvasho will know. This will paint a target on them."

She grips his arm tighter. "You did that by caring about them. Now the Olvasho will know what they will have to contend with if something happens to either of them. Your face says it all."

Lathe pulls out of Emily's grip. He holds tight to the railing as he watches Ashley and Deja travel the room much slower than he prefers. He rolls his neck, and when he can't stand it anymore, a surge of wind blows through the room, clearing a path from his girls to the balcony stairs.

Ashley lifts her head to look at him. Patrick closes his eyes, shaking his head and Emily laughs under her breath. "Way to be subtle."

"I don't do subtle."

Patrick pushes Ashley and Deja forward, afraid of what else Lathe might do if the girls don't make it to him soon.

Deja peers up at Lathe. Before Evelyn died, Deja didn't think there was anything Lathe couldn't handle. She hadn't seen him since that day and seeing him now has her swallowing back tears. She left him when he needed her most. Deja doesn't let her nerves show as she travels through the room of potential threats. She doesn't care if she has to fight every single one of them; she would do it just to be here for Lathe.

With a determined scowl, she rushes down the path he created and up the stairs. She feels hundreds of eyes on her as she stops just in front of Lathe, her shoulders lifting with her controlled breaths. She avoids his eyes as her small voice trembles with her apology, "I'm sorry, Lathe. I'll never run away again. I'll be brave next time, I promise."

With a finger, he lifts her chin and at the same time he kneels down. "Deja, what are you talking about? You are without a doubt the bravest person I know, but even the bravest warriors need a tactical retreat, sometimes."

Her lips tremble, and Lathe opens his arms to embrace her. She doesn't hesitate to throw her little arms around his neck as he wraps her in a hug. Soon she backs out of his arms, wiping away her tears before people see. She promises, "I'm here now, so if there is anything you need, just tell me."

He meets those dark eyes of hers, saying, "You being here is enough." When she doesn't look satisfied with that, he adds, "But if you could keep an eye out for anything suspicious, I would appreciate it."

She gives him a firm nod and goes into lookout mode.

Lathe stands to his full height as Ashley reaches the top of the steps. She walks to him with a singular focus. He takes a step toward her as the whole world disappears around them. He dips his head, his forehead resting on hers. Her palms cup his cheeks to guide his lips down to meet hers, and he pulls her closer.

Deja gives dirty looks to everyone staring up at them, while Emily steps away, giving them as much privacy as a room full of observing Olvasho will allow.

PATRICK COMES to stand next to Emily, asking, "How are you?"

She lifts her head to look at him, jealous that Ashley and Lathe make loving one another look so simple, while her feelings for Patrick are so complex. She needs him too much to let herself openly love him, yet he's the only one she feels understands her. The incident in the shower remains an isolated occurrence, but they haven't talked about it. The Olvasho barely accepted Patrick as one of her advisors. There is no way they would support them as a couple.

She can't risk upsetting the balance. She needs their support to make a difference for all the innocent people.

She looks down to the casket.

"These people have no idea," she says. "They have no idea what we lost."

"I know." He threads his fingers through hers, sending a red-hot spark through her that she diligently ignores while she holds onto him.

"We've already learned this lesson, Patrick."

"I know, love."

"We already knew life wasn't fair and good doesn't always win. We've already grieved the deaths of our mothers. I thought Lathe would be spared."

Patrick leans in to place a kiss at her temple, saying softly, "Lathe isn't the only one who is grieving. She was important to you, too."

Emily turns her body into his, and he drops her hand to wrap his arms around her. She tucks her face into his shoulder while he buries his face in her hair, breathing her in.

"Patrick . . ." Indecision has her hesitating. "I was in love with Ben. I thought it was a forever kind of bond that we shared. If that couldn't last, then what chance do we have?"

When she starts to pull back, he holds her tighter. His words are soft but unyielding, "I know you're not ready for a relationship, love. You're not leading me on. I know where we stand, and I'm okay with it, but don't let guilt pull you away from me. My love for you is not contingent upon our relationship status. I will love you because I will always love you, but we are friends before everything else."

Her eyes close as she holds onto him, saying, "I love you, Patrick. I don't know what I'd do without you."

JERRICK LEADS Mark and Morgan through the mansion toward the upper entrance to the balcony. He opens the door for them but hesitates in the doorway. He knows he should be with his friends, but after watching Ashley and Lathe kiss, and Emily and Patrick embrace, he steps back and closes the door. He had lost the woman that made him feel so much. He had lost everyone, and he isn't in the mood to be social, so he isolates himself further by escaping to his room.

Patrick sees the newcomers and whispers into Emily's ear, causing her to break their embrace. She turns to hug Morgan before greeting her dad who motions with his head toward the door, and Emily and Mark disappear.

Ashley and Lathe are no longer kissing but are still holding one another. Morgan wraps an arm around Patrick, asking, "How's everyone doing?"

"None of us took her death well."

She notes, "Jerrick seems to be holding it together."

Patrick gives a dry laugh. "He can't even stand to be in here with the rest of us. He's someone you want next to you in a disaster because he keeps his cool and functions logically, but after the trauma, he isolates himself. I suspect so he can fall apart in private. I'm glad he was there the day Evelyn died, but her death may be bringing up some of his past demons."

"He has past demons?"

"He spent a year of his life being blackmailed by Sky. We all have our demons, Jerrick more than most."

"He seems so level-headed."

"Remember, Morgan, the Olvasho are master manipulators. You can't take anything at face value."

Morgan swallows. "How's Emily?"

"She's grieving about more than Evelyn. She's grieving Ben, grieving her freedom. With Evelyn gone, all the Olvasho leadership remains on her shoulders. It isn't what she wants, but she can't risk having someone like Sky lead the Olvasho."

"Sacrificing for the greater good," Morgan says.

MARK AND EMILY step out into the hall. Mark looks both ways to make sure they are alone before asking, "How are you holding up?"

"I'll be okay, Dad. Thanks for coming."

He pulls her in for a hug. As she's huddled up close, she says, "I wish I didn't have so much on my shoulders. Evelyn would've known what to do about Latovia."

Mark pulls back suddenly. "What did you say?"

Confused, Emily repeats, "I wish I didn't have so much on my shoulders."

Mark shakes his head. "You said Evelyn would've known what to do about Latovia."

"She would. She was half-Latovian."

His face loses its color, as he repeats, "Latovian?"

Emily searches her memory and realizes they'd been so focused on the Trinity group that she hadn't mentioned Latovia to her dad. "What do you know about Latovia?"

"Your mom . . . umm," he hesitates. "Sometimes she would have moments of confusion, especially after she exerted herself mentally. She had times when she seemed to forget who and where she was, spouting all kinds of crazy theories like powerful sorcerers being locked underground in a magic world called Latovia. She spoke of magic moons, royalty hiding among us, and dragons. I thought it was just a creation from her overstimulated mind. When she snapped out of it, she couldn't remember what she had said. I started recording her so she could listen to herself later. She never understood it. The recordings are gone, but she wrote some notes in a journal. I went through them after she died and . . ." His face twists with concern. "Emily, if Latovia is real, if any of the things she said were true, do not get involved." He pulls out his phone. "I'll have Chris scan the pages and send them over."

"Dad," Emily lays a hand on her dad's wrist. "It can wait." She looks back toward the balcony door. "The funeral will be starting soon."

He lowers his phone, shaking his head. "You're right, of course. Sorry. If I had known Latovia was real, I would've given you this information months ago."

CHAPTER TWENTY-NINE ~

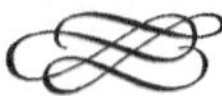

April ~

From across the table, Cindy asks, "Molly, how is school going?"

Molly grins, her edges softening since she left the Cetrone mansion. "I love it."

Sitting next to her Ben runs a hand over his face. "She only loves it because it has boys." In her all-girl private school, she rarely had the opportunity to meet guys and now all the guys at her new school are drawn to the new girl.

"There is nothing wrong with liking boys," his sister argues.

"Oh, dear," says Cindy while Alec laughs.

A knock at the door interrupts their conversation and Morgan lets herself in. "Sorry, I'm late. I got held up at school."

Cindy had started inviting the group over for Sunday dinners, and nobody could say no to Cindy or her cooking. Not to mention, Ben is thankful for the bond Cindy has created with Molly.

Morgan sits next to Alec and he turns all his focus to her. He turns into a lovesick puppy when Morgan is around, and although she isn't unaffected by him, she is not ready to go there with Alec. Not yet.

Two weeks have passed since Evelyn's death, and it still feels fresh. Lathe is itching to get out of this place that reminds him so much of his mother, and he would follow Ashley anywhere, so she returns to school with Lathe at her side. She even takes him to meet her parents where she finally has the strength to stand up to her mother, breaking the news that she will not be going to law school. They hash it out, and though nobody leaves happy, Ashley feels like she and her mom are one step closer to repairing their complicated relationship.

Ashley's skin doesn't show any more signs of petrifying, and she has never been happier or felt like she had more of a purpose. Instead of a graduation celebration, Ashley takes Lathe with her to visit Jacob's grave. Then, she says her goodbyes to friends and family before heading back to the Fort Wayne mansion where she will begin working to repair Latovia and eventually set her people free.

In the weeks following Evelyn's death, Emily stays busy cleaning up one Olvasho mess after the another. When she finally has a moment to breathe, she opens her private email. She had forgotten about her conversation with her dad until she comes across his email.

She opens it and finds the attached file. She clicks on the file, and the pages from her mother's journal appear on the screen.

She skims through, searching for something. It isn't until the last page that Emily understands why her dad looked so worried. An unsettling feeling takes over. She pushes back from the desk and stands to pace as her stomach churns. She forces a deep breath and sits down to reread her mother's words.

"She must've been confused," Emily justifies, but the quivering in her gut tells her otherwise.

Patrick bursts into the room. "Emily! What's wrong?"

Oh, shit, cloaking her emotions was second nature, and yet she realizes she let her emotions slip. Perspiration beads across her face and back. She stands, stripping out of her sweatshirt. In her tank top and jeans, she paces the room again. "Ashley's not really one of them. She isn't Latovian, just like Evelyn wasn't really Latovian," she says, trying to separate her friends from Latovia.

"Emily, what are you going on about?"

She waves a hand at the computer. "My dad sent me my mother's journal. My mom knew about Latovia."

Patrick bends to read the screen. His eyes flick up to her's when he's finished reading, and he says, "We don't know if this is true."

"God, I hope it's not, but we'd better figure it out before Ashley and Lathe get back. What if they are all lying? What if we don't really know them at all?"

From across the room, Patrick says, "Calm down, love. These are our friends. Lathe is your brother. If they know something, they would have told us."

She turns to face Patrick, offering, "Then it's just Wolfe lying to us. He is the king of Latovia, even if none of the others know, even if Evelyn didn't know, Wolfe knows!"

Patrick grimaces. "Lathe and Ashley are close to Wolfe. One of them can get the information out of him."

"But can we trust them?" she asks, taking a seat.

Patrick kneels in front of her. He takes her hands in his and promises, "If there are still dragons in Latovia, we will find out."

"It's not the dragons I'm worried about," nausea rolls through her, "it's how they're creating them."

⁓

ASHLEY LIES next to Lathe in his king-sized bed, both panting from exertion, she doesn't remember ever feeling so complete. Cuddled together, Lathe eventually falls asleep, and Ashley pries herself from his arms to go to the bathroom.

She is wearing only her robe and a satisfied smile. She flicks on the light and catches her reflection in the full-length mirror. She freezes, and her smile dissolves, along with her heart. She stumbles back, turning off the light. Pulling her robe tight around herself, she slips out of the bathroom and escapes Lathe's bedroom, wanting to hide from him until she understands what this means. She wanders next door to the moonlit library. Taking a seat in front of the window, she curls her legs up beneath her.

After a while, Lathe comes looking for her. He finds her sitting in the dark, moonlight glistening off her blond hair. He moves her hair to the side and bends to kiss her neck. She stiffens, and Lathe's lips come away dusty.

Dread runs up his spine like a razor-sharp scalpel, slicing him open to expose his biggest fear come to life. He flicks on the nearest lamp and Ashley flinches as the window before her reveals her reflection. She witnesses Lathe's reaction. His beautiful face contorts with the pain that is so clearly consuming him.

He turns away.

Ashley unfolds herself from her seat and rounds the chair. "Lathe," she pleads, "Lathen, look at me."

Lathe turns to her, his movement slow as guilt presses down on him, smothering him. "This is my fault. I never should have let you go to Latovia."

Ashley reaches out. "We don't know what this means, Lathe. It may be easily fixed. It doesn't hurt, and the moon didn't seem to make it worse. We don't know yet, so don't write me off."

"Never," he says. "I will never write you off, but you are the rightful princess of Latovia. It is meant to be your home."

"My home is here, with you."

ACKNOWLEDGMENTS ~

There are so many people to thank.

To my readers who have stuck with me this far, thank you for following Emily's story. You guys are amazing, and I couldn't do what I do without you.

Mary Catherine Kline, writing will not be the same without you. Through the editing process, you have become such a dear friend, and I will miss you terribly. You encouraged me to grow and taught me so many important points that will stick with me forever. Even when I self-edit, I hear your voice in my head questioning my wordy sentences and whether a scene is relevant to the overall story. You've made an enormous impact on my writing and an even more significant impact on my life. I feel blessed to know you.

Thank you to my husband who had to deal with me acting crazy while I was working on publishing my first three books at the same time. You continue to hold me together when I fall apart, and I don't know how I tricked you into marrying me, but I'm so happy it worked.

To my mom, my self-proclaimed number one fan and promoter, thank you for believing in me so much.

To my good friend, Melissa, I love it when you say *we* while talking about these novels because it is *we*. You've been in it with me from the beginning, encouraging me to get my book out there. You continue to give me your feedback, answer my random questions, and even help me package books to send out. You've been there to celebrate with me every step of the way. Thank you! Friends like you don't come around often, and now you're stuck with me.

To my favorite sister, Sarah, you are the light in a dark world. Everything I have accomplished is all because of you. Maybe that's a bit much, but seriously we've shared so much together. Thank you for everything.

To my favorite sister, Heather, I'm so happy my brother married such a beautiful soul. You have been an inspiration, a friend, and a fellow book nerd. I'm so glad he brought you into our family and into my life.

To my favorite sister, Marissa, who gives my mom a run for her money when it comes to being my number one promoter. You are fierce and loyal, and I'm so glad to have you on my side, rooting for me. Thank you for cheering me on and reading all 1000 plus pages of my books even though you're not a reader.

To my favorite sister, Jenna, thank you for your enthusiasm, feedback, and encouragement. Your excitement over my books makes me eager to write the rest of the story. You always give me the best book recommendations, and I'm so glad we can share our favorite books with one another.

To my grandmothers, Lois, Jessi, and Dee, thank you for encouraging me to write. You may not have had the chance to read my books, but I know you were all proud of me.

Thank you to the rest of my family. You have all been so supportive. Thank you for happily answering all my random questions when google fails me.

To Quata Merit, thank you for your editing and proofreading skills. You are always a pleasure to work with.

There are many more people I would like to thank and please don't be offended if I didn't list you personally. You all mean so much to me. Thank you!

With *Broken Alliance*, the fourth book in the Valla Series.

PROLOGUE ~

SIX MONTHS AGO ~

LATHE LIT UP HIS PHONE, *holding it out to see in front of him. He found his mother curled on the floor by the sofa in her modified basement apartment. She whimpered when the light illuminated her features.*

"Mother, what do you see?"

"Gore," Evelyn whispered, uncurling from the fetal position to look at him with cloudy eyes. "Gore . . . and an army of horned beasts and fire. Fire burning everything." Her eyes grew wider as if what she was seeing was happening right in front of her. "Fire burning everything!" She folded back into a ball, covering her head with her arms. "No, no, no, no, no, no, no."

Lathe breathed out a sigh and put his phone away. He crouched to sit on the floor next to her, his back resting against the side of the sofa while he placed a reassuring hand on his mother's back hoping she was only having a delusion and not a vision of the future, but he knew better. Delusions didn't incite such an emotional reaction from her. Lathe knew something bad was coming, but how could he possibly prepare when the details were so vague.

BROKEN ALLIANCE

CHAPTER ONE ~

FIRE RAINS down from the heavens as winged demons fly through the night sky, exhaling flames. The mansion and stables burn while frightened horses run wild across the vast landscape. In the center of the chaos, riding fearlessly on the back of a snow-white horse is the scarred face of a warrior. Lathe shouts at the night sky, his face contorting with anger as he lashes out with violent winds.

Emily's blond hair flows out behind her, her beautiful face dusted with soot and streaked with tears as she comes from the woods riding on the back of a giant horned elk. Following her is a horde of horned beasts leaping out of the woods. She joins up with Lathe in the meadow just as a hippo sized dragon swoops down from the sky, breathing fire. Emily grabs the horns of her massive elk and rises to her feet on its back. She thrusts her arm out, shooting white-hot flames from her palm. There is no chance for the dragon to dodge the blaze, and as it strikes the beast, its cringe-worthy screams penetrate the air, sounding almost human. The creature spirals to the earth, breaking the ground and silencing its cries forever.

Hearing the call of their fallen brother, the dragons swarm, circling the meadow. Their sizes vary, from two-hundred pounds to two-thousand with bat-like wings that span from ten to twenty feet. Dozens of the hideous creatures come from all directions.

Lathe uses the air around him as a weapon, using sharp winds to throw his enemy off course, while Emily uses her gifts to leap onto the back of a deformed dragon flying too close. Her fingers grip onto the slimy skin of the beast, and before it throws her, she melds her mind with it.

Its stench is overwhelming, like a rotting corpse mixed with spoiled milk and mold. She forces the dragon up, flying higher into the sky. Her body slips down the creature as a chunk of the dragon's flesh sloughs off in her hand. She cringes, gagging as she drops the fleshy piece and grabs another area of the beast.

Once she's up high enough, she looks around, searching beyond the burned mansion and plumes of smoke covering the ground. Over the next hill, Emily spots what she's looking for and sends the dragon into a dive.

The mother dragon sits on the hillside looking regal. Its forty-foot wingspan dwarfs the others, and her flesh is covered in glistening purple and green scales making her body shimmer. The scales make the dragons flame-retardant, but none of the other dragons have them.

Emily dives through the sky, silent except for her heartbeat hammering. She realizes her dragon's stench is giving her away as the scaled beast sniffs the air and turns to face her. She swerves to the side and her dragon loses its balance and spirals. Emily lets go and pads her fall, using the air to cushion her landing, while the deformed beast that was once human dies upon impact. These creatures weren't built to last. They were created to kill. Emily rolls up to her feet and the ground rumbles as the mother dragon stalks towards her.

As it comes closer, Emily notices what she didn't before. On the back of the mother-dragon sits a Latovian warrior. Ashley turns her blond head, pinning Emily with her dark glare.

Emily shouts, "Ashley, don't do this!"

Ashley shakes her head, disgust curling her lips. "You've forced our hand!" She spits, "It's the only option you've left us!"

"Lathe is over there!" Emily warns, shouting to be heard. "Your dragons will kill him!"

Ashley's gaze flicks down for a moment before returning to Emily, her voice vibrating with rage, "Then let him die!"

Ashley yanks on the dragon's reins, and a thunderous rumbling begins inside the beast. Its neck stretches up, and its mouth opens, filling the heavens with the fires of hell. Then the creature turns her flames to engulf Emily.

Ashley cries out, her triumph tainted with grief.

The present comes back to Ashley as a cold sweat breaks out across her skin. It's always a little too chilly down here for her liking, but Latovia stayed a mild fifty to sixty degrees.

Hundreds of years ago, the Olvasho made it so the sun—the very source of Latovian magic—would kill Latovians should the sun or its shadow touch their skin, so now they are stuck here, underground in Latovia.

The glow of magic gemstones in the cave walls illuminates the room. They still glow gold, the color of Evelyn's magic. Evelyn was half Latovian, half Olvasho which is how she survived both sides of the portal, but even her immense power didn't stop a bullet from killing her.

Ashley doesn't have an ounce of Olvasho blood, but she has twice the amount of power a Latovian usually holds, which allows her to absorb the sun's energy. At least for now.

She sits on a hard seat with her back ramrod straight, holding her composure. Her visions are coming more frequently, and each time they feel more alive than they did before. She tries to hide her trembling, remaining stoic as the needle repeatedly bites into her wrist.

Latovian tattoos are inscribed without the use of modern

technology. Each stick of the needle burns like a swarm of bee stings, because mixed in the tattoo's ink, is Latovian magic.

First, a Latovian gemstone is melted down, the magic extracted and mixed with the ink. Then a custom-made needle, wielded by the precise hand of a carver, pierces the skin over and over again. The process is grueling, taking hours to complete two of the three thin bands around Ashley's wrist. She stays strong through the first two bands but feels faint by the end of the third.

"We'll finish in the morning," Wolfe announces in his gravelly voice. He speaks a little more stern, using the voice of authority —the voice of a king. People don't question him.

The carver is already packing up supplies. Ashley's shoulders stay ridged, her posture perfect as the surrounding group ready themselves to leave. Wolfe stands across from Ashley as everyone files out. His nearly black eyes meet hers, communicating understanding and compassion. His ebony skin and long dreadlocks almost match his black dragon skin jacket and pants. He looks like a shadow—one you wouldn't want to cross in a dark alley.

When Wolfe was sixteen, he killed the previous king, not in the traditional battle challenge, but by slicing the king's throat as he slept. What Wolfe did was ruthless, illegal, and punishable by death, but it didn't stop the Latovian people from demanding Wolfe take kingship. He was the only Latovian king voted into his role.

Wolfe closes the door after the last person exits the room. As soon as he flips the lock, Ashley's shoulders slump, her head falling back, while she lets go of her tears. Wolfe walks over to her, encouraging, "You did good today."

She lifts her head to glare at him, her inky eyes furious. "These traditions are barbaric!"

"It is the Latovian way."

"That doesn't mean it's right!"

"No, but traditions take time to break. You didn't cry. They will respect you more for your bravery."

Strands of blond hair fall in her face as she inspects the simple lines around her wrist. She expects her skin to be swollen and red, but her pale skin is flawless, marked only with the delicate black bands around her wrist.

She pushes her hair back, tucking it behind her ear as she looks up at Wolfe. "Can I go?"

"The tattoo is not complete, but I'm not holding you here."

She wipes her tears as she stands. "Where is Deja?"

"I told her to stay with him."

Deja is Lathe's favorite Latovian, aside from Ashley. The eight-year-old has more courage and gumption than any adult Ashley has met. Her spirit seems unbreakable, especially given the way her life began. When Deja was a toddler, her father challenged Wolfe in a fight to the death. When Deja's father lost, Deja's mother was ashamed and took Deja with her as she walked out into the sunlight. The sunlight killed Deja's mother instantly as the curse the Olvasho placed against those with Latovian blood burned through her body. Children were immune to the curse, so after Deja watched her mother die, she found shelter in the stables behind the Vallor mansion. Lathe was the one who found her and cared for her until Wolfe came to retrieve her during the new moon, the only time the Latovian curse is suspended. Lathe handed Deja over, but the two had already bonded, and their bond had only grown over the years.

Wolfe walks Ashley to the portal door. She has not yet completely succumbed to her Latovian blood, but things are getting worse, and she knows it is only a matter of time until she can no longer leave Latovia.

Before she walks out of the portal, Wolfe reminds her, "Set your timer. Remember to watch your tattoos."

She nods. "See you soon," she says, holding back the tears that always threaten.

Lathe and Deja are right outside the portal, waiting on her.

The once dank unwelcoming tunnel below the mansion was becoming a livable space thanks to all of Lathe's hard work. The biggest problem is its massive size. The arched stone ceiling above them is easily thirty feet high, and the tunnel itself is the size of a football field. Yet, Lathe works tirelessly on the space to make it more comfortable for Ashley.

Deja runs to Ashley. Her jet-black hair and eyes nearly as dark are stark in contrast to her pale skin. She is tiny for an eight-year-old, but her size only makes her more fierce.

Ashley thinks she's going to get a hug, but Deja pushes Ashley's sleeve up to view the new black bands around her wrist. "So cool! I can't wait to get my own," she says, looking at her own wrists.

Ashley barely holds back her wince. The day she gets her tattoo will be the day she can't come visit Lathe anymore, and she's afraid that will hurt him even more than her own absence.

"You still have some time, Deja. Enjoy your freedom while you have it," Ashley reminds her.

Deja wraps her little arms around Ashley in a quick hug, before leaving through the portal door.

Ashley looks up to find Lathe staring at her from ten feet away. Others may call him intimidating or sinister because of the horrific scars along the left side of his face and torso, but all Ashley sees is the beautiful man she fell in love with. Without his scars, she fears he would be too pretty. She loves every rough part of him, and the scars speak volumes about what kind of man he is. He was a teenager when he deformed himself in order to save his mother. It was one of many sacrifices. He has spent his whole life protecting those who can't defend themselves.

Seeing him now, Ashley is reminded of the vision she had earlier, the vision of him riding horseback across a burning lawn with dragons flying above.

Her visions began shortly after Evelyn died. She didn't think much of them at first, just vivid daydreams, completely inconsequential, but then her little daydreams started coming to life.

They were small, little snippets of reality before they happened. Now her visions have grown elaborate and ominous.

Lathe's eyes don't miss a thing as he steps forward. "You had the vision again?"

She nods, her eyes blurring.

He pulls her against his chest, and she takes in his scent as her finger claw into his back, holding onto him as if it will hold off the inevitable.

Visions of the future were Evelyn's thing, but when Evelyn killed Ashley, she merged their souls to save Ashley's life. Now, Ashley sees pieces of the future.

"What are we gonna do, Lathe?"

Continue Reading **_Broken Alliance._**

Valla Series:

Unraveling Emily ~ book one
Descendant of Valla ~ book two
Guardian of Latovia ~ book three
The Thorn ~ *Valla Series Novella 3.5*
Broken Alliance ~ book four

*Pink f*cking Moscato*

ABOUT THE AUTHOR

Anna Rezes has been passionate about writing since she was a child. When she's not busy honing her superpowers or traveling to other worlds full of fictional characters, she is spending time with family and friends. She lives in Central Ohio with her husband, their two dogs, and the cat they love and hate. Anna is the author of *Unraveling Emily*, *Descendant of Valla*, *Guardian of Latovia*, *Broken Alliance*, and *Pink f*cking Moscato*.

For more from Anna Rezes visit:
www.annarezes.com
www.instagram.com/anna_rezes
www.facebook.com/annarezesauthor
www.twitter.com/annarezes

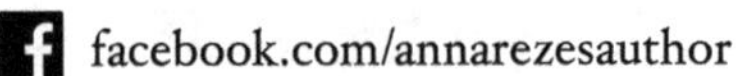 facebook.com/annarezesauthor

 twitter.com/annarezes

instagram.com/anna_rezes